Acknowledgments

It is with great gratitude that I like to acknowledge and thank my son Alex for helping me to pull my book together as a whole. Thank you, Alex.

And as always, I thank God for anointing me with the gift of writing, giving me the ability to envision a story in my head then be able to transpose that story onto paper. It is truly a blessing! Thank You Lord.

Contents

Chapter One

Sixteen year old Raynetta stood in the enormous country kitchen, lined with starch white cupboards, watching intently as her mother Josephine, maid to the Cutter Family, demonstrated the art of kneading dough. Wearing a plain black, white collared maid's uniform with an apron around her waist, Raynetta's eyes shifted from her mother's hands when hearing the harmonious voice of Jonathan and Winifred Cutter's only child, twenty three year old Jonathan Jr., nicknamed Sonny, as the musical words of Elvis' "Can't Help Falling in Love" flowed from his lips with a slight southern drawl. Handsome with slightly tanned skin accenting the thick dark hair on his head, his water blue eyes captivated any female daring enough to look into them. Raynetta's anticipation heightened as Sonny's voice moved from the front entrance of the mansion growing louder as he drew near the kitchen.

"How you doing on this fine day Josephine?" Sonny asked stopping in the doorway of the kitchen, curiously shifting his eyes over at her attractive young daughter displaying two ponytails on each side of her head. Josephine noted his stationary smile as he stared into Raynetta's chestnut brown eyes, captivated by his flirtatious gaze. "I see Mother's hired a new girl." He said turning his attention briefly to Josephine then back to Raynetta. "I keep telling her if she ever stops comparing every girl she hires to the great Josephine White—" Josephine giggled. "—maybe she'd find someone she can keep in here longer than thirty days." He cunningly chuckled as he continued his gape at Raynetta, flashing her a seductive smile. She blushed—awestruck by his charm.

"Mr. Sonny that's my daughter Raynetta." Josephine said with motherly pride. "But we call her Netta for short." Sonny's smile widened.

"Your daughter . . . now Josephine why on earth would you be telling me a lie like that, pretending this grown up young lady's your daughter?" He looked at Raynetta and winked. She girlishly blushed. "Why you hardly look old enough to have a daughter age enough to be working at all." He said playfully teasing. Josephine again giggled.

"Mr. Sonny . . . Raynetta's my oldest—getting ready to celebrate her seventeenth birthday in a few weeks."

"Is that right!" He said continuing his lustful gawk. "Well Raynetta since you're gonna be working here with your momma it looks like you and I are gonna have to become good friends." Her blushing smile widened.

Sonny's flirtatious moment ended at the sound of his father, Jonathan Sr. entering the house through the main entrance headed for the kitchen, curious of his son's preoccupation with the going on's in there. He strolled through the foyer and dining room stopping directly behind his much adored son.

"Why on earth are you in here disturbing Josephine son when you know—" She interrupted.

"Now Mr. Jonathan your boy ain't causing us no harm!" She said in Sonny's defense as she dropped the smooth round midsized ball of dough on the floured butcher's block. "I was just introducing him to—" Jonathan politely interrupted.

"Well I'm sure you don't need Sonny in here disturbing you gals while you're preparing our supper." He said placing his hand on Sonny's shoulder, looking over at Josephine. "I know I certainly don't . . . I'm hungry enough to eat the whale that swallowed Jonah!" Jonathan said bursting into laughter, taking note of Sonny's infatuation with Raynetta.

"Poppa did you know this attractive young lady was Josephine's daughter?" He asked continuing to eye Raynetta's curvaceous figure.

"Why yes son your mother and I met Anita—"

"Raynetta Poppa."

"Huh?"

"Josephine's daughter's name is Raynetta—not Anita." The smile on Sonny's handsome face broadened.

"Yes . . . yes of course it is." Jonathan said forcing an illegitimate chuckled, embarrassed by Sonny pointing out his mispronunciation of Raynetta's name. He momentarily gazed at his beloved son then looked over at Josephine as she proceeded to flatten the dough with a wooden rolling pin. "Well son, why don't we let Josephine and her daughter uh, uh—"

"Raynetta Poppa?" Sonny stated.

"Yes of course . . . let them finish preparing our supper." He briefly shifted his eyes to Raynetta then back to Josephine. "By the way Josephine do you have any idea how much longer we're gonna have to wait for our supper?" Jonathan asked glancing over at Sonny troubled by his continuous lustful gaze at Raynetta. Josephine suddenly stopped and looked at him, the rolling pin still in her hand as she stared into his greenish brown eyes, looking at him as if preparing to chastise a naughty child.

"Now Mr. Jonathan you know I ain't ever in all my years of working for the Cutter family ever placed your supper on the table no later than half pass five—not a minute early or a minute late." She said feeling dishonored. "And if you want your supper the same time this evening I suggest you and Sonny get on out of my kitchen and let me do my work!" Jonathan's face turned bright red.

"Now Josephine you know I wasn't trying to upset you none—" She cut him off.

"If Mother Cutter was alive . . . God rest her soul, she'd—"

"I know Marietta, she'd be mad as hell and she'd be ready to skin my hide raw." He looked at Josephine with apologetic eyes. "Mother loved you Josephine up until the very day she died, I guess I must have let my growling stomach do my speaking for me, I deeply apologize."

"I guess you did!" Josephine said hurt.

"Come on Sonny . . . let's get on out of Josephine and her daughter way." Josephine intervened.

"That is if you want your supper by five thirty."

"Then I guess we'll be seeing you and Raynetta at five thirty." Jonathan said turning to leave. He abruptly stopped. "You know the only reason I allow you scold me like I'm a six years old little boy is because I've fallen in love with your magnificent cooking."

"I can see that from that pot gut hanging over them pants you didn't have before I started working here." They laughed. "Now you and Sonny go 'head on and get washed up and at a half pass five me and Netta's gon be placing your favorite foods right there on the dinner table." Marietta said smiling. "Go on now."

"Thank you Josephine." Jonathan stated humbly as he noted Sonny's eyes again fixated on Raynetta. "Let's go son!" He said breaking his son's lustful gaze.

"Do we have to Poppa?" Sonny said smiling, excited by Raynetta's giddiness.

"You heard Josephine son."

"No Poppa I'm afraid I didn't . . . for some reason I can't seem to take my eyes off of Josephine's beautiful daughter. " Sonny again winked. Raynetta blushed.

"Now you be sure and put lots of butter on them mashed potatoes Josephine." Jonathan said diverting from the subject of Raynetta. "You know how much I love butter!" He laughed.

"Don't I always Mr. Jonathan? There'll be two bowls of mashed potatoes on the table as always—the yellow potatoes are yours and the white potatoes are for Ms. Winifred because you know she ain't about eat potatoes looking more like butternut squash than white potatoes." She laughed.

"I don't know why, she eats everything else!" Jonathan burst into laughter as he and Sonny exited the kitchen on their way to the parlor. Josephine quickly turned her attention to her young daughter seeing the blushing smile on her face, smitten by the charismatic Sonny Cutter.

"Momma—"

"Shhhhh." Josephine said quieting her.

"What Momma?" Raynetta whispered. Josephine silently listened, waiting to hear the sound of the parlor doors close before speaking. She shifted her eyes to Raynetta when hearing the familiar click she'd become accustomed to when the Cutter's spoke on subjects not intended for her ears to hear.

"What Momma?"

"First thing you gon need to learn working here is you don't speak on nothing accept work until the Cutter's enter the parlor and lock the door."

"What you mean Momma?" Josephine looked at her naive daughter.

"You gon learn when the Cutter's are behind closed doors it's because they speaking on something they don't want you to hear." She looked at Raynetta with seriousness. "Now you listen to what I'm about to tell you Netta?"

"What Momma?"

"I'm gon say this one time and one time only."

"Say what Momma?"

"Sonny Carter—" Raynetta Blushed when hearing his name. "—I've known that boy since he was in diapers and his meals came from his momma's breast."

"Momma!"

"Listen to me Netta!" Josephine snapped, upset by her young daughter's obvious attraction to Sonny. "When puberty hit, that boy went on the hunt like a fox in a hen house!" Raynetta giggled. "I watched with my own eyes how he went through girls like a roaring tornado through a small town!" Marietta paused and looked into Raynetta's vulnerable eyes. "And I ain't ever seen one of them look like you or me."

"Well Momma maybe Sonny Cutter's ready to change the hens he's been hunting." Raynetta said blushing.

"Hush, just hush!" Josephine said frightened by the possible consequences. "Whatever you thinking you best clear your head of it right now."

"I'll be seventeen in a few weeks Momma then I'll be old enough to make my own decisions." Josephine grabbed her young daughter by the arm and looked her sternly in the eyes.

"Don't you let that charming smile and them water blue eyes get you nine months of trouble you understand me girl!" Raynetta girlishly smiled as her thoughts continued to be on the striking Sonny Cutter. "You hear what I'm saying to you Netta?"

"Yeah Momma I hear you . . . and that man ain't done nothing except smile." She said blushing. "But I ain't ever known a girl to get pregnant from a smile."

#

"Look here son—" Jonathan said behind the locked parlor doors as he walked over to the bar and poured himself a glass of sherry. "There are rules that us Cutter's have always lived by."

"And what rules are those, Poppa?" Sonny asked, amused.

"You never help yourself to the 'Help.' Jonathan said tossing a shot of sherry in his mouth. "The 'Help' is here son to do our cooking, cleaning, and all those other nasty little things we don't want to do for ourselves." He scowled as he swallowed the sherry. "So as long as we keep that in mind we don't ever have to worry about bringing shame on the Cutter's reputable name."

"Is that why Uncle William and Aunt Lucille's maid Roberta has a son that's a spitting image of Uncle William?" Sonny asked, laughing. "Oh, that's right there is one little difference . . . he has his mother's color?" Jonathan slightly choked.

"You alright Poppa?"

"Now that's a lie spun straight out of the pits of hell!" He said nervous as he poured himself another glass of sherry. "Besides nothing's ever been proven and I've never heard Roberta name my brother as that boy's daddy not once!" Jonathan said hurling the drink into his mouth. "As far as anybody's knows that boy belongs to Roberta's husband Richard." Jonathan said filling his glass a third time. "Why Richard himself would be the first one to tell you that Richard Jr. looks just like him!"

"Of course he would Poppa he knows Aunt Lucille would fire Roberta's ass quicker than a snowball could melt in hell if she knew the truth, and we also know Uncle William would never want that to happen." Jonathan's jaw dropped.

"Now don't you go speaking on stuff you know nothing about, Sonny Cutter!" Jonathan said raising his voice. "My brother William's no different than any other man in his male weaknesses."

"Yes Poppa apparently he isn't." Sonny chuckled. "And his weakness' name is Roberta."

"Now you hush up with that kind of talk Sonny Cutter, my brother—" Jonathan abruptly stopped when hearing the sound of the doorknob turning followed by knocking.

"Jonathan?" Mrs. Cutter said calling through the door. "What on earth could you boys possibly be discussing that would require you to barricade yourselves in the parlor?" Jonathan shifted his eyes to Sonny, cautioning him to say nothing further then hurried over to open the door. Winifred Cutter, an exquisitely dressed, fortyish, full figured red head entered the parlor looking at her nervous husband with suspicion then glanced over at her adored son then back to her eerily silent husband. Sonny looked at his father and silently grinned saying nothing further.

"You didn't answer me Jonathan." He gave no reply

#

"Ahhhhhhhhhhh!" Raynetta cried out as she lay in bed preparing to deliver her unborn child. "It hurts Momma!"

"I know baby but that's just the way God made it." Josephine said shifting her nervous eyes to her sixty year old mother Mildred Koffee also present in the room. Standing at Raynetta's right stood her two aunt's Irene and Ilene watching as they awaited Ms. Vera, Midwife to the African American community in the county to bring Raynetta's child into the world.

"Momma?"

"Yeah baby?"

"You mad at me?" Raynetta asked as beads of sweat saturated her face. Mildred intervened.

"Ain't no point in you worrying 'bout what's going on in your momma's head."

"That's right Netta all you need to be thinking about is bringing this baby in the world." Ms. Vera said as she placed a white bath towel between Raynetta's legs when seeing the crown of the infant's head emerging.

"Where Daddy at Momma?" Raynetta asked through her pain. "He ain't coming in to see his first grandbaby be born?" Mildred looked at Josephine with disappointed eyes and awaited her reply.

"Netta you know your daddy—" Josephine said shifting her eyes over at her two younger sisters. Ilene quickly intervened.

"Now Netta you know Ray Arthur ain't getting ready to watch no baby be born."

"Yeah Netta—" Irene said. "—he wasn't even in the room when his own babies, was born." She chuckled.

"I guess your daddy thinks bringing a baby in the world is woman's work." Josephine said masking her nervousness. "Besides, if your daddy's in here who gon look after Ray Arthur Jr. and your baby brother Joseph?" She said trying to ignore the disciplining look in Mildred's eyes. "I'm sure your daddy's out there now just wondering if he gon have a grandson or a granddaughter." Josephine said forcing a giggle.

"Ahhhhhhhhhhhhhhhh!" Raynetta screamed out as excruciating pain ripped through her pelvis. "I'm scared Momma!"

"I know Netta but listen to Ms. Vera and do what she say and that baby gon be here before you know it okay?"

"Ahhhhhhhhhhhhhhhhhhhhh!"

"Push Raynetta push!" Ms. Vera coached from the foot of the bed. "I can see the head on the way out—your baby gon be making his or her way into this world real soon now."

"It hurt Momma!" Raynetta screamed out drenched in sweat. "Ahhhhhhhhhhhhhhhh!" Ms. Vera grasped hold of the infant's emerging head.

"I need you to push with all your might Netta."

"I can't it hurt!"

"That hurting ain't gon stop 'til that baby come out, so you just keep pushing 'til it do."

"Push Netta . . . you can do it baby" Josephine said.

"I'm trying Momma—ahhhhhhhhhhhhhhhhhhh!!!"

"I got the head right here in my hands, all I need for you to do is keep on pushing!" Ms. Vera stated. Raynetta closed her eyes and grimaced as she vigorously pushed, thrusting her newborn baby into the world. The room suddenly filled with pin dropping silence as each woman laid eyes on the infant. Ms. Vera shifted her eyes to Josephine then quickly swaddled the newborn in a white bath towel and rushed from the room. Josephine looked over at Mildred both women looked one to the other, neither said one word.

"Momma where's my baby?" Raynetta asked slightly lifting her head.

"Lay still Netta." Josephine said as her mind race for an answer to her daughter's reasonable question. She again shifted her eyes to Mildred noting her disciplining gaze.

"Where did Ms. Vera take my baby Momma?" Raynetta asked, uneasy by her momma's silence. She looked over to her left seeing her grandma Mildred. "Grandma why Ms. Vera ain't brought me my baby yet?" Raynetta asked looking into Mildred's unreadable eyes. "Is it alright?" Mildred flashed Josephine a look of disappointment then placed a kiss on Raynetta cheek.

"Your momma's got all the answers you need Netta." She looked at Josephine then walked away exiting the room, closing the bedroom door.

"Momma, wait!" Josephine said hurrying behind her.

"You and Ray Arthur gon rule the day y'all done what y'all done to Raynetta!" Mildred said glaring angrily into Josephine's eyes.

"Raynetta's our child Momma and we gon do whatever we believe gon be best for her."

"Nothing goods gon come from taking that child from Netta."

"Where's my baby Momma!" Raynetta called out from inside the room. Mildred looked at Josephine with persecuting eyes as Ilene rushed out in tears.

"Where's my baby Momma!" Raynetta repeated attempting to sit up.

"Lie still Netta wait for Ms. Vera to come back." Irene said placing her hand on Raynetta's chest lowering her back down as she anxiously waited to see her newborn child. "You gon need your strength when you start pushing that afterbirth out, keep you from bleeding to death . . . you gon have plenty enough time to hold that sweet baby after all that gets done." Irene said trying to calm her anxious niece.

"Ms. Vera ain't even tell me if I had a boy or a girl." Irene gave no reply as her eyes drew to the opening door. "What should I name my baby Momma?" Raynetta asked when seeing Josephine enter the room accompanied by Ilene.

"Don't worry about that right now Netta, you got plenty enough time to give that baby a name." Josephine said handing Ilene several large bath towels, nonverbally instructing her to go to the foot of the bed and assist Raynetta in expelling the remaining evidence of childbirth.

"Netta I'm gon help you get all that afterbirth out since Ms. Vera gon be a while cleaning up your baby." Ilene said placing a metal bowl on top of the white towels as she prepared to receive the placenta.

"Netta why don't we sing your favorite church hymn while your Aunt Ilene clean you out?" Josephine said shifting her eyes to Irene.

"Yeah Netta that way it'll take your mind off the pain from your body pushing."

"Okay auntie." Raynetta stated.

Josephine began singing.

"I'm going home on the morning train oh, oh, oh . . . I'm going home on the morning train—" Raynetta and Irene joined in.

• • • •

Ms. Vera stood in the kitchen and applied the customary slap on the infant's bottom to ensure the child was alive and breathing. Hearing the tiny cry of the infant while waiting on the front porch, Ray Arthur hurried around to the back of the house and prepared to lay eyes on his newly born grandchild. He stopped just outside the door and wiped the tears from his eyes then took a deep breath before entering. Ms. Vera looked into Ray Arthur's frightened eyes as he slowly pulled back the towel covering the infant, laying eyes on the on his first grandchild. He looked at Ms. Vera unable to speak as tears filled his hurting eyes. Ray Arthur threw his hands up in defeat and walked over to the back to leave. He suddenly stopped.

"I want that child out of my house now!" He stated in fury as tears streamed down his cheeks. "I don't care where you take it, but it ain't staying in here!" He yelled. Ms. Vera's jaw dropped, stunned by his malicious words.

"Ray Arthur, what about Netta?" She said trying to reason with him. "Taking this baby from that girl is gon kill the child!"

"She should've thought about that before she let herself get pregnant!" Ms. Vera's eyes widened, appalled.

"Let herself get pregnant, Ray Arthur you know damn well what happened to Netta!" She said infuriated.

"I got plans for my daughter!" He said looking Ms. Vera sternly in the eyes. "And it ain't for her to be cleaning rich folk's houses like her momma . . . and I'll rot in my grave before I let my baby girl raise that bastard child in my house!" He yelled glaring at his illegitimate grandchild before turning and walking away.

"Ray Arthur!" Ms. Vera called out as he stormed out the back door. "Ray Arthur!"

"What Netta have Daddy?" Ray Arthur Jr. asked when seeing him emerge from the left side of the house. "A boy or girl?"

"Yeah Ray Arthur—" His brother Charlie said. "—you got a grandson or granddaughter in there in the house?" Ray Arthur ignored their inquiries as he walked onto the dirt road—disappearing in the night. Their attention suddenly drew to Ms. Vera hurrying out the front door, the infant bundled in her arms.

"Is that Raynetta's baby, you carrying Ms. Vera?" Charlie asked.

"You do best to forget this child was ever born." She said swiftly walking away. Charlie's mouth abruptly opened, shocked by her reply.

"Forget? What you mean forget?"

"If you want to know more than that you gon have to speak to your brother." Ms. Vera said as she scurried down the dark dirt road, clueless on what to do with the infant.

Chapter Two

"Damn!"

Thirty year old Thomas Lee Simms said to himself as he sat perched on the bank of the Mississippi River fishing. "I been sitting out here in this hot sun all day and ain't caught a damn thing!" Attractive with a passion for fishing and a love for women outside of his marriage—especially Delores Clarkston, Thomas Lee reached over and opened the large red cooler and took out a brown bottle of beer. "I guess I'll head on home call it a day." He said thinking out loud before turning the beer up to his mouth consuming its contents then tossing the bottle in the river. "Whew! It's so damn hot even the fish won't come from under water." He said removing his propped fishing pole from the ground. "I could've spent a little quality time with Lucille, the fish may not be biting but I know Lucille is." A cunning smile stretched across Thomas Lee's face as he thought about it. "She's always happy to see Thomas Lee . . . and her husband's working out of town this week too!" He grinned as he began reeling in his fishing line from the water.

A peculiar look formed on Thomas Lee's face when seeing a wet, muddy object floating near the riverbank. "Now what the hell is that?" He asked himself using his fishing pole to pull the object closer to the bank. He identified it as a cloth, frowning as he looked it over. "Now what the hell is a baby blanket doing out here in the river?" He said continuing to exam the blanket. His eyes again drew to the river seeing what looked like a pale baby doll dressed in a muddy white undershirt and diaper. "How in the hell did that doll get out here?" Thomas Lee asked himself watching as the object floated towards him. His eyes widened as his mouth flung open when realizing what he'd pulled ashore. "Naw! Naw! Naw!" Thomas Lee shouted realizing he'd discovered a dead bi-racial, newborn baby boy. He dropped his fishing pole and fled. "Help! Help! Help!!!!"

One Year Later

"We the Jury find the defendant Thomas Lee Simms on the count of kidnap and murder in the first degree—Guilty!"

"Noooooooo!!" Dorothy Jean Simms cried out as the word *guilty* repeated continuously in her head. The wife of Thomas Lee for the past ten years, tears soaked her face as she believe her husband had been wrongly convicted of a crime she knew he could never have committed. Thomas Lee's heart pounded in his ears as Dorothy Jean's voice seemingly echoed throughout the jam-packed, highly charged southern courtroom comprised of eighty percent Blacks and twenty percent Whites—all who'd anxiously awaited the verdict of the accused in the murder of one day old Baby boy Doe.

"Order in the court!" Judge Wilbert C. Clarke shouted pounding his gavel as the courtroom exploded in an angry outburst. "Order in the court!" Observing from the very rear of the court room sat Mildred Koffee watching as two uniformed officers led Thomas Lee out in handcuffs. She subtly shook her head in opposition to the verdict knowing it had been unjust, due to fact there simply had not been enough evidence to sustain a guilty verdict. Mildred also had knowledge of vital information withheld by the prosecutor that would've resulted in reasonable doubt by the jury thus possibly resulting in an acquittal.

She slowly rose to her feet, shifting her eyes to the right of the courtroom when sensing the gaping stare of Detective Andrew Stokey, a middle-aged, average height, plain faced slightly overweight White male who'd testified in the trial for the Prosecutor, twenty nine year old William Michael Shelby III, grandson of Baton Rouge's blue blood Michael Shelby Sr. He looked into Mildred's tell-tale eyes leading him to wonder if perhaps the information she attempted to provide to the police, being dismissed as the ramblings of an eccentric old woman, now had merit. Familiar with her reputation as the eyes and ears of the Black community where she resided, Detective Stokey lessened his doubt of her reputation as being beneficial in solving a multitude of the unsolved homicides in the city. Mildred broke her mutual gaze with the detective then exited the courtroom. Detective Stokey's mind raced as he now marveled over whether his certainty of Thomas Lee's guilt may have been wrong.

#

Sitting on the front porch of her modest, somewhat aged country home where she sat every day, most of the day watching the comings and goings of her neighbors, Mildred absorbed the Sunday afternoon sun as she mechanically rocked in her wooden, weather beaten rocking chair, her rocking ceased when sensing the presence of an individual moving through the thickness of the large oak trees blanketing the exterior of her home. Mildred watched, unmoved as Detective Stokey emerged from the left side of her home coming to a stop in front of the house.

"Evening to you." Mildred said not surprised by his visit.

"Evening, Mrs. Koffee."

"You that detective testified in the case of Baby boy Doe ain't you?"

"Yes Mrs. Koffee I am . . . my name's Detective—"

"I know who you are Detective Stokey." She asked looking at him with persecuting eyes. "What is it you think I can do for you Detective

Stokey?" He swallowed the newly formed lump in his throat. "That is why you come all the way out here ain't it?"

"I uh, know I didn't exactly treat you—"

"Like a person that had good sense when I tried to tell you Thomas Lee ain't murdered that baby?" Mildred stated sarcastically. Detective Stokey's face flushed red with guilt.

"I uh, have since learned that you're uh, considered the eyes and ears around here." He nervously chuckled. "They say if you ever want to know anything about anything, just ask Mildred Koffee."

"I'm sure that ain't all folks around here saying about Mildred Koffee now is it?"

"Ahem!" Detective Stokey cleared his throat. "Yep that's what they say alright." He momentarily looked at her electing not to reply to her loaded question as he grew impatience with their fruitless conversation. His attention suddenly drew to the odd aroma flowing from inside the house through the screened back door. "Are they uh, correct Mrs. Koffee?"

"I don't know . . . you tell me."

"Ahem!" Detective Stokey again cleared his throat annoyed by Mildred's lack of cooperation and the smirk on her face. "To be honest with you Ms. Koffee—" His anger and impatience heightened. "—I don't think you know diddly squat about that dead baby." He said agitated! "And if it weren't for the fact that in the past you lucked up on minor evidence that happened to resulted in solving a few homicides—"

"A few?"

"That's right—a few!" Detective Stokey said raising his voice. Mildred abruptly stood, offended by his blatant disrespect.

"Good day detective."

"Go ahead leave . . . see if I care, but when you go to bed tonight I want you to ask yourself Mrs. Koffee if you're a contributor to an innocent man rotting in prison!"

"If I was you detective I'd be careful yelling at a old woman in these parts, folks around here don't take to kind to city folk coming around asking questions."

"Well I'm not just city folk I'm—"

"Lawmen included." Mildred stated. Detective Stokey looked around seeing a crowd congregating on the dirt road in front of Mildred's house.

"So I guess that crowd's supposed to frighten me—is that how that works?"

"That's a question only you can answer detective."

"Well it doesn't . . . you people don't scare me!" He said with boldness. "I'll have a mirage of officers out here so fast you won't—"

"Is that man bothering you Mildred?" A man called out from the middle of the road. Detective Stokey turned to the angry crowd looking at him then again looked at Mildred.

"I'm warning you Mrs. Koffee—"

"Warning me about what detective?" Mildred said staring him in the eyes. "What you gon do lock me up same as you done Thomas Lee?"

"Ain't that the detective put Thomas Lee in prison for something he ain't done?" A woman yelled out from within the crowd.

"Yeah that's him!" Another woman said.

Detective Stokey again looked out at the crowd, masking his uneasiness.

"You tell them detectives you work with when they ready to hear the truth about who really murdered Baby boy Doe come see me."

"Well I think a jury of Mr. Simms' peers decided that a few days ago Mrs. Koffee!" He stated pessimistically.

"Well that jury got it wrong."

"Yeah well, until you or anybody else can prove different the verdict stands!" Detective Stokey nervously massaged his neck as he looked Mildred sternly in eyes, suddenly remorseful for his angry words. "Look Ms. Koffee I didn't come here to argue with you, I'm on your side . . . I guess uh, this didn't go well at all?"

"What you think?"

"So uh, where do we go from here?"

"I don't know where you going—" Mildred stated. "—but I'm going in my house and eat my supper." She walked over and opened the back door. "Good day detective."

"Yeah well . . . good day to you too Mrs. Koffee." He watched feeling defeated as Mildred entered the house allowing the screen door to slam shut behind her. "Bitter old lunatic." He stated underneath his breath as he walked away. "Wait until I see Detective Fish . . . I'm going to give him a good what for sending me all the way out here to talk to that old voodoo priestess!" Mildred watched through the kitchen window as he journeyed back through the thicket of trees.

"Just like the all the others—" She chuckled. "—you'll be back Detective Stokey."

#

Detective Stokey glanced around squad room seeing Detective Seymour Fish's chair empty, the detectives that urged him to follow-up with Mildred Koffee after he'd mentioned his unusual encounter with her at the courthouse, an anomaly that left Detective Stokey second guessing the guilty verdict of Thomas Lee Simms. He shifted his eyes to the left of the room seeing his partner, Detective Roger Abernathy, one of the many Black detectives working at the precinct, seemingly too busy to notice his return. Detective Stokey walked quickly to his desk located mid-center of the room, believing he'd been unnoticed as he lowered his rear end into his chair. He breathed a sigh of relief.

"Hey Stokey!" Detective Abernathy called out from behind his computer screen.

"Oh hey what's up Abernathy?" He said pretending to be engrossed in reading the notes he'd obtained from Mildred Koffee.

"How'd things go with old lady Koffee?" Detective Abernathy asked waiting to hear the bad news. Detective Stokey's mouth quickly dried.

"It uh, it went well."

"So did she know anything we didn't already know?" He asked getting up from his desk headed over to him.

"It's just like you said—she had nothing of significance to offer to the case."

"Hahahahahaha!" Detective Abernathy burst into laughter. "So in other words you blew it with the old gal!" Detective Stokey's face reddened.

"That's not what I said Abernathy—"

"You didn't have too man!"

Detective Stokey looked into his partner's chestnut brown eyes.

"So what makes you think I blew it Abernathy?" He said trying to save face. "Like I said Mrs. Koffee didn't know anything the prosecutor didn't already have knowledge of."

"Threw you off her property huh?"

"Where are you getting all this from? I said no—" He looked in Detective Abernathy's humored eyes. "Yes."

"Don't worry about it Stokey, if it'll make you feel better we've all blown it with the infamous Mildred Koffee."

"Why in hell didn't somebody warn me about that old racist woman and how she hates Whites."

"Whoa . . . is that what you think man?" Detective Abernathy said bothered by his partner's conclusion. "Newsflash Stokey that old woman don't like nobody . . . Black, White, green or red!" He said, lightly chuckling. "The first time I went out there she didn't treat me no different than she treated you and the same goes for Detective Fish and every other detective that's been out there to that 'forest' she calls home." Detective Abernathy looked at him with seriousness. "Naw man with Mildred Koffee it ain't about race it's about respect!" An odd look displayed on Detective Stokey's face.

"Respect?" He looked Detective Abernathy in the eyes. "I never disrespected that old woman." He said trying to convince his partner. "Well, maybe just a little at first but then—"

"So tell me man . . . what exactly did you said to upset old lady Koffee?" Detective Stokey massaged his neck.

"I uh, guess I did tell her I didn't believe she knew diddly squat about who murdered that baby."

"Hahahahahaha!" Detective Abernathy again burst into laughter. "Stokey man, please tell me you're joking—you did not tell Mildred Koffee that she didn't know diddly squat!" A pathetic look showed on Detective Stokey's face.

"Well she provoked me!"

"Provoked you?" Detective Abernathy shook his head. "Like I said man it's respect, that's the key to getting anything out of Mildred Koffee—plain and simple."

"Respect?"

"That's something you gon have to learn about my people Stokey—"

"And what's that Abernathy?"

"In Mildred's Koffee's generation respect means everything man."

"So why didn't you tell me that before I went out there and made a complete ass of myself?"

"That would've taken all the fun out of it!" Detective Fish said entering the squad room laughing. "What happened, old lady Koffee threw you off her property?" Detective Abernathy intervened.

"Yeah she threw his ass off."

"I never said that Abernathy."

"You didn't have too Stokey—" Detective Fish stated. "—we know how that old lady works, but Abernathy thought it best we let you find out for yourself." Detective Stokey's shifted his eyes over to his partner.

"That was your idea Abernathy?"

"Yeah . . . teach your ass a lesson so when you go back out there—"

"Oh no, I'm not going back out there to that crazy old woman's house!"

"What's the matter Stokey you scared of an old woman?" Detective Fish asked, laughing.

"No Detective Fish I'm not afraid of—"

"How about it Abernathy—" Detective Fish said grinning. "—two tickets to a Saints game that he won't go back out there."

"Bet man." Detective Fish and Abernathy shook on it.

"Well Fish I hope you enjoy the game." Detective Stokey said.

"Whoa . . . Stokey man I know you ain't gon do me like that!"

"It's not my fault Abernathy you made a bet on the impossible." Detective Stokey said massaging his neck looking slightly intimidated at the thought of facing Mildred Koffee again."

"Of course he is Abernathy . . . he's afraid can't you see it in his those beady eyes of his?" Detective Fish said chuckling.

"Stokey man, how long have I known you?" Detective Abernathy asked.

"I don't know twenty years give or take a few, what does that have to do with me going back out to Mildred Koffee's house?" Detective Fish intervened.

"Nothing . . . your partner wants to make sure he's got his facts right when he gives your eulogy, I read somewhere it really is possible for a man to die of fright!" Detective Fish burst into laughter. A pathetic look formed on Detective Stokey's face.

"Very funny, Fish."

"I know you Stokey man—" Detective Abernathy said looking him in the eyes. "—and I know you won't sleep one wink until that little something that's telling you that old woman knows something is satisfied that she does or doesn't have something!"

"And just what do you think that something is Abernathy?"

"You tell me man."

"I'll tell you what it is—" Detective Fish said intervening. "—it's about a detective who helped put away a baby killer and now he's having buyer's remorse." He looked at Detective Stokey and shook his head. 'I'm telling Stokey don't waste your time, that old woman doesn't know squat!"

"I never said she did Detective Fish—"
Detective Abernathy interjected.

"If that's what you believed Stokey we wouldn't be having this conversation and you know it."

"Okay, say you're right Abernathy?"

"I am." He stated with confidence. "I know you Stokey and I know when your curiosity is peaked you won't rest until it's nil and null." Detective Abernathy said looking inside his partner's ambiguous eyes. "Am I right?"

"Dammit Abernathy!" Detective Stokey said massaging his neck, getting up from his desk.

"Where you going man?"

"Where the hell you think I'm going Abernathy . . . I'm going back out there with egg on my face with puckered lips to kiss that old woman's ass!"

"Mildred Koffee's no lightweight." Detective Fish said amused. "It's gonna take more than one pair of lips to kiss that wide ass. He burst into laughter. "I would let you borrow mines Stokey but I gotta hot date tonight."

"Very funny, Fish." Detective Stokey said stuffing his black notepad in his jacket pocket.

"Naw Stokey man . . . she ain't gon like that!" Detective Abernathy said shaking his head.

"What the hell's wrong this time?"

"Boot licking." Detective Abernathy said. "Old lady Koffee hates bootlicking just about as much as she hates disrespect."

"Boot licking?" Detective Stokey stated. "Who the hell said anything about boot licking? I was simply going back out there to show the old gal some respect?"

"If I were you Stokey man I'd give her a day or two—let her cool off then I'd go back out there." Detective Abernathy said looking in his partner's water blue eyes. "But that's just what I'd do." He shifted his eyes over to Detective Fish and silently chuckled. A look of ambivalence displayed on Detective Stokey face. "But you do what you thinks gon work for you Stokey man."

"Maybe I'll go ahead Abernathy and do what you would do."

"Smart boy." Detective Fish stated, chuckling. "Because I'd hate to have to arrest an eighty three year old Black woman, it wouldn't look good for the department."

"Arrest?" Detective Stokey said puzzled by the statement. "Arrest her for what?"

"Assault on an officer."

"What?"

"If you go back out there today—" Detective Fish said laughing. "—I guarantee Mildred Koffee's gon take a broom to your ass, therefore leaving us no other choice but to arrest her old ass for assaulting an officer!" He burst into laughter then walked away. Detective Stokey watch unamused as Detectives Fish and Abernathy laughed on their way back to their desk.

Chapter Three

Detective Stokey locked eyes with Mildred as he pulled in her dirt driveway and stopped. Seated in her old rocking chair on the front porch she quickly stood and prepared go into her house.

"Mrs. Koffee—wait!" He said through his open car window. Mildred turned and looked at him through the windshield.

"You got more guts than folks round here gave you credit for." She said watching as he got out of the car. "Didn't expect to see you back here no time soon."

"I came back to apologize Mrs. Koffee . . . I think I may have uh, disrespected you when I said you didn't know diddly squat about who murdered that baby." Mildred gave no reply. "So uh, Detective Abernathy thought maybe I should—" She cut him off.

"Look like I'm gon need to talk to Roger about always running his mouth thinking he know me."

"So I guess I uh, should go ahead and apologize." Mildred sarcastically smiled.

"That would be a good place to start."

"I uh, know we kind of got off to a rocky start—" He said trying to find the right words. "—but I'm here and I'm hoping we can uh, start over." He stood next to his car hoping Mildred would ask him to join her on the porch.

"That depends on what you came here to say."

"How about I don't say anything Mrs. Koffee and I just listen to you?" She returned to her rocking chair and sat down.

"First thing you can do is stop calling me Mrs. Koffee." A peculiar look displayed on Detective Stokey's face.

"Okay, I can do that." He said trying not to sound like he was bootlicking. "What would you uh, like for me to call you?"

"My name is Mildred."

"Okay Mrs. Koff—" He stopped and looked into Mildred's scolding eyes. "—Mildred."

"Second thing you can do Detective Stokey—" He interjected.

"Andy."

"What?"

"Andy . . . my name is Andy Stokey and since you've instructed me to call you Mildred, I'd be obliged if you would drop the Detective Stokey and just call me Andy." They laughed then exchanged a mutual smile. "You do want our relationship to be informal don't you Mildred?"

"Yes I would Detective—" She hesitated. "—Andy."

"Thank you Mildred."

"You welcome Andy." She took note him standing idly next to his car. "Ain't no point in you standing out there in that hot sun when you can take shade up here on this porch." Detective Stokey noted the two kitchen chairs placed at Mildred's right and the lone chair to her left. He walked towards the house stepping on the slightly leaning stairs joining Mildred on the porch being seated in one of the two chairs to her right.

"So tell me Andy what is it you want to know 'cause I got information on just about every crime happened in these parts for the last twenty years or so." Detective Stokey's eyes widened as he looked at Mildred, curious of her self-incriminating words.

"Mildred, do you know something about homicides you haven't reported to law enforcement?" He asked, troubled by her possibly withholding evidence of previous crimes.

"I ain't saying I do and I ain't saying I don't."

"You do know withholding evidence about a crime is a crime don't you Mildred?" She grinned, ignoring his question.

"So do that mean you want me to tell you which of your officer friends been spending time over at Ms. Verna Mae's whorehouse?" Detective Stokey's jaw dropped.

"Ms. Who's . . . what?" He said disturbed by the accusation.

"But that ain't the reason why you here now is it?" Mildred giggled.

"Do you know something about other crimes Mildred that—"

"We can talk about that another day, right now I believe you here to find out who murdered Baby boy Doe." Detective Stokey momentarily stared at her—his curiosity peaked as he now wondered of Mildred's own criminal status. "But if you really want to know about Ms. Verna Mae's whorehouse best thing for you to do is be back here come Friday evening see for yourself."

"Would uh, one of those officers happen to be Seymour Fish?" He asked remembering Detective Fish's mention of an upcoming hot date. She giggled.

"Why don't we just move on Andy?"

"Maybe it's best we do." He said as thoughts of his colleagues frequenting Ms. Verna Mae's whorehouse troubled his moral fibers. "Ms. Verna Mae's whorehouse?" He muttered to himself. Mildred continued giggling. "I couldn't help but notice you in the courtroom on the day Thomas Lee Simms was convicted for the murder of Baby boy Doe."

"Yeah I saw you looking at me Andy."

"You shook your head as if you believed the jury had gotten it wrong."

"They did."

"You want to tell me uh—" He hesitated not wanting to sound disrespectful. "—you uh, think you can tell me why you believe the verdict was wrong Mildred?"

"Because it was."

"Do you know something a jury of twelve men and women and everybody else in the courtroom listening to the evidence don't know?"

"I do."

"Do you mind telling me what that is Mildred?" Detective Stokey asked becoming irritated by her brief responses. Mildred sensed his increasing agitation, but ignored it.

"Have you had breakfast this morning Andy?"

A puzzled looked formed on his face in response to her irrelevant question.

"What?"

"I asked if you'd eaten breakfast yet."

"As a matter of fact Mildred I haven't, but what does that have to do with anything?"

"Because I ain't so much as had a glass of water this morning and I'm—" He cut her off.

"Well don't let me stop you—"

"I don't eat alone Andy when there's somebody here to break bread with."

"Break what?" He asked, confused.

"I want you to join me for breakfast this morning."

Detective Stokey looked into Mildred's insistent eyes hoping his refusal wouldn't be seen as disrespectful.

"Uh, don't worry about me Mildred—" He half-heartedly chuckled. "—truth is I'm not really a breakfast person, in fact my first meal of the day usually begins with lunch." He said swallowing the lump forming in his throat, uneasy by the skeptical look on Mildred's face.

"You look mighty round about the waist for a man claiming not to eat breakfast." Detective Stokey discretely shifted his eyes down at his protruding belly as he tried to close his suit jacket, suddenly feeling self conscious about his plump physique.

"Well believe it or not Mildred, I don't." He again tugged at his jacket. "But that doesn't mean I uh, don't eat." She giggled.

"I can see that."

"Can we get back the topic at hand Mildred?" Detective Stokey said shifting his eyes again at his belly.

"It's a good thing Roger called me this morning—"

"Ahem!" Detective Stokey clear his throat. "Did you say Detective Abernathy called you this morning?"

"That's right." Mildred said smiling. "Told me you'd be coming back out here—thought I needed to fix you some breakfast." She glanced over at his enlarged belly. "I don't know why . . . you don't look like you missing no meals to me."

"Good Ol' Abernathy." Detective Stokey stated with sarcasm. "I'll be sure to thank him when I get back to the precinct." He said thinking out loud.

"I was thinking about having you take Roger a plate of this food back with you." Detective Stokey's face lit up.

"Why not Mildred I'd love to do that?" He said sounding vengeful. "It would be an honor for me to hand Detective Abernathy a plate of your food."

"I sure would appreciate it Andy, but right now, I need you to do me favor." A huge smile formed on Mildred's face. "You married Andy?" His anxiety heightened, uncertain exactly what the smile on Mildred's face meant.

"Uh, wait a minute Mildred—" He said believing her smile to be of an intimate in nature. "—I uh, don't think it would be appropriate for us to—" Mildred laughed out loud.

"I don't know where your mind is Andy but I'm a old woman—"

"Old? You're not old Mildred." He said searching for a respectable way to put it. "I would say that you're an original template of mankind." She chuckled.

"If that's your way of saying I'm old I accept it."

"Exactly how old are you Mildred?"

"Only thing you need to know about me is which cupboard I keep my plates in so you can fix us both some breakfast." Detective Stokey silently looked at her, masking his agitation of her insistence on him eating breakfast, but held his temper as he remembered Detective Abernathy's lesson on respect.

"I tell you what Mildred . . . why don't you go ahead and let me fix that plate for Abernathy and while I'm taking it back to the precinct you enjoy whatever it is you've prepared." Mildred giggled as his words fell on deaf ears.

"I got grits, scrambled eggs with a little onion, green pepper and cheese . . . ham, fried pork chops and a pan of fried potatoes." Detective Stokey massaged his neck.

"I uh don't mean to sound judgmental Mildred, but that seems like an awful lot of food for one meal." She giggled.

"You don't look to me to be a man afraid of food." He rose from his chair, offended by her candid words. "And I don't take to kind to folks shunning my hospitality especially when they want something from me."

"What the hell why not?" He said relenting. "I guess an oversized fat filled, greasy, unhealthy breakfast won't kill me." Mildred chuckled.

"I hope you like onions Andy?"

"Sure why?"

"I dropped a few in the fried potatoes." Detective Stokey looked through the screened back door.

"I uh, guess I'll go in here in this unfamiliar kitchen and fix us both a plate." He stated with reluctance.

"You like hot sauce Andy?" His mouth abruptly opened.

"With breakfast Mildred?" She laughed, humored by the sour look on his face.

"I eat it on anything ain't sweet, kind of gives food a extra burst of flavor." A perplexed look formed on Detective Stokey's face.

"Flavor . . . it's hot! Who wants everything they eat to be hot?" Mildred giggled gesturing him with her hand.

"Run on now so we can eat!" Detective Stokey opened the back door, subtly shaking his head as he entered the house, allowing the screen door to slam shut behind him.

"Damn you Abernathy!" He mumbled underneath his breath as he went in search of the cupboard containing Mildred's plates.

#

Dorothy Jean glanced nervously around the crowded visitation room at the Louisiana State Penitentiary as she awaited Thomas Lee to enter. Her attention drew the steel door guarded by two officers seeing Thomas Lee as he entered, his eyes searching throughout the room. She raised her hand hoping to get his attention.

"Thomas Lee!" Dorothy Jean called out.

"Ma'am!" A guard said cautioning her with a stern gaze. "No shouting." Thomas Lee looked over at him then again turned to Dorothy Jean, comforted by her loving eyes as he sat in a chair across the table from her. Tears rolled down her cheeks as she reached over and touched his hand.

"No touching!" A guard yelled out. Dorothy Jean swiftly pulled back her hand, startled by the forceful voice. Thomas Lee looked again over at guard, angered by his aggressive enforcement of the rules then turned back to Dorothy Jean.

"How you been doing Dorothy Jean?"

"I've had more bad days than good if that's what you asking." He gazed in her tear filled eyes and tried to read her thoughts. "The way Rita's been over to the house helping out . . . you'd think I'd had baby or something." She said forcing a chuckle.

"You believe I did what they say I done Dorothy Jean?" Thomas Lee asked. She looked into his frightened eyes.

"I don't believe that no more than I believe you can grow wings and fly." She quietly laughed, masking her fears with humor. "Thomas Lee you got to be one of the gentlest men I've ever known." Dorothy Jean said reaching across the table and touching his hand.

"No touching!" A guard shouted. Thomas Lee shook his in aggravation.

"Damn!" He said keeping his voice low. "This ain't no place for a human being to be Dorothy Jean—we men not animals.

"I heard that detective who testified against you been talking to Ms. Mildred." Dorothy Jean said diverting the subject of the stringent conditions.

"I need to talk to you about something Dorothy Jean?" Her eyes widened with fear.

"If you getting ready to tell me you murdered that baby Thomas Lee I don't want to hear it." She whispered, nervous.

"This ain't got nothing to do with that baby Dorothy Jean." Thomas Lee said sensing her fear.

"Then why you looking at me like a fly caught in a spider web?"

"If I get murdered in here Dorothy Jean I want you to know I truly do love you." She looked at him with doubt.

"I know I ain't ever been faithful and maybe this is my punishment for it but—" She cut him off.

"If this about you and Delores Clarkston—" His eyes widened, shocked by her knowledge of his affair.

"Dorothy Jean I—"

"You think I didn't know about you and Delores?" She shifted her eyes briefly over at the guard then turned back to Thomas Lee. "Gossip around town moves faster than a rushing river."

"Dorothy Jean you know I—"

"Ain't nothing folks like more than spreading other folks hurt, and if you getting ready to tell me how sorry you are Thomas Lee, don't!" Dorothy Jean suddenly chuckled. "Seem more like I was the one who was your mistress and Delores was Mrs. Thomas Lee Simms." Thomas Lee looked at her loss for words. "First time I heard about you and Delores I just about died inside." He reached over and attempted to take her hand as he looked in her moistened eyes. Dorothy Jean snatched it away. "Don't touch me Thomas Lee." She said hurt by his betrayal. "Don't you ever touch me again!"

"I'm sorry Dorothy Jean—"

"Do you love her Thomas Lee?"

He looked in Dorothy Jean's her pained eye as his stomach rumbled with butterflies. "Answer me!" She yelled.

"Keep it down!" A guard shouted looking over at her with demanding eyes. Thomas Lee quickly stood. He looked at the guard with defiance. Dorothy Jean's eyes widened, terrified of the consequences for his sudden action.

"Sit down Thomas Lee!" She said panicked.

"What for Dorothy Jean they gon kill me anyway!"

"Thomas Lee please sit down baby!"

"Prisoner!" A guard shouted. "Sit you ass down before I come over there and sit you down!" Thomas Lee continued standing. Dorothy Jean abruptly stood.

"I ain't getting ready to sit here and watch them beat my husband to death!" She screamed out hurrying toward the exit.

"Dorothy Jean—wait!" Thomas Lee called out. "Baby, don't leave!" She turned and looked into his pleading eyes. "Come on baby we ain't finished talking yet". She shifted her eyes over to the guard then walked over to him being seated at the table. "Thank you baby."

"That murdered baby boy Thomas Lee—" Dorothy Jean said. His heart pounded in his ears as he awaited her question. She took a deep breath. "—was he yours Thomas Lee birthed by Delores?"

"Naw Dorothy Jean . . . me and Delores ain't had no baby I swear!" She looked at him unconvinced. "I ain't been nowhere near Delores in over a yea you know that!" Thomas Lee said trying to convince her. "Not since Charles told me if I went near his wife again he would kill me and Delores!" Dorothy Jean looked at him—hurt by his thoughtless words.

"So it took Charles Clarkston threatening your life for you to leave his wife alone?" She said raising her voice.

"Naw, yeah . . . ain't no woman worth dying over Dorothy Jean."

"Do that include me Thomas Lee?"

"Naw baby, you know I ain't talking about you!" Dorothy Jean looked at him with uncertainty. "You my wife baby, I love you Dorothy Jean!"

"Do you Thomas Lee?"

"You know I do baby!"

"When I married you Thomas Lee I thought I was taking them vow with a man—not a dog."

"A dog?" Thomas Lee said bothered by her low opinion of him. "Is that what you think me Dorothy Jean?" She rose from the table.

"I'll be back next week Friday." A desperate look formed on Thomas Lee's face.

"Delores ain't meant nothing to me Dorothy Jean she was just something to do that's all . . . don't abandon me baby please!"

"You still my husband Thomas Lee and I would never turn my back on you no matter how wrong you done me."

"Thank you Dorothy Jean, I know you don't believe me, but I am sorry for everything I done to you." She momentarily looked in his eyes wanting desperately to believe him.

"Are you Thomas Lee?"

"Yeah Dorothy Jean I am."

"I'll see you next week." Thomas Lee watched from the table as Dorothy Jean exited through the steel door.

"Simms!" A guard yelled. "Return to your cage!"

#

Charles Clarkston III obscured his face behind the morning newspaper ignoring the cup of black coffee and glass of orange juice located to the right of his gold trimmed plate containing a vegetable omelet covered with a Cajun sauce, grits, ham steak and two beignets prepared by Marietta, the Clarkston's maid who've spent the better part of her now middle aged life working for the Clarkston family dating back to the days when Charles, often compared to Red Butler was a youth. Seated at the end of the enormous, rectangular dining room table, Charles awaited his wife Delores to join him. Marietta's also the mother of Thomas Lee, Delores Clarkston's former lover. Charles lowered the newspaper when hearing his wife enter the room still wearing her pink satin nightgown and holding a glass of red wine in her hand as she stumbled over to the table, plopping down in one of the satin covered dining room chairs at the opposite end of the table.

"Uh-uh I see queen lush is up." Carrie, also one of the Clarkston's maids, whispered as she assisted Marietta in prepping the family's evening supper. A fortyish Black female, Carrie's been in the Clarkston's employment for the past ten years.

"This early in the morning and that poor child's already drunk." Marietta said cutting vegetables.

"So you already know she getting ready to give Mr. Charles hell!" Carrie said amused. Marietta intervened.

"And it ain't gon be long before he—" Carrie interjected.

"Start calling us to take her drunk ass back upstairs."

"Hush Carrie!" Marietta stated. "Don't you let Mr. Charles hear you—"

"It ain't our job to be picking Ms. Delores' drunk as up off the floor everytime she fall Marietta!"

"Good morning dear." Charles said.

"We been doing it all this time why should anything change—"

"Shhhhh!" Carrie said quieting Marietta when hearing Charles' Louisiana southern drawl. "Mr. Charles just stepped in the ring with Ms. Delores and round one is about to begin." Carrie said finding the Clarkston's marital discord entertaining.

"I would offer you some breakfast Delores dear, but I see you're still adhering to your liquid diet." Charles said barricading his face behind the newspaper. "What do you call it again? Oh that's right it's called the fall on my ass again red wine diet."

"And it's doing exactly what it's supposed to Charles." Delores said slurring.

"And what would that be dear?"

"It keeps me so drunk I don't have to think about anything except which floor in this big boring house I'm going to pass out on next." Charles lowered the newspaper and stared at her.

"And after her drunk ass pass out . . . he gon be calling to scrape her ass up off the floor."

"Hush now Carrie." Marietta said whispering.

"Now that sounds like a total waste of gravity usage and a misuse of an expensive wine." Charles said. Delores looked at him with defiance then turned her glass of wine up to her mouth and consumed its entire contents. Charles looked momentarily at her and again obscured his face behind the newspaper. Carrie looked at Marietta and quietly giggled.

"Uh-oh here it comes." Carrie said underneath her breath as she sat at the kitchen table peeling potatoes pretending to be uninterested in the Clarkston's bickering.

"Maybe if I had children to fill the rooms in this big empty dungeon I wouldn't need to drown myself in your expensive red wine." Delores said raising the empty glass preparing to throw it at Charles.

"I wouldn't do that if I were you dear." He said from behind the newspaper.

"And if she do I bet her ass gon clean up every piece of glass that's on that floor!" Carrie said in a low voice.

"You go to hell Charles!" Delores shouted. He again lowered the paper and subtly smiled.

"I'll make you a deal dear." He sarcastically grinned. "How about I met you there?" Carrie's mouth flung open.

"TKO!" She whispered with excitement. "I see Mr. Charles getting better at playing the dozens with her drunk ass."

"Hush Carrie!" Marietta said. "One of these days Mr. Charles gon hear you."

"No he ain't . . . don't you hear me whispering Marietta?"

"I hate you Charles!" Delores bellowed.

"Oh, it must be—I hate you Charles day again." He said chuckling. "Before you agreed to be my wife Delores you knew we'd never have children and you knew the reason why." She stared at him but gave no reply. "If you didn't agree with it you should've never allowed me put that extremely expensive ring on your finger."

"He got a point there." Carrie said quietly instigating. Delores burst into tears, infuriated by Charles' painful reminder of the deal she made with 'the devil'.

"Why don't you excuse yourself dear and go find a floor in this big boring house to pass out on."

"Damn!" Carrie said trying to keep her voice low. "It won't be long now before his ass start calling one of us to take her drunk ass back upstairs."

"Well I hope he call you this time Carrie, I need to finish this big supper Mr. Charles want me to cook." Carrie's mouth flung open.

"Me!" She stated with objection. "I took Ms. Delores' drunk ass back upstairs last night and my back still hurting from halfway carrying that heifer up them steps!"

"Today Delores dear I would really like to enjoy one of Marietta's delicious breakfast without looking at you sitting across the table from me inebriated." She gave no reply. "It somehow diminishes my ability to enjoy it." Charles said with a bitter look on his face.

"I hate you Charles!" Delores again screamed out.

"Then I guess that makes two of us because I sometimes can hardly stand myself." He contemptuously laughed then again raised the newspaper obscuring her from his view. "Marietta!" Charles called out. She shifted her eyes to Carrie and shook her head.

"Yes, Mr. Charles?" Marietta said entering the dining room taking note of Delores slumped over on the table.

"Would you please take my drunken wife upstairs to her room and pour her back into bed?"

"I'm telling you now Mr. Charles if Ms. Delores start fighting, you gon have to take her up there yourself." Marietta said as she cautiously approached her. "Come on Ms. Delores let me to take you upstairs so you can go back in bed."

"Hey Marietta!" She said slurring as Marietta assisted her up from the table. "Where's Roosevelt?" Delores asked unbalanced. "I need him to bring me another bottle of red wine."

"I don't think Mr. Charles gon let you have any more wine Ms. Delores." Marietta said guiding her through the vestibule over to the staircase.

"Well Charles is not my father, he's my husband—" Delores burst into laughter. "—and not a very good one at that." Charles lowered the newspaper and looked at her.

"And Marietta try to get some food in my wife would you please? She's skin and bones and she looks like something not even the dogs would drag in." Marietta looked at him with chastising eyes.

"Now Mr. Charles you should be shame talking about your wife like that."

"Perhaps not Marietta, but I think it's something my wife needs to hear."

"I'll see what I can do, but you know how Ms. Delores is when it comes to eating solid food.

"Yes Marietta I'm afraid I do." Charles looked at his wife and shook his head with antipathy before again burying his face behind the paper. "I see there's an article in the paper announcing that a Detective Stokey is on a mission to prove your son innocent of murdering that poor innocent baby." Charles said bothered by the news.

"My boy ain't killed that baby Mr. Charles and you know it!" Marietta said as she escorted Delores up the stairs.

"Well Marietta it seems a jury of your boy's peers said different, are you saying twelve competent people were all wrong?"

"I think it best we dropped the subject Mr. Charles don't you?" Marietta said angered. Charles lowered his newspaper. He looked at Delores and frowned.

"Would you please inform Roosevelt that I'd like my wife to remain sober until I return home from the work this evening? I'd like to enjoy my supper just once with the woman I married, sober."

"Maybe if you let her have some babies like she keep asking she'd put down that wine bottle and pick up a baby bottle." Charles looked at Marietta offended by her unsolicited comment.

"I don't believe that's a matter to be discussed with staff."

"Well you remember that the next time you want staff to go drag your wife out of some bar or some man's bed." Charles gave no reply as he began eating his breakfast.

#

"You find anything yet that the prosecutor didn't already have Stokey?" Detective Fish asked quietly standing over him as Detective Stokey sat engrossed in the notes he'd taken during his visit with Mildred.

"Dammit Fish!" He yelled. "Why in the hell are you sneaking up on me like that?"

"A little jumpy aren't you Stokey?" Detective Fish said humored. "All I asked was if old lady Koffee had given you anything that would make a judge overturn the guilty verdict of a baby killer?"

"Well next time you have a question Detective Fish, how about you ask it from over at your own desk." Detective Fish quietly laughed. "And don't be sneaking up on me like that . . . I do carry a loaded weapon you know." A surprised look displayed on Detective Fish's face.

"So you're gonna shoot me for asking a damn question Stokey?"

"No Detective Fish I'm not going to shoot you for asking me a question and that's not what I said anyway I said—oh never mind." Detective Stokey's attention remained on his notes. "Well the answer to your question is no I haven't found anything new, but I'll tell you what I have learned Fish since you're so inquisitive—"

"And what's that Stokey?" He asked looking over Detective Stokey shoulder trying to decipher his badly written notes.

"Never eat pigtails, buttermilk and grits for breakfast."
A sour look formed on Detective Fish's face.

"I'll keep that in mind the next time I have a taste for food loaded with saturated fats." He continued frowning. "Well don't be surprised when you end up in an emergency room Stokey needing to have your stomach pumped." Detective Fish said still looking over Detective Stokey's shoulder.

"Don't you have a case or something you need to be working on detective instead of standing over here bugging me?" Detective Stokey asked, annoyed.

"Look who's talking . . . a detective wasting good time trying to solve a case where the defendant's already been proven guilty."

"Detective Fish!" Lieutenant Porter said when seeing the agitated look on Detective Stokey's face in response to his coworker's unwanted presence.

"Yeah Lieutenant?"

"Has crime slow down to the point where you have nothing you need to be working on?" Detective Fish looked at him then returned to his disorganized desk.

"Well I bet you a steak dinner Stokey that nothing changes, and that baby killer remains locked up where he belongs." Detective Fish said being seated at his desk. "Just remember I like my steak medium rare."

"And you remember that I like mines rare." Detective Stokey said.

"You're on!" Detective Fish said shifting his eyes briefly to Lieutenant Porter still watching the two detectives. "Oh and uh, Fish—"

"Yeah—"

"I think I'd like to have a bottle of champagne with that steak when I celebrate my victory."

"No problem Stokey." Detective Fish said from behind his computer monitor. "Just so long as you know when you lose I expect the same thing."

"May the best man win!" Detective Stokey stated certain he'd be the victor. Detective Fish watched with curiosity when seeing his opponent suddenly hurry from the squad room.

#

"Good morning Mildred, beautiful day isn't it?" Detective Stokey said enthusiastically as he got out of his car.

"Since the day ain't been long started I think I'll wait and see." She said watching through the screen door as he walked towards her house. "What's got you so bright eyed this morning Andy?" She asked as she walked out onto the porch. "Smiling like you just hit the numbers over at Big Daddy Andrews number house." A perplexed look formed on Detective Stokey's face.

"Big daddy's who?" He asked walking up the three crooked stairs leading to the porch. "Am I going to have to arrest you Mildred when all this is over?" She cunningly smiled on her way to the old rocking chair being seated.

"You gon tell me why you here or are we gon waste time speaking on what information you think I might be withholding?" He silently looked at her before speaking.

"I was reviewing my notes on the information you gave me and I saw that—"

"Only thing keeping you from sitting in one of these chairs is you." She said giggling. He hesitated then sat in a chair to her right.

"I was looking through my notes and I noticed—" Mildred interrupted.

"I can't wait to hear what you think you got." She said smiling.

"Good because I can't wait to—"

"Well before you get started I got a pan of roasted rutabaga in there on the stove with some fried cabbage, cornbread and a honey glazed ham still hot in the oven." A look of disbelief appeared on Detective Stokey's face.

"For breakfast Mildred?"

"Food is food ain't it?"

"Mildred is it healthy for you to be eating that kind of—"

"Cooked it for supper last night, but I messed around and fell asleep before I got a chance to eat it!" She giggled. "So I figured I'd eat this morning for breakfast."

"Did you uh, leave that food out overnight Mildred?" She again giggled.

"Not all night . . . I did wake up some time in the wee houses of the morning and put it in the ice box." A lump formed in Detective Stokey's throat as he anticipated Mildred inviting him to 'break bread' with her. "Would you uh, happen to remember exactly what time that was Mildred?"

"I can't say I do but—" She tried to recall. "—I'm pretty sure it's still good to eat." Detective Stokey swallowed the lump. "So why don't you run on in the house and fix us both a plate?"

"As much as I'd love to join you for breakfast Mildred—"

"Liar."

"Ahem!" Detective Stokey cleared his throat trying to think of how to get out eating Mildred's possibly contaminated food. "Lunch!" He blurted. "I uh, almost forgot . . . I have plans to meet with Detective Abernathy for lunch and—"

"Why don't you call Roger then y'all both can have lunch with me!" Mildred said delighted at the thought. He looked at Mildred seeing the loneliness behind her excited smile.

"Oh hell why not." Detective Stokey said to himself. "Like you said breakfast is whatever you choose to eat right?"

"I got some leftover pig feet that'll go good with them rutabagas!" She giggled. Detective Stokey smiled as his stomach twinged with nausea. "Ain't no point in letting good food go to waste now is it?"

"Of course not Mildred."

"And after breakfast we'll have all the time in the world for me to hear what you think you done found while we eating some of that peach cobbler I threw together this morning."

"Peach cobbler Mildred?" Detective Stokey discreetly looked at her two hundred pound, five foot one frame. "For breakfast?"

Chapter Four

Detective Stokey wiped his mouth with the white paper napkin as he finished the unusual breakfast, licking his lips as he savored the flavor.

"Well Mildred I must say that was an interesting breakfast—what did you say those roasted things were again?"

"Rutabagas."

"Rutabagas?" He again licked his lips. "Taste kind of reminds me of turnips . . . and again Mildred I'd like to apologize for Abernathy not being able to make it." He said electing not to tell her of his partner's blatant refusal.

"You tell Roger I said the next time somebody bring a dozen donuts to the office it ain't meant for him to eat half of them by his self!" She giggled.

"That's Abernathy for you he has a tooth for sweets like a bear has for honey." He chuckled.

"Now I know you didn't come all this way to discuss rutabagas, so let me hear what you think you got that's gon put the real murderer of that baby behind bars."

"Okay, when I was looking over my notes—" Mildred interjected.

"You know Andy its two things for sure gon leave its mark on a female—having her innocence stolen and losing a child." An odd look showed on Detective Stokey's face.

"I'm sure there's some validity to what you're about to say Mildred but—" He stopped when noting the blank stare in her eyes. "—you alright Mildred?"

"Some twenty or so years ago I had a granddaughter." An endearing smile formed on Mildred's face as her eyes began to moisten with tears. "My Raynetta was a beautiful child." Mildred said turning briefly to Detective Stokey. "One thing about having beauty . . . it can serve a woman well at times and at others it can bring the worse kind of evil on her she could ever imagine." Mildred again stared into nothingness.

"Raynetta?" Detective Stokey said looking at Mildred with a peculiar look in his eyes.

"Mildred did something happen to Raynetta?"

"She was seventeen and trying to grow up faster than life would let her." Mildred half-heartedly grinned. "Josephine, that was her momma and my eldest daughter . . . decided she was gon take Raynetta to the Cutter's mansion to work with her cooking and cleaning house, ain't gave no thought to how Ray Arthur felt—" Detective Stokey interjected.

"Ray Arthur?"

"Josephine's husband." Mildred paused. "Ray Arthur hated my daughter cooking and cleaning house for rich folks."

"Cutter?" A perplexed look formed on Detective Stokey face as he contemplated the name. "Why does that name sound familiar?"

"Probably because he thinks he's the most important man in all of Louisiana."

"Cutter . . . Congressman Cutter?" He said readjusted his rear end on the uncomfortable chair. "I uh, know this might sound strange Mildred, but what does the congressman have to do with any of this?" He asked not sure where her story was headed. "Oh, I know Sonny Cutter right? I'm sure his name is written all over whatever happened to your granddaughter, but I'm still not making the connection." Mildred gave no reply as she shook her head becoming upset. "How old did you say your granddaughter was again Mildred?"

"Old enough for them to get my grandbaby pregnant."
Detective Stokey's jaw dropped.

"Mildred did you just say pregnant?"

"I remember my granddaughter lying there trying to bring that child in this world—cried something awful, but all she could think of was disappointing her momma and Ray Arthur." Tears ran down Mildred's cheeks. "Seem like her crying wasn't ever gon stop."

"Mildred I'm sorry about your granddaughter—" She looked him firmly in the eyes. "—but . . ."

"After she had done pushed that child in the world you could've heard cotton hit the floor when we laid eyes on the child, it was white as snow." Detective Stokey eye's quickly widened.

"Did you say white as snow?"

"Look like you could've birthed it." She said noting the cynical look on his face. He lightly chuckled with skepticism.

"White baby? Is that even possible Mildred?" Detective Stokey said challenging her story.

"Black women been doing it since slavery . . . birthing the master's child, some look like the momma others White just like the master."

"Is that right?" He said unconvinced by her entire story.

"Black folks been passing for years—" He cut her off.

"Passing?" He said confused. "What do you mean by passing?"

"Black folks passing themselves off as White 'cause they could, knowing they was Black." He momentarily looked at Mildred then laughed. "Are you serious Mildred?" He asked amused by her unbelievable genealogy.

"When my granddaughter gave birth to that White baby wasn't no way Ray Arthur was gon allow her keep it, and the Cutter's wasn't 'bout to claim it as their own."

"So if I'm hearing you correctly Mildred, you're telling me Sonny Cutter impregnated your granddaughter and—" She cut him off.

"That ain't what I'm telling you at all Andy." A baffled look formed on his face.

"I don't understand, didn't you just say Raynetta was impregnated by a Cutter, if not Sonny Cutter then who?" Detective Stokey asked suspicious of Mildred's story. "That only leaves—"

"Jonathan Cutter . . . he was the one got my grandbaby pregnant." Mildred said. Detective Stokey's stomach rumbled with butterflies as he tried to digest Mildred's damming allegation.

"That's uh, one hell of an accusation to make Mildred." He said uneasy. "Do you understand the trouble you could get yourself in by making such a claim?"

"It ain't no claim it's the truth!" Mildred said raising his voice.

"Truth or not—" He said disturbed by the allegation. "—you're accusing a very wealthy, influential, highly respected congressman of having been intimately involved with your seventeen year old granddaughter resulting in a child!"

"That's right."
Detective Stokey looked at Mildred, afraid to believe her story.

"Uh, how long ago did you say this happened, Mildred?"
"It was over twenty years ago."

"Over twenty years ago?" Detective Stokey shook his head as he sarcastically chuckled. "Maybe Detective Fish was right." He mumbled to himself.

"About me being crazy—"

"Now Mildred I didn't say that I uh—"

"You ain't had to say it, me and Detective Fish done had plenty words on my sanity.

"Okay Mildred, let's say what you're telling me is true—"

"It is!" She yelled. Detective Stokey took a deep breath and nervously massaged his neck.

"Then where is this child Mildred?"

"If my granddaughter says Jonathan Cutter impregnated her then that's just what happened!" Mildred said furious. Detective Stokey looked at her, unable to believe her controversial story. "When Ray Arthur found out that child was pregnant he whipped her 'til she ain't had a tear left in her eyes—" A look of horror displayed on Detective Stokey's face.

"Whipped her?"

"That child never changed her story that Jonathan Cutter was the one who got her with child." Detective Stokey's heart pounded in his ears as he listened to Mildred's allegations about Congressman Jonathan Cutter impregnating her seventeen year old granddaughter.

"Do you hear what you're saying Mildred?"

"I ain't deaf!"

"Do you realize the trouble words like that could get you in?"

"I'm eighty-three years old Andy and if the good Lord allows me to keep breathing I might just live to see ninety—" He interjected.

"And if I repeat what you just told me, you may not live to see eighty four!" He said deeply concerned. "And as for me I'll be lucky to find a job as a short order cook!"

"You may be afraid of Jonathan Cutter but—"

"You're damn right I'm afraid!" Detective Stokey said raising his voice. "And you should be too!"

"Well I ain't!"

"Congressman Cutter is an extremely powerful man Mildred, and if I were you I'd forget all about that story your granddaughter told you!"

"Get off my property!" She shouted.

"Mildred—" He said afraid to accept Mildred's story as truth. "I don't mean to sound insensitive but I'm not here trying to establish paternity of Raynetta's illegitimate child—" He sated without remorse. "I'm not about to destroy a man's reputation on something that has absolutely nothing to do with who killed that baby!"

"I believe I told you to get off my property!" Mildred shouted.

"Mildred please try and understand—" She abruptly stood then entered her house slamming the door shut. "Dammit" Detective Stokey yelled.

#

"A penny for your thought?" Detective Abernathy said breaking his partner's concentration when seeing him sitting at his desk nervously massaging his neck, deep in thought as he recalled his conversation with Mildred regarding Raynetta and Congressman Cutter.

"Dammit Abernathy!" He yelled, startled by the intrusion. "Why in the hell are you sneaking up on me like that?"

"Man all I said was a A penny for your thought, how in hell is that sneaking?" Detective Stokey looked at his partner with apologetic eyes.

"I'm sorry Abernathy it's just that this thing with Mildred—"

"Stokey man you need to let it go!" He said raising his voice, concerned about his partner's involvement in the controversial case. "Because contrary to what you might believe Thomas Lee Simms is guilty as hell man and he did murder that baby!" Detective Stokey's mouth abruptly opened, astounded by his partner's opposing opinion.

"Well thanks for your honesty Abernathy." He stated sarcastically. "Well before you throw away the key to Thomas Lee's cell maybe you can help me to make sense of the story Mildred told me yesterday." Detective Abernathy shook his head no.

"No! I don't want hear nothing that has to do with Mildred Koffee and all her 'unsubstantiated' I witness accounts."

"Just hear me out Abernathy then tell me what you think."

"No!" Detective Abernathy said as he began walking back to his desk.

"I'll take you to lunch . . . your choice of restaurants." Detective Abernathy abruptly stopped.

"My choice?" He said looking him in the eyes. "You buying man?"

"Why is it everytime I invite you to lunch I end up paying for it?"

"I don't know you tell me?"

"Could it be because I'm a sucker for your company?" Detective Stokey said cynically.

"Wrong . . . it's because the only time you invite me to lunch is when you want to discuss something with me that's gon give me the worst damn headache I could ever imagine!"

"You know Abernathy you just might just be right."

"You know damn well I'm right Stokey!" Detective Abernathy said reconsidering the offer. "Maybe you should tell me what it's about before I accept your offer."

"I'm only asking for your expert opinion because this thing's been nagging the hell out of me!"

"Let me guess, Mildred Koffee told you some story about officers frequenting Ms. Verna Mae's whorehouse and now you trying to figure out who they are?" Detective Stokey's eyes widened with surprise.

"You uh . . . you know something about that Abernathy?"

"About what? I don't know what you talking about man." Detective Abernathy said electing not to disclose his fellow officers weaknesses. Detective Stokey rose from his desk.

"Ready?"

"Ready for what man?

"What do you mean for what . . . Lunch!"

"Whoa . . . I don't recall agreeing to that Stokey man."

"Of course you did, now let's go!"
Detective Abernathy shook his head, relenting.

"Stokey man I don't want spend my lunch listening to some off the wall story you heard from old lady Koffee—"

"How about I let you order dessert?"

"Dessert?" Detective Abernathy took a second to contemplate on his partner's offer.

"Anything on the menu."

"Anything?"

"Anything." A huge smile formed on Detective Abernathy's face.

"Let go man. The two detectives headed for the elevator arriving just as the doors opened.

"You guys going somewhere?" Detective Fish asked as he stepped off the elevator.

"Lunch." Detective Abernathy said as he and Detective Stokey entered the elevator. "My partner's feeling generous this morning." Detective Fish glanced at his watch.

"Lunch? It's nine O'clock in the morning, and since when did you start eating breakfast Stokey?" He asked as the elevator doors closed. "Now I wonder what that's all about." He said to himself in response to Detective Stokey's out of character behavior. "I hope he's not spending the money for my steak dinner and bottle of champagne."

#

Detective Abernathy glanced around the half empty restaurant then looked at his partner with pessimistic eyes as the two men seated themselves in the very back of the Appetite Pleaser Café having arrived ahead of the lunch crowd.

"What?" Detective Stokey said noting his partner's silent gaze.

"You want to tell me why in the hell we sitting all the way in the back like we staking out the joint?"

"What do mean staking out the place?" Detective Stokey said massaging his neck and looking around.

"Man by the time the waitress gets back here with our food it's gon need to be reheated!" Detective Stokey ignored his partner's gripes as he leaned in towards him.

"I need to warn you Abernathy—"

"Warn me about what man?" He asked looking into his partner's troubled eyes."

"That what I'm about to tell you, could cost both of us our careers if any ears besides yours heard it." Frowns formed on Detective Abernathy's forehead.

"Then I'm out of here man!" He stood and prepared to leave.

"Sit down Abernathy, please!"
He looked around with apprehension then again sat down.

"Man what the hell could that old woman, have told you that could cost us our careers?" He asked staring Detective Stokey in the eyes. "Naw man forget it . . . I don't want to know."

"Wait a minute Abernathy just hear what I have to say!" Detective Stokey said looking at him with pleading eyes.

"Stokey man I ain't trying to hear nothing that gon cost me a career I spent over twenty five years building!" Detective Abernathy momentarily looked at him. "Man I thought we were friends!"

"We are friends Abernathy . . . at least I thought we were."

"Then why in the hell would you want to ruin my career? Why don't you tell whatever it is you're trying to tell me to Detective Fish?"

"I would but I don't like that guy well enough to buy him lunch." They laughed.

"Go ahead man, tell me what is it you're about to tell me that's gon cost me everything—my career, my wife, my family, my life?"

"Thanks Abernathy now tell me what you make of this, I was talking to Mildred—" Detective Abernathy's eyes widened.

"So you gon tell me anyway after I told you all that I stood to lose?"

"Of course I'm going to tell you."

"Why you doing this to me man?" Detective Abernathy asked as he made eye contact with one of the five waitresses in the café. "Waitress!" He yelled out.

"I'll be with you in a minute sir." A red haired, twentyish waitress said from across the room.

"Can we get a couple cups of black coffee over here please?" He asked agitated.

"I'll bring those coffees over in just a minute sir." Detective Abernathy nodded.

"Can you make one of those with lots of sugar, no cream?" Detective Stokey stated. The waitress stopped and stared at him.

"You hard of hearing old man, I said I'd be there in a minute!" He quickly turned to Detective Abernathy insulted by her belittling words.

"Did you hear that Abernathy?" He said watching as the waitress grabbed a pot of coffee and headed in their direction. "You can bet she won't be getting a tip from me."

"How are you today sir?" She asked looking at Detective Abernathy before turning to Detective Stokey. She smiled. He ignored her little too late kindness as she placed two coffee cups on the table and filled them. "Let's see now . . . one black coffee and one coffee with sugar, no cream." She said dropping a handful of sugar packs on the table. "Are you gentlemen ready to order?"

"I think if we had menus that would make the task a little easier don't you?" Detective Stokey stated cynically. She shifted her eyes to Detective Abernathy then back to Detective Stokey.

"Kinda picky aren't you?" Detective Stokey's eyes widened.

"Did she just call me picky?" He said. Detective Abernathy quickly intervened.

"Whenever you can get a couple menus over here that would be just fine uh, what's your name?"

"Darla." She looked at Detective Stokey and rolled her gray eyes then turned to Detective Abernathy. "Thanks for asking handsome I'll be right back with those menus." Detective Stokey quickly looked over at his partner.

"You know Abernathy on second thought I think I will leave her a tip."

"Oh yeah, what made you changed you mind?"

"Why not?" He reached inside his pants pocket and removed a nickel. "You got change for this Abernathy?" Detective Abernathy silently grinned, humored by his partner's spiteful behavior. "You think a penny's too much?"

"I know you don't want to hear this Stokey—" Detective Abernathy said sipping his coffee. "—but I think you should walk away from this whole damn Thomas Lee Simms mess before it leads you into no man's land."

"I can't do that Abernathy, especially after what Mildred told me."

"Well I think you should know something."

"What's that?"

"I'm not in this with you man."

"I think you've already made that perfectly clear Abernathy." Detective Stokey looked at him as he opened multiple packs of sugar, dumping them in his coffee then stirring the hot beverage with his finger. "And, I guess I'm a little surprised to hear you say that."

"Why?" Detective Abernathy said offended. "Because I'm Black?"

"Partly."

"Is that how you think justice should work Stokey? Because I'm Black I'm supposed to dismiss a guilty verdict simply because me, and the defendant happen to be of the same race?"

"Of course not Abernathy and you know that's not what I'm saying."

"Then what are you saying man?"

"I'm just saying . . . given the injustice experienced by Blacks, I would think you'd—" Detective Abernathy cut him off.

"You know what I think Stokey I think you need to stay the hell away from Mildred Koffee and stop trying to solve a case that's already been decided on by a jury!"

"Point taken." Detective Stokey said agitated. "And I hope you'll understand when I say that both you and that damn jury are wrong!" He looked Detective Abernathy firmly in the eyes. "Thomas Lee Simms is no more, guilty of murdering that baby than I am, and I'll say that all the way to my grave."

"Point taken." Detective Abernathy stated. The two detectives stared one to the other, both trying to cooled down.

"Well I'm glad to see we can both agree to disagree." Detective Stokey said. "So can I tell you what I learned from Mildred—"

"Coffee." Detective Abernathy said.

"Of course, Mildred Koffee!"

"Naw man I was saying I needed another cup of coffee to help me digest the information you're about to share with me that's gon destroy both our—" He silenced when the Darla returned to their table handing them each a food stained paper menu.

"Here you go gentlemen—two menus." Detective Stokey shifted his eyes over to Detective Abernathy. "As soon as y'all make up your mind which one of our tasty meals you'd like to order just raise your hand and I'll be right over."

"We'll be sure to do that Darla." Detective Abernathy stated, quickly intervening before Detective Stokey could speak. "You think we could get a pot of coffee over here?"

"For you sir no problem." She looked at Detective Stokey and rolled her eyes. Detective Abernathy quietly chuckled. "Now don't you gentlemen be acting all stingy when it comes time to give me my tip." She said giggling. Detective Stokey watched with aggravated eyes as she walked away.

"I'll give her a damn tip alright find another line of work because you stink as a waitress." Detective Abernathy briefly grinned.

"Okay Stokey man so what was it Mildred Koffee told you?"

"You ever eat pigtails before Abernathy?" An confused look appeared on Detective Abernathy's face.

"Pigtails?"

"Yes pig tails."

"I know damn well you didn't bring me out to this greasy spoon, and remember it is your treat—to talk about some damn pig tails!"

"What about rutabagas?"

"I'm giving you five seconds Stokey to tell me what the hell pigtails and rutabagas have to do with the murder of that baby or you'll be eating lunch by your damn self . . . I got other things I can be doing."

"I ate some for the first time and they weren't half bad." Detective Abernathy looked at his watch.

"Detective Stokey I'm telling you man—"

"So anyway, after the pigtails and rutabaga Mildred tells me this story about her granddaughter Raynetta."

"Her granddaughter?" A perplexed look appeared on Detective Abernathy's face as he sipped from his coffee. "You sure she didn't say her daughter?" He asked confused. "Because to my knowledge Mildred Koffee never had, a so-called granddaughter."

"Yes, I'm definitely sure she said grand—"

"One pot of coffee freshly brewed!" Darla said interrupting their conversation as she returned.

"Thank you Darla." Detective Abernathy said watching as she filled both cups. "And don't worry about the tip you'll definitely be compensated for your excellent service." He said shifting his eyes over to his partner. "Ain't that right Stokey?" Darla smiled and awaited his reply.

"Yes Darla . . . I guarantee you'll get a tip you'll never forget."

"Thank you gentlemen." She said excited. "Well, don't forget if you gentlemen need me just raise your hand and I'll be right over."

"We'll be sure to do that Darla." Detective Abernathy said as she walked away.

"The nerves." Detective Stokey stated.

"Will you calm down man and tell me what I've been waiting thirty three minutes to hear?"

"It was what she said about her granddaughter that could get us both in trouble." Detective Abernathy's anger heightened as he listened, puzzled by his partner's mysterious impending statement.

"How the hell, can Mildred's granddaughter hurt us and we ain't never even heard of her?"

"It seems when Mildred's granddaughter was seventeen she had a baby—" Detective Abernathy burst into laughter.

"And that's what's gon cost us our careers Stokey?" He continued laughing. "Mildred's granddaughter having a baby at seventeen—seriously man?" He shook his head in disbelief. "Hell, my momma had me when she was seventeen should I be worried?"

"Here's the thing Abernathy, she's accusing Congressman Cutter of being the father of her granddaughter's child." Detective Abernathy began choking on his coffee in response to the allegation.

"What the hell did you just say?"

"Mildred said her granddaughter told her that the baby she'd gave birth to had been fathered by Congressman Cutter." Detective Stokey said whispering. A skeptical look displayed on Detective Abernathy's face.

"Tell me you don't believed that Stokey?"

"At this point Abernathy I don't know what to believe, but what I do believe is that Mildred certainly does." Detective Abernathy subconsciously watched as his partner dumped six packs of sugar in his coffee and again stirred it with his finger.

"Okay, now I understand." Detective Abernathy said nodding.

"Understand what?"

"That you've fallen off the damn wagon again and you we're drunk the last time you talk to Mildred right?"

"What?"

"When was the last time you went to an AA meeting Stokey?"

"What the hell are you talking about Abernathy?" He said disturbed by the accusation. "I haven't fallen off the wagon, what are you talking about?" Detective Stokey momentarily stared at his partner. "And for your information I went to a meeting last night, but I'm telling you Abernathy—"

"Telling me what man?" Detective Abernathy said raising his voice. "The quickest way for you and me to in up in the bread line—"

"Ain't nobody in their right damn mind gon believe Congressman Cutter would be crazy enough to father a child with a seventeen year old Black girl knowing the scandal would demolish his political career!" Detective Abernathy said picking up his coffee and sitting it back down without drinking. "I need a drink and it's gon needs to be a hell of a lot stronger than this cup of coffee!"

"Why do you think I went to an AA meeting last night?" Detective Abernathy said looking at him, uncertain how to respond to the outrageous allegation made by Mildred.

"Stokey man don't you let that old—"

"What? Crazy woman?"

"If she believes Congressman Cutter fathered her granddaughter's baby that's exactly what she is."

"Then you tell me this Abernathy, what would Mildred have to gain by accusing a powerful man like Congressman Cutter of impregnating her granddaughter and after all these years?"

"And you're thinking what Stokey . . . Baby boy Doe is the bastard child of Congressman Cutter and Mildred Koffee's granddaughter?"

"Of course not Abernathy!"

"Then what man? I don't understand!" Detective Abernathy looked at him puzzled by his reasoning for even bringing it up.

"That was over twenty years or so ago and the gender of the child was never revealed." Detective Abernathy's mouth abruptly opened.

"Are you serious man, over twenty year ago?" He said raising his voice. "Then why in the hell are we even discussing something that happened that long ago and what the hell does it have to do with Baby boy Doe found last year by Thomas Lee Simms?"

"That's what I'm trying to figure out Abernathy." Detective Stokey said sipping his coffee. "I've heard rumors about a number of politicians over the years but never anything involving Congressman Cutter."

"Maybe that's because Cutter only became a Congressman twelve years ago, and besides we both know family secrets can be a normal occurrence in some southern households."

"Oh that's right I forget, you yourself married your first cousin once removed or was it your second cousin twice removed?" Detective Stokey said trying to add humor to the distressing conversation.

"Very funny Stokey." Detective Abernathy said unamused. "And you said Mildred Koffee told you this incident with her granddaughter Raynetta, that nobody seems to know ever existed is somehow directly related to Baby boy Doe . . . tell me how?" Detective Stokey gulped down the last of his coffee then opened two additional packs of sugar and dumped them inside the empty cup then began massaging his neck.

"That's just it, Mildred didn't say how."

"Okay, then why bring it up?"

"I don't know Abernathy . . . I think maybe she just wanted somebody to talk to."

"Did she even say one thing had anything to do with the other?" Detective Abernathy asked, his frustration growing.

"Yes, no . . . I'm not sure."

"Man what the hell you mean you ain't sure?"

"She threw me off her property when I indirectly accused her granddaughter of being a liar." Detective Abernathy shook his head.

"Stokey man, have you lost your damn mind?" He asked rhetorically. "I don't blame Mildred Koffee for kicking your ass off her property, especially if that story had any truth to it." Detective Stokey picked up his cup and prepared to drink, pouring sugar onto his lips. Detective Abernathy's eyes widened.

"Stokey man what the hell you doing?"

"You gentlemen ready to order yet?" Darla asked as she again returned to the table. Detective Abernathy looked at his partner and the sprinkles of sugar on his lips and shook his head.

#

Dorothy Jean looked from behind the flowered bed sheet she hung on the line when seeing a silver automobile pull in her driveway and park. She continued watching as Detective Stokey got out of his car and began walking towards her.

"Are you Dorothy Jean Simms?" He asked. "I'm Detective—"

"I know who you are." She said looking at him with contempt. "Did you think I wouldn't remember the man that helped put my husband in prison?" She sated, solemnly.

"Mrs. Simms that's the reason I'm here—"

"Say your piece then get off my property!" Detective Stokey briefly massaged his neck as he continued walking towards the house.

"I think your husband's innocent Mrs. Simms." She dropped the sheet back in the laundry basket and stared at him.

"It's kinda late for you to be saying you believe in Thomas Lee's innocence after they've locked my husband up in behind bars don't you think detective?"

"You're right Mrs. Simms, but at that time I believe that Thomas Lee was guilty."

"So what happen to make you change your mind?" She looked at him with mistrust as she again retrieved the sheet and hung it on the clothesline.

"You see Dorothy Jean—" Detective Stokey hesitated. "—it is alright if I call you Dorothy Jean isn't it?"

"Naw it ain't." She stated with coldness. "My friends and family call me Dorothy Jean and you ain't either one."

"Ahem!" Detective Stokey cleared his throat. "To answer your question Mrs. Simms the day Thomas Lee was convicted I saw something that made me wonder if—" She interrupted.

"Mildred Koffee? Is that the something you saw detective?"

"As a matter of fact Mrs. Simms it was."

"If you think my husband's innocent of murdering that baby detective you won't get no objection from me, but if you expect to prove it through Mildred Koffee then I guess its gon be a while before Thomas Lee see the light of day again."

"Mrs. Simms I happen to think Mildred—"

"Mildred?" She looked at him with oddity. "Why's that old woman letting you call her Mildred?"

"What do mean?"

"I ain't ever known Mildred Koffee to let anybody call her Mildred before." She peered over at him. "What's so special about you?"

"Ahem!" Detective Stokey again cleared his throat. "It's uh, it's a long story.".

"I bet it is." She said with suggestion."I heard that old woman had a sneaky side to her, but I didn't believe it until now." Detective Stokey flushed with redness

"Uh no, it's uh . . . not what you think."

"What you and Mildred do is y'all business."

"There's uh, nothing going on between Mildred and me uh—"

"Say your peace detective!" Dorothy Jean yelled.

"Mrs. Simms is there anything you can tell me about your husband that would convince an appellate judge that a jury of his peers got the verdict wrong the first time?"

"My husband ain't murdered that baby Detective Stokley and that's all you need to know." His eyes slightly widened in response her mispronunciation of his name.

"I know that's what you and I believe Mrs. Simms, but it's going to take a hell of a lot more than that to get Thomas Lee an appeal." Dorothy Jean looked at him with skepticism as she removed another sheet from the laundry basket and prepared to hang it.

"You crazier than Ms. Mildred if you think a court gon listen to what she got to say?" She said pinning the sheet on the line. "I know my husband a lot better than Mildred Koffee."

"Then Dorothy Jean what can you tell me about him that I don't already know?"

"Do you know my husband Detective Stokley?"

"No, but that doesn't stop me from believing in his innocence."

"I ain't got no problem with what you trying to do for Thomas Lee, but maybe you ought to go to that prison and talk to him for yourself before you start trying to prove him innocent." A worried look appeared on Detective Stokey's face.

"Is there something in particular about your husband I should know Mrs. Simms?"

"Why don't you go ask Mildred Koffee since she seems to have eyes and ears everywhere when it comes to other folk's business?"

"Are you trying to tell me Mildred knows something about Thomas Lee that could hurt his chances of free—" She cut him off.

"You do best to go ask her that!" Dorothy Jean said hanging a matching flowered pillowcase on the line. Detective Stokey massaged his neck as his patience lessened in response to her fruitless words.

"You'll excuse me Mrs. Simms if I say that Mildred's has shown more interest in clearing your husband's name than you." Dorothy Jean stopped and stared at him.

"Detective Stokley—"

"Stokey." He said correcting her. "My name is Detective Stokey!" She gave no reply as she retrieved a second pillowcase and hung it on the line.

"Well Detective Stokey let me ask you this."

"What's that Mrs. Simms?"

"You a married man detective?"
His eyes widened curious of her personal question.

"What does that have to do with—"

"Just answer the damn question!" She said raising her voice. "You married or not?" Detective Stokey massaged his neck, uncertain if he should answer her intrusive question.

"As a matter of fact I'm not."

"Divorced?" She asked. He readjusted his composure, uncomfortable with her probing questions.

"Yes, I am."

"You ever cheat on your wife detective? Is that why she divorced you?"

"If you must know Mrs. Simms it was my wife who was doing the cheating, it was also her who filed for divorce." He said ill at ease with disclosing the intimate details of his life. "Now can we move on and stop all the nonsense?" Dorothy Jean dropped the wet blouse she's just retrieved, back into the basket and looked him angrily in the eyes.

"I got two German Shepherds been trained to kill, detective." His mouth slightly opened. "I keep them right here on the side of the house." Detective Stokey shifted his eyes over at the dog pen seeing the growling canines. "If you don't get in your ass off my property and get back in that car of yours and leave here, your detective friends gon have to come pick your bones up out of my yard."

"If I didn't know better Mrs. Simms I'd say that sounds like a threat."

"That's what it sounds like to me too."

"I don't understand!" Detective Stokey said losing his tempter. "I'm trying to prove your husband's guilty verdict was wrong and you're threatening to feed me to your dogs!" He yelled. "What am I missing?"

"You got as long as its gon take me to walk over to that pen and unlatch that gate for you to get off my property." He looked momentarily at her then turned and walked away shaking his head in defeat before climbing in his car and driving away.

Chapter Five

Thomas Lee forced a smile as he watched Dorothy Jean enter the visitor's room, a bitter look in her eyes. His apprehension grew as she approached.

"Thanks for coming back Dorothy Jean." He said ambivalent about her return.

"What you thanking me for Thomas Lee, I said I'd be back didn't I?" A timid look appeared on his face.

"I wasn't sure after the way you left here last time."

"After all these years and you still don't realize I'm a woman of my word?" She said seeing the guilt in his eyes. "Something you wouldn't know nothing about." Thomas Lee briefly lowered his eyes as he thought of his multiple affairs, his latest being with Delores Clarkston.

"I know you probably hate me Dorothy—" She cut him off.

"How you expect me to feel Thomas Lee knowing my husband's been out there lying up with other women?"

"I don't know what made me do that Dorothy Jean . . . it must be something wrong in my head!"

"It ain't your head got you in trouble Thomas Lee."

"I'm telling you Dorothy Jean, I tried like hell to resist all them women!" He said forcing a look of helplessness on his face. "They just wouldn't leave me alone!" Thomas Lee reached over and took hold of her hand.

"No touching!" A guard shouted. Thomas Lee glanced over at him then released Dorothy Jean's hand.

"Dorothy Jean I may have been with other woman, but you the only woman I loved." She suddenly stood. His eyes widened. "What I say?" He asked in response to her unexpected move. "Come on now baby, sit down." Thomas Lee pleaded. "I know what I done wasn't right and you should hate me but right now baby I need you to stand by my side like a wife suppose to do." She silently looked at him then returned to her seat.

Thomas Lee's Affair

Delores lay in Thomas Lee's arms after a morning of intimacy, believing their rendezvous at The Hidden Palace Motel, located in a neighboring county had remained discrete.

"So tell me Tommy—" She kissed him intimately on the lips. "—what do you think your wife Dorothy Mae would say if she—" He interjected.

"Jean."

"What?"

"My wife's name is Dorothy Jean and I told you we don't talk about my wife when me and you together Delores!" She again kissed him.

"Okay, but I wonder what would Dorothy Mae would say if she knew her husband was here making love to me?"

"Come on now Delores find something else to talk about or stop talking!" Thomas Lee said placing a quick kiss on her lips. "I feel guilty enough as it is for being here."

"Guilty?"

"Yeah Delores guilty!" He shook his head with remorse.

"You're so silly Tommy." She giggled. "To think after all this time we've been coming here to this cheap motel and you're just now feeling guilty."

"I been feeling guilty!"

"So tell me Tommy just how guilty could you feel? We've only been doing this now for three years now." He embraced her in his arms and romantically kissed her.

"Girl you got me so crazy in love with you, I couldn't stop seeing you if I wanted to." They passionately kissed.

"Say that again Tommy." Delores said smiling.

"Say what?"

"That you're crazy in love with me."

"You know I am Delores." They again kissed."

"Do you love me enough to leave Dorothy Mae?" A blank look appeared in Thomas Lee's eyes.

"Do you love me enough to leave Charles?"

"Love has nothing to do with it silly." Delores girlishly giggled. "Charles is rich and even though it's you I love with all my heart—" She lovingly kissed him. "—you're a poor Black man and you could never provide for me the lifestyle Charles gives me." Thomas Lee looked her in the eyes surprised by her statement. He half heartedly laughed.

"Now you see why I stay with my wife . . . she loves the hell out of this poor Black man!"

"And you know what else Tommy?" Delores said ignoring his words.

"What's that baby?" He asked kissing her on the neck and lips.

"I could never live the life you and your people do nor could I ever be happy being poor." He shook his head and grinned, humored by her view of Black people.

"Are you happy being a rich White woman Delores?"

"Only when I'm on the town spending Charles' family money and living the life of a snobbish, rich White socialite." She said bursting into laughter. Thomas Lee looked at her with love in his eyes and humorously grinned then resumed kissing her on the neck and lips.

"Why don't you let me show you what this poor Black man can do for a rich White socialite woman?" He said seductively kissing her.

"You naughty boy." Delores said giggling as she pulled him over on her to again engage in intimacy.

· · · ·

"I cried many nights Thomas Lee thinking about you and Delores being together—" He interjected.

"Come on now Dorothy Jean, let's not talk about that." Thomas Lee said trying to keep from thinking about how much he missed his intimate rendezvous with Delores.

"I spent many day wondering why my husband seem to prefer being in another woman's bed over his own wife's."

"Naw Dorothy Jean it wasn't like that baby." He became fidgety as his anxiety heightened listening to Dorothy Jean's reminders of his infidelity.

"So I started telling myself maybe I wasn't pretty enough or woman enough because I couldn't give my husband children—"

"You a good woman Delores!" Thomas Lee stated. His eyes abruptly widened when realizing he'd inadvertently said Delores' name in place of his wife's. "Baby you know I didn't mean to say that, it was a slip of the tongue." He said trying to read the look in her eyes. "I'm just nervous being locked up in this place that's all." Dorothy Jean looked around the room making eye contact with one of the guards overseeing the multitude of inmates and their visitors then turned her attention back to Thomas Lee looking into his frightened eyes.

"Do you love Delores, Thomas Lee?"

"What you mean do I love her?" He asked trying to mask his feelings. "Baby you the only woman I love you know that."

"When a married man steps outside his wife's bed, most times it ain't because of her it's because he don't give a damn about nobody but his self." Thomas Lee lowered his eyes in shame.

"You right Dorothy Jean, me being with other women wasn't something I needed to do." He looked inside her hurting eyes. "It was something I wanted to do and I'm sorry Dorothy Jean." She suddenly chuckled.

"That's something else I've learned Thomas Lee."

"What's that?"

"Sorry ain't nothing but a word." A dazed look entered Dorothy Jean eyes. "Can it take away the pain in my heart?" Thomas Lee looked at her loss for words. "Can it give me back the trust I lost in the vows I took with the only man I ever loved?" Tears rolled down her cheeks. "Can it take away the thoughts haunting me everytime I see in my head, my husband making love to Delores Clarkston?"

"Dorothy Jean why you—"

"And you know what's funny Thomas Lee it ain't a dictionary in all the world can define the hurt you feel knowing your husband's taking pleasure in another woman."

"Why you bringing all this stuff up Dorothy Jean?" Thomas Lee said with a pitiful look on his face. "I'm in here caged up like a animal and you talking about what was." He said trying to divert the conversation from his adulterous ways. "I already said I was sorry what more you want Dorothy Jean?"

"That detective that's been talking to Ms. Mildred came snooping around the house yesterday." A puzzled look formed on Thomas Lee's face.

"What Detective you talking about?"

"The one helped put you in this place."

"What hell he want?"

"Say he trying to prove you didn't murder that baby, asked me what kind of man you were."

"What you tell him Dorothy Jean?"

"I told him if he didn't get his ass off my property I was gon put the dogs on him." She said amused. Thomas Lee looked at her in disbelief.

"You hate me that much Dorothy Jean?" He said raising his voice. "That man's trying to prove I didn't murder that baby and you threaten to put the dogs on him?" He shook his head feeling helpless.

"If he really trying to prove you innocent he'll be back." Thomas Lee abruptly stood.

"What? You trying to punish me because you jealousy of Delores?" He said infuriated. A stunned looked formed on Dorothy Jean's face."

"Jealous?"

"That's what I said ain't it?" He said speaking out of fear.

"Is that supposed to hurt me Thomas Lee?"

"I don't give a damn what it do Dorothy Jean." Thomas Lee gazed at her with angry eyes then walked away. She watched with satisfaction as he exited through the steel door.

#

Marietta's attention diverted from the pot of gumbo simmering on the stove as Delores staggered in the kitchen, a tall glass of red wine in her right hand. She shifted her eyes quickly over to Carrie standing at the sink running cold water over several pieces of raw chicken wings, tossing them in a bowl of seasonings. ,

"Did you need something Ms. Delores?" Marietta asked taking note of her intoxicated state. Delores plopped down in one of the four chairs at the kitchen table.

"Yes Marietta I do . . . I need Tommy!" Carrie looked over at Marietta and shook her head.

"Now Ms. Delores you know better than to be talking like that in your husband's house." Marietta said shifting her eyes over at Carrie who elected to not to speak as she placed the seasoned chicken wings in a preparation for Cajun chicken.

"I don't think Mr. Charles would like it much if he heard you asking about another man—"

"Especially one you been slapping the sheets with behind his back." Carrie said underneath her breath. Marietta looked at Carrie chastising her with her eyes.

"Why would Charles be upset if I talked about Tommy, because he's Black?" Delores stated with defiance. "Well the hell with Charles!" She slurred taking a drink from the glass of wine. "You know as well as I do Marietta, Charles doesn't love me anymore."

"Now Ms. Delores you know that ain't true."

"Probably be better for him if he didn't." Carrie said speaking just above a whisper. "As many men as her ass done laid down with." Marietta flashed a second disciplining look.

"The only thing Charles Benjamin Clarkston the third cares about is his family's money and their precious name."

"Ms. Delores you need me to call Roosevelt so he can help you back upstairs?" Marietta asked.

"You know Marietta my Tommy loves me." Delores slurred. Marietta motioned Carrie with her head to get Roosevelt. "I miss my Tommy!" Delores cried out.

"Now Ms. Delores you know you could get Thomas Lee in a whole lot of trouble if Mr. Charles heard you talking like that." Marietta said frightened for her son.

"Why did Tommy have to be Black?" Delores said insensitive to the fact that both Marietta and Carrie were also Black. Carrie's jaw dropped.

"Let me hurry up and go get Roosevelt so he can get that drunk heifer out of here before I slap her ass and get every damn body fired!" Carrie said looking at Delores slumped over the table. "In here talking about why Thomas Lee had to be Black . . . what the hell kind of question is that?"

"Hush Carrie." Marietta said trying to quiet her. "Let's just get Roosevelt to take her back upstairs before Mr. Charles get home from work and find her in here like this." Carrie intervened.

"So he can blame us for her ass being drunk!" She said shifting her eyes to Delores. "What I can't figure out is why Mr. Charles ain't divorce her ass yet!"

"Carrie!" Marietta said disturbed by her mean words. "Hush."

"Her drunk ass can't hear what I'm saying." Carrie said looking at Delores. "Girl she passed out."

"Is she?" Marietta said looking at the wine glass in Delores' hand. "She still holding that glass ain't she?"

"What about it?"

"You ever seen Ms. Delores hold onto a glass after she's passed out?" Delores raised her head.

"You know what Marietta?" She said slurring. "I bet you Charles killed that baby himself so he could blame Tommy so we couldn't be together." Marietta's mouth flung open. She looked over at Carrie.

"Roosevelt!" Carrie hollered out. "Marietta needs you to come get Ms. Delores before she get all our asses threw in jail!" She said amused.

"No!" Delores yelled. "I want to stay down here and talk to Marietta about Tommy." Carrie shifted her eyes to Marietta and pointed to the yellow circular clock hanging just above the sink displaying a time of half past four p.m.

"I'm not going back to bed!" Delores said raising her voice. "I want Tommy." Carrie intervened.

"Ms. Delores you didn't know?"

"Know what Carrie?"

"Tommy's upstairs in the bed waiting on you girl, he naked and everything . . . didn't you know that?" Marietta looked at Carrie and shook her head in disapproval. Carrie snickered.

"Tommy!" Delores called out trying to stand. "Don't leave Tommy I'm on my way!"

"Ol' tramp."

"Hush Carrie!" Marietta said upset by her inappropriate actions.

"Girl I ain't doing nothing but having fun with Ms. Delores' drunk ass."

"You keep on, one day she gon hear you—" Marietta silenced when seeing Carrie's eyes widened as she look over at the stove. "What?"

"Unless you plan on serving that gumbo off the stove—"

"Damn!" Marietta yelled then hurried over to the stove removing the pot from the burner. "Where's Roosevelt?"

"Right here." He said entering the kitchen. "You need me Marietta?"

"Why couldn't Tommy be White, Marietta?" Delores said. Roosevelt's eyes widened. He looked at Marietta.

"Because his momma and daddy's Black, that's why!" Carrie said taunting her. Roosevelt looked at Carrie with scolding eyes as he assisted Delores up from the table.

"Come on Ms. Delores let me help you upstairs to your room."

"Thank you Roosevelt." She said staggering.

"Mr. Charles gon be home soon Ms. Delores and you know how he gets when he see you drunk."

"I'm not drunk Roosevelt!" Delores said turning the empty wine glass up to her mouth. "How can I be drunk if my glass is empty?" She burst into laughter. Roosevelt looked at Marietta and subtly shook his head. "I think Ms. Delores gon need a bowl of that gumbo and plenty of coffee if we expect to have her anywhere near sober by the time Mr. Charles gets here." Marietta walked over to the cupboard and retrieved a soup bowl.

"Go ahead and take her on up Roosevelt, I'll be there shortly with this gumbo and that pot of coffee." He nodded as he led her up the back stairs located off the kitchen. Marietta dipped a ladle in the pot and filled the bowl with gumbo. "Roosevelt!" She called out.

"Yeah Marietta."

"Just take her in the bathroom and let her wash her face, Carrie can get her dressed and bring her back down for supper."

"Supper!" Roosevelt's eyes widened with surprise. "You sure about that Marietta?"

"Then we got an hour to try and get Ms. Delores sober and at the dinner table."

"Well that gumbo better be a miracle worker." Roosevelt said continuing up the stairs with a drunken Delores. "Because I don't see that happening." Carrie shook her head in aggravation as she placed the pan of Cajun chicken in the oven.

"Mr. Charles know Ms. Delores ain't nothing but a damn drunk!" She stated loudly. "And Thomas Lee messing around with her head ain't done nothing but made matters worse!" Marietta looked quickly at her, offended by her distasteful words.

"Ms. Delores ain't innocent Carrie!" Marietta said in her son's defense. "Thomas Lee ain't no different than no other man that's laid down with Ms. Delores!"

"Uh huh—" Carrie stated. "—but its Thomas Lee's ass that's locked away in prison because of it." Marietta momentarily stared at her then resumed dipping gumbo from the pot.

"I'm sorry Marietta it's just that—"

"Keep an eye on my gumbo." Marietta said dismissing her apologetic words. "I need to go help Roosevelt." Carrie watched as Marietta walked up the stairs, feeling guilty for her careless words.

#

Thomas Lee entered the visitor's room looking around with his left eye, his right eye black and swollen. His fury magnified when seeing Detective Stokey, recognizing him from the courtroom.

"Thomas Lee." Detective Stokey said extending his hand to shake as he rose from the table.

"Ain't you that bastard helped put me in here for a crime I didn't commit?" Thomas Lee said ignoring the detective's extended hand. "Man what the hell you want?"

"Please Thomas Lee . . . won't you sit down and let me—"

"Let you what man?" He said looking at Detective Stokey with contempt. "Man I ain't trying to hear a damn thing you got to say!"

"And I can understand why you would feel that way Thomas Lee—"

"Then why the hell are you here?"

"Would you please just hear me out?" Thomas Lee's anger magnified. "What is it . . . they kicked your ass out of the good Ol' boys club so to teach them a lesson you trying to free the Black man convicted of killing a baby?"

"If you'll just let me explain—"

"Oh I know, you fell in love with a susta and now you trying to clear your guilty conscience from all the dirt you done to Black folks over the years."

"How have they treating you in here Thomas Lee?" Detective Stokey asked electing not to respond to his heated words. Thomas Lee's eyes widened, surprised by the detective's sincere words.

"How the hell you think they treating me!" He yelled. "You don't see this black eye?"

"I'm uh, sorry for—"

"Or did you think I walked into a door?" Thomas Lee stated sarcastically. "You being sorry ain't gon do a damn thing when one of these crazy ass men in here decides a baby killer ain't got no right breathing the same air as the rest of the convicts!" He said slightly raising his voice. Detective Stokey gave no reply as he thought of the dilemma he faced in trying to convince an appellate court of Thomas Lee's innocence. "So why you all of a sudden got a change of heart?"

"If you calm down for a minute Thomas Lee I'll tell you." He watched as Thomas Lee's rigid body language slowly yielded. "Are you calm?" Thomas Lee looked over at the guard then again to Detective Stokey.

"Yeah man I'm calm."

"You sure?"

"I said I was didn't I?" Thomas Lee said raising his voice.

"Keep it down!" The guard yelled. Thomas Lee shifted his eyes over at him and again looked at Detective Stokey appearing calmer.

"Good, now we can talk—"

"Talk about what man?" Thomas Lee said again raising his voice.

"Calm, remember?" Detective Stokey stated softly.

"Yeah alright.

"The day you were convicted I was in the courtroom—" Thomas Lee cut him off.

"You think I don't remember seeing how happy your ass was when that jury found me guilty!" Detective Stokey massaged his neck.

"Well something happened that day—" Thomas Lee again interjected.

"You damn right something happened that day . . . they locked my ass up that's what happened!" Detective Stokey's mouth dried as he glanced over at the guard watching in the distance.

"Are you still calm Thomas Lee?"

"Yeah man I'm calm."

"Do you know Mildred Koffee?"

Thomas Lee half-heartedly grinned.

"Who don't know that old lady, what about her?"

"Well that old lady is the reason why I'm here."

"How so?"

"After the verdict she gave me a look I'll never forget."

"Yeah that sounds like her." Thomas Lee chuckled.

"You know what that look said to me?"

"As a matter of fact detective I don't so why don't you tell me 'cause I ain't in much of a mood for playing no damn guessing games."

"That look told me I had just helped the prosecutor convince a jury that an innocent man was guilty."

"Man get the hell out of here . . . you think I'm a fool?" Thomas Lee said unconvinced of Detective Stokey's explanation. "You want something but I'll be damn if I know what it is."

"You probably don't believe me Thomas Lee, but I'm only trying to right the wrong—"

"Because of a look you seen on, Mildred Koffee's face?" Thomas Lee said agitated. "And that scared ass look on my face didn't say nothing to you?"

"You have to understand Thomas Lee I've seen that look on defendant's faces for as long as I've been in law enforcement, why should I believe yours over anybody else's?" Frowns stretched across Thomas Lee's forehead.

"Because I'm innocent man, that's why!" He yelled.

"Hey!" The guard shouted. Thomas Lee looked over him. "Keep it down or you'll go back to your cage!"

"I'm calm man."

"Keep it that way."

Thomas Lee shook his head and again turned to Detective Stokey.

"I guess it's pretty tough in here."

"What the hell you thought it was gon be like for me when you convinced them people I murdered that baby . . . do I look like I'm capable of killing a baby?"

"That's why I'm here Thomas Lee I was hoping you could answer that question for me." Frowns again formed on Thomas Lee's forehead.

"I thought you said you believed I was innocent?"

"I do but—"

"But what man?" Detective Stokey looked him directly in the eyes.

"I think you know more about Baby boy Doe than you admitted to at your trial." Thomas Lee stared back at him, but neither confirmed nor denied the detective's allegation. "I also think it was a huge mistake for your attorney to put you on the witness stand knowing the prosecutor would rip you to shreds."

"Time's up!" The guard yelled.

"I can't say why detective—" Thomas Lee look at him with hope. "—but I trust you and that's something I don't do with just anybody."

"Thank you Thomas Lee." Detective Stokey said relieved.

"You come back here next week and I'll tell you everything I know." A puzzled look appeared on Detective Stokey face in response to the time delay.

"Next week? Why next week?"

"I got to talk to my wife first." Detective Stokey looked at him with curiosity.

"Oh?"

"Naw man, Dorothy Jean ain't had nothing to do with that baby being murdered if that's what you thinking."

"Then why?"

"Man I ain't ever been faithful to my wife." Thomas Lee said with guilt. "And I don't want to bring no more shame on her than I already have."

"I can understand that."

"She'll be back on Friday I'll talk to her then." Thomas Lee rose from the table and began walking away.

"You take care, Thomas Lee." Detective Stokey said watching as he walked pass the guard and disappeared through the steel doors.

#

Mildred smiled when seeing Detective Stokey's car pull in the driveway and park. She waited at the screened door watching as he got out of his car and headed for the house.

"You braver than I thought." She said speaking through the door as he stepped on the porch and sat in one of the chair to the right of her rocker.

"It's too beautiful of a morning Mildred for you to be cooped up in the house, why don't you come on out and join me?"

"And why would I want to do that?"

"For one it's your porch." He half-heartedly chuckled. "And for another . . . you being the hospitable southern woman you are you would never leave a guess sitting all alone on your porch." Detective Stokey watched as she pushed open the door, coming out onto the porch being seated in her old rocker.

"I see you been doing some checking up on that information I gave you." A mysterious look formed on his face, stunned by her knowledge of his actions.

"As a matter of fact Mildred I have and you know what else—"

"I'm listening."

"I've found a lot of pieces to the puzzle." She cleverly smiled. "Problem is I haven't quite figured out how they fit together yet."

"You will."

"Is it alright if we eat breakfast first Mildred I'm starving." A surprised look formed on her face.

"Since when you start eating breakfast Andy?"

"For some reason Mildred I've changed . . . as a matter of fact quite a few things about me have changed since I met you."

"Is that so?" She giggled.

"You wouldn't happen to have any more of those rutabagas would you?" She laughed. "And you know what would taste good with that?"

"I'm listening."

"Some eggs over easy and some of your award winning homemade biscuits and maybe even some buttermilk." Mildred's laughter intensified.

"You like ham Andy?"

"Love it!"

"Then I think I'll add some ham to make that breakfast even better!" She looked at him with cautioning eyes. "But you need to stay away from that buttermilk." A puzzled look showed on Detective Stokey's face.

"And why's that Mildred?"

"Your stomach and buttermilk don't get along." His mouth flung open. 'cause the last time you drank some I was all day trying to get that smell you left behind out of my house." He burst into laughter. "Had to open every window in my house!" He continued laughing as Mildred entered the house to prepare his breakfast minus the buttermilk.

#

"Good morning Mr. Charles." Marietta said pouring his morning cup of coffee then sitting it next to the plate of pork sausage links, Cajun grits, a vegetable omelet and two beignets as he entered the dining room being seated. He immediately picked up the morning newspaper.

"And indeed it is a good morning Marietta." He said opening the paper as Marietta returned to the kitchen to retrieve a glass of freshly squeezed orange juice. "Is my wife up yet?"

"I ain't seen her this morning." Charles slightly lowered the paper and looked at her with curiosity.

"You know if I didn't know better Marietta I'd think you were hiding something from me." He said looking at her. "I happen to know you get my wife up every morning after Roosevelt has poured her in bed the night before so where is she?"

"Now Mr. Charles you know I don't meddle in you and Ms. Delores' personal affairs, but since you asked I'll tell you."

Carrie and Roosevelt huddled in the butler's pantry listening to Marietta and Charles' conversation.

"I don't know what you said to Ms. Delores last night, but after she finished her first bottle of red wine she ordered Roosevelt to bring her another one and she drank half of that before passing out drunk in the living room." Charles showed no interest in his wife's dilemma as he again buried his face behind the newspaper turning to the business section.

"That because she ain't nothing but a damn drunk." Carrie whispered to Roosevelt.

"Hush Carrie!" He said shaking his head as she silently chuckled.

"And when I tried waking her up this morning I could've set a grenade off in that room and Ms. Delores wouldn't have budged."

"Then let her sleep Marietta, I hope your preoccupation with my wife's deplorable behavior hasn't resulted in you forgetting about the business dinner I have planned this evening with a dozen or so people." He looked briefly from behind the newspaper.

"Naw Mr. Charles I ain't forgot about your business dinner." Marietta said taking note of his stiffening grits as they grew cold. "Just let me know what you want and I'll get started prepping it." Charles lowered the newspaper and smiled.

"You're wonderful Marietta." He said picking up his coffee taking a sip. "That's why despite your dishonorable son sleeping with my wife I've allowed you to stay on here as my maid." She silently stared at him masking her anger, offended by his belittling words.

"Uh oh!" Roosevelt said whispering, hoping Marietta wouldn't lose her temper and say something she'd regret.

"Mr. Charles done lost his damn mind saying some mess like that to Marietta?" Carrie said trying to keep her voice down. "He know damn well what kind of woman his wife is!"

"Hush Carrie I can't hear." Roosevelt said holding his hand to his ear.

"Like Thomas Lee was the only man sleeping with that slut!"

"Hush!"

"Now Mr. Charles you know I ain't had nothing to do with what went on between Thomas Lee and Ms. Delores."

"I never said you did Marietta."

"I was just as surprise as you when I learned he was seeing her." Charles took another sip of coffee.

"Seeing her?" He again obscured his face behind the paper. "I would hardly call taking my wife to some cheap motel as merely seeing her?" Charles stated sarcastically. "Your son treated Mrs. Charles Clarkston the third no better than a common whore."

"Mr. Charles you know that ain't how I raised Thomas Lee." Marietta said trying to hold her temper.

"Perhaps if you had kept a closer eye on my wife—" She interjected.

"Mr. Charles you pay me to clean your house and cook your food!" Marietta said raising her voice. "I ain't seen nothing in my duties said it's my responsibility to keep Ms. Delores from dropping her draws after she done got drunk herself silly!" Carrie's mouth flung open.

"Go get her Roosevelt before she get all our asses fired!"

"Uh-uh Mr. Charles needs to hear that." He said excited by Marietta's provoked tongue lashing. Charles again lowered the newspaper and looked at her.

"Thomas Lee ain't no different than any other man, if Ms. Delores offering it him being a man he gon take it."

"How about you cook some of your famous Catfish Étouffée and uh, put that over a bed of rice?" Charles said diverting from the subject of his badly behaved wife. "I can never seem to get enough of your amazing Étouffée." He said apologizing in his own way.

"Not even when you were a little boy!" Marietta said calming down as she reminisced.

"And to go with that Étouffée how about some blackened redfish, snap peas, oh and I couldn't help but notice those big red tomatoes Roosevelt has growing outback in the garden, so why don't you have him pick some cucumbers and tomatoes and Carrie can prepare a colorful salad." He said as if his hurtful words to Marietta had never been spoken.

"Alright Mr. Charles you can stop laying it on so thick now, you're forgiven."

"Well I'm just being honest Marietta." She giggled. "Besides, you know yourself not a word I've said about your marvelous cooking wasn't true."

"I ain't saying I don't agree with it, but if I'm gon have supper ready for your guest this evening I need to get started."

"Then I won't hold you a minute longer." He said gazing at her.

"Did you need something else Mr. Charles?"

"Would it be a bother if I asked you to make that delicious red wine vinaigrette dressing I love so much, you do such a great job at making it?" Marietta humorously grinned.

"Yeah Mr. Charles I can do that." She said waiting to hear his dessert request.

"And Marietta for dessert—"

"How about I make my lemon and chocolate doberge cake with a scoop of vanilla ice cream on top?" A boyish smile formed on Charles' face.

"Another one of my favorites since I was a little boy."

"And how many times did I sneak you an extra slice even after your momma said you'd had enough after your third slice." Charles winked then buried his face behind the newspaper.

"And Marietta—" He said poking his head back out. "—could you see to it that my wife is appropriately dressed and sober so she can respectfully receive our guest this evening?"

"Is there anything special you want Ms. Delores to wear?"

"How about I let you decide." Marietta watched as his head again disappeared behind the newspaper.

Chapter Six

Mildred stood watering the vegetable garden to the right of her house when her attention shifted to a late model white Lincoln Continental pulling in her driveway and parking. She looked through the windshield and attempted to identify the driver before he opened his door and got out. She watched from underneath her straw sun hat trying to read the look on the gentleman's face as he walked towards her home.

"Mildred Koffee?"

"I am."

"Do you know who I am Mrs. Koffee?"

"Yeah I know who you are Mr. Clarkston."

"Then I guess there's no need for introductions." Charles stated with authority.

"My niece Marietta been caring for you since you was wet behind the ears." She half-heartedly grinned.

"Then I guess you do know me." Mildred released the water hose allowing it to drop to the ground as she walked towards him.

"What business you got with me Mr. Clarkson?"

"I hear you've been speaking to a Detective Stokey about that murdered baby."

"How's that any business of yours?"

"Well actually Mrs. Koffee it's not—"

"Then why you here?"

"To tell you for your own good to stay out of it!" Mildred looked at him, undaunted by his threatening words.

"I don't work for you Mr. Clarkston so that mean I don't take orders from you either." Charles walked slowly towards her. "I'm eighty-three years old and I've lived long enough to know if you come all this way trying to intimidate me it's because you must know something about what happened to that baby."

"If you think for one second I'd allow you to free the man who treated my wife like some cheap saloon girl—" He grabbed Mildred by the arm. "— I'd see you rot in hell first old woman, do understand what I'm saying?" He stared Mildred angrily in the eyes. "After all an eighty three year old woman dying from a heart attack is nothing out of the ordinary—at least that's what the coroner's report will say?"

"I ain't afraid of dying or you Mr. Clarkston!"

Charles cunningly grinned.

"I'll keep that in mind."

"Me dying ain't gon change the truth about your family, truth that would knock you right off that high-horse you been riding on all these years if your high society friends knew the truth." Charles quietly chuckled.

"I have absolutely no idea what truth you're referring to Mrs. Koffee."

"If you don't take your hands off me I'll see to it your friend's read all about your secret in tomorrow's society column whether you claim to know it or not." He gazed momentarily at her before releasing her hi-jacked arm. "Thomas Lee ain't murdered that baby and you know it." Charles cleverly smiled.

"Well a jury of his peers said different."

"A jury of your peers is more like it." Mildred stated. "I ain't seen not one of them folks sitting on jury look like Thomas Lee."

"Never the less he received a fair trial." She looked at him with disdain.

"Is that what you tell yourself Mr. Clarkston when you think of Thomas Lee making love to your wife?" Mildred said rubbing his nose in it. "Thing is I don't recall that being the reason why Thomas Lee was on trial."

"Any man that uses another man's wife as his personal whore deserves whatever he gets!" Charles yelled.

"Then you better get prepared to spend a whole lot of days in court 'cause from what I hear it's been many men walked in Thomas Lee's shoes!" Charles raised his hand to slap her. He abruptly stopped when hearing the sound of a gun cocking.

"You alright Mildred?" A man from across the road called out from his front porch holding a shot gun. Charles quickly looked over at him then turned back to Mildred.

"Just so you know old woman, freedom for Thomas Lee Simms could actually be a death sentence for him after all."

"Sound as if you just made a threat on Thomas Lee's life Mr. Clarkston."

"No Ms. Koffee that wasn't a threat at all." He looked her sternly in the eyes. "No, not a threat I'd say that was a definite promise."

"Then I'd say Mr. Charles Clarkston it's time for you to be getting off my property, going back to wherever you came from."

"Perhaps you're right Ms. Koffee." Charles cunningly chuckled. "But before that happens I think I'd better warn you." Mildred looked him boldly in the eyes.

"And I'm warning you Mr. Charles Clarkston I don't take to kind to folks giving me warnings." He laughed.

"Not too many of the important folks around town would be to pleased with you being instrumental in setting a baby killer free." He said shifting his eyes over at Mildred gun toting neighbor. "But if you insist on doing so I can assure you that after the dust has settled there's definitely going to be some landing at your doorstep."

"Good day Mr. Clarkston."

"You keep trying to free that baby killer old woman and I can assure you I'll be back." Mildred turned and walked away picking up the water hose. She watched from the corner of her eyes as Charles climbed back in his car, staring at her through his windshield as he backed out onto the dirt road and drove away.

#

"You say you had something urgent you needed to tell me Mildred?" Detective Stokey said quickly climbing out of his car as he walked towards her, following her visit from Charles Clarkston. "You have another piece to the puzzled?" He noted the infuriated look on Mildred's face as she rocked back and forth in her rocking chair.

"You okay Mildred?" He asked concerned.

"Yeah I got another piece you can add to your puzzle that's gon help you in your investigation." She said brewing from Charles' visit. Detective Stokey's eyes lit up.

"I'm listening."

"Families can sometimes hide deep secret—" Mildred said incensed by Charles' threats. "—secrets that could change how they friends look at them." Detective Stokey's eyes widened as he listened with intrigue. "Charles Clarkston—"

"Clarkston?" His anxiety heightened. He massaged his neck. "Wait a minute Mildred . . . where's this coming from and what does Clarkston have to do with that murdered baby?"

"You want to hear what I got to say or are you gon let your fear of Charles Clarkston deafen your ears?" He looked at her with apprehensive eyes.

"Mildred I—"

"Maybe when you grow yourself some bigger balls—" Detective Stokey's mouth flung open.

"That's a pretty cheap shot Mildred."

"I just call it like I see it." She said looking at him as a coward.

"You have to understand Mildred, I have a career to think about and Charles Clarkston's a very powerful man—"

"I thought you wanted to prove Thomas Lee didn't murder that baby?"

"I do Mildred, but Charles Clarkston—"

"Good day Andy." Mildred said noting the immense fear in his voice.

"Mildred—"

"I said good day Andy!" She said raising her voice.

"Is that detective bothering you again Mildred?" Her neighbor from across the road hollered. Detective Stokey looked over at him as he walked away, headed in the direction of his car. He looked up on the porch at Mildred then climbed inside his car and drove away.

#

The Clarkston's mansion filled with the town's elite as the sound of classical music filled the acoustics of the elegant home. Included amongst the many guest were Congressman Jonathan Cutter, his wife Winifred and their now forty six year old son Sonny. Charles made his grand entrance into the drawing room where he greeted his guest.

"Congressman." He said as he approached Jonathan and extended his hand.

"Charles!" The congressman replied delighted to see his biggest supporter both financially and politically. The two men shook. "Don't be so damn formal Charles—" Congressman Cutter whispered. "—in case you hadn't heard . . . that nasty little rumor some disgruntle employee started about an imaginary affair she and I allegedly had was cleared up and determined to be a lie." He leaned towards Charles ear. "That little indiscretion cost me ten thousand dollars of tax payer's money of course."

"How in the hell am I supposed to keep supporting you Jonathan when every year there's a new allegation with your name written all over it?" Charles asked in a low voice.

"Where's that exceptionally beautiful wife of yours?" Congressman Cutter asked cunningly smiling, diverting from the subject of his many indiscretions. "You two are still happily married aren't you?"

"Of course we are Jonathan I couldn't ask for a better wife than Delores." Charles said forcing out the words as he noticed Roosevelt in the doorway of the drawing room. "As a matter of fact Delores and I will be celebrating our fifth anniversary here shortly, I'll make certain you and your wife Winifred are on the guest list." He said masking his true feeling behind an illegitimate smile.

"Well make sure you do." The congressman said. "And be sure to add Sonny to that list as well . . . he just loves social events."

Charles again shifted his eyes to Roosevelt who nodded indicating Delores was ready and sober.

"Sonny?" Charles stated. "Shouldn't those apron strings be slashed by now?" He said turning to the congressman seeing an enormous smile displayed on his face as he looked in the direction of the stairs.

"Here comes that extraordinarily beautiful woman now!" Congressman Cutter said removing a handkerchief from his shirt pocket wiping the drool from his mouth. Charles eyes widened, mesmerized when seeing Delores dressed in a sleeveless, V-neck fuchsia evening gown accented with elongated diamond earrings and a diamond studded choker highlighting her vanilla neck and sandy brown hair.

Charles smiled as he fondly reminisced on the day they were married, finding himself unable to remove his eyes from his unfaithful wife's face— momentarily forgetting their daily marital battles as he hurried over and extended his arm as he prepared to escort her in the drawing room to welcome their guests, despite his apprehensiveness of what the evening would bring.

"Thank you Charles." Delores said displaying an insincere loving smile. He kissed her on the cheek as their distinguished guest watched them enter the drawing room. Charles smiled, impressed by Roosevelt, Marietta and Carrie keeping his wife sober.

"Congressman Cutter you remember my wife don't you?"

"Oh Charles don't be so formal." He said fixating his eyes on Delores taking hold of her arm. "Please . . . call me Jonathan." He cunningly smiled.

"It's a pleasure to meet you Jonathan." She said blushing as he took her hand and raised it to his lips softly applying a kiss to it, gazing in her greenish/brown eyes. Winifred Cutter watched from across the room then hurried over bothered by the lust beaming in her husband's eyes as he looked at Charles' wife.

"Jonathan?" She said interrupting. "Are you going to introduced me to that beautiful woman who seems to have captured my husband's undivided attention?"

"Winifred dear this gorgeous creature is the adorable wife of our gracious host Mr. Charles Clarkston the third!" Delores' blushing smile widened."

"Please to meet you uh—" Winifred shifted her eyes to her husband and awaited him to provide a name. He turned to Charles.

"Delores—" He said in response to the congressman's nonverbal request for Delores' name.

"Delores yes of course." He grinned. "How could I forget such a lovely name for such a lovely specimen?" Delores continued blushing as she turned to Winifred Cutter.

"I'm pleased to me you as well Mrs. Cutter."

"Please dear call me Winifred." She said extending her hand to Delores as the congressman maintained his grasp. Delores gently slid her hand from his hold then shook hands with the congressman's wife as Charles fondly looked at her, captivated by her poise and grace. His attention drew to Marietta standing in the vestibule alerting him that dinner was ready to be served.

"I see our cook's informing me the wonderful meal she's prepared is ready so if you'll all join me and my lovely wife in the dining room we can eat." He turned to Delores and smiled, delighted with her behavior thus far. "Are you ready dear?" He asked taking hold of her arm. "Dinner awaits us." Delores lovingly smiled as he escorted her in the dining room and assisted her in being seated at the table before walking to the opposite end and sitting down.

Roosevelt and four additional butlers hired for the event entered the dining room and began filling each guests long stemmed glasses with Bordeaux. Charles nervously observed as Roosevelt approached Delores leaving her glass unfilled per his instructions.

"Roosevelt?" She said as the butlers began exiting the room without filling her glass. He shifted his eyes quickly to Charles then turned to her.

"Yes Ms. Delores?"

"Aren't you forgetting someone?" She asked holding her glass up. Roosevelt again shifted his eyes to Charles. "Roosevelt?" Delores repeated. Charles quickly intervened.

"Delores dear have you forgotten what happened the last time you drank red wine?" He asked trying to make light of the situation as he masked his fear. "Roosevelt had to practically carry you upstairs and put you to bed. She glanced over at him, unamused by his untruth as her eyes remained on the bottle of Bordeaux.

"Don't you to pay any attention to Charles, Roosevelt." She stated. "My digestive system will be just fine." Delores again glanced over at Charles as she continued holding her glass up awaiting Roosevelt to fill it with red wine. He again looked at Charles then began filling her glass. Delores' mouth slightly watered as she watched the wine enter the crystal wineglass that Roosevelt filled only halfway. "Roosevelt?" She said urging him to continue filling it. He shifted his eyes to Charles then reluctantly filled it. A huge smile displayed on Delores' face as she raised the glass to her lips and took a swallow. "Thank you Roosevelt you may go now."

"Yes Ms. Delores." He shifted his eyes to Charles a final time before exiting the room and returning to the kitchen.

"Sometimes I feel sorry for Mr. Charles." Marietta whispered looking at Roosevelt with worried eyes.

"Don't be feeling sorry for Mr. Charles!" Carrie stated without compassion. "Hell, feel sorry for us, we gon be the ones having to take Ms. Delores' drunk ass upstairs and pour her in the bed after this big shot dinner is over." Marietta quickly looked over at her.

"Carrie!"

"What Marietta, you know damn well that's what gon happen!"

"Look here Roosevelt—" Marietta said hoping to avoid a catastrophe. "—when you start serving dinner make sure you fix Ms. Delores' plate first, I want to get as much food in her as possible before she drink a whole bottle of that red wine."

"I'm telling you now Marietta, once Ms. Delores starts drinking she ain't getting ready to eat no food." Roosevelt stated with certainty. "And you best believe she's already drank half what I just poured her, if not all."

"Damn!" Marietta said speaking just above a whisper. "I sure hope she don't embarrass Mr. Charles I know how much the Clarkston's name means to him.

"Well after tonight them fancy friends of his gon be calling him Mr. Fool—" Carrie said bursting into a quiet chuckle. "—'cause that's just what Ms. Delores getting ready to make him out of."

"Hush Carrie!" Marietta said reprimanding her.

"Marietta you know yourself how Ms. Delores gets when she start drinking—"

"Well unless you got something better that's gon help the situation just hush!" Carrie looked at her and rolled her eyes.

"Then I guess it ain't nothing left for me to say."

"Good!" Roosevelt said. Marietta hurried over to the refrigerator and retrieved two bowls of cucumber and tomato salad then shoved them into Carrie's hands.

"Here . . . take these out there and start serving them folks." Carrie looked at the four other females standing idle in the kitchen.

"I know damn well you don't think I'm getting ready to serve all this salad by myself?"

"Did you hear me say that Carrie?" Marietta said slightly raising her voice, aggravated by Carrie adding fuel to the fire. "What I do expect is you to do is take some of these women with you and start serving that stuff!" She said authoritatively. A look of defiance showed on Carrie's face.

"Yes ma'am!" She stated cynically. "Come on ladies let start serving this salad." She shifted her eyes to Marietta before exiting the kitchen. Marietta ignored her cynicism then turned to Roosevelt.

"I need you to do everything you can to keep from pouring Ms. Delores another glass of wine." An uneasy look formed in his eyes.

"I'll try Marietta, but that's all I can say."

"Roosevelt!" Delores called out. Marietta grabbed a plate from the stack sitting on the kitchen table and dumped a couple spoons of rice on it then covered it with the Étouffée.

"Here—" She said handing the plate to Roosevelt. "—take this in there to Ms. Delores." He stared briefly at the plate of food then looked at Marietta.

"What am I suppose to do with this Marietta?"

"Take it out there and give it to her!"

"Then what, spoon feed her?"

Marietta's agitation grew.

"If you have too!" She said raising her voice. Roosevelt looked at her with worry then shook his head.

"Marietta this ain't your battle." He stated with reason. "Ms. Delores is Mr. Charles' responsibility—let him handle it."

"Just do it Roosevelt!" Marietta demanded. He exited the kitchen without further dispute and entered the dining room.

"Here you go Ms. Delores." Roosevelt said sitting the plate of food in front of her trying to figure out how he would persuade her to eat it. "Marietta wanted you to try Mr. Charles' favorite childhood meal before you spoil your appetite with that red wine." He said shifting his eyes briefly over at Charles. Delores looked at it.

"I don't know what it is Roosevelt but it looks and smells delicious!" She said shifting her eyes briefly to Charles. He quickly intervened.

"It's Étouffée spooned over a bed of rice, Delores dear." He said trying to hide his anxiety. "It's absolutely delicious you really should taste it dear it's one of Marietta's best dishes."

"Go on Ms. Delores taste it." Roosevelt said smiling.

"Maybe I'll try some after I've had another glass of that delicious red wine." She said dismissing Roosevelt's suggestion as she looked at her empty glass.

"Delores dear why don't you go ahead and taste it so Roosevelt can let Marietta know what you think before she serves it to our guest."

"I will Charles, but first I'd like another glass of wine." Charles continued smiling as he tried not to draw his guest's attention to his wife's unquenchable thirst for red wine.

"You wouldn't want Marietta to think you didn't like one of her most delectable dishes would you dear?"

"Of course not Charles!" Delores said shifting her eyes to Carrie as she and two female servers placed cucumber and tomato salad on each guest's gold trimmed salad plate. "So as soon as Roosevelt pours me another glass of wine I'll eat." He looked at Charles and awaited his permission. Charles subtly nodded.

"Ms. Delores why don't you go ahead and eat a few bites before I leave to get another bottle of wine that way I can at least tell Marietta what you thought." Delores giggled then placed a few spoons of the Creole cuisine in her mouth and swallowed.

"So what should I tell Marietta?"

"Tell her it's absolutely divine Roosevelt!"

"She'll be pleased to hear it." He said shifting his eyes to Charles before leaving the room seeing the apprehensive look on his face. Marietta watched as Roosevelt again entered the kitchen shaking his head with worry. "It's gon be a long night Marietta so if I were you I'd hurry up and start feeding them folks so they can discuss whatever it is they gon discuss and get the hell out of here before Ms. Delores fill herself up with red wine!" He said grabbing a bottle from off the table. "Something tells me Ms. Delores getting ready to put on a real show!" Marietta looked at him with distressed eyes as she began to emotionally crumble, her eyes moistening with tears.

"I don't know what else to do Roosevelt." She said. He sat the bottle of wine back on the table and took her in his arms.

"It ain't your battle Marietta." Roosevelt said placing a light kiss on her cheek before picking up the bottle of wine.

"Did she eat any of that food I sent her?"

"Barely enough to taste and not enough to keep her sober."

"Well take this fish and—" He cut her off.

"It ain't you battle Marietta and beside if I don't get back out there with this wine Ms. Delores gon—" Carrie interrupted.

"Embarrass the hell out of Mr. Charles!" She said laughing in a low voice. "Mr. Fool may never show his face in high society again." Marietta looked at her and rolled her eyes.

"Take this miss mouth—" She said shoving the serving tray of Étouffée covered rice in Carrie's hands. "—go do your job and keep your opinion to yourself." Carrie passed the dish to the woman standing next to her and began walking away. "Where you going?" Marietta asked.

"Any place where you ain't." Marietta's mouth flung open, watching in disbelief as Carrie swiftly walked away. She turned to the woman holding the tray of food.

"I need you to start with Mr. Charles and work your way around the table." She pointed to the female next in line. "Get that tray right there it's got blackened redfish inside . . . make sure you give everybody at least two pieces." The woman picked up the tray and exited the kitchen.

"Roosevelt!" Delores called out speaking over the chattering voices of their guests growing louder as they consumed multiple glasses of the Bordeaux.

"Delores dear I'm sure if you just give Roosevelt time he'll return." Charles said growing impatient, infuriated by her less than refined behavior and insatiable thirst for wine. "Why don't you go ahead and eat a little more of the food Marietta prepared?"

"I'll be more than happy to Charles—" She looked down at her plate. "—right after Roosevelt pours me another glass of wine." Charles silently gazed at her before picking up his own glass of wine and taking a drink. Marietta watched from the kitchen as the hired maids and butlers carried food in and out of the kitchen serving the Clarkston's many guests.

"How we doing so far?" She asked when Carrie again entered the kitchen carrying used plates from the dining room.

"All I can say Marietta is I hope these folks get a chance to at least eat dessert before all hell breaks loose."

"Roosevelt!" Charles called out.

"Aw hell . . . here we go." Carrie said putting the dirty dishes in the dishwasher.

"Hand me a bottle of wine off the table so I can get back out here before Ms. Delores start telling Mr. Charles to go to hell in front of his guests." Roosevelt said lightly chuckling as he hoped for the best but sensed the worst was yet to come. He looked in Marietta's concerned eyes as she grudgingly handed him the bottle. "Its gon be alright Marietta." He said. "It's almost over." Roosevelt smiled then exited the kitchen, returning to the dining room with the bottle of Bordeaux.

"Oh there you are!" Delores said slurring as she picked up her empty glass. "If you would pour me some more wine Roosevelt I'd be eternally grateful." She giggled. He shifted his eyes to Charles before popping the cork on the bottle.

"Roosevelt would you please let that be my wife's final glass of wine for the evening?"

"I sure will Mr. Char—"

"Nonsense!" Congressman Cutter intervened. "If that beautiful woman wants to enjoy this delicious Bordeaux you keep it coming, I insist." Roosevelt glanced over at Charles as he filled Delores' glass. "So you go ahead Delores dear and drink up." Congressman Cutter stated. Charles's nervously watched as she picked up the glass, drinking its entire content then again raised her glass. "And Roosevelt—" Congressman Cutter again interceded. "—I do believe that's what I heard our delightful hostess call you . . ."

"Yes sir."

"Would you please give my compliments to the chef?"

"I sure will congressman."

"Uh, Roosevelt—" Winifred Cutter said quickly drinking the contents of her glass and holding it up. "—if it's not a bother I'd like another glass of wine as well." She sat her glass on the table and awaited a refill. "Thank you Roosevelt." She said as he filled her glass.

"You welcome ma'am." He shifted his eyes to Charles when seeing Delores' raised glass.

"Delores dear . . . why don't you try to eat a bit more of your food?" Charles said discretely scolding her.

"I guess I have to be the wife of a congressman to get another glass of wine." She said slurring her words. Roosevelt again filled her glass in response to Charles' reluctant nod. "Thank you Roosevelt."

"You're welcome Ms. Delores." He said preparing to leave the room.

"Roosevelt!"

"Yes Ms. Delores?

"Why don't you go ahead and leave the bottle so our guest won't have to wait so long for you to bring it back—" Charles cut her off.

"That'll be all Roosevelt."

"Yes Sir Mr. Charles." Delores watched as Roosevelt exited the dining room taking with him the bottle of Bordeaux.

"Well now that we've eaten that wonderful meal—" Congressman Cutter stated taking a swallow from his glass with wine. "—I can hardly wait to see what's for dessert."

"Dessert!" Delores giggled. "All I want is another glass of wine." Charles quickly intervened, diverting attention away from his drunken wife.

"Uh, why don't we all retire to the drawing room and I'll have my staff serve desert in there?"

"That sounds like an excellent idea." Congressman Cutter said. Charles rose from the table and watched as Roosevelt escorted his guest into the drawing room. He turned his attention to Delores.

"Could you not let me enjoy one evening without your drunkenness Delores?" Charles said infuriated, speaking in a low tone.

"And why on earth would I want to do that Charles?" She said turning her empty glass up to her mouth. "Roosevelt!"

"Yes Ms. Delores?" He returned to the dining room.

"I need another bottle of red wine?" He looked at Charles seeing the fury in his eyes. "You can bring it upstairs to my room, I think I'll retire for the evening." Delores said slurring.

"And what about our guest Delores?" Charles asked looking at her with contempt.

"Let them get their own bottle." She burst into laughter.

"Marietta!"

"Yes Mr. Charles?"

"Would you please take my wife up to her room?" Marietta shifted her eyes briefly to Roosevelt. "I don't want our guest seeing the elite Mrs. Charles Clarkston the third in her second-rate drunken state."

"Come on Ms. Delores let me help you upstairs." Marietta said looking at her with sympathetic eyes as she approached her.

"Hey Marietta!" Delores slurred. "Can you have Roosevelt bring me a bottle of red wine?" Marietta looked over into Charles' eyes as she took hold of Delores' arm assisting her up from the table then headed in the direction of the vestibule.

"Marietta, why don't you take my wife up the kitchen stairs?" Marietta turned around.

"Come on Ms. Delores." She said guiding her towards the kitchen. "Mr. Charles want you to take the back stairs." Delores looked over at him.

"I hate you Charles!" She shouted. He looked quickly in the direction of the drawing room hoping his guests hadn't heard her venomous words.

"Marietta please!"

"Keep walking Ms. Delores you can hate Mr. Charles from upstairs, right now you need go to bed and sleep it off." Charles watched with disgust as his wife staggered through the kitchen and up the stairs escorted by Marietta.

"You alright Mr. Charles?" Roosevelt asked.

"Would you please make sure my wife stays in her room throughout the evening please?"

"You know the only way I'm gon be able to do that is by giving her a bottle."

"Do whatever you have to!"

Roosevelt's eyes widened surprised by Charles' response.

"You sure?"

"Yes Roosevelt . . . anything to keep her from embarrassing me in front of my guests."

"If that's what you want."

"It is!" Charles said on his way to the drawing room to join his guests. Roosevelt watched with disappointment as he returned to the kitchen to retrieve a bottle of red wine.

"I'm too old for all this mess." He said.

"Age ain't got nothing to do with it Roosevelt." Carrie stated scraping uneaten food off plates then loading them in the dishwasher. "I'm tired as hell myself, and I'm a lot younger than your old ass!" They simultaneously laughed as Roosevelt continued up the stairs with the bottle of Bordeaux.

#

"Thomas Lee!" Dorothy Jean yelled, abruptly getting up from the table when seeing him enter the chatter filled visitation room, his right eye black and swollen.

"Ma'am sit down!" A guard shouted. Dorothy Jean lowered herself back into her chair watching in horror as Thomas Lee walked over to the table being seated. She reached over and touched his eye.

"No touching!" A guard's voice hollered out.

"What happened, Thomas Lee?"

"What the hell you think happened, Dorothy Jean?" He snapped. "They think I'm a baby killer . . . it ain't gon be long Dorothy Jean before somebody kill me up in here!" Thomas Lee said as he looked nervously around the room as beams of sweat formed on his forehead.

"What you mean kill you Thomas Lee?" Dorothy Jean said looking at him with nervousness. "What about the guards?"

"What about them, Dorothy Jean?"

"They can't just let these men hurt you like that!" Thomas Lee looked at her with cynical eyes.

"Who the hell you think did this?" Dorothy Jean gasped. "I'm telling you Dorothy Jean I got to be the most hated man in this whole damn place!"

"Did that detective ever come see you?" Thomas Lee's ears deafened to Dorothy Jean's voice as he thought about the possibility of being murdered. "You hear me Thomas Lee?"

"Huh?"

"Did that detective come see you yet?"

"Yeah he came."

"Did he say if he could get you out of here?"

"It won't be long now." Thomas Lee said shifting his eyes nervously over at the guard standing at the door watching him with angry eyes.

"What you talking about Thomas Lee?"

"What the hell you think I'm talking about Dorothy Jean!" He said increasing the tone. "They gon kill my ass that's what I'm talking about." Dorothy Jean anxiety heightened as she glanced around the room at the multiple men in orange jump suits.

"Don't be talking like that Thomas Lee."

"It won't be long before they find me hanging in my cell." He said, again shifting his eyes over at the guard. "Don't believe it Dorothy Jean if they say I hung myself I didn't do it!" He said emotionally unraveling. "I wouldn't kill myself you know that Dorothy—"

"Thomas Lee!" Dorothy Jean yelled.

"Keep it down!" A guard shouted.

"Can't they put you somewhere safe?"

Thomas Lee's eyes widened, in response to her naïve question.

"Safe!" He said slightly raising his voice. "In a damn prison Dorothy Jean!" He looked anxiously over at the guard. "Ain't no safe place in here— talk to him Dorothy Jean." Thomas Lee stated with desperation.

"Talk to who Thomas Lee?"

"That detective."

"What you want me to say?"

He looked her in the eyes, gradually calming down.

"He said he want to talk to me, hear my side of the story."

"What he mean hear your side of the story?"

"He think I know more about that baby than I said when I was on the witness stand." Thomas Lee hesitated. "I told him I wanted to talk to you first—"

"What you got to say to him Thomas Lee that you need to speak with me first?" Dorothy Jean looked at him with suspicion.

"He think I was somehow connected to that baby."

"What make him think that Thomas Lee?"

"If you think I murdered that baby Dorothy Jean—" Thomas Lee said diverting from her question. "—you might as well walk on out of here right now."

"I didn't say that Thomas Lee but—"

"You don't have too I can see it in your eyes."

"Thomas Lee I don't know what to believe."

"Get your ass out of here Dorothy Jean I don't need you!" He said raising his voice.

"Thomas Lee—"

"Leave me alone!"

"Thomas Lee I said—"

"I said leave me alone Dorothy Jean!" He shouted.

"Your visit's over baby killer! A guard's voice yelled out. Thomas Lee looked over at the guard standing at the door then turned back to Dorothy Jean.

"I said your visit over baby killer!" A guard walked over and grabbed him by the arm and snatching him up. "It's time for you to go back to your cage!"

Dorothy Jean's eyes filled with tears as she watched her husband being forcefully escorted from the visiting room, disappearing through the steel door.

Chapter Seven

"Hey Stokey!" Detective Fish called out seeing him engrossed in reading the transcripts from Thomas Lee's murder trial.

"What is it Fish?"

"You got a visitor!" Detective Stokey looked up seeing Detective Fish escorting a well dressed White male towards him.

"Detective Stokey?" The man said as he approached.

"Yeah that would be me, who are you?" He asked looking briefly up from the transcripts.

"Charles Clarkston the third." Detective Stokey's eyes slightly widened as he looked at Charles, shocked by his visit. His attention suddenly drew to Detective Fish watching and waiting, curious of Charles' visit.

"Did you need something Detective Fish?" Detective Stokey asked breaking his stare.

"Uh, need something, no." He looked at Charles. "It was uh, a pleasure meeting you Mr. Clarkston." Detective Fish said looking at Charles with admiration.

"Likewise Officer—"

"That's uh, Detective . . . Detective Fish."

"Thank you Detective Fish." Detective Stokey said breaking the detective's *star struck* gawk at Charles. "That'll be all you can go back to doing whatever it was you weren't doing."

"I uh, guess I'll get back to work then." Detective Fish said backing away, his eyes still fixated on Charles.

"Good!" Detective Stokey said as he removed the enormous stack of papers from the chair to his right of his desk, dropping them on the floor to his left. "Won't you please have a seat Mr. Clarkston?" Charles looked at the worn metal framed, brown leather chair and scowled.

"Is there a more suitable place where we can talk detective?" Detective Stokey noted the arrogant look in his eyes.

"I guess we can go in Lieutenant Porter's office he's out sick today—"

"Sick?" Charles again scowled.

"Oh it's nothing contagious if that's what you're worried about, it's just his allergies." Charles glanced around the squad room.

"I do hope the lieutenant's décor is far more inviting than what I'm seeing out here."

"Only if you remember this is a police precinct and not some fancy country club." Detective Stokey stated sarcastically as he rose from his desk, dismissing the condescending look on Charles' face.

"I know you wouldn't know Detective, but there's no comparison by far." Charles stated, unamused by Detective Stokey's cynical words.

"If you'll follow me Mr. Clarkston." Detective Stokey stated. Detective Fish watched from his desk as Charles followed Detective Stokey into the lieutenant's office. Charles glanced around the office as they entered taking note of the leather Queen Anne chairs and cherry wood desk, complimented by fine artwork displayed on the walls.

"Your Lieutenant Porter appears to have the taste of a man of means."

"I'll be sure and let him know that you approve."

"I understand you've been re-investigating the Thomas Lee Simms case?" Charles said being seated.

"And you heard that from who?" He looked Detective Stokey sternly in the eyes.

"Does it matter detective?" He said. "What does matter is why the detective who testified against Mr. Simms would suddenly give a rat's ass about a convicted baby killer."

Detective Stokey's eyes slightly widened in response to Charles' apparent disdain for Thomas Lee. He wondered if Charles' visit to the station could be another piece to the puzzle and how did it fit.

"You'll uh, have to understand Mr. Clarkston if my curiosity is somewhat peaked as to why the prosecutor never called on you as a witness since you speak like a man who may have had pertinent information that could've possibly kept an innocent man from being sent to prison for what may be the rest of his life." Charles half hearted grinned.

"An innocent man Detective Stokey? Last I heard a jury of Mr. Simms' peers found him guilty of murdering that poor, innocent baby." Detective Stokey's intrigue magnified.

"You uh, know Thomas Lee Simms personally Mr. Clarkston?" Charles looked at him, but ignored his question then stood.

"Do you like your job Detective Stokey?" Charles asked in a threatening manner. Detective Stokey gave no reply. "You probably didn't know this but right now I hold your job in the palms of my hands detective." Charles smirked. "One call to the right people and you're out on your ass without a pension."

"Ahem!" Detective Stokey cleared his throat as he watched Charles walked over to the door concluding his visit. "Do I make myself clear Detective Andrew Stokey?" He said opening the door, flashing him a cunning smile before walking out.

"I wonder what the hell that was about." Detective Stokey said to himself as his eyes remained on focused on Charles through the opened office door as he journeyed back through the squad room without looking back.

Detective Stokey's eyes met with his partner's as he exited Lieutenant Porter's office, puzzled by Charles' peculiar visit. He glanced over at Detective Fish when sensing his gapping stare as he walked back to his desk.

"Stokey man was that who I think it was?" Detective Abernathy asked astounded.

"I don't know Abernathy . . . I don't know who you thought it was?" Detective Stokey said as he again sat at his desk, astonished by Charles's interest in the Thomas Lee Simms' case.

"The extremely wealthy, high sadity Mr. Charles Clarkston the third?"

"Yep that was him." Detective Abernathy looked at his partner and awaited an explanation.

"What Abernathy?"

"So what did he want man, for you to fix a parking ticket or something?" Detective Abernathy said humored.

"If only it were that simple." Detective Stokey said deep in thought.

"I'm listening?"

"Tell me what you make of this Abernathy?"

"Make of what?"

"Mr. Money bags came here to tell me to cease with my investigation of the Thomas Lee Simms case."

"What the hell does that have to do with him?" Detective Abernathy asked walking over to his partner's desk.

"That's the million dollar question Abernathy." Detective Stokey said looking at him with questioning eyes. "Whatever it is he apparently thinks it worth trying to ruin my career over."

"What?" A look of astonishment appeared on Detective Abernathy's face. "Did he say something about ruining your career man?"

"Is that odd or what?"

"It's unusual to say the least, but I warned you to leave this thing alone didn't I?"

"And you know I can't do that."

"Didn't I tell you not to be listening to all that craziness old lady Koffee was feeding you?"

"This has nothing to do with Mildred—"

"The hell it don't!"

"Quiet I'm thinking." Detective Stokey said ignoring his partner's ranting as his mind remained occupied on the possible relationship between Charles and Thomas Lee.

"You know damn well Charles Clarkston and Congressman Cutter are thick as two thieves, he'll have your ass out the door before you can sit your shield on Lieutenant Porter's desk!" Detective Stokey cunningly smiled. "Man this ain't funny!"

"He knows something Abernathy."

"What?" Detective Abernathy said puzzled. "About the congressman?"

"Stay with me Abernathy this has nothing to do with the congressman."

"Then what?"

"I'll be damn!" A clever grin formed on Detective Stokey's face. "He knows something about Baby boy Doe." Detective Abernathy's jaw dropped. He looked quickly around the squad room hoping none of the other officers present heard his partner's consequential words.

"Stokey man, are you crazy!" He said raising his voice. "If you want to ruin your career that's on you, but I'll be damn if I let you ruin mines!"

"Well I'll just be damn." Detective Stokey said dismissing his partner's fear, convinced that Charles knew something. "You know what Abernathy—"

"No and I don't want to know."

"I think Mildred's put me on to something big."

"Well, leave me out of it man." Detective Abernathy said uneasy. "I don't want nothing to do with you or that old woman and her crazy accusations."

"I think we're going to find that old woman—" Detective Abernathy interjected.

"Is crazy as hell and not we Stokey, you . . . I told you to leave me out of it man I don't want nothing to do with you or Mildred Koffee—you hear me Stokey?" Detective Stokey again grinned.

"You know what else I think Abernathy—"

"No!" He yelled.

"How do you like that?" Detective Stokey said thinking out loud. "Mr. Money bags Clarkston has his hands in that baby's murder all the way up to his shoulders." Detective Abernathy looked at him and shook his head in response to his foregone conclusion.

"Listen to yourself Stokey man do you hear what you saying?" He looked at him in disbelief. "Charles Clarkston's a powerful man with powerful friends—people you don't want to find yourself on their bad side." Detective Stokey glanced briefly at him, deafening his ears to his forewarning. "Are you listening to me Stokey?"

"As a matter of fact Abernathy I'm not."

"Well you should be!"

"Why Abernathy because you're afraid of Clarkston and his powerful friends?"

"And unless you ready to throw away a thirty year career you damn well better be afraid too!"

"You worry too much Abernathy?" Detective Stokey stated. "And I'm surprised, a big strapping fella like yourself who looks like you could take Mike Tyson out in round one—" Detective Abernathy interjected.

"You just keep on joking Stokey, and you know damn well men like Charles Clarkston don't fight with their fist." He looked at Detective Stokey with seriousness. "They hand your ass a shovel and let you determine how deep a hole you can dig before they push your ass in it!" Detective Stokey looked at him with frustration.

"Well that hole, Detective Abernathy is about an innocent man rotting in prison while the real killer of that baby walks the streets free."

"It ain't your fight Stokey, I'm telling you to leave it alone."

"Lunch?"

"What?" Detective Abernathy said confused.

"I'm hungry . . . you want to discuss this over lunch?"

"No!" Detective Abernathy yelled.

"Is the Appetite Pleaser Café okay?"

"No!"

"I'll meet you there say—" Detective Stokey looked at his watch. "—noon?"

"No!"

"If you get there before I do feel free to go ahead and order for the both of us."

"No!"

#

"Lovely day don't you think Mildred?" Detective Stokey said walking up her driveway.

"Just because the sun is shining now don't mean its gon stay that way."

"How's that?"

"I'm guessing you didn't see the news this morning?"

"As a matter of fact Mildred I didn't." Detective Stokey chuckled. "So what did I miss?" He said humored as he stepped on the porch being seated to Mildred's right.

"Weatherman said a storms' on the way." He looked up at the sky and humorously smiled.

"No way . . . do you see that sky Mildred? Not a cloud in it."

"Well I hope you got an umbrella, weatherman said you gon need one." He ignored Mildred's warning as he thought only of his visit from Charles. "Judging from the look in your eyes Andy you must've found another piece to the puzzle."

"I got him Mildred!" Detective Stokey stated with confidence. "And you're never going to guess who it—"

"Charles Clarkston?" He momentarily looked at Mildred, disturbed by her reply.

"Mildred is there something you're not telling me?"

"I guess it won't be no need in me watering my garden today if it's gon rain."

"Are you telling me that you knew Clarkston murdered that baby?"

"I don't recall saying that he did Andy."

"Look Mildred—" Detective Stokey said massaging his neck. "—if you know anything about what happened to that baby you're legally obligated to report it." He said trying to remain respectful.

"Can you prove Charles Clarkston murdered Baby boy Doe?" Mildred asked looking at him, challenging his theory.

"Of course I can . . . Clarkston all but confessed." He said believing his unsubstantiated claim to be fact.

"Did he?"

"His threat to ruin my career if I didn't back off is confession enough to me."

"Well before you put the cuffs on Charles Clarkston, you better make sure you can prove what you saying."

"Are you saying Clarkston didn't do it Mildred?" He asked losing confidence in his assumption. "Okay then Mildred you tell me why a man of Clarkston's societal standing would take interest in a case involving a poor Black man and a murdered Black baby?" Detective Stokey asked, unintentionally disregarding Mildred's ethnic background. An apologetic look suddenly formed in his widened eyes. "Uh, Mildred I uh, I didn't mean to uh, I wasn't trying to—" She cut him off.

"You don't have to apologize to me Andy for being Black." Mildred said amused. "I been Black for eighty three years and I don't recall once wanting to be anything other than what I was."

"Thank you Mildred for uh, taking my foot out of my mouth."

"You ever heard the expression everything that glitter ain't gold?"

"Yeah who hasn't?" Detective Stokey said in a matter of fact tone. "My grandma Stokey use to say it everytime I—" He stopped and looked Mildred in the eyes realizing she'd given him another piece to the puzzle in her riddled words. A large smile formed on his face. "Mildred are you trying to tell me something?" She cunningly smiled.

"I'm gon let you figure it out."

"Come on now Mildred that's not fair, you give me a puzzle piece and then you don't explain what it means!"

"You're a smart man Andy you'll figure it out." She giggled. "You just keep putting them puzzle pieces together and when you done you gon find the light of truth shining on a whole lot of folks." Detective Stokey looked mysteriously at her.

"You don't say?" He said convinced Charles Clarkston would be one of them.

"I scratched your back Andy—" Mildred looked him in the eyes and smiled. "—now it's turn to scratch mines." An uncomfortable look appeared on Detective Stokey's face unsure exactly what she meant. He massaged his neck as he remembered what Dorothy Jean said about Mildred being sneaky.

"Uh, Mildred I uh—" He continued massaging his neck. "—I don't uh, think we should uh be—" Mildred giggled.

"I'm eighty three years old Andy and I ain't enjoyed a man's company in so long if it was possible I might even be a virgin again." His face turned bright red.

"So uh, when you say scratch your back that didn't mean—" She burst into laughter.

"What it means Andy is that I ain't had lunch yet." His face remained flushed with embarrassment. "I was hoping you'd run in the house and fix us both a plate of that food I cooked this morning." He swallowed the lump forming in his throat.

"I uh, sort of promised Abernathy I'd meet him for lunch today or I would uh—"

"I got food enough for him too!"
Detective Stokey's anxiety increased.

"As hospitable as that sounds Mildred I uh, don't think—" She cut him off.

"Why don't you run on in the house and call Roger tell him to join us." He again swallowed. "Telephone's right there in my sitting room just inside the door to your right and down the hall." Detective Stokey's mind raced as he tried to think of an excuse not to eat Mildred's undoubtedly, unhealthy lunch.

"What uh, exactly did you prepare for lunch Mildred?" He asked, uneasy.

"Oh let see . . . I've got barbeque spare ribs, potato salad, macaroni and cheese, and a pot of mustard greens." A smile slowly stretched across Detective Stokey's face.

"Where'd you say that phone was?"

Chapter Eight

Detective Stokey followed the guard down the concrete corridors on his way to the infirmary to see Thomas Lee. His mouth slightly open, when arriving at a dingy white, slightly odorous room consisting of twenty sheet covered beds—all occupied.

"Oh my God!" He yelled out when seeing Thomas Lee asleep in bed, his head wrapped in bandages and his right arm supported by a sling. "Thomas Lee." Detective Stokey said trying to awaken him—observing the excessive bruising and swelling on his face. Thomas Lee gradually opened his eyes bringing Detective Stokey into view.

"Hey— man."

"I hope this wasn't the result of you talking to your wife." Detective Stokey said trying to add humor to the extremely serious situation.

"I wish it was?" Thomas Lee said speaking through the right side of his swollen mouth. "What's up?" Detective Stokey tried to mask his fear of the reality of Thomas Lee's possibility of being murdered.

"I guess from looking at you things haven't gone well for you in here."

"They tried to kill me man!" Thomas Lee said forcing the words through his bloated lips.

"I'm sorry that happened to you Thomas Lee—"

"Man I don't need you to be sorry for me!" He suddenly grimaced from pain as he tried to frown. "I need you to get my ass out of here!"

"I'm sorry Thomas Lee it's not that simple, as much as I would love to be able to just open up the door and let you walk out it's impossible without proving your innocence." Thomas Lee stared at him with tears in his eyes.

"Man, get the hell out of here and leave me alone!" He yelled. "And don't you bring your ass to my funeral either, because if you do I'm gon kill you!" Detective Stokey silently chuckled. "Man it ain't funny!"

"I'm not laughing because I think it's funny, Thomas Lee."

"Then what the hell, you laughing at?"

"I can't get you out, but I can keep you in." A confused looked showed on Thomas Lee's face.

"What the hell's that supposed to mean?"

"I have a few favors owed to me so that means I can have them keep you in the infirmary a little while longer."

"Then what?" Thomas Lee asked shifting his eyes with suspicion over to the female nurse seated in the nurses' station.

"Why don't we uh, just focus on proving you're not the murderer of Baby boy Doe?" Thomas Lee's ears deafened as his anxiety magnified.

"Huh?"

"Just hold tight Thomas Lee—"

"Hold tight?" He said repeating Detective Stokey's discouraging words. "If they put me back on the block somebody gon shank my ass!"

"Try to calm down Thomas Lee—"

"Calm down!" He said emotionally falling apart. "How the hell I'm supposed calm down when the whole world think I killed that baby, even my wife!" Thomas Lee shouted.

"Well believe it or not Thomas Lee I'm on your side so let's just see if we can figure out who had a reason for wanting that baby out of the way."

"Did you hear what I said man?" Thomas Lee asked trying to frown through his swollen face and pain.

"I heard you Thomas Lee, but let's just concentrate on how we can keep you safe, and in the mean time I'll see what I can do to keep you from being put back out on the block."

"Yeah right." Thomas Lee said unconvinced.

"Can you tell me what reason Charles Clarkston would have, to want to see you behind bars?" Thomas Lee stared briefly at him hesitant to disclose their history. "You providing me the truth could make the difference between you going free or spending the rest of your life in here."

"Alright . . . before they locked me up—" A guilty look formed on Thomas Lee's face. "—me and Delores Clarkston were lovers." Detective Stokey's jaw dropped.

"Clarkston's wife?" He said shocked.

"You know Delores Clarkston detective?" Thomas Lee asked, humored. "'cause you don't look like her type." Detective Stokey's looked at him perplexed by his statement.

"Uh, her type?"

"Yeah . . . Delores like her meat dark." An odd look appeared on Detective Stokey's face, clueless to Thomas Lee's unusual analogy.

"Likes her meat dark?"

"She likes Black men." Detective Stokey's mouth slightly opened.

"But, she's married to uh—"

"Charles?" Thomas Lee grimaced with pain as he laughed through his distended lips. "Delores also like, being rich."

Thomas Lee's Story

Delores' lay in Thomas Lee's arms following an afternoon of intimacy.

"Tommy?" He kissed her lightly on the lips.

"Yeah baby."

"What's it like being Black?" He looked at her, surprised by her childlike question.

"What you mean what is it like?"

"I sometimes watch my maids and how they interact with each other—" She gazed into his eyes. "—they always seem to be so happy, it just made me wonder what it's like to be Black."

"The answer to that depends on what Black person you ask." Thomas Lee said thinking of his own complicated life. "I'm sure most Black folks would probably answer the question different in some ways but the same in others." He kissed her on the forehead.

"What do you mean Tommy?"

"Just because a person's Black or even White don't mean they experience life in the same way." He placed a light kiss on Delores' lips.

"I don't understand Tommy."

"Sometimes Delores it seems like being a Black man is one of the hardest things in this world to be but when we get together with friends and family you just feel like a man . . . not a Black man but just a man."

"And how do you feel when you're with me Tommy?" A huge smile stretched across Thomas Lee's face. He kissed her on the forehead, nose then applied an intimate kiss to her lips. "To be honest Delores—" A blank stare entered his eyes. "—I feel like one day all this wrong gon catch up with me and when it do—" She interjected.

"Do you feel like you're doing wrong when you're with me Tommy?" He embraced her in his arms then passionately kissed her. She giggled. Guilt flashed briefly through Thomas Lee's mind as he thought about her question. "You know what we doing ain't right Delores." He said becoming agitated. "You want to know how I really feel when I'm with you Delores—" She raised his hand to her lips and kissed it. "—guilty as hell!" She pulled out of his embrace. "What's wrong baby?"

"I thought you loved me Tommy!" Delores said pouting.

"Come here baby." Thomas Lee said pulling her back in his arms kissing her intimately on the lips. "You know I love you, but sometimes I ask myself what it is you see in me."

"I love you Tommy!"

"I know you do Delores but why?" She smiled then kissed him lightly on the lips. "You got it all Delores . . . a rich White husband, status in society, a mansion you call home with my people waiting on you hand and foot—" She gave no reply. "—and instead of being here laid up with me in some cheap motel, you should be at home with Charles raising kids and planning a family vacations in France, Spain, somewhere!" Thomas Lee half-heartedly grinned.

"You and Dorothy Jean don't have children Tommy."

"I've done told you now Delores—" He said upset. "—when me and you together we don't talk about my wife!"

"I'm sorry Tommy." He placed a quick kiss on the lips. "You know what Tommy?"

"What that baby?" He seductively kissed her.

"I would love to have children!" Delores stated with enthusiasm. "But not with Charles." A confused look showed in Thomas Lee's eyes.

"See . . . that's what I'm talking about Delores, now why wouldn't you want to have children with your husband?" He asked trying to read the look in her eyes. "I know Charles's arrogant ass and as selfish as he is I know he would love to have a Charles Clarkston the fourth." Thomas Lee laughed as he placed another seductive kiss on Delores' lips.

"Tommy?"

"Yeah baby." He said kissing her on the neck and shoulders.

"Can we have a baby?" He abruptly stopped. Frowns formed on Thomas Lee's forehead.

"What the hell you talking about, Delores? Do you know what you saying?" He asked disturbed by her request. "You must want to see me dead!" A naïve look appeared on Delores' face.

"Nobody would have to know you're the—" He cut her off.

"Think about it Delores!" He said raising his voice. "Who in the hell you think Charles gon come after when you give birth to a Black baby?"

"What do you mean Tommy . . . I know Charles can sometimes be mean, but I don't think he's capable of hurting anyone." Delores said looking at him with childlike eyes.

"Then you tell me Delores, what you think Charles would do if he walked in here right now and caught me in the bed with his wife?" Thomas Lee asked trying to open her eyes to reality. "I can tell you now he damn sure ain't gon say don't let me stop you Thomas Lee, you just keep doing what you doing to my wife." Delores giggled then kissed him on his bare chest.

"You're so silly Tommy."

"Right now I don't want to think about Charles or nobody else." He kissed her suggestively on the lips.

"Good, because all I want to do is make love to the man that gives my heart a reason to beat." She said placing another kiss on his chest. "Then I need to get home in time for dinner, Charles just hates it when I'm late." Thomas Lee quietly grinned then took her in his arms and prepared to again engaged in intimacy.

#

"Well Thomas Lee—" Detective Stokey said bowled over by his blatant love affair with Mrs. Charles Clarkston the third. "—that's a hell of a confession." He said with a huge smile on his face. "So did it ever happen?"

"Hell yeah it happened . . . a woman lay down with Thomas Lee and you damn straight something's gon happen?"

"I don't uh doubt that Thomas Lee but I uh, meant did Mrs. Clarkston ever get pregnant with your child?"

"Naw man, not that I know of." Thomas Lee said trying to read the look on Detective Stokey's face. "After Charles threatened to kill me about Delores, I never touched her again I—" Detective Stokey cut him off.

"Clarkston knew about you and his wife?" He asked, astounded.

"Yeah he knew."

"Mind if I ask how he found out?" Detective Stokey asked unable to keep from prying.

"You know the best way to keep a secret detective?"

"How's that?"

"Keep your own damn mouth shut." Thomas Lee said grimacing from pain as he laughed.

"Yeah I've heard that once or twice before." Detective Stokey said amused.

"You ever seen Delores detective?"

"No I uh, haven't." He noted the enormous smile forming on Thomas Lee's face."

"Man Delores is beautiful!"

"You don't say."

"She's what most men would call a trophy!" Thomas Lee said continuing to smile through his pain. "When she showed interest in me it made me feel like I was the man!" He cunningly grinned.

"But Thomas Lee you were a married—"

"You think I didn't know that!" Thomas Lee said raising his voice. Detective Stokey momentarily looked at him.

"Is that who uh, Baby boy Doe was Thomas Lee?" He asked with caution. "The love child of you and Mrs. Clarkston?"

"I told you man!" Thomas Lee yelled. "Me and Delores ain't had no baby and if we did ain't no way in hell she would've ever killed it!"

"You sure about that Thomas Lee?" He looked at Detective Stokey with angry eyes.

"Man get the hell out of here."

"So tell me Thomas Lee—"

"What?"

"Say by some chance Mrs. Clarkston did give birth to your son—" Thomas Lee interjected.

"I told you man I didn't kill that baby!" He shouted. "And as far as me and Delores making a baby—you been to my house detective you seen any kids there?"

"So if I ask your wife she'll say the problem lies with you?"

"Man I didn't kill that baby!" Thomas Lee said shaking his head in anguish. "I thought you said you believed in me?"

"I do Thomas Lee." Detective Stokey hesitated. "I don't know why but I do."

"Thanks man."

"I'll see what I can do about having you put in isolation." Thomas Lee's eyes widened.

"Isolation!"

"I know it's not what you wanted Thomas Lee, but it's better than being in the general population, right?"

"Much better." Thomas Lee said with little hope as Detective Stokey began walking away. "Hey?" Detective Stokey turned back around. "Man you probably the only person in the world that believe I'm innocent."

"I am—" Detective Stokey said amused. "—now I just need to be able to prove it." He again turned and walked away.

#

Mildred relaxed as she rocked in her old rocking chair on the front porch. She humorously smiled when seeing Detective Stokey pulled in her driveway and parked then get out of his car, walking eagerly towards the house.

"It's kind of soon for you be coming back ain't it?"   She said curious of his early return.

"Mildred . . . I think I've found another major piece to the puzzle."

"Is that so?" She chuckled. "Why don't you come on up here and sit down, tell me what you think you got." He joined Mildred on the porch being seated to her right.

"I went to the prison yesterday to see Thomas Lee—"

"How he doing?" A troubled look showed in Detective Stokey's eyes.

"Not too good Mildred, but he's managing."

"They ain't hurt him too bad up in that prison did they?" He looked Mildred in the eyes then shook his head in pity as he thought of his recent visit with Thomas Lee.

"Yeah Mildred I'm afraid they did." He eyes widened with fright. "He sustained a pretty good beating."

"Is he gon be alright?"

"I wish I could say he was, but at this point I just don't know."

"Anything happen to that boy it would kill Dorothy Jean even though goodness knows Thomas Lee ain't ever been faithful to that child."

"Speaking of which Mildred, do you know if the Simms ever had children?"

"Naw—" A sympathetic looked showed on her face. "—never could."

"Do you know if the problem was with Thomas Lee or—" She cut him off.

"Seems to me Andy that's a question you need to be asking Thomas Lee . . . it ain't my place to say."

"So there's nothing wrong with Thomas Lee that would keep him from—"

"Why you asking?"

"Did you know that he and Delores Clarkston were having an affair?" Mildred laughed out loud.

"I think everybody who knew Thomas Lee knew about him and Delores including her husband."

"So I've heard." Detective Stokey hesitated. "Mildred have you heard anything about Mrs. Clarkston giving birth to a baby?"

"I've known Thomas Lee since before he was ever born." A perplexed look displayed on Detective Stokey's face in response to Mildred's odd words.

"Before he was born Mildred?"

"And it ain't no way in this world he would ever hurt anybody, let alone kill a baby."

"Can you be sure about that Mildred?"

"He may not have been the most faithful man when it came to Dorothy Jean, been running 'round on her since before she ever married him, but it ain't in Thomas Lee to hurt a baby no more than it is in me or you . . . so you just keep on collecting them puzzle pieces Andy."

"I hope you're right Mildred."

"Now how about me and you have some of them pig feet I got simmering on the stove?" Detective Stokey swallowed the newly formed lump in his throat as he massaged his neck.

"Pig's feet? He subtly shifted his eyes to her rounded physique. "Do you uh, eat those every day Mildred?"

"You know maids and butlers working for rich folks been known to see and hear a whole lot of things most folks wouldn't know." She said dismissing his critique of her unhealthy eating habits.

"Are pig feet even healthy to the human body?" Detective Stokey asked then suddenly stared at Mildred, a clever smile forming on his face. "Are you giving me another puzzle piece Mildred?"

"I sure would hate for them pig feet to burn." She said looking at him. He took a deep breath then stood. "Make sure you grab a bottle of hot sauce from the cupboard on your way out?"

"Hot sauce?" Detective Stokey opened the back door and entered. "Why not?"

#

"Hey Stokey." Detective Fish called out from across the room. "You still trying to free that baby killer?" He said laughing. Detective Stokey ignored his colleagues taunting as he continued examining what he believed to be pieces to the puzzle in solving the murder of Baby boy Doe. "Maybe you should make a sign and stand outside of the prison saying "Free the Baby Killer! Free the Baby Killer!" Detective Fish said laughing out loud.

"Very funny Detective Fish."

"I wouldn't laugh too hard if I were you Fish." Detective Abernathy said in defense of his partner as he sat at his desk devouring powdered donuts from a box of a dozen. "He might just be on to something."

"Yeah . . . an early retirement if he keeps trying to set that baby killer free." Detective Stokey's ears deafened to his coworker's criticisms as he thought of his newest clue.

"Maids and butlers—maids and butlers." He said to himself trying to figure out how those words fit into the equation. "Dammit Mildred!" He said thinking out loud.

"You alright man?" Detective Abernathy said in response to his partner's sudden outburst that interrupted his feast on the box of donuts.

"You better be careful Stokey." Detective Fish stated. "I hear Charles Clarkston's been talking to the mayor, the governor, and Congressman Cutter about you." Detective Stokey gave no reply. "He's outraged at how you've been trying to retry the Simms case in your own court of law disregarding a jury that found him guilty." Lieutenant Porter's office door suddenly opened.

"Detective Stokey!" He said standing in the doorway glaring at him. He shifted his eyes from his notes looking into Lieutenant Porter's water blue eyes.

"You called me Lieutenant?"

"I do believe it was your name I heard coming from my lips."

"Don't say I didn't warn you Stokey." Detective Fish said looking at him with cautioning eyes. Detective Abernathy glanced over at his partner and gave him thumbs up as powder from his donut fell onto his navy blue shirt. Detective Stokey's eyes drew to the powder sugar on his partner's shirt as he rose from his desk and headed for Lieutenant Porter's office.

"Be sure to wipe that off your shirt Abernathy—" Detective Stokey stated. "—it takes away from your integrity as a detective." Detective Abernathy looked at his shirt seeing the powder sugar.

"Damn." He said attempting to brush it off with his hand, smearing it.

"Go ahead and have a seat detective." Lieutenant Porter said as Detective Stokey entered his office. "I received a call at home yesterday from Congressman Cutter—"

"I already know what you're going to say lieutenant but—" "Then I guess this conversation's over."

"Huh?"

"If you know what I'm about to say then there's no need for me to waste time repeating it."

"I can tell you right now Lieutenant . . . it's Clarkston having Congressman Cutter do his dirty work for him!" Lieutenant Porter's eyes abruptly widened.

"Did I just hear you call Charles Clarkston the third, Clarkston?"

"Yes lieutenant you did."

"If you value your career Detective Stokey I'd be careful calling a man like Mr. Charles Clarkston anything less than that!"

"I'm not afraid of Clarkston." Detective Stokey stated. Lieutenant Porter's eyes again widened. "I'll tell you what I am afraid of lieutenant, seeing an innocent man rot in prison or possibly be murdered for a crime he didn't commit!"

"Are you finished Detective Stokey?" Lieutenant Porter said raising his voice.

"That depends on what you're about to say."

"I've known you for over twenty years Detective Stokey and I've never seen you run off halfcocked on any case, but I'll have to admit you have me worried on this." He said notably nervous. "If you believe Thomas Lee Simms is innocent, and I believe you do . . . trying to prove him innocent after a jury found him guilty won't come without an enormous cost and pressure from Congressman Cutter and Charles Clarkston both breathing down my neck!" Lieutenant Porter suddenly chuckled. "To be honest I never really liked either one of those stuff shirts nor did I vote for Congressman Cutter." They laughed. "But I think you should know Detective Stokey—" He noted the beads of sweat forming on Lieutenant Porter's forehead. "—trying to prove the innocence of one of the most hated men in the state of Louisiana could cost you your career, but if you really think you have something an appellate court will take into consideration—"

"I do lieutenant but—" Detective Stokey stopped as he debated within himself if he should disclosed the information he had thus far with the lieutenant.

"But what?"

"I think I need to give you a heads up lieutenant—"

"A heads up?" A lump formed in Lieutenant Porter's throat as he removed a handkerchief from his shirt pocket and wiped his forehead.

"I'm pretty certain when this thing comes to light, Clarkston, Congressman Cutter and maybe even a few other prominent people will be highlighted front and center, something the prosecutor either ignored or didn't want to make known." Lieutenant Porter swallowed the lump.

"You tread lightly Stokey because if I see for one minute you're jeopardizing the integrity of this department I'll feed your ass like a steak to a hungry lion to both Congressman Cutter and Charles Clarkston!" He said looking Detective Stokey sternly in the eyes. "Do you understand?"

"Yes lieutenant I understand well." Detective Stokey said wondering if he should inform him of his suspicions of who Baby boy Doe's mother possibly might be.

"Now get out of here."

"Lieutenant?"

"Yeah."

"I think I should let you know—"

"Know what?"

"I think I know who the mother of Baby boy Doe is." Beads of sweat again covered the lieutenant's forehead.

"I'm almost afraid to ask."

"It's Mrs. Clarkston." Lieutenant Porter's jaw dropped. He opened his mouth to speak but nothing came out. "Did you hear me lieutenant?"

"You want to say that again Detective Stokey?" He said bewildered by the accusation.

"I'm pretty certain Mrs. Clarkston's was that baby's mother."

"Just what the hell are you saying detective?" Lieutenant Porter said raising his voice. "Have you forgotten Baby boy Doe was Black? So how in the hell could—"

"Thomas Lee Simms was the father lieutenant, they were lovers?" Lieutenant Porter again wiped sweat from his forehead.

"Get the hell out of my office Detective Stokey!" He shouted.

"Listen to me Lieutenant—"

"Do you know what a rumor like that would do to your career—hell to my career if a rumor like that ever reached the ears of Charles Clarkston?" Lieutenant Porter looked at Detective Stokey with outrage. "I don't know where you got that tainted information from detective, but until you have proof those words do not leave this office!"

"When I spoke to Mildred today, she—"

"Koffee!" Lieutenant Porter shouted. "Please tell me that nut case is not you're information source!"

"She's been right thus far lieutenant and I trust—"

"Get the hell out of my office Stokey!"

"Give me a couple of month's lieutenant and if I don't hand you that baby's killer by then—" Detective Stokey looked him in the eyes. "—I'll resign." Lieutenant Porter momentarily stared at him.

"You have ninety days to give me something other than what that jury decided detective or—"

"Thank you, lieutenant."

"Don't thank me just yet Detective Stokey I may have to fire your ass if this doesn't go the way you've planned." Detectives Fish and Abernathy watched as the detective exited the lieutenant's office and again sat down at his desk, turning his focus back to the puzzle pieces.

"Hey Stokey!" Detective Fish called out. "You need a box and some help packing all of your personal belongings before you leave here at the end of the day?" He said laughing. "I hear the burger joint up the street's hiring fired police detectives if you're interested." His laughter intensified.

"Very funny, Fish." Detective Stokey said merely responding to his coworker's humorless words. "Let's see who'll be laughing the loudest when I prove to all of Louisiana that Thomas Lee Simms didn't murder that baby."

"That's right Detective Fish." Detective Abernathy said in his partner's defense, masking his own doubt of Thomas Lee's innocence. Detective Fish looked over at him.

"Is it right Abernathy?" He stated sarcastically. Detective Abernathy shoved the last of the dozen donuts into his mouth.

"Yeah it is Fish." He said with his mouth full. "You just make sure you bring enough steak sauce for that T-bone you'll be buying my partner and uh, don't forget his champagne."

"It'll never happen Abernathy because there's no way in hell Stokey's gonna be able to prove Thomas Lee Simms is not a baby killer!"

"You just be prepared to stand clear of the debris when Stokey blows the lid off this entire thing!"

"Yeah right." Detective Fish stated, doubtful. "Well I hope for your partner's sake Charles Clarkston's not included in whatever 'blowing the lid off' consist of . . . or you better start looking for another partner and Detective Stokey a good lawyer, one that's not country club buddies with Charles Clarkston the third." He burst into laughter. Detective Stokey looked up from his puzzle pieces when sensing Detective Fish approaching.

"What is it Fish, mocking me from your desk wasn't good enough?"

"I just wanted to warn you up close and personal of the danger of probing into the Clarkston's family affairs." He said looking over Detective Stokey's shoulder trying to read his notes.

"And I'm warning you Detective Fish to keep your fears to yourself."

"Okay fine, but don't say I didn't warn you." Detective Fish said peeping at the notes Detective Stokey carefully scrutinized. "That family has enough money and influence to make your thirty year career null and void."

"Believe me Detective Fish I am well aware of the status, power and money that blankets the Clarkston family."

"So tell me Stokey . . . just what is it you have that your partner seems to thinks going to blow the lid off of this free Thomas Lee Simms crusade?" Detective Stokey looked up from his notes and into the inquiring eyes of Detective Fish.

"What I've known all along, Thomas Lee Simms is innocent."

"So have you figured out who else had a reason to murder that baby besides Thomas Lee Simms?"

"I'll say this much Fish—" He looked him in the eyes. "—Thomas Lee is probably the only person who didn't have a motive to want that baby dead."

Detective Fish shifted his eyes over at Detective Abernathy who humped his shoulders. "The only dilemma now is getting him out of prison before his housemates kill him."

"I can imagine." Detective Fish said with genuine concern. "Let's just hope you can prove your theory before it's too late."

"Well right now he's in the infirmary—" Detective Fish burst into laughter.

"Newsflash Stokey, if an inmate puts a hit out on Thomas Lee Simms being in the infirmary is only a technicality."

"Don't you have an unsolved homicide you need to be working on Officer Fish?" Detective Stokey said taunting him.

"That's Detective Fish, and I'm just saying—"

"Well say it over at your own desk, now beat it you're disturbing me."

"Well excuse me!" Detective Fish said walking away. "You just make sure you have money to pay for my T-bone steak and bottle of champagne." Detectives Stokey's eyes widened when looking over at his partner, his shirt covered with powder sugar.

"Did somebody say it was more donuts in the break room?" Detective Abernathy asked trying to brush the white substance off of his shirt.

Chapter Nine

"I take it you've been staying safe." Detective Stokey asked Thomas Lee as he entered the infirmary a week later noting his reduced facial swelling and bruises.

"I'm still alive ain't I?" Thomas Lee said sitting up. Detective Stokey lightly chuckled. "I want to thank you man—" Thomas Lee said through his partially swollen lips.

"No Thomas Lee it's me who should be thanking you."

"Thanking me for what?"

"For being honest with me about you and Mrs. Clarkston." Detective Stokey reddened as he slightly blushed. "Most men wouldn't admit—"

"Hold on man."

"Is something wrong Thomas Lee?" A guilty look formed on his face as he lowered his head.

"Yeah it is." He again looked up and into Detective Stokey's attentive eyes. "I lied man."

"Lied?"

"Yeah I wasn't honest!"

"I understand what lying means Thomas Lee, but you want to tell me what it is you lied about?" Thomas Lee shook his head with remorse.

"It wasn't me with the problem it was Dorothy Jean she couldn't get pregnant."

"Dammit Thomas Lee!" Detective Stokey yelled believing his efforts had been sabotaged.

"Look man I'm sorry—"

"I don't need you to be sorry Thomas Lee!" Detective Stokey shouted. "I need you to be honest!"

"When Delores talked about us having a baby—" Thomas Lee half-heartedly smiled. "Man, it made me feel something I ain't ever felt before."

"So what are you telling me Thomas Lee?"

"I pulled off my jimmy . . . I could've been the one who got Delores pregnant and Baby boy Doe could've been my son." Detective Stokey took a deep breath and vigorously massaged his neck.

"Do you realize that makes you look guilty as hell Thomas Lee for the murder of that baby?" He shouted.

"Hell naw!" Thomas Lee said raising his voice.

"Can you see how that gives you a motive for wanting that baby dead?"

"How so?"

"You're a married man Thomas Lee getting another woman pregnant—" Detective Stokey's heart pounded in his chest. "—but not just any woman the wife of Charles Clarkson who wouldn't hesitate to destroy you if he knew!"

"Man what the hell you trying to say, that I murdered my own son?" Thomas Lee yelled. "You crazy as hell if you think I could kill my child or anybody else's!"

"Well when you lie to me Thomas Lee it makes it difficult for me to trust anything you say!" Detective Stokey said trying to hold back his anger. "How do I know even now that you're being honest?"

"Man you never trusted me in the first damn place!" Thomas Lee yelled. "You ain't trying to help me!" He looked at Detective Stokey with suspicion. "What? You working for Charles now?"

"You're wrong Thomas Lee." Detective Stokey said shaking his head. "I put my ass on the line because I believed in your innocence."

"Man I'm telling you that baby was already dead when I found him floating in that river!" He looked Detective Stokey in the eyes trying to convinced him. "It was almost like he wanted his daddy to see what somebody had done to him." Thomas Lee's eyes filled with tears. Detective Stokey's eyes filled with skepticism as he tried to sympathize with Thomas Lee.

"I'm sorry Thomas Lee I know finding that baby—"

"He wasn't that baby, man!" Thomas Lee shouted as tears rolled down his cheeks. "He was my son!"

"I need you to calm down Thomas Lee and tell me if there's anything else you haven't told me?" He looked at Detective Stokey and shook his head with shame.

"Yeah man it is."

"Dammit Thomas Lee!" Detective Stokey shouted, infuriated by his dishonesty. "Let me tell you one damn thing, if I find out one more time that you've lied to me about anything—" He stared Thomas Lee in the eyes. "—I'm off this case do you understand me?"

"Yeah man I understand."

"Good!" He said maintaining his gaze at Thomas Lee waiting to hear his truth.

"Alright man . . . when I pulled my son out of the river I knew he was the baby, my baby Delores had just gave birth to a few days ago." Detective Stokey took a deep breath and massaged his neck. "I was there man the day my son was born." A confused look formed on the detective's face.

"What do mean you were there?"

"Upstairs in Delores' bedroom." Detective Stokey's eyes widened, shocked by Thomas Lee's report.

"Did Clarkston know that?"

"He knew Delores was up there having a baby, but he didn't know I was there." Detective Stokey opened his mouth to speak, stunned by Thomas Lee's admission, but nothing came out.

"I watched my son come into this world man." A fatherly smile formed on Thomas Lee's face. "I couldn't believe it . . . I was a daddy and that little boy laying there crying was mines and I wasn't gon let nobody stop me from being his daddy—not Dorothy Jean and damn sure not Charles!" Detective Stokey sympathized with the tears in Thomas Lee's eyes as he now tried to figure out what direction he would take his investigation given the information he'd just received.

"Did your uh, wife ever find out about your son Thomas Lee?"
He shook his head no.

"Naw man I couldn't hurt Dorothy Jean like that, I'd hurt enough over the years." Thomas Lee stated with remorse. "I thought I'd wait before telling her—" He shook his head. "—I guess I was hoping when I did tell her she'd be ready to love my son as much as I did."

"When was the last time you saw your son Thomas Lee?" He lowered his eyes and shook his head before answering.

"The day I fished him out of that river."

"Did you and uh, Mrs. Clarkston continue seeing each other after that?"

"Naw . . . . for some reason she didn't want to have nothing to do with me." Thomas Lee said thinking back. "The next time I saw Delores it was at my trial—" A puzzled look form on his face. "—I knew something wasn't right when she wouldn't even look at me, but I assumed it was because she was with Charles even though that never stopped her before from sneaking a peek." Thomas Lee cunningly grinned. "You know detective it was something funny about the way Delores was acting."

"Funny? What do you mean by funny Thomas Lee?"

"She acted as if our son had never been born!" An angry look appeared in Thomas Lee's eyes. "Man she didn't shed one tear the whole time they was showing his pictures or talking about him at the trial."

"Do you think she could've—" Thomas Lee cut him off.

"Naw man, Delores ain't killed our son if that's what you thinking . . . I'd stake my life on it."

"In a way Thomas Lee you are." Detective Stokey said massaging his neck. "What about your wife?"

"Hell naw!" Thomas Lee yelled. "Dorothy Jean never even knew my son was born!"

"Then you tell me Thomas Lee who do you think could've murdered your son?"

"I wish I knew—" Thomas Lee shook his head in anger. "—then me being in this place for murder would be justified."

"What about Clarkston?" Detective Stokey said grasping at straws. "You think he could've killed your son?"

"That man hated me so much detective I wouldn't put it pass him if—"

"Enough to kill a baby?"

"Naw." Thomas Lee stated with certainty. "Charles would've probably made Delores give my son away to a Black family who couldn't have a babyd of their own."

"Give him?" Detective Stokey looked at him, astounded by Thomas Lee's casual response to the illegal adoption. "You are aware it's illegal to simply give a child away right?"

"I loved that little boy detective." Thomas Lee said dismissing his lesson on the law. "I should be watching him taking his first steps." He said shaking his head in frustration. "Not sitting in prison being convicted of his murder."

"I agree Thomas Lee."

"Man who would be heartless enough to just throw a baby in the river like fish bait?" Detective Stokey's eyes widened, in response to Thomas Lee's vulgar description.

"That's a good question Thomas Lee and I wish I had an answer to your question."

"Well it damn sure wasn't me!" Thomas Lee said wiping away his tears. "Maybe you should be talking to Delores's husband he had more of a reason to murder my son than anybody." Detective Stokey looked at him with ambiguity considering he'd just declared Charles incapable of committing such an act.

"I'm sure Clarkston's attorney, the mayor, Congressman Cutter and anybody else with clout would see me in hell before they'd let me arrest him— you got any other suggestions?"

"Talk to my momma man, I bet she probably knows something." A perplexed look displayed on Detective Stokey's face.

"Your momma? Who's uh, your mother Thomas Lee?"

"Her name's Marietta, she's maid and cook for the Clarkston family, been there since before I was born." Thomas Lee said half heartedly chuckling. "You ain't gon believe this detective but me and Charles grew up together." Detective Stokey looked at him with humored eyes.

"You're teasing me right?"

"Naw man I'm serious . . . when my momma would go to work she always took me with her."

"You are serious aren't you?"

"Yeah I am, as a matter of fact me and Charles were just like cousins or something." Detective Stokey's eyes lit up.

"Cousins?" A cunning smile formed on his face. "Well I'll be damn, so that's what Mildred meant."

Charles buried his face behind the morning paper as Marietta sat a plate of waffles, ham steak and a vegetable omelet in front of him.

"Marietta—"

"Yes Mr. Charles."

"Has my wife gotten up yet this morning?"

"Who? Ms. Delores?" Marietta said stalling.

"Of course Delores, she's the only wife I have isn't she?" He said aware that his wife had already left the house. Charles lowered the newspaper. "You're not keeping anything from me are you Marietta?"

"Anything like what Mr. Charles?" She said avoiding eye contact with him.

"Where's Roosevelt I haven't seen him this morning?" Marietta shifted her eyes in the kitchen, looking in the humored eyes of Carrie as she waited to hear Marietta's explanation.

"Ms. Delores had Roosevelt take her in town, I guess she felt like doing some early morning shopping." Marietta said trying to make light of her absence. She again shifted her eyes to Carrie in the kitchen watching. Charles looked down at his watch.

"And just what kind of shopping do you think my wife would be doing Marietta since the really expensive stores, and Delores does likes to frequent expensive stores . . . don't open their doors for another four hours?"

"Maybe she wanted to get off to a early start before—"

"Before what Marietta?" She again glanced in the kitchen seeing Carrie silently laughing.

"Mr. Charles you know Ms. Delores ain't been right since—"

"You can bring me my coffee now Marietta." He said avoiding the subject of his wife's murdered baby boy. Charles again raised the newspaper. "When my wife gets back from wherever it is she didn't want me to know she was going, would you please let her know I'd like to speak with her?" Marietta shifted her eyes a third time in the kitchen at Carrie doubled over in silent laughter.

"Now Mr. Charles you already know when Ms. Delores get home she probably gon already be drunk as a skunk." Charles lowered the newspaper and looked her sternly in the eyes.

"I want to talk to my wife and I want to do it with her sober!" He demanded. Carrie's eyes widened, offended by his aggressive tone. "That's not too much for a husband to ask is it?" Marietta momentarily stared at him before turning to leave to retrieve his coffee. "Tell her it's about her visit up to the prison to see Thomas Lee." Marietta turned to him, shocked by the news.

"You sure about that Mr. Charles? Ms. Delores ain't said nothing to me about going to see Thomas Lee."

"Stupid whore!" Charles shouted, disgusted by his wife's behavior. Marietta's mouth abruptly opened.

"Mr. Charles you know that ain't no way for a husband to be talking about his wife."

"Then my wife shouldn't be presenting herself as such." He said burying his face behind the newspaper. "When Thomas Lee and I were little boys I remember how I would share anything I had with him because I knew you were too poor to afford him the luxuries I was privileged to." Marietta silently stared at the newspaper concealing his face, offended by his belittling words. "I guess I never dreamed that one day my sharing would include my wife." She looked quickly in the kitchen at Carrie seeing her mouthing the word:

"Bastard."

"Let me go get your coffee."

#

"So tell me Stokey man, what could be so important you would treat me to lunch in a restaurant you hate?" Detective Abernathy asked.

"I never said I hated the Appetite Pleaser Cafe." He said glancing around the half empty restaurant. "What I hated was that waitress."

"I thought she was pretty good."

"That's because she treated you like king of the day." Detective Abernathy grinned.

"Well maybe that day I was."

"I'll be sure to tell your wife Regina the next time I see her." Detective Abernathy's eyes widened, surprised by his partner's unofficial threat.

"Stokey man would you really be that petty?"

"Nevermind that, just answer me this—how do I find a person that's impossible to find because I don't know who I'm looking for to begin within the first place?" Detective Abernathy looked at him, confused by his riddled words.

"Now what the hell kind of question is that Stokey?" He asked picking up his menu. "And furthermore how in the hell am I suppose to answer it?"

"I know it sounds confusing Abernathy—"

"You think." Detective Abernathy said looking over the lunch menu. "What you ordering man?"

"What?"

"For lunch, what are you ordering?" Detective Stokey stared at him bothered by his dismissal of the question he'd just asked him.

"Just give me a ham and cheese sandwich platter on wheat." Detective Abernathy lowered his menu and looked over at him, puzzled by his request.

"Wheat?"

"That's what I said."

"Earth to Stokey." Detective Abernathy said in response to his partner's careless order.

"What?" He said looking at his partner. "I said I'll take the ham and cheese sandwich on wheat . . . what the hell's wrong with that?"

"You tell me."

"Tell you what Abernathy?" Detective Abernathy laid his menu down on the table.

"Why don't you go ahead and order the Ruben sandwich?"

"Because I don't want a damn Rueben sandwich Abernathy!" Detective Stokey removed his notes from his jacket pocket. "What the hell's wrong with a ham and cheese on wheat?"

"Hey, if that's what you want man, feel free."

"What?"

"I said if you want the ham and cheese on wheat knock yourself out."

"Why the hell would I want ham and cheese on wheat Abernathy?" He said looking at him with cynical eyes. "You know damn well I have an allergy to gluten?" Detective Abernathy's mouth opened in disbelief as he stared at him and shook his head before again picking up his menu.

"That's what I was trying to—"

"Just order me the damn Ruben sandwich platter and a coffee, oh and Abernathy will you make sure she brings lots of sugar, you think you can do that?" Detective Abernathy looked quickly at him from behind his menu.

"If it wasn't for the fact you were paying for my lunch man I'd make you order your own damn food." He said looking around the restaurant in search of a waitress spotting a red haired female with a ring in her nose coming out of the kitchen. "Waitress!" Detective Abernathy called out.

"Did you need something sir?"

"Can we get a couple Ruben sandwich platters and two coffees, black?'

"I'll bring that right out sir." Detective Stokey looked up from his notes.

"Uh, waitress?"

"Yeah."

"Can you put one of those Rubens on wheat instead of rye?" Detective Abernathy's mouth abruptly opened as he looked across the table at his partner and shook his head.

"Wheat instead of rye Stokey—really man?"

"That's right, is something wrong with that?"

"No, not if that's what you want but don't be complaining to me when those stomach pains hit and diarrhea make you feel like crap."

"It's my body why can't I just have what I want, wheat?" Detective Abernathy threw his hands up in defeat.

"I give up . . . if you want to mess up a perfectly good Rueben sandwich by having them put it on wheat knock yourself out man."

"Can you just order the damn sandwiches so we can eat?" Detective Stokey said agitated turning to the waitress as she approached.

"Hey it's no skin off my behind." Detective Abernathy said knowing the consequences his partner would face.

"Did you get that sweetheart?" Detective Stokey stated.

"One Ruben on rye for your friend and a second Ruben on wheat for you." She looked at Detective Abernathy and scribbled the order on her order pad and walked away.

"I need two Ruben platters . . . one on rye and the other on wheat!" The waitress said handing the order slip to the gentleman in the kitchen.

"Wheat?" He stated loudly. "What kind of a bozo eats a Ruben sandwich on wheat?" Detective Abernathy shifted his eyes to Detective Stokey and quietly chuckled.

"So what do you think Abernathy?"

"About the wise guy in the kitchen?"

"No, about the question I asked you earlier."

"If it were my investigation Stokey I guess I'd first want to speak to anybody who might know anything about anyone who might've had a baby around the time Baby boy Doe turned up in the river who no longer has that baby."

"What if I told you that I knew who the mother was." Detective Abernathy's eyes widened, shocked by his partner's words.

"Wait a minute . . . did I just hear you say—"

"I know who the mother of that baby was, yes Abernathy you did." Detective Abernathy looked at him, unconvinced.

"Now how in the hell could you know that Stokey?"

"It's Mrs. Clarkston." Detective Abernathy's jaw dropped.

"Whoa . . . hold on one damn minute man!" He said aggravated. "I think you better check your facts before you go putting something like that out there!" An uneasy look showed on Detective Abernathy's face. "Have you forgotten that Baby boy Doe was Black?"

"Thomas Lee Simms was the father." Detective Abernathy's jaw dropped a second time.

"Do you know what the hell you saying Stokey? And can you prove it?"

"Thomas Lee told me—" He cut him off.

"Thomas Lee?" Detective Abernathy said shaking his head seeing his partner as naïve. "Stokey man have you forgotten Thomas Lee's ass is the one who was convicted of murdering that baby?"

"Exactly . . . so what reason would he have to lie now?"

"It's my guess Thomas Lee Simms would say anything to get his ass out of prison!" Detective Abernathy said bothered by his partner preparing to do battle with one of the town's most prestigious, powerful and wealthy citizens. "Stokey man, do you realize you're putting your career on the line messing with Charles Clarkston?" Detective Stokey dismissed his partner's concern. "And from what you just told me man, Thomas Lee Simms had more reason than anybody to want that baby to disappear!"

"Marietta?" Detective Stokey said looking at him. "Do you know her?"

"Yeah that's Thomas Lee's mother what about her?"

"He suggested I talk to her—"

"About what man? Detective Abernathy said raising his voice."

"Thomas Lee tells me she's worked for the Clarkston—"

"Since Thomas Lee was a baby, okay what about it?"

"He seems to think she might have information on Mrs. Clarkston giving birth to a baby—" Detective Abernathy interjected.

"Listen to what you saying Stokey!" He looked around the restaurant hoping his partner's derogatory words had not been heard. "You don't have proof that Delores Clarkston gave birth to that baby or any other baby!"

"But Marietta would." A skeptical look displayed on Detective Abernathy's face.

"Stokey man it sounds to me like you playing a game you can't win."

"What if Thomas Lee's right?"

"And what if he's wrong?"

"Thomas Lee told me he was there when the baby was born." Detective Abernathy's mouth flung open.

"And you believed him?" He shook his head in disbelief. "Ain't no way in hell Charles Clarkston stood by while his wife gave birth to Thomas Lee Simms' son!"

"He said Clarkston was downstairs while he hid out upstairs in Mrs. Clarkston's bedroom."

"Hell naw!" Detective Abernathy said looking at him with strong objection. "Think about that Stokey . . . does that sound right to you man?"

"I believe him."

"You what!" Detective Abernathy yelled. "I've known you a lot of years man and—" He cut him off.

"Twenty five to be exact."

"And this is the first time I've ever heard you say anything that makes me think you losing your damn mind!"

"Okay."

"Okay? Man when was the last time you been to see your doctor? I hear mental illness can happen to anybody."

"Then you go talk to him."

"I'm not the one who's talking like I don't have any damn sense!"

"Not the doctor Abernathy, Thomas Lee."

"Why in the hell would I want to do that Stokey? I'm not convinced that Thomas Lee's innocent."

"Well I don't recall asking you what you thought Abernathy." Detective Stokey said insulted by his comment.

"Thomas Lee Simms is guilty as hell and it's time you accept that man!" Detective Abernathy said increasing his tone. "The hell with your bet with Detective Fish, I'll buy him a damn steak dinner and two bottles of champagne it that's what it'll take for you to drop this whole damn thing!"

"Go talk to him Abernathy."

"Man I'm not talking to that baby killer!" Detective Abernathy yelled. "So what Stokey I can start sounding like I'm ready for the Looney bin like you?"

"Two Ruben platters?" The red haired waitress said as she returned with the food. "One Rueben on rye and the other on wheat?" She sat white plates containing mounds of fries and Rueben sandwiches in front of each man. "I'll be right back with your coffee." Detective Stokey examined his sandwich then looked over at Detective Abernathy.

"Does this look like wheat bread to you?"

"Naw it looks the same as mines, rye."

"Two black coffees one with lots of sugar." The waitress said placing two coffee cups on the table.

"Uh, waitress." Detective Stokey said trying to hold his temper.

"Yeah."

"There's been a mistake."

"What mistake?" She said filling their cups with hot coffee. "You ordered two Rueben platters right? And that's what I brought you, so what's the mistake?"

"It looks like the cook made both Rubens with rye, I ordered one on wheat."

"That wasn't a mistake." She said chewing gum. Detective Stokey looked over at Detective Abernathy and began massaging his neck as his anxiety soared.

"Did I or did I not request my Rueben be made with wheat?"

"You did." She said looking at him. "Oh yeah that right, the cook said historically the Ruben's been made with rye and he's not breaking tradition for some jerk who doesn't know the difference." Detective Stokey's mouth flung open. "If you have a problem with it take it up with the cook, I don't make the food I just serve it." She dropped two packs of cream on the table. "Will there be anything else?"

"Yeah you can get me some damn sugar like I asked and take back this damn cream!" He stated with insolence.

"Make up your mind!" She said annoyed. "First you ask for cream and now you're crying for sugar." The waitress reached inside her apron and grabbed a handful of sugar packets and tossed them on the table." Detective Abernathy watched in amusement as his partner and the waitress glared angrily at one another before she walked away.

"You gon be alright Stokey?"

"You think I can make a case for arresting her?"

"Arresting her?" A perplexed look formed on Detective Abernathy's face. "For what man, serving you a traditional Ruben sandwich and giving you cream instead of sugar?"

"No for impersonating a waitress!"

Detective Abernathy laughed.

Chapter Ten

Pacing out front of Night Owl Nightclub, a Black owned bar and grill located in the Black community, Detective Stokey nervously massaged his neck as he prepared to meet with Marietta. His stomach bundled with nerves as he worried she'd be unable to provide him with anything of significance. He took a deep breath then opened the door and entered, his ears quickly being hijacked by the explosive sound of the Blue's filling the bars acoustics. His anxiety heightened when all eyes drew to him as he looked around the dimly lit room of Black patrons engaged in drinking and dancing.

"You looking for somebody?" A man asked coming up from behind. Detective Stokey quickly turned, looking in the face of a sixtyish Black male. "You Detective Stokey?"

"As a matter of fact I am, who are—"

"Come with me." Detective Stokey reluctantly followed as the man lead him towards the rear of the establishment through a darkened room which ultimately ended at a closed door. The man knocked twice and awaited an answer. Detective Stokey watched with curiosity as the door slowly opened.

"Come on in detective." A woman's said from inside. He cautiously looked in seeing two Black women sitting at the lone round table in the center of the room. "Come on and sit down." The female in charge stated. He shifted his eyes over to the man who escorted him to the room, seeing him close the door before joining the women at the table.

"I'm Marietta . . . Thomas Lee's momma." Detective Stokey smiled.

"I can see the resemblance." Marietta turned to the other female.

"This here's Carrie she works with me at the Clarkston's."

"Nice to meet you Carrie."

"And the man that brought you back here that's Roosevelt." Detective Stokey greeted him with a nod of the head.

"Thank you all for agreeing to meet with me, I—" Carrie interjected.

"So you're that detective trying to prove Thomas Lee didn't kill that baby huh?" She asked looking at him with mistrust. "My baby brother went to school with Thomas Lee, said he ain't ever so much as seen Thomas Lee slap a biting mosquito." Detective Stokey quietly grinned. "So I know ain't no way in hell he killed that baby."

"That's uh, what I'm trying to prove Carrie."

"What you need from us detective?" Marietta asked.

"I understand you all were working for the Clarkston at the time Baby boy Doe was discovered?"

"Yeah that's right." Carrie said shifting her eyes briefly to Marietta.

"I been working for the Clarkston since I was sixteen, I'm forty eight now." Marietta said looking briefly at Roosevelt. "I started working for Mr. Charles Clarkston the second when Mr. Charles was still in diapers.

"I've been working for the Clarkston's for ten years—" Carrie stated. "—long before Mr. Charles ever married Ms. Delores, but four years of working with that crazy ass woman feels like it's been a lifetime." She burst into laughter.

"Well I've been working for the Clarkston family before either of these women." Roosevelt stated. "Started there when Charles Clarkston Sr. was the man of the house and when he died I worked under Charles Clarkston the second and after he died I've been working for Mr. Charles the third." Detective Stokey's eyes widened with amazement.

"Is that so?"

"My mother and aunties worked for the Clarkston's that's how I came to work for the family." Roosevelt suddenly grinned. A curious look displayed on Detective Stokey face.

"What?"

"The Clarkston family got more skeletons in their closets than the graveyard got bones." Roosevelt said continuing to laugh.

"Is there something specific you know about the Clarkston family, Roosevelt?" Detective Stokey asked snooping.

"Plenty . . . but it'll be going to the grave with me." Roosevelt stated. "The Clarkston's been like family to me and they always treated me well." Detective Stokey's concern grew as he worried if Roosevelt's loyalty to the Clarkston's would result in him being less than forthcoming.

"Ahem!" He cleared his throat. "Well the reason I've asked you all here is because I need some personal information about that family." He looked quickly to Roosevelt. "I promise I won't ask you anything that's not relevant to my investigation. Roosevelt nodded. "Good, so do any of you remember Mrs. Clarkston giving birth to a baby?" They looked one to the other.

"Before we answer any of your questions, detective—" Roosevelt said speaking on behalf of everybody. "—we need to know that whatever we say here in this room today the Clarkston's won't know it came from us." Carrie nodded in agreement.

"The last thing we need is to be fired over speaking on the Clarkston's personal business with the police."

"I got to agree with Carrie." Roosevelt stated. "I'm too old to be starting over."

"I understand . . . and believe me I would never put your jobs in jeopardy." Detective Stokey said looking at Marietta, taking note of her silence and the ambiguous look in her eyes. "Marietta?"

"All I know is it was bad blood between Mr. Charles and Thomas Lee." She said opening up. "Only reason I stay there working is because I feel bad how Thomas Lee started carrying on with Ms. Delores." Roosevelt intervened.

"I want you to know detective if anything comes out that shines a dim light on the Clarkston family, before I let either one of these ladies take blame I'll own it all, you remember that." Detective Stokey nodded as he removed his tablet from his inside jacket pocket.

"Agreed, now what can any of you tell me?"

"I'll go first." Marietta said. "When Mr. Charles married Ms. Delores—" She smiled as she reminisced. "—He seemed to be the happiest man in the world!" Roosevelt likewise smiled.

"That was before Ms. Delores started drinking all that damn red wine!" Carrie stated, unsympathetically. "Damn drunk!" Detective Stokey's mouth slightly opened.

"Did uh, something happen to make her—" Carrie interjected.

"Yeah something happened alright." She looked at Roosevelt then shifted her eyes to Marietta before speaking. "Mr. Charles wouldn't or couldn't give her ass babies." Marietta looked at her with scolding eyes.

"Let's not start telling the detective stuff we don't nothing about Carrie."

"Well it had to be Mr. Charles who couldn't have babies Marietta, 'cause Ms. Delores ain't had no problem getting pregnant even if it wasn't her husband!"

"Carrie!"

"What Marietta? You know I'm right!"

"It wasn't a thing wrong with Mr. Charles either." Roosevelt stated with assurance. "And that's all I'm gon say." Carrie's eyes widened, surprised by his mysterious words.

"You know something we don't know Roosevelt?" She asked. He ignored her prying then continued speaking.

"About two months into the marriage, Ms. Delores started nagging Mr. Charles about wanting to have babies, but it just seem to fall on deaf ears—" Detective Stokey listened, but sensed Roosevelt withheld additional facts. "—after that, instead of nursing a baby with a bottle Ms. Delores started nursing herself with that bottle of red wine." Detective Stokey lightly chuckled. "Had me bring her a one every day starting with breakfast."

"That was also about the time Ms. Delores started hating Mr. Charles' ass too!" Carrie said amused. "But it wasn't until one day when they was eating supper and Mr. Charles told Ms. Delores he ain't had no intentions on ever giving her children that she seem to have lost her damn mind!" A odd look appeared on Detective Stokey's face.

"Uh, lost her mind?"

"Yeah, that's when she started stepping outside of her and Mr. Charles' marriage—" Marietta said.

"That was also when she started messing around with Thomas Lee's ass." Carrie stated. Marietta looked over at her, but ignored her biting words.

"She only done it 'cause Mr. Charles hurt her so bad." Roosevelt stated in Delores' defense. Detective Stokey intervened.

"I know this may not mean much coming from me Marietta—" He stated with compassion. "—but I want to know how sorry I am about how things turned out for Thomas Lee." Marietta looked at him with skeptical eyes considering he testified on behalf of the prosecution. "Do any of you know if Mrs. Clarkston was pregnant around the time Baby boy Doe would've been born?" They again shifted their eyes one to the other uncertain if they should answer.

"Yeah her ass was pregnant." Carrie stated. "And Mr. Charles knew that baby wasn't his too!"

"Hush Carrie!" Marietta said uneasy by her revealing unsolicited information.

"You want this man to help Thomas Lee or not Marietta?" Carrie said raising her voice. Marietta shifted her eyes to Roosevelt but gave no reply. "Look like she had swallowed a damn bowling ball too!" Carrie said bursting into laughter. Roosevelt quietly grinned.

"After she became pregnant Mr. Charles wouldn't have nothing to do with her." Roosevelt said shaking his head. "Put her out of the marriage bed too . . . made her sleep in one of the guest rooms like she wasn't even his wife!"

"Things got even worse when Mr. Charles seen that baby was born Black!" Carrie said looking into Detective Stokey inquisitive eyes. "Mr. Charles wasn't no fool!"

"Did he know his wife's baby belonged to Thomas Lee?" Detective Stokey asked. Carrie again burst into laughter.

"Hell naw!" She said continuing to laugh. "Thomas Lee wasn't the only Black man riding that bus." A perplexed look formed on Detective Stokey's face.

"Huh?"

"It was another Black man Ms. Delores was laying up with." Carrie said shifting his eyes over to Roosevelt. Detective Stokey's mouth abruptly opened, he looked at Roosevelt with inquiry.

"You and uh, Mrs. Clarkston—"

"Naw—" Roosevelt said cunningly grinning. Ms. Delores once offered, but that ain't my thing detective . . . too young, too married, too drunk."

"You're saying somebody other than Thomas Lee was—"

"Yeah but Thomas Lee didn't know it though." Roosevelt stated.

"But I bet you a damn dollar Mr. Charles knew!" Carrie said amused.

"Carrie!" Marietta said trying to censor her coworker's busy mouth.

"What Marietta?" She looked over at her then turned back to Detective Stokey. "Ms. Delores thought Mr. Charles didn't know about her new lover, but the only person blind to that relationship was Ray Charles!" She burst into laughter. Detective Stokey tilted his head as his curiosity continued to peak.

"Ms. Delores didn't know it but— " Roosevelt said shifting his eyes to Marietta then again to Detective Stokey. "—but Mr. Charles knew every move that girl made, had a private investigators following her." Detective Stokey's eyes widened, surprise to learn about Charles' extreme measures.

"Is that so?"

"Hired Tony as his private investigator." Roosevelt stated.

"Uh, Tony?" Detective Stokey asked, curious. Carrie quickly interjected.

"Phony Tony is more like it!" She said. Detective Stokey slightly grinned.

"So uh, what was phony about Tony?"

"Everything!" Roosevelt said chuckling. "After he started working for Mr. Charles, watching Ms. Delores, Ol, Tony became a big shot." Roosevelt said humored. "Wearing expensive suits and driving a Cadillac, but what Mr. Charles didn't know was Tony wasn't no different than Thomas Lee." He shifted his eyes Marietta with apology. "I'm sorry Marietta."

"Go on Roosevelt—" She stated with disappointment. "—speak your piece." Detective Stokey subtly smiled, fascinated by Roosevelt's story.

"For all we know Ms. Delores' baby could've been Tony's." Roosevelt said again shifting his eyes to Marietta then back to Detective Stokey.

"You uh, mean—"

Carrie intervened.

"Yeah, her trifling ass started messing around with Tony's phony ass too!"

"Carrie!"

"What Marietta? You know she was!"

"Wow." Detective Stokey said astonished. "So why did you say they call him Phony Tony?"

"Tony and his whole family was phony!" Roosevelt said.

"That family's been selling Black folks fake insurance policies for years." Carrie said joining in the conversation. Detective Stokey's eyes widened.

"Fake insurance policies?"

"Yeah, but didn't nobody know they were fake until old Mrs. Williams died and her family tried to use the policy to pay for her funeral." Roosevelt said chuckling. A humored smile formed on Detective Stokey's face.

"So uh, what happened?"

"Old Mr. Williams took a shot gun to Mr. Jerry's ass!" Carrie said laughing.

"Mr. Jerry?" Detective Stokey asked.

"Yeah that's Tony's Ol' crooked ass daddy!" Carrie stated. "Mr. Williams told his ass if he didn't see to it that his wife got a proper funeral and burial he was gon shoot him dead!" Detective Stokey's eyes widened with shock.

"Uh, shoot him dead?"

"And Mr. Jerry knew Old Mr. Williams wasn't playing with his ass either!" Carrie stated. Detective Stokey's eyes again widened, stunned by what sounded like a crime.

"Would he uh, really have shot—"
Carrie burst into laughter.

"Hell yeah he would shot Mr. Jerry's crooked ass!" She said with certainty. "I bet if y'all check into some of these murders ain't ever been solved you'll find—"

"Carrie!" Marietta cut her off. Detective Stokey's curiosity heightened.

"You folks uh, know something about homicides that Mr. Williams' may have committed?" Roosevelt shifted his eyes to both Marietta and Carrie.

"No . . . can't say we do."

"Like Roosevelt said, we don't know nothing about no unsolved murders." Carrie said looking into Roosevelt's disciplining eyes realizing she'd said too much.

"You folks know it's a crime to withhold—"

"Are you done speaking to us detective?" Roosevelt asked. "We need to get back before Mr. Charles gets home from work."

"Did Thomas Lee ever know Mrs. Clarkston's child may not have been his?"

"What you trying to say detective?" Marietta asked becoming nervous. "That Thomas Lee learned Ms. Delores' baby wasn't his and murdered it?"

"I know the hell he ain't!" Carrie said looking at him, upset by the thought. "I thought you was trying to help Thomas Lee?" Detective Stokey massaged his neck.

"I uh, I am." He looked at Marietta. "If I didn't think Thomas Lee was innocent believe me I wouldn't be here."

"Sounds to me like you trying to give my son a reason for wanting that baby dead." Marietta said with mistrust. Detective Stokey shifted his eyes to Roosevelt then turned back to Marietta.

"You have to understand Marietta why I have to ask the hard questions—" He again looked at Roosevelt. "—because if Thomas Lee's fortunate enough to get an appeal the appellate court certainly will."

"We understand detective." Roosevelt said.

"I can tell you this much Detective Stokey—" Carrie said grinning. "—Ms. Delores loved her some Black men and plenty of them!" She burst into laughter. "Make sure you tell the judge that too!" Detective Stokey's face reddened.

"If that's the case then how do you know it was Phony Tony who fathered Mrs. Clarkston's son?"

"That little boy was a spitting image of Tony's Ol' Phony ass." Carrie said with assurance. Marietta intervened.

"Mr. Charles knew Tony could've fathered that child same as we did the minute he laid eyes on him."

"Clarkston saw the child?"

"Yeah he saw him." Marietta stated with bitterness.

"Came in the room right after hearing him crying." Roosevelt said. "Wouldn't lay a foot in that room all while Ms. Delores was crying out in labor, sat downstairs eating his supper—" Carrie intervened.

"And reading that damn newspaper—"

"Just like he didn't hear her." Roosevelt stated.

"Marietta?" Detective Stokey said preparing to ask her of Thomas Lee's fertility status. "Was uh, Thomas Lee able to father children?" Marietta lowered her head then again looked at him.

"I know it was wrong, but I ain't ever told Thomas Lee the doctor said he would never father a child due to his testicles not moving in place before he reached puberty." Roosevelt and Carrie's eyes met, stunned by Marietta's first time admission. "Let him believe Dorothy Jean was the one had the problem." Detective Stokey swallowed the lump forming in his throat, wondering if Thomas Lee could have found out, giving him a motive for murdering the son he thought was his.

"You all have been very helpful." He said getting up from the table.

"Detective Stokey?" Marietta said frightened. "Is my boy gon be alright in that prison? I heard he got beat real bad in there." Detective Stokey massaged his neck.

"I wish I could say yes Marietta, but I can't." Her eyes watered. "What I can say is that I'm going to do everything in my power to keep your son alive."

"Thank you."

"If it's anything else we can do to help Thomas Lee just let us know." Roosevelt said extending his hand.

"I'll remember that and thank you Roosevelt." The two men shook.

#

"He did it Mildred!" Detective Stokey said with certainty, joining Mildred on her front porch as she rocked in her old rocking chair. She looked over at him with inquisitive eyes and waited to hear his theory. "Clarkston . . . he murdered that baby as sure as we're breathing air."

"Well if you thinking about arresting him Andy you better make sure you can prove what you saying." Mildred said troubled by his foregone conclusion.

"It was Clarkston and I can prove it!" He stated, convinced.

"Can you Andy?"

"Baby boy Doe was his wife's son fathered by another man, but not just any man Mildred . . . a Black man—" Detective Stokey suddenly silenced. He looked at Mildred with apologetic eyes. "Mildred I uh, didn't mean to—"

"Ain't no point in you apologizing for stating facts Andy." He nervously massaged his neck. "Don't bother me none you calling a Black man—Black."

"I uh, really shouldn't have—" She again interrupted.

"That prison gate ain't gon swing one way or another to free Thomas Lee by you apologizing to me." Detective Stokey remained loss for words. "I've lived eighty three years and I done heard Black folks called a whole lot, worse things than that." Detective Stokey gave no reply. "So you convinced Charles Clarkston murdered that baby?"

"Yes Mildred I am."

"Now what?"

"Now, I go over there and arrest his ass, see how he likes being locked up for life!"

"You really think you gon be able to do that?" Mildred asked calmly.

"Dammit Mildred!" He yelled. "I thought we were on the same side."

"If you think you gon lock Charles Clarkston up, you gon need more than your bad temper to do it."

"Bad temper? What do mean bad temper?" He yelled. "I don't have a bad temper!" Mildred looked at him with confirming eyes. "Do I?"

"I was under the impression you was trying to prove Thomas Lee was innocent."

"I thought that's what I was doing Mildred!"

"What you doing Andy is going on what you believe and not what you can prove."

"Alright . . . then what do you suggest I do Mildred?" He asked curious of the mysterious look on her face. "Do you know something you're not telling me?"

"I know a whole lot that you don't know Andy." He looked at Mildred with doubt, convinced she was wrong about Charles. She cleverly smiled.

"I got some fried green tomatoes, wild rice, fried pork chops and lemon meringue pie in the kitchen!"

"At the risk of sounding disrespectful Mildred—" Detective Stokey said losing his temper. "—I don't want any of your damn fried green tomatoes or any of that other junk you call food!"

"Why don't you go on in the house and fix us both a plate?" She said ignoring his angry outburst. Detective Stokey shook his head with remorse then took a deep breath, repentant for his deliberate disrespect.

"I'm uh, I'm sorry Mildred . . . I uh, haven't had much sleep or an appetite lately—"

"That all the more reason you need to put something in your stomach." She giggled.

"If it's okay with you Mildred I think I'll uh, take a rain check?" Detective Stokey said standing, walking over to the stairs preparing to leave.

"I'll let you get away with it this time Andy, but after you solve this case I expect you to come over here so we can have us a celebration dinner!" A huge smile formed on Mildred's face.

"As tempting as that sounds Mildred—" He massaged his neck. "—me solving this thing is not going to happen." Mildred again giggled.

"I hope you ain't giving up Andy when you so close to solving it." Mildred said noting the look of defeat in his eyes. "Thomas Lee's counting on you, but if you give up who he gon have left." Detective Stokey hesitated then again sat down.

"Coming from you Mildred, that's encouraging." She smiled. "So tell me . . . where do I go from here?"

"You may not have an appetite Andy, but ain't nothing wrong with mines." Mildred said laughing.

"Would you like me to fix you a plate Mildred?"

· · · ·

"You sure you don't want a piece of this pie Andy? Mildred asked as she placed a spoonful in her mouth. "I put my foot in it too!" She giggled. An odd look appeared on Detective Stokey's face.

"Your uh, foot Mildred?" He said watching as she ate a second slice of lemon meringue pie after consuming a second helping of the fattening meal she'd prepared.

"That's just what us folks around here say when we've cooked something that taste better than it's ever tasted before!" She giggled.

"I uh, didn't really think you had actually put your foot in—" Detective Stokey said slightly embarrassed.

"If we gon talk Andy we better do it now 'cause you got about thirty minutes before these old eyes of mines gon need resting." Mildred said putting more pie in her mouth. "That's just something I do that after eating a big meal." Detective Stokey removed a pad and pen from his shirt pocket.

"Okay, so where were we Mildred?" He asked trying to mask his disappointment in her dismissing Charles Clarkston as a suspect. "Oh that's right . . . you were saying you didn't believe Clarkston murdered his wife's baby, but you didn't say why."

"You don't know the Clarkston's do you Andy?"

"Do you Mildred?" He asked, curious.

"I know Charles Clarkston well enough to know he had many ways to cover up the shame Delores brought on him with that baby, so wouldn't be no reason for him to kill it."

"Okay, let's say you're right Mildred then who else had reason to murder that infant?"

"That's what you about to find out Andy."

"Clarkston could've easily murdered his wife's love child then framed Thomas Lee—" He said rationalizing. "—it would be like killing two birds with one stone."

"Charles Clarkston knew how bad his wife wanted a child, he also knew that any child she brought in this world no matter who the daddy was, would kill her inside if he took that child away—" Detective Stokey interjected.

"Will you stop with the riddles Mildred?" He yelled then abruptly stood. "How can I understand what you're trying to say if you're speaking in gibberish!" Mildred chuckled.

"Charles loves Delores and he would never lay hands on a child she brought in this world knowing he'd lose her."

"You can't know that for sure Mildred." He said challenging her unproven theory. "If he arranged to have Thomas Lee put in prison for murder, how, do you know he's not capable of—" She cut him off.

"Did you ask about the midwife that helped bring Delores' child in this world?"

Dammit!" Detective Stokey shouted. "It never crossed my mind to do so." He looked at Mildred with objection. "And how is that important and where would I even begin to find this midwife, I doubt very seriously Mrs. Clarkston's going to give me her name."

"She'd be the only one beside his staff can give you answer about what happened to Delores' baby besides Delores."

"Okay so where I can find this mysterious woman Mildred?"

"You go right back to the same eyes and ears that told you all know now." A smile stretched across Detective Stokey's face.

"Of course, why didn't I think of—" He silenced then looked at Mildred with inquisitiveness. "How did you know I talked to—" She cleverly smiled.

"Marietta's my niece Andy, my oldest brother Marvin's granddaughter." His eyes widened, amazed by the connection. "Who was it you think told her to speak with you in the first place?"

"Then that means you're related to Thomas Lee also."

"I guess it do." Mildred giggled.

"So once I find this midwife how do I get her to talk?" He hesitated. "You uh, know Black people aren't exactly forthcoming with law enforcement." He looked Mildred in the eyes. "What I'm uh, trying to say Mildred is certain people aren't eager to talk to uh—"

"I wouldn't worry much about that Andy . . . if that midwife think in any way that baby's blood gon find its way to her hands she gon talk." Detective Stokey smiled, regaining his confidence.

"You know what Mildred?"

"What's that Andy?"

"I think I'll have a plate of that delicious meal you prepared after all."

"I thought you said you didn't have an appetite?"

"It just came back." They laughed.

Chapter Eleven

"I see you back huh, detective?" The bartender said when seeing Detective Stokey enter through the front door of the Night Owl Nightclub.

"How are you?" Detective Stokey said as his ears absorbed the sound of the blues blasting throughout the patron filled establishment. He headed, unescorted in the direction of the backroom there to with Marietta. Detective Stokey stood momentarily outside the closed door then took a deep breath and opened the door seeing Marietta sitting at the table alone, awaiting his arrival.

"How are you Marietta?" Detective Stokey asked being seated at the table.

"I don't know why Aunt Mildred told you to come questioning me again." She said agitated and nervous. "I already told you everything I know."

"And I thank you for doing that Marietta but—"

"But what?" She said raising her voice, frightened as she glanced over at the closed door.

"It seems I forgot to ask you—"

"Ask me what . . . we answered every question you asked, so I don't know what more I can tell you."

"And believe me Marietta I'm grateful for that but—"

"But what?" She yelled. "I ain't got nothing else to say that ain't already been said."

"I need the name of the midwife who delivered Mrs. Clarkston's baby and how to go about finding her." A look of terror displayed on Marietta face. She stood.

"I can't do that!" She yelled.

"Marietta please!"

"Please my foot!" She said again shifting her eyes over at the door. "I've raised two children on money I made from working for the Clarkston's and—" Detective Stokey interjected.

"Marietta, don't you want to see Thomas Lee proven innocent for the murder of that baby?" He asked appealing to her as a mother.

"Of course I do, but right now I got four grandbabies I'm raising while my daughter's somewhere up in Ohio with some no good man who ain't had no interest in being daddy to her kids!"

"I understand that Marietta but—"

"Do you Detective Stokey?" She shouted looking at him with nervous eyes.

"Please Marietta . . . all I'm trying to do is prove Thomas Lee's innocent of murder before—" He silenced and began massaging his neck. Her eyes watered with tears.

"Before what detective?"

"Before somebody in that prison declares himself a hero by killing a convicted baby killer." He looked at her with compassionate eyes.

"Don't let them kill my boy detective!" Marietta cried out.

"I'm trying everything in my power Marietta to keep that from happening that's why I need your help!"

"And how you gon keep my boy safe?" She said weeping. "You gon trade places with him?" She asked upset. Detective Stokey's stomach filled with butterflies.

"All I'm asking Marietta is for you to give me a chance to find the real killer."

"And if you do get Thomas Lee out, proving he didn't murder that baby—" She looked him in the eyes. "—who gon keep you safe?"

"I appreciate your concern Marietta, but that's a chance I'm willing to take."

"Why? Thomas Lee don't mean nothing to you." Detective Stokey looked into her frightened eyes, feeling helpless. A slight smile suddenly formed on his face when he remembered Mildred's words of encouragement.

"Despite what you might think Marietta, I can't let an innocent man die in prison for something he didn't do." He looked at her with sincere compassion. "Could you?" She hesitated then again sat down.

"I don't want my son in prison for something he didn't do no more than you do Detective Stokey, but Thomas Lee made his bed hard the day he chose to lay down with Mrs. Delores." Marietta stated in anger. "Lowdown just like his daddy—" She abruptly stopped." Detective Stokey's mouth slightly opened in response to her harsh words regarding Thomas Lee's father. "The woman you looking for is Anna Louise Foster you can find her at New Bethel Missionary Baptist Church."

"Thank you Marietta." Detective Stokey said displaying a sigh of relief. "How will I know who she is?"

"Just look for a woman with the floppy yellow hat." A peculiar look showed on his face.

"Floppy yellow hat?"

"Calls it her good luck piece." Marietta half heartedly laughed. "Anna Louise been wearing that yellow hat since the time she delivered a baby where the momma had so many complications nobody believed her or that baby would survive."

"Is uh, Anna Louise a nurse?" Detective Stokey asked not sure he wanted to know the answer.

"A woman, don't have to be a nurse to bring a baby in this world detective."

"I think uh—" Marietta cut him off.

"Anna Louise brought that baby in the world and kept it and the momma from dying."

"Is that so?"

"The next day she went to the department store and bought that yellow hat and been wearing it ever since." She chuckled then stood, walking over to the door. "After you get Thomas Lee out and I believe you will . . . do me a favor?"

"Anything Marietta."

"Tell Thomas Lee to look me up in Ohio, Cincinnati." A perplexed look formed on Detective Stokey's face.

"Ohio?"

"You can also tell him I said thank the Lord for giving him a second chance and take Dorothy Jean and get as far away from here as he can." She looked Detective Stokey in the eyes. "Mr. Charles is a vengeful man."

#

Charles looked briefly in the kitchen as he entered the dining room seeing Marietta and Carrie as they prepared his breakfast. He picked up the morning newspaper as he sat down at the table, opening it up, his attention being drawn to an article on Detective Stokey vowing to prove Thomas Lee's innocence.

"What the hell does he think he's doing?" Charles said raising his voice. "Marietta!" She shifted her eyes to Carrie standing over at the oven placing a pan of beignets inside. "Were you aware of this Detective Stokey's insistence on continuing his crusade in proving your son's innocence?" Carrie watched as Marietta nervously exited the kitchen and entered the dining room.

"Did you need something Mr. Charles?" Marietta asked.

"Yes, this Detective Stokey—" He stated from behind the newspaper. "—has he said anything to you about what he's trying to do?" Marietta's stomach bundled with nerves.

"Yeah he did." She shifted her eyes in the kitchen at Carrie who listened afraid Charles would discover their cooperation with Detective Stokey. "I figured he just trying to help Thomas Lee get out of there since he was the one who helped put him in." She said as her mouth dried.

"Do you believe Thomas Lee is innocence?"

"That's my son Mr. Charles you know I do." Marietta said insulted by his question. "You know I didn't raise Thomas Lee to be no killer!" Charles lowered the newspaper in response to her aggressive tone. "Only thing Thomas Lee's guilty of is lying down with your wife, but he ain't murdered that baby!"

"Would you bring me my breakfast now please?" He said choosing to ignore her anger as he again concealed his face behind the newspaper.

"You know yourself Ms. Delores chased after Thomas Lee, wouldn't let him alone until she got him in her bed."

"I believe I asked you to bring me my breakfast Marietta and I won't ask you again." She momentarily stared at him, his face still hidden behind the paper. Carrie watched with sympathetic eyes as Marietta returned to the kitchen.

"You alright Marietta?" She whispered, removing the pan of beignets from the oven.

"Put a couple of them on this plate." Marietta said scooping Cajun grits onto Charles' plate next to the Cajun butter steak and vegetable omelet. "Carrie looked in her co-worker's hurt eyes as she placed two beignets on the plate. "I ain't gon be here much longer." Marietta said. Carrie's mouth abruptly opened.

"What you mean you ain't gon be here much longer?" She asked, shocked. "Girl you just upset right now . . . and where you gon go anyway?"

"I been thinking about taking my grandbabies and moving up to Ohio—"

"Ohio!" Carrie's eyes widened. "Marietta you ain't got no family up there do you?"

"My daughter's up there somewhere, but Anita that use to work here—" Carrie interrupted.

"Ol' lazy ass Anita?" Marietta looked at her with chastising eyes and shook her head.

"Anyway . . . she said I could stay there with her until I can find a job and get a place for me and my grandbabies to live."

"Where's all this coming from Marietta?" Carrie asked troubled by her out of the blue decision. "You been living in the south all your life, how in the hell you talking about moving up north?"

"Marietta!" Charles called out. "I'm waiting."

"I been thinking about it for a while and I figure now might be the right time for me to do it."

"Why?" Carrie said upset. "Because Mr. Charles getting on your damn nerves?"

"Mr. Charles, been getting on my nerves since he was a boy." Marietta stated.

"Then why you talking about leaving here now?"

"I don't want my grandbabies growing up like me and my children, I want them to know it's someplace in this world with more freedom."

"Freedom?" Carrie said trying to keep her voice low. "Marietta freedom is in the mind and the heart and if you expecting to find it in a city or state you ain't ever gon find it!" Marietta looked momentarily at her then walked away and again entered the dining room placing the plate of food in front of Charles.

"Thank you Marietta."

"You welcome Mr. Charles."

"Don't forget my coffee."

"Do I ever?" She said walking away. Carrie approached her as she again entered the kitchen.

"You leave here Marietta and Mr. Charles' ass ain't gon know what to do with Ms. Delores." She said quietly laughing.

"Well maybe it's time he learned." Marietta said angry. "Ms. Delores is his wife and his responsibility, not mines, yours or Roosevelt's."

"And what about Roosevelt?"

"What about him, he was here long before I got here—"

"Marietta—" Carrie said looking at her with tell-tale eyes. "—girl don't act like you don't know that man is in love with you, and he been in love with you since his wife passed away years ago!" Marietta ignored Carrie's truthful words.

"Well I ain't got time for Roosevelt or no other man." She said pouring coffee in the gold trim cup. "Besides, I got grandbabies to raise."

"Well your grandbabies gon grow up one day and move on, leave your lonely ass all by yourself then what?"

"Does it really take that long to pour one cup of coffee Marietta?" Charles stated in chastising tone. Carrie looked at Marietta and shook her head annoyed by Charles' nagging.

"I wonder what Ms. Delores done this time that's got his ass in such a bad mood?" Carrie asked, rhetorically.

"I'm coming Mr. Charles." Marietta said nervously spilling coffee on the kitchen counter. "Clean that up for me would you Carrie?"

"You think Ol' lazy ass Anita got room for me, Buster and the kids?" Carrie said teasing. They quietly laughed as Marietta walked away headed for the dining room, with the cup of coffee.

#

"Hey Stokey!" Detective Fish called out from behind his computer monitor when seeing him enter the squad room. "Solved that big case yet?" He said chuckling. "Oh that's right . . . it's already been solved and the defendant's been sent up the river for life!" He burst into laughter.

"Very funny, Fish." Detective Stokey said sitting down at his desk. "You just make sure you have that bottle of champagne and T-bone steak ready when Thomas Lee walks out of prison a free man."

"Yeah, and you make sure you do the same when he doesn't."

"And keep your negative opinion to yourself Detective Fish."

"And you stop trying to set a baby killer free Detective Stokey."

"Let's just see how that T-bone steak tastes after you've had to add a little crow to it."

"Well it won't be me being served crow Stokey—"

"Whoa!" Detective Abernathy said as he stepped off the elevator hearing the two men bickering. "What the hell's going on in here? I could hear y'all clean downstairs on the first floor."

"Yeah well, tell that to your partner who still thinks he gonna free that baby killer!"

"I don't think Detective Fish, I know!"

"Yeah, yeah so you say."

"Well right now you both have a fifty-fifty chance of being right." Detective Abernathy said bringing the dispute to an end. "So why don't you save the insults until you see what actually happens?"

"I owe you lunch Abernathy." Detective Stokey said looking at him before turning his attention back to his notes, trying to figure out how the pieces of the puzzle fit together.

"Have you learned anything you didn't already know Stokey?" Detective Abernathy asked as he approached him.

"You wouldn't believe it if I told you."

"Try me." Detective Stokey glanced around the squad room then to Detective Fish and again to his partner.

"You have to promise me Abernathy whatever I tell you remain between me and you okay?" Detective Abernathy noted the intensity in his partner's eyes.

"Wait a minute man, this sounds serious."

"Baby boy Doe—"

"What about him?"

"I found the midwife that delivered him." He whispered. Detective Abernathy's jaw dropped.

"What?" He stated out loud drawing the attention of Detective Fish and others officers in the room.

"How about we discuss this over lunch?" Detective Stokey said observing the inquisitive eyes of their coworkers.

"Where you want to go man?"

"The Night Owl Nightclub." Detective Abernathy's jaw again dropped.

"Man did you just say the Night Owl?"

"That's right."

"Stokey man what the hell you know about the Night Owl?" He said shocked by his partner's knowledge of the Black owned establishment.

"We can discuss that over lunch too, but first we need to go by Mildred's to see if she has anymore pieces—"

"Whoa . . . hell naw!" Detective Abernathy said. "You gon have to do that without me man, I ain't about to set foot on that old woman's property!"

"Then I guess I'll meet you at the Night Owl—"

"You serious man?" Detective Abernathy asked making sure his partner wasn't joking. "The Night Owl?"

"You got a problem with that Abernathy?"

"Naw I'm cool . . . if that's where you want to go then I guess I'll meet you there say at around—" Detective Abernathy glanced at his watch. "—eleven thirty?"

"Eleven thirty's fine with me." A curious look showed on Detective Abernathy's face.

"How long you been hanging out at the Night Owl Stokey?"

"Oh, not that long." He stated with vagueness.

"You ever had the jerk chicken there man?"

"No, I can't say that I have."

"Then you got to try it man!" Detective Abernathy stated with enthusiasm. "They got the best jerk chicken I ever had!"

"Is that so."

"I'm serious man you got to try it!"

"I'll be sure to tell Mildred you said hello." Detective Stokey said getting up from his desk.

"Yeah Stokey you do that." He said looking at his partner with curious eyes as he climbed on the elevator. "Now what the hell Stokey doing hanging out at the Night Owl?"

#

"Wait until I tell Mildred I have the name of the midwife who deliver Mrs. Clarkston's baby." Detective Stokey said thinking out loud as he turned down the dirt road leading to her house, excited about his discovery. "But I'm sure she already knows?" He looked at his watch and chuckled. "Damn, I bet that old woman's getting ready to eat breakfast!" He scowled when thinking of what she might have prepared. "Maybe I should come back after I've eaten lunch that way when she offers me some pig ears—" He chuckled. "—I can tell her I've already eaten." He continued in self talk as he pulled in Mildred's driveway and parked. "That woman eats more pig than Abernathy eats donuts." He said laughing then looked up on the porch, surprised when not seeing Mildred sitting in her old rocking chair.

Detective Stokey got out of his car and walked towards the house. "Mildred!" He called out as he stepped on the porch and knocked on the door. "Mildred, I'm back for more pieces to the puzzle. He said excited. "Mildred!" His concern grew when not smelling the aroma of pork flowing from the kitchen and Mildred not yet appearing. "Now where is that old woman?" Detective Stokey said talking to himself. "I hope nothing's wrong." He attempted to look through the back door window skewed by a yellow curtain. "Mildred you in there?" He walked over to the window to the right and looked inside. "Oh my God! Mildred!" Detective Stokey yelled out when seeing her lying on the floor unconscious. "Mildred!" He pounded on the window then rushed over to the door and turned the knob, it opened. He hurried inside, ultimately finding his way through the maze that led to Mildred's bedroom. "Mildred!" He said kneeling at her side and shaking both shoulders, watching as she took shallow breaths. "Mildred!" Detective Stokey rushed from the room in search of a phone, finding an old black desk phone sitting on a small wooden table in Mildred's outdated sitting room. He snatched the receiver off its base and called for an ambulance.

"I need an ambulance out here at—" He suddenly realized he didn't know Mildred's address. "This is Detective Stokey and I just found Mildred Koffee in her home lying unconscious on the floor, please can you get an ambulance out here?" He nervously hung up then hurried back to Mildred's side watching as she seemingly clung onto life.

#

Carrie stood at the sink draining water from the pot of macaroni she'd just removed from the burner. "Ms. Delores keep drinking the way she do, I'm telling you Marietta something bad gon happen to her, she already look like she ain't but a hundred pounds and that's with her carrying a forty pound bag of quarters in her pocket!" Carrie said bursting into laughter. "Make that a ninety-five pound bag." Her laughter ended when seeing Marietta standing at the counter deep in thoughts as she dumped three pounds of ground beef and a pound of pork sausage in a large bowl. "You alright Marietta?"

"I ever tell you about my husband, Thomas?" Marietta stated.

"Thomas?" A peculiar look appeared on Carrie's face. "Girl I didn't know Thomas Lee was a junior." Marietta looked briefly over at her and humorously smiled.

"He ain't."

"Didn't you just say your husband's name was Thomas?"

"Leroy—Thomas Leroy Simms, but everybody called him Leroy." Marietta half-heartedly chuckled as she mixed in onions, green peppers and celery in a separate bowl. "And he was a good looking too!" Marietta said smiling. "He was also a heavy drinker and a skirt chaser."

"I guess Thomas Lee followed right in his lowdown daddy's footsteps." Carrie said insensitive to Marietta's feelings regarding her son.

"It wasn't until Leroy left me for the girl living up the road that I learned folks like him and Ms. Delores drink for a reason, usually got something bottled deep inside that's bothering them."

"Well I know what's bottled up inside Ms. Delores." Carrie said sitting at the kitchen table cubing cheese for her macaroni. "Thomas Lee murdering her—" She abruptly stopped then looked over into Marietta's stunned eyes glaring at her.

"Is that what you think Carrie?" Marietta asked offended. "That Thomas Lee murdered Ms. Delores' baby?" Carrie looked at her with remorseful eyes.

"You know what I'm trying to say Marietta, he was convicted of it and—" Marietta cut her off.

"You getting ready to use that oven anytime soon?" She asked, angry over Carrie's belief that Thomas Lee actually could have murdered Baby boy Doe. "I got a few more things to add to my meatloaf then it'll be ready to go in the oven."

"I was getting ready to put my macaroni and cheese in there once I add the cheese to my white sauce."

"That's fine." Marietta stated dryly.

"Well I did preheat the oven for my macaroni and cheese in the first damn place." Carrie said carrying the bowl of cheese over to the stove to add to the simmering white sauce. "I can turn the other oven on for you if you want me to?" Marietta momentarily looked at her.

"I can do that myself."

"Suit yourself." Carrie said noticing Marietta grimacing with pain as she worked her fingers through the meatloaf mixture.

"You alright Marietta?"

"It's my arthritis . . . it's been bothering me all morning." She said looking at her fingers.

"You need me to finish mixing that meatloaf for you?"

"I'll be alright I just need to soak my hands in some warm water." Their attention suddenly drew to Roosevelt rushing in through the back door, a frightened look on his face.

"What's going on Roosevelt?" Carrie asked. He shifted his eyes to Carrie then turned to Marietta.

"Nooooooo!" She cried out as her knees buckled. "They killed my boy!" Roosevelt rushed over to her.

"Thomas Lee's fine Marietta!" He said assisting her into a chair. He glanced over at Carrie and again turned to Marietta seeing the horrified look in her eyes. "It's Ms. Mildred . . . that detective found her in her house on the floor unconscious." Carrie's mouth abruptly opened.

"Is she dead Roosevelt?" She asked expecting the worse.

"They thinking she might've had a stroke."

"Is she gon make it Roosevelt?" Carrie asked.
A look of uncertainty showed on his face.

"Right now it's hard to say what's gon happen." Marietta hung her head and wept. "That's something only God knows." Roosevelt stated.

"If Aunt Mildred dies—" Marietta looked Roosevelt in the eyes with despair. "—my boy gon die in that prison."

"Don't talk like that Marietta—" Roosevelt said rubbing her back. He shifted his worried eyes over to Carrie.

"You know as well as I do Roosevelt that detective ain't gon be able to prove Thomas Lee didn't murder that baby without Aunt Mildred's help." Roosevelt again shifted his eyes to Carrie.

"Didn't you say he was making some kind of progress Marietta?" Carrie asked.

"Yeah, but he gon need Aunt Mildred to figure everything out." "You sure she even gon be able to figure it out?"

Marietta looked over at Carrie upset by her unsolicited opinion.

"Sometimes Carrie you just need to keep your mouth shut!" Roosevelt said scolding her as Marietta continued weeping.

Chapter Twelve

Detective Stokey parked outside of New Bethel Missionary Baptist Church waiting for Wednesday night Bible Study to dismiss, hoping to catch Anna Louise as she departed from the church. His eyes lit up when seeing the door open and members of the congregation exiting. He visually searched through the multitude of people as they walked in various directions, some going to their cars, others gathering in small groups chatting amongst themselves. His eyes widened when seeing the floppy yellow hat highlighted on the head of a middle aged woman emerging from the church. He watched as Anna Louise stopped on the sidewalk and began talking to a middle aged female who also exited the church. He got out of his car and began walking towards her.

"Hello ladies." Detective Stokey said as he approached. They shifted their eyes over at him, suspicious of his intent.

"Are you lost sir?" A woman standing in the doorway of the church yelled out.

"No I uh, I don't think so." He said thinking of how to approach Anna Louise without scaring her off.

"I kind of uh, got myself in a little trouble and uh—" Anna Louise cut him off.

"Trouble?" An odd look displayed on her face. "What kind of trouble you talking about mister?" She asked.

"We got enough troubles of our own." The woman standing with Anna Louise stated looking at him with mistrust. "The last thing we need is to be getting involved in some White man's troubles."

"Hold on a minute, Sister Joanne—" Anna Louise said curious of his visit. "—let him speak.

"Thank you uh, Ms.—" Detective Stokey said.

"I'm Anna Louise."

Sister Joanne intervened.

"Just what kind of troubles you talking about mister?"

"Stokey."

"You got a first name Mr. Stokey?" Anna Louise asked looking at him with suspicion.

"It's uh, Andy—" Sister Joanne intervened.

"Andy Stokey?" She looked at him with recognition. "Ain't you that detective been hanging around at Ms. Mildred trying to get Marietta's boy Thomas Lee off for killing that baby?" He massaged his neck.

"As a matter of fact I am Ms. uh—"

"You don't need to know my name." Sister Joanne said turning up her nose.

"What make you think Thomas Lee ain't kill that baby like that jury said he done?" Sister Joanne asked.

"If that's why you here, I'm telling you now we don't know nothing about nothing!" The woman standing in the doorway yelled.

"Actually that's not why I'm here at all." Detective Stokey said turning his attention to Anna Louise. "Believe me this has nothing to do with Thomas Lee Simms."

"Then why you here?" Sister Joanne asked, unconvinced.

"It's more of a personal matter."

"Personal?" The woman standing in the door said. "What you bringing your personal business around here for?"

"Yeah, what make you think we care about your personal business?" Anna Louise asked, suspicious.

"We don't know you!" The woman standing in the door shouted.

"You go ahead on Sister Joanne." Anna Louise said certain she knew what Detective Stokey's troubles consisted of. Sister Joanne's eyes widened.

"What?" She said shocked by Anna Louise's request. "You sure that's what you want Sister Anna?" She looked at Detective Stokey with suspect.

"The man said he had a personal problem Sister Joanne—" Anna Louise said with a cunning smile on her face. "—what I'm wondering now is how much he willing to pay for his problem go away."

"You be sure to call me Sister Anna when you done speaking with that policeman, let me know you alright." She glared at Detective Stokey. "I hope it ain't what I think it is—" Sister Joanne said looking him over. "—'cause he looks too damn old for that!"

"How you gon say that Sister Joanne?" Anna Louise said grinning. "You know a man don't ever get too old for that."

"I disagree 'cause this man here is too old, too fat and too tired for anything that's gon get him in trouble." Detective Stokey's mouth slightly opened as Sister Joanne continued scrutinizing him.

"Thank you uh, Sister Joanne for your candid words." He stated with sarcasm.

"No problem." She said rolling her eyes. "You be sure and call me Sister Anna let me know what he wanted." She gave Anna Louise a farewell hug. "You be careful with that one there he got them beady blue eyes." The woman standing in the doorway watched as Sister Joanne walked away then slowly closed the door.

"Speak your peace detective." Anna Louise stated.

"Why don't you let me give you a ride home, Anna Louise?" She looked at him with caution.

"I ain't too comfortable riding in the car with a man ain't married."

"I promise you Anna Louise I won't bite." Detective Stokey said teasing.

"And I promise you if you do I'll bite you the hell back!" His eyes widened. "You also might want to change your mind when you find out where I live." She said following him over to his car.

"Oh, don't worry about it." He stated without reservation.

"I'm one of Mildred Koffee's neighbors."

Detective Stokey's jaw quickly dropped.

"One of uh, Mildred's—neighbors?"

"That's right, and if you got a problem with driving me out that far it's too late, Sister Joanne was my ride home." He massaged his neck.

"I guess that should uh, certainly give us plenty enough time to talk." He said thinking out loud as he opened the passenger side door. Anna Louise got in. "Me and my big mouth." Detective Stokey said underneath his breath as he walked around to the other side and got in then started the engine.

"So what kind of problem you got detective?" He gazed through the windshield trying to think of how to ask Anna Louise about Delores Clarkston without her clamming up.

"You might not believe this but I'm sort of a lady's man—" Anna Louise looked quickly over at him.

"Hah!" She laughed out loud. "And the sun is green." She said humored. "You about much of a lady's man as I am the Queen of England, don't try to play me detective just tell me what it is you want!"

"Well I can see that I can't fool you—"

"So don't even try."

"I uh, kind of got myself in trouble with a young lady and I was telling Mildred—" She shifted her eyes over at him. "—and she told me you're a midwife?"

"Yeah that's right . . . when she due?"

"Soon."

"How soon is soon?"

"I take it you're use to doing these spur of the moment deliveries?" Detective Stokey said leading up to his intended conversation. Anna Louise's suspicion heightened.

"Often enough why you asking?"

"I think you should know Anna Louise you came highly recommended by Mildred." A glowing smile displayed on her face. "As a matter of fact I heard you were the one who delivered Mrs. Clarkston's baby." Anna Louise's boastful smile dropped.

"Mildred told you that too?" She asked becoming uneasy.

"Were you the midwife that delivered Mrs. Clarkston's son?"

"Well ain't this some mess!" She said realizing she'd been setup. "That's why you really here ain't it? Your old ass ain't got nobody pregnant!" She said looking at him, upset. "Just wait 'til I get back home, I'm gon call Mildred's old ass and give her a piece of my mind telling you I delivered Delores' baby."

"Did you?" Detective Stokey asked looking briefly over at her then back onto the dark road. "Baby boy Doe?" Her eyes widened, frightened by his subtle interrogation.

"I ain't had nothing to do with that baby ending up in the river if that's what you thinking!"

"I never said you did."

"Then why you asking me if I was the one who brought him in this world?"

"Because Anna Louise you were one of the few people to see that baby alive before Thomas Lee Simms found him floating in the river." Her jaw dropped.

"Now you hold on just one damn minute detective!" She said frightened. "After I brought that boy in this world even the colorblind could see he was Black!" She said becoming uneasy. "His skin may have been white, but he had Black folk features." Anna Louise said staring through the windshield as she spoke. "He was a beautiful baby too!" A smile formed on her face. "Head full of curly black hair, full lips and eyes that looked like black pearls." She said. "But as much as Ms. Delores wanted to keep that baby she knew Mr. Charles wasn't gon let that happen." Anna Louise's empathetic eyes filled with tears. "Wouldn't come near that room all while Ms. Delores was laboring in pain." Tears rolled down Anna Louise's cheeks. "It wasn't 'til after that beautiful baby boy entered this world that dirty dog came to see if he was Black or White." Detective Stokey held his tongue as he listened. "When seeing him Black, he walked out the room as if that child had never been born—sent word by Roosevelt for me to get him out of his house." Anna Louise looked in Detective Stokey's heartfelt eyes. "But Ms. Delores fought like a mother bear hanging on to her cub, and try as I might I couldn't take him from her hold." She stated, again staring through the windshield. "My heart just wouldn't let me do it." Anna Louise said turning to Detective Stokey. "God as my witness, when I left that house detective that baby boy was in his momma's arms as he was alive!" She stated with sincerity. "Next time I heard anything about him—" Anna Louise began sobbing. "—they was saying Thomas Lee had done fished him out of the river."

"Are you uh, going to be alright Anna Louise?" Detective Stokey asked when seeing tears flowing from her eyes. She shook her head, no.

"I sometimes lay awake at night thinking about the day I brought that beautiful baby in this world . . . only thing help keep my eyes shut now is that bottle of whiskey I keep next to my bed." Detective Stokey reached over and gently rubbed her on the back as she continued weeping.

"I promise you Anna Louise I'm going to find whoever murdered that baby."

"Who would throw an innocent baby in the river like his life had no meaning?" She asked through her tears.

"I was uh, hoping you could tell me Anna Louise." Detective Stokey said hopeful she had the answer. "You have any idea who would've wanted that baby dead?"

"I don't know, but what I do know is it wasn't Thomas Lee." Detective Stokey wondered why she hadn't testified.

"Did the prosecutor ever speak to you about it testifying?"

"Mr. Charles is a powerful man Detective Stokey." Anna Louise said looking at him with timid eyes. "I'm a poor Black woman and I ain't no match for Charles Clarkston the third."

"Thank you for speaking with me Anna Louise." Hurt displayed on her face as she continued weeping.

Chapter Thirteen

Thomas Lee sat up in bed when seeing Detective Stokey enter the infirmary noting the satisfactory look on his face.

"Man you look like Christmas came early for you this year." Thomas Lee teased.

"Not for me Thomas Lee . . . for you." Thomas Lee's eyes widened with anticipation of Detective Stokey's news.

"You serious man?"

"I just spoke to the midwife that delivered Mrs. Clarkston's son—"

"Anna Louise?" Detective Stokey's mouth abruptly opened.

"You uh, you knew who she was?"

"Yeah man, I was there remember!" He said grinning. "Besides, everybody know if you need a baby delivered Anna Louise is the one to call, she been delivering baby around here for years."

"What?" Thomas Lee said seeing the judgmental look in Detective Stokey's eyes. "I guess you wondering why a man of Charles Clarkston's means need to have his wife's child delivered by—" He stopped. "Thomas Lee I uh, didn't say—"

"An old country Black woman?" Thomas Lee said completing the detective's thoughts.

"Think about it detective . . . Charles knew Delores' baby was gon be Black and he damn sure wasn't gon have no White doctor deliver it!" He said rationalizing. "So what did Anna Louise have to say? Did she know anything?"

"Only that you didn't do it."

"I told you that before y'all arrested me!"

"Knowing it Thomas Lee and proving it are two different things."

"You think that prosecutor proved I murdered that baby?" Thomas Lee asked agitated.

"Roosevelt . . . what do you know about him?" A bothered look formed on Thomas Lee's face.

"You can get that out your mind right now." He said in Roosevelt's defense. "That old dude got to be one of the most decent men I ever knew—" Detective Stokey interjected.

"He's also extremely loyal to the Clarkston family."

"That man's just doing his job detective just like my momma and Carrie, ain't no way in hell Roosevelt would ever kill a baby!" Thomas Lee noted the suspicious look in Detective Stokey's eyes. "And don't you even think about blaming my momma!"

"Calm down Thomas Lee, remember I'm on your side." Detective Stokey said at loss for suspects. "I would never think of blaming Marietta."

"And like I said before Detective, Delores would never hurt her own baby." Thomas Lee said with insistence. "After Ol' selfish ass Charles told her he would never give her kids, it done something to Delores."

"Something like what Thomas Lee?" Detective Stokey asked curious.

"It just seem like it killed something on the inside of her, lead her straight to that wine bottle and into my arms." A smile displayed on Thomas Lee's face. "One day after we had—" He stopped and looked at Detective Stokey with slightly remorse. "—well anyway when Delores told me she was pregnant." Detective Stokey said electing not to tell him he wasn't the father. "Man you should've seen her . . . she was like a kid in at the county fair with all the cotton candy she could eat!" He laughed. "As much as I'd like to see Charles get his—" Thomas Lee said looking Detective Stokey in the eyes. "—he didn't kill my son."

"I'm not convinced of that Thomas Lee." Detective Stokey said disappointed to hear Thomas Lee's belief in Charles' innocence.

"Charles loves Delores more than he even knows and he would never hurt her like that."

"Are you sure Thomas Lee?"

"I grew up with Charles remember?"

"Somehow Thomas Lee, that doesn't convince me of his innocence." He said noting the troubled look in Thomas Lee's eyes.

"That look in your eyes, what's uh—"

"I know this gon sound crazy detective, but if you find out Delores had anything to do with killing that baby, before I'd let her serve one day in jail I'd die in here man." Detective Stokey's eyes widened as he looked at Thomas Lee momentarily loss for words.

"You uh, you love Mrs. Clarkston, Thomas Lee?" He lowered his head before answering.

"Yeah man I do—" He again looked up at Detective Stokey. "—just as much as Charles and more than Dorothy Jean know."

"Is that so?"

"When Delores told me we was having my baby, my love for her grew like a wild fire!"

"Well before you make a decision like that Thomas Lee I uh, think there's something you should know."

"What's that?"

"There's rumors that Mrs. Clarkston—" Thomas Lee cut him off.

"Was seeing other Black men besides me?" Detective Stokey's eyes again widened, surprised by Thomas Lee's knowledge of Delores's additional indiscretions.

"You uh, knew that Thomas Lee?"

"Yeah man I knew." He half heartedly grinned. "I can't get mad at Delores for doing her thing when I'm out there doing mines." Thomas Lee cunningly grinned.

"Well I guess you can't."

"You know detective it was a time when I had a woman for every day of the week." Detective Stokey's mouth opened in amazement.

"A woman for uh, every day Thomas Lee?" He flushed with redness. "Seven days a—"

"Week!" Thomas Lee said completing his sentence. "Yeah." A look of astonishment displayed on Detective Stokey's face.

"Wow." He looked at Thomas Lee with wonder. "Seven days a week huh? Wow."

"How's my momma holding up?"

"She's holding the best she can—she uh, told me to let you know she has plans to move to Ohio, Cincinnati."

"What the hell she mean she's moving to Cincinnati?" Thomas Lee said upset.

"She also told me to tell you that once you're free to take your wife and get out of Louisiana."

"Man I don't understand, we ain't got no family in Cincinnati!"

"I don't know if Marietta wanted me to tell you this but—" A frightened look displayed in Thomas Lee's eyes.

"But what?"

"She's concerned Clarkston might want revenge once you've been released."

"Man I ain't worried about Charles!" Thomas Lee said undaunted.

"Well maybe you should be Thomas Lee."

"Man I can't worry about what Charles might do, you just keep talking to Mildred"

"About Mildred—" Detective Stokey hesitated. "—I didn't want to have to tell you this Thomas Lee but—" Thomas Lee's eyes widened with panic.

"Hell naw . . . man don't tell me she dead!" He said emotionally unraveling. "Man they gon kill me!"

"Calm down Thomas Lee, Mildred's not dead but—"

"But what!" He yelled. "What's going on?"

"If you calm down I'll tell you." Detective Stokey said trying to mask his own dread.

"Just tell me!" Thomas Lee shouted. "They gon kill me as soon as they find out Mildred's dead."

"She's not dead Thomas Lee it looks like she may have had a stroke." Thomas Lee laid down and threw the covers over his head.

"They getting ready to shank me man the minute the nurse turn her back . . . they gon drive that blade straight through my heart."Thomas Lee stated losing hope. Detective Stokey looked at the silhouette underneath the covers.

"Don't give up Thomas Lee there has to be somebody out there who knows what happened to that baby and as soon as I know anything, I'll be sure and let you know."

"Tell my momma I need to see her." Thomas Lee said through the covers.

#

"How's she doing?" Detective Stokey asked he entered Mildred's room seeing the nurse taking her vital signs. A lump formed his throat as he looked at Mildred lying in bed with her eyes closed. "Was it a stroke?"

"No . . . not this time." The nurse said removing the cuff from Mildred's arm after taking her blood pressure. "Ms. Koffee's diabetic and apparently she hasn't been taking her medication or following the diet prescribed by her doctor." Detective Stokey withheld his knowledge of Mildred's unhealthy eating habits as he listened. "She also has high blood pressure and based on her excessively high readings it looks like she hasn't been taking her medication for that either or following her sodium restricted diet."

"Is she uh, in a coma?" He asked looking at Mildred with sorrowful eyes.

"No, right now she's asleep." The nurse said pulling the white sheet and blanket up around Mildred's neck. "It looks like her guardian angel was really looking out for her." She turned to Detective Stokey and smiled. "If you hadn't found her when you did you might've been identifying her downstairs in the morgue." His eyes slightly watered as the nurse left the room.

"You just wait until you get out of here old woman." Detective Stokey said softly scolding Mildred as he looked down at her. "I'll make damn sure you never eat another pig foot, pig tail or anything else on the pig." He momentarily stared at her then removed her hand from underneath the cover and gently squeezed it.

#

Dorothy Jean sat on her front porch drinking beer and absorbing the warmth of the hot afternoon sun with her next door neighbor Rita.

"Dorothy Jean, girl if I was you I'd divorce Thomas Lee's trifling behind." Rita said rolling her head and gesturing with her hands. "Let Delores Clarkston have his ass, let him do the same thing to her he been doing to you."

"Well you ain't me Rita and Thomas Lee ain't your husband." Dorothy Jean said taking a drink from the clear bottle of beer.

"Lucky for him I ain't because I—" Rita silenced when seeing a car pull in Dorothy Jean's driveway. "—look like you got company, maybe it's somebody from the prison coming to tell you they done killed Thomas Lee up there."

"Shut up Rita—" Dorothy Jean said becoming nervous by Rita's chilling words. "—let me see what this man wants." A surprised look displayed on Rita's face.

"You know who that is Dorothy Jean?"

"Yeah . . . that's the detective I was telling you about been trying to help Thomas Lee."

"Why he coming out here bothering you?" Rita asked drinking the last of her canned beer then opening up another, taking a drink as she waited for Detective Stokey to get out. "Here he come Rita." She said when seeing the driver's side door open.

"Good evening Mrs. Simms." Detective Stokey said as he began walking towards her house. "Beautiful weather we're having."

"Could be better—could be worse." She replied.

"You got a minute to talk?" He asked continuing to walk towards the house shifting his eyes briefly to Rita then back to Dorothy Jean.

"That depends on what you want to talk about."

"Thomas Lee, your husband?"

"What about him?"

"Solving his case could get personal."

"What case?" Rita yelled out. "Thomas Lee's ass was found guilty you the only person believe he's innocent!" Detective Stokey stared briefly at her then turned his attention back to Dorothy Jean.

"You sure you want to talk in front of your friend there?"

"Rita's my next door neighbor." She turned to Rita. "Let me see what he want Rita, I'll talk to you later."

"Okay girl, but if you need me—" She peered at Detective Stokey. "—you know I'm right next door." Rita stood. "You know you can't be too careful these days." She said continuing her gaze at Detective Stokey as she walked off the porch and headed towards her own house. He watched Rita as she stepped onto her front porch being seated on her stairs. He again turned to Dorothy Jean.

"May I uh, join you on the porch?"

"You look alright from where you standing to me." He quietly chuckled in response to her rudeness.

"I uh, wanted to update you on what I've found so far proving Thomas Lee had nothing to do with murdering that baby."

"And what proof is that?"

"I'd rather not shout it where everybody can hear." She shifted her eyes over at Rita then turned back to Detective Stokey.

"Come on up."

"Thank you." Dorothy Jean watched with suspicious eyes as he walked up on the porch and sat down. "How have you been doing Mrs. Simms?"

"How you think I been doing knowing my husband in prison for murdering a baby he didn't kill while Delores Clarkston and her husband wasn't even considered suspects?" Dorothy Jean said skeptical about his loyalty to Thomas Lee. "Everybody know that baby Thomas Lee found floating in the river belong to Delores Clarkston, so you tell me how he end up in the river without her knowing?"

"That's uh, what I'm trying to figure out—"

"Figure out my ass!" Dorothy Jean said raising her voice. "Then why wasn't Delores and her husband . . . Mr. Charles Clarkston the third even considered suspects?" He nervously massaged his neck.

"There wasn't enough evidence—" She interjected.

"And what damn evidence did you have on my husband?"

"He uh—"

"None!" She yelled.

"Oddly enough Mrs. Simms, Thomas Lee doesn't think either Mr. Clarkston or his wife had anything to do with what happened to that baby."

"You think Delores Clarkston's newborn baby crawled in the river by his self detective?" Dorothy Jean stated sarcastically. "Because I guarantee you Delores knows exactly what happened to her baby and so do her rich husband!"

"I assure you Dorothy Jean—"

"You can't assure me a damn thing Detective Stokley!" He took a deep breath, frustrated by her routinely discourteous attitude.

"To answer your question . . . Charles Clarkston has credible witnesses that swears he wouldn't hurt a fly let alone a child—"

"Credible!" Dorothy Jean shouted. "Like who Roosevelt, Marietta and Carrie who ask how high everytime Mr. Charles Clarkston tells them to jump?" She looked at Detective Stokey as a fool.

"I've talked to the Clarkston's staff and they didn't appear to have reason to lie about Clarkston murdering that baby."

"Charles Clarkston's White wife gives birth to a Black baby and you think what detective?" Dorothy Jean said infuriated. "He just gon look the other way?" She yelled.

"Do you know anything about who might've fathered Mrs. Clarkston's son Mrs. Simms?"

"You got five minutes to get your ass off my property!" Dorothy Jean said enraged by his question. "Then I'm letting my dogs loose on your ass." He quickly stood and began walking swiftly away.

"I think you should know Dorothy Jean—" Detective Stokey said feeling ornery. "—Thomas Lee said he'd be die in prison before he'd let Mrs. Clarkston spend a single day in jail!" He looked back at her as he reached for his door handle. "That's a hell of statement for a married man to say about his mistress."

"Get your ass away from here!" Dorothy Jean shouted standing to her feet. Detective Stokey quickly climbed inside his car. He hoped by repeating Thomas Lee's selfless words regarding his lover would provoke Dorothy Jean into confronting Delores Clarkston and possibly getting her to confess what she knew about who murdered her infant son.

"Mission accomplished." He said to himself as he drove away.

#

Dorothy Jean's anger mounted as a guard led her through the cement corridors of the infirmary where Thomas Lee lay in bed asleep.

"Thomas Lee!" She yelled. His eyes abruptly opened startled by her loud voice.

"Hey Dorothy Jean when you get here?" He asked still half asleep. She watched with disdain as he slowly sat up.

"That detective brought his ass back out to the house yesterday bothering me!" Thomas Lee noted the rage beaming in her eyes.

"Bothering you, what you mean?"

"Came to tell me what you been saying." His heart pounded in his chest.

"Did he tell you about what happened to Aunt Mildred?" He said diverting from Dorothy Jean's impending conversation. A look of alarm appeared in her eyes.

"What you mean what happened to Ms. Mildred?"

"He didn't tell you?" Thomas Lee said trying to think of what Detective Stokey could've told her.

"If he had told me would I be asking you Thomas Lee?" Dorothy Jean said raising her voice.

"He stopped by her house a few days ago and found her—"

"Found her!" Dorothy Jean cried out bursting into tears.

"Yeah, found Mildred in there unconscious on the floor."

"Is she—"

"Come here baby." Thomas Lee said extending his opened arms. Dorothy Jean entered his arms, resting her head against his chest. "Stop crying Dorothy Jean, Mildred gon be alright."

"Ms. Mildred's been like a momma to me Thomas Lee—"

"I know baby."

He kissed her gently on the forehead.

"When Momma passed I wasn't but fifteen, Ms. Mildred took me in and raised me like I was her own blood."

"I know baby." Thomas Lee again kissed her forehead. "That old woman's strong . . . she gon pull through." He said placing a comforting kiss on her cheek. "They said it was her sugar diabetes and blood pressure, but the hospital got it under control now." He wiped Dorothy Jean's tears with his sheet. "You know that old woman part human and part cat." Thomas Lee said laughing. Dorothy Jean lightly chuckled. "And I bet you she got lives just like a cat!" They continued laughing. Dorothy Jean suddenly stopped and looked at him.

"Do you love Delores, Thomas Lee?" He released her.

"Now why in hell you asking me something like that Dorothy Jean?"

"It is true what that detective said?"

"How am I supposed to know what he said to you, let alone if it's true?" Thomas Lee said trying to think of what Detective Stokey could have told her.

"Said you told him you would die here before you'd let Delores spend one day in jail." He looked up at the ceiling and shook his head before again looking into his wife's heated eyes.

"Damn! I thought he was on my side, why in the hell would he tell you something like that?"

"Would you die in here for me Thomas Lee?" Dorothy Jean asked pained by his words. He looked momentarily at her then turned away. She rose from the bed and began walking away. "I guess you not answering said all needed to be said."

"Dorothy Jean, wait!" She again turned. "What you want me to say?"

"I want my husband to say what he would do for another man's wife he would do for his own!"

"I don't know what I was thinking Dorothy Jean when I said that, these folks got me so drugged up in here!"

"Maybe I should do like Rita said—" He cut her off.

"Rita?" A frustrated look appeared in Thomas Lee's eyes. "What the hell Rita got to do with us?"

"She thinks I should divorce you."

"I know Rita better mind her own damn business stay out of ours!"

"This ain't about Rita, Thomas Lee . . . it's about my no good cheating ass husband that ain't been faithful to me since the day I met him!"

"Then why the hell did you marry me then Dorothy Jean?" Thomas Lee asked raising his voice. "You know what kind of man I was."

"I thought if you really loved me Thomas Lee you would change!" She yelled. "But I guess I was wrong."

"Then why the hell after ten years you still with me?"

"I knew I was making a mistake when I caught you in bed with my cousin Gina the day before we got married—" He cut her off.

"I ain't getting ready to argue with you about all this old mess Dorothy Jean." She burst into tears. "I explained to you then how I end up in the bed with your cousin . . . She came after me!"

"And I was fool enough to believe you over my own eyes!" She stared Thomas Lee in the face. "Why did you marry me Thomas Lee if you didn't loved me?"

"You want to know why I married you Dorothy Jean, I'll tell you why." He gazed into her tear filled eyes. "When you married me after catching me in bed with your cousin you showed me I could have my cake and eat it too." Thomas Lee said confirming his words with a nod of the head. "And you know what Dorothy Jean . . . you never challenged me on that."

"I hate you Thomas Lee!" Dorothy Jean screamed out. The nurse quickly turned in response to her bellow.

"Ma'am?"

Thomas Lee said quickly intervened.

"She just learned her momma's in the hospital from having a stroke."

"I'm sorry to hear that, but she'll have to keep it down." He nodded.

"I understand."

"Maybe I should tell that detective I saw you with that baby just before you supposedly fished him out of the river." Dorothy Jean stated, spitefully as she walked away. A horrified look appeared on Thomas Lee's face.

"Now you know that's a damn lie Dorothy Jean, don't tell that man that lie!" He yelled. "Come back here Dorothy Jean!"

#

"A penny for your thought?" Detective Abernathy said when seeing his partner sitting at his desk deep in thought. Detective Stokey gave no reply. "Earth to Stokey." He said approaching him. "Stokey man you alright?"

"Huh?"

"You were so still, for a minute there I thought maybe you had sleepwalked into work this morning."

"Sleepwalked?" He half-heartedly grinned. "I can think of a lot of places I'd go if I were sleepwalking Abernathy and believe me, this place wouldn't be one of them." Detective Abernathy laughed then noted the troubled look lingering in his partner's eyes.

"You alright man?"

"No Abernathy I'm not . . . it's hunting me."

"What hunting you man?"

"This case."

"Whoa!" Detective Abernathy said disturbed by his partner's words. "This case Stokey? Man ain't no damn case!" He said slightly raising his voice. "If memory serves me right this case you've allowed to take over your life is closed man!" He stated realistically. "In fact, I'm pretty sure a jury of twelve already decided Thomas Lee Simms was guilty as hell!"

"If, your conscious allows you to sleep at night Abernathy knowing an innocent man's rotting away in prison then—"

"Whoa . . . uh-uh man you ain't getting ready to make me feel guilty about how the judicial system works." Detective Abernathy said raising his voice. "I'm not the one who convicted Thomas Lee Simms for the murder of a baby he just happened to have fished out of the river!" Detective Stokey sarcastically applauded.

"Let's give a hand to the detective without a conscious."

"You hold one damn minute Stokey!" Detective Abernathy said, offended. "I got a conscious just like you man, but when a jury says a defendant is guilty I accept that verdict!"

"Hey hey hey!" Detective Fish said getting up from his desk, walking over. "Will you two cool it?" He looked at his coworkers as feuding children. "Some of us are around here are trying to work." They looked at him and then to each other. "You two sound like the Saints just lost the Super Bowl costing one of you a bundle!"

"Stokey's over here all bent out of shape because I don't agree with him on the Thomas Lee Simms—" Detective Fish interjected.

"If Stokey wants to believe Thomas Lee Simms is innocent that's his prerogative." Detective Abernathy's eyes widened, stunned by Detective Fish's two-faced words.

"I know damn well I didn't just hear what my ears thought they heard." Detective Abernathy said looking at Detective Fish as a hypocrite. "Aren't you the one who bet Stokey a steak dinner that he wouldn't be able to prove Thomas Lee Simms' innocence?"

"Whether we agree or disagree with Detective Stokey—" Detective Fish stated with sincerity. "—the fact remains we're all on the same side of the law aren't we?"

"I use to think so Detective Fish—" Detective Stokey said looking at Detective Abernathy. "—but lately I'm not so sure."

"Maybe it's because when a certain detective saw a peculiar look on an old woman's face, he now believes that it's evidence enough to overturn a guilty verdict!"

"You mean to tell me Abernathy if you felt in your gut that Mildred had information to prove what she was saying, you wouldn't follow that lead?"

"Evidence!" Detective Abernathy stated, cynically. "What damn evidence Stokey?" He looked at his partner with pessimism. "Show me any evidence old lady Koffee gave you that prove somebody other than Thomas Lee Simms murdered that baby."

"Now just hold on a minute Detective Abernathy." Detective Fish said instigating. "I don't think I like how you're talking to my friend Stokey."

Detective Abernathy's mouth flung open. "If Andy wants to believe a convicted baby killer is innocent then—"

"Whoa!" Detective Abernathy stated. "That's my partner you're mocking man, and if he says Thomas Lee Simms is innocent then he's innocent."

"Then what's all the yelping about?" Detective Fish said humored. Detective Stokey intervened.

"Who's yelping?"

"Well whatever it is you and Abernathy are belly aching about keep it down so I can work on a real case, one that a jury hasn't already given its verdict." He looked at Detective Stokey then shifted his eyes to Detective Abernathy. They watched as he turned and walked away returning to his desk, again barricading his face behind the computer monitor.

"How's the case coming along anyway Stokey man?" Detective Abernathy asked as if their altercation had never occurred.

"You sure you want to know?" Detective Stokey asked with skepticism.

"I wouldn't ask you man if I didn't."

"Is that so?"

"Yeah it's so, besides it bothers the hell out me to think Detective Fish could actually win that bet you foolishly entered into with him."

"The only thing missing are the clowns." Detective Stokey said. A puzzled look formed on Detective Abernathy's face.

"What the hell is that suppose to mean Stokey?"

"It means this entire thing is turning into one big circus."
Detective Abernathy's confusion accelerated.

"What?"

"Just when I think I'm proof positive about one person as a suspect the fat lady sings."

"Stokey man what the hell you talking about, that makes no since and who the hell is the fat lady?" Detective Stokey looked at his partner but gave no reply. "Man you been working cases long enough to know that cases can go in any direction."

"I'm aware of that Abernathy, but you haven't heard the worst of it."

"You telling me that it gets worse?"

"Thomas Lee's now vowing to die in prison rather than to let his mistress spend one day behind bars."

"Damn!" Detective Abernathy half heartedly grinned. "Did he say she murdered her baby?"

"No quite the opposite, he contends there's no way Mrs. Clarkston would've ever murdered her baby."

"Even if she did it Stokey do you actually think Charles Clarkston would allow you to arrest his wife?" Detective Abernathy asked challenging by his partner's reasoning.

"He may not have a choice."

"What you mean he may not have a choice man?"

"I talked to the midwife who delivered Mrs. Clarkston's son—"

"Whoa!" Detective Abernathy said stunned. "You know who the midwife is that delivered Baby boy Doe?"

"As a matter of fact I do Detective Abernathy." Detective Stokey stated proud of his investigative work. "You want to know what else I discovered?" He said cunningly smiling. "It turns out Mrs. Clarkston had quite an appetite for Black men." Detective Abernathy's jaw dropped.

"Are you serious man?"

"Very."

"So that's where Thomas Lee fits into this whole mess, so is he, Baby boy Doe's father?" A tell-tale look appeared on Detective Stokey's face.

"Thomas Lee's not the father." A look of surprise showed on Detective Abernathy face.

"Come again?"

"According to the Clarkston's staff, Ms. Clarkston was slapping the sheet with some guy name Phony Tony—"

"I know Tony." Detective Stokey looked at him, curious of his relationship with Phony Tony. "How does he fit into all this?"

"You know Phony Tony, Abernathy?"

"Yeah I just bought some life insurance from him for the wife and kids." Detective Stokey's eyes widened.

"Is that so?"

"Yeah." Detective Abernathy said innocently. "What's wrong with that?"

"Anyway—" Detective Stokey said evading the question. "—I didn't have the heart to tell an imprisoned man the woman he's willing to die for is a jezebel and the kid wasn't his." Detective Abernathy's mouth flung open.

"Jezebel?" He laughed. "Man that's cold, but don't that make Clarkston and his wife two good suspects?"

"So you would think Abernathy."

"So what you gon do man?" He looked at his partner then began massaging his neck.

"I guess that's the million dollar question Abernathy—one I don't have an answer to." Detective Stokey stared momentarily at his inquisitive partner. "Until I can prove which one did it Abernathy, all I can do is, keep gathering pieces to the puzzle until the big picture emerges."

"Only thing I got to say Stokey man is that you damn well better have those pieces in place before you go after Charles Clarkston or his wife Jezebel" The two detectives burst into laughter.

Chapter Fourteen

"You said this Mildred person is Tommy's Aunt?" Delores asked as she and Marietta stepped off the elevator on their way to Mildred's hospital room.

"Mildred's my grandfather's sister, she helped me raise Thomas Lee when his daddy was out in the streets doing who knows what—" Marietta silenced as they approached Mildred's room. "Knock, knock." She said poking her head inside. A large smile stretched across Mildred face when seeing her.

"Is that you Marietta?"

"Yeah it's me Aunt Mildred—how you feeling today?" Marietta asked walking over and hugging her then placing a kiss on her cheek. Delores followed. Mildred shifted her eyes to Delores then back to Marietta.

"As long as I'm still above ground I guess I'm doing fine."

"Hi Mildred." Delores said extending her hand. "I'm Delor—"

"I know who you are Delores."

"You do?" She said surprised. "I guess Tommy must've told you all about me." Delores giggled. Mildred glanced over at Marietta as she shook Delores' hand. "Since me and Tommy are special friends—"

"Tommy?" Mildred said shifting her eyes briefly to Marietta. Delores again giggled.

"Oh, that's just what I call Tommy since we've been—"

"Aunt Mildred . . . Delores is Mr. Charles' wife." Marietta said uneasy by Delores' conversation on her relationship with Thomas Lee. Delores turned quickly to her.

"Marietta—" She looked at her with chastising eyes. "—I don't think Mildred's interested in knowing that—are you Mildred?" She said not wanting to speak on her marital status with Charles. "Marietta tells me you helped her raise my Tommy?" Marietta's jaw dropped in response to Delores' choice of words.

"Ms. Delores!"

"What Marietta . . . I just told Mildred that Tommy and I were special friends." Delores blushed.

"Well don't you forget, you and Thomas Lee are both married to other people." Delores shifted her eyes briefly over at her, ignoring Marietta's subtle reprimand.

"Go on Mildred—" Delores said turning to her. "—tell me about my Tommy." Mildred shifted her eyes briefly to Marietta seeing the anxious look on her face.

"Raising Thomas Lee wasn't an easy thing to do." Mildred said chuckling as she reminisced.

"Well I must say you did a fine job in raising Tommy to be such a wonderful man."

"Thank you Delores but I didn't do it by myself, Marietta—" Delores cut her off.

"I sometimes think if I hadn't married Charles Clarkston the third, I just know I would be Mrs. Thomas Lee Simms." She giggled. Marietta's mouth slightly opened.

"Now Ms. Delores you know them ain't proper words for a married woman to be saying, especially the wife of a Clarkston." Mildred's eyes drew to the door when seeing Detective Stokey preparing to enter.

"Now tell me this Delores—" Mildred said distracting her, allowing the detective time to back out of sight. "—since you're a special friend of my nephew why don't you go come on over here and give Ms. Mildred a nice big hug." Delores' eyes lit up.

"Can I Mildred? I would love to hug the woman who helped raised my Tommy." Mildred alerted Marietta with her eyes that Detective Stokey stood just outside the door as Delores lovingly embraced her. Marietta nodded. "I just know one day that jury going to kick themselves for convicting my Tommy of murdering my—" She abruptly stopped. "—that baby."

"Do you know something about what happened to that baby Delores?" Mildred asked as they ended their embrace.

"All I know is Tommy wasn't the last person to see my—" She again silenced then looked at Marietta before again turning to Mildred.

"Did you tell that to the prosecutor Delores?"

"Of course not Mildred, don't be silly." She said amused by the question. "Charles would never allow me to do something like that, in fact when the prosecutor asked Charles told him I didn't know anything that would prove Thomas Lee wasn't the murderer of that poor baby." Marietta shifted her eyes over to the door, desperately needing to distance herself from Delores' upsetting words.

"Aunt Mildred is it a bathroom around here somewhere?" Marietta asked walking swiftly towards the door.

"I'm sure a nurse can tell you where you can find one if you ask."

"Alright then I'll be back." She turned to Delores. "Ms. Delores you don't mind staying in here with Aunt Mildred while I run to the restroom do you?" A huge smile formed on Delores' face.

"Of course I don't mind Marietta, don't be silly!" Marietta held back her tears, upset by Charles' refusal to allow Delores to speak with the prosecutor.

"I won't be gone long."

Detective Stokey watched as Marietta hurried from the room, her eyes filled with tears as she scurried down the hall.

"How long you and Thomas Lee been special friends Delores?" Mildred asked subtly interrogating her. Detective Stokey's heart pounded with anxiousness, hoping to hear a confession. Delores girlishly blushed.

"Well . . . between me and you Mildred I guess you could say me and Tommy we're a little more than just friends." Delores giggled.

"Did you and Thomas Lee ever talk about Baby boy Doe before they arrested him?"

"Since you're Tommy's aunt and Tommy and I are practically married—" Delores said blushing. "Is it alright if I call you Aunt Mildred?" Mildred's eyes slightly widened, surprised by Delores' unexpected request.

"Of course you can Delores I bet you Tommy would love that." Mildred said smiling.

"You think so Aunt Mildred?" Delores said suddenly hugging her. Mildred glanced over at the door seeing Detective Stokey peeping inside and pointing at his wristwatch indicating he needed to leave soon.

"I sure wish I knew who the mother of that precious baby was, I would like to give her my condolences."

"Can you keep a secret Aunt Mildred?" Delores said ending their embrace. Detective Stokey's eyes lit up.

"I guess as best as the next person." A proud smile stretched across Delores's face.

"Then I'll tell you."

"Go head I'm listening." Detective Stokey stepped out of the doorway seconds before Delores looked in that direction checking for Marietta. "That beautiful baby boy was mines and Tommy's."

"It was?" Mildred stated sounding surprised. Detective Stokey peeped in the room with widened eyes.

"The day after our precious son was born I awakened that morning and my baby boy was gone." Delores' eyes moistened. "I assumed that monster Charles had given him to the midwife to take him away from me." She silently cried.

"Aww baby I'm sorry to hear that." Mildred said embracing Delores as her own eyes watered with tears.

"I thought maybe he'd given my son to a nice Black family somewhere, but when I heard Thomas Lee found a baby boy out in the river, I just knew Charles had something to do with it." Mildred glanced over at the door seeing the victorious smile on Detective Stokey's face.

"Did you ever ask Charles what happened to your baby Delores?"

"Of course I did Aunt Mildred, but I didn't expect Charles to tell me the truth!" Detective Stokey's eyes again lit up, certain a confession would be imminent. "But I knew from how angry Charles was there was no telling what he wouldn't have done to me and Tommy's son." Mildred again shifted her eyes to the door seeing Detective Stokey peeping inside. "Why did Charles have to kill my baby boy Aunt Mildred?" Delores cried out pulling from Mildred's hold, removing a silver flask filled with red wine from her purse.

"We probably should be getting back to the house Ms. Delores." Marietta said returning to the room seconds after Delores screwed the cap off the flask and took a drink. "Now Ms. Delores I don't think Mr. Charles want you out here at this hospital drinking."

"Well unless you tell him Marietta, Charles will never know." She said turning the flask up to her mouth a second time taking a swig. "You know Aunt Mildred whenever me, and Tommy would lie in each other's arms—"

"Ms. Delores!"

"Well Marietta it's not like Charles wasn't aware of me and Tommy's love for one another."

"Now Ms. Delores what you think Mr. Charles would say if he heard the way you talking right now?" Marietta asked disturbed by Delores revealing the details of her and Thomas Lee's love affair. Marietta watched as Delores displayed no shame as she took another swallow from the flask.

"Tommy and I loved each other and I don't care what Charles or anybody else has to say about it!" Marietta watched in anger as Delores again turned the flask up to her mouth and drank.

"Aunt Mildred let me get Ms. Delores out of here while she can still stand." She said infuriated.

"When Thomas Lee Jr. was born—"

"Ms. Delores!" Marietta said scolding her. Detective Stokey's eyes widened as he mouthed the words:

"*Thomas Lee Jr.?*"

"That was the best day of me and Tommy's life!" Delores said crying. Marietta looked at Mildred and shook her head.

"Come on Ms. Delores before you say something that's gon get Mr. Charles arrested and threw in jail."

"The only reason Charles wouldn't let me keep Tommy Jr. was because he was Black!" Delores yelled out slurring before taking another drink from the flask. "Because of me, Aunt Mildred my beautiful Black baby is dead." Mildred shifted her eyes to Marietta with concern. "You know what Aunt Mildred—" Delores said continuing to slur. "—I wouldn't be surprised if Charles murdered my son himself."

"Ms. Delores!" Marietta yelled. "Now you know dog gone well Mr. Charles ain't had nothing to do with killing that baby." Detective Stokey poked his head in the room, elated by what sounded like Delores confirming his theory that Charles murdered Baby boy Doe.

"I'll give you a call tomorrow Aunt Mildred." Marietta said taking hold of Delores's arm.

"I'm sure I'll be here since my doctor ain't talking like he in no hurry to let me go home." Delores placed a light kiss on Mildred's cheek.

"Bye Aunt Mildred."

#

Detective Abernathy looked around smiling with approval as he and Detective Stokey convened at the Sizzle and Serve Steak House, a Four-Star restaurant selected by Detective Stokey.

"Yeah Stokey man, I like this place." Detective Abernathy said admiring the laminated menu. "It's a little expensive for my taste, but it's nice."

"Don't worry about the cost Abernathy don't I always pay for lunch?"

"You want to tell me now what it is we're celebrating?"

"I got him Abernathy." Detective Stokey said convinced.

"Got who man?" He asked from behind his menu.

"Clarkston . . . he murdered that baby."

"Whoa . . . hold on Stokey!" Detective Abernathy said lowering his menu.

"Mrs. Clarkston practically admitted that he did it."

"Did she say those exact words Stokey?" Detective Abernathy asked looking at him with doubt. "Or did you hear what you wanted to hear?"

"I heard Mrs. Clarkston say as clear as day that her husband murdered that baby just like I've said all along." A big smile stretched across Detective Stokey's face. "And that means Mildred was wrong about money bags Clarkston and I was right, and that's why we're celebrating Abernathy!"

"You're joking right?" Detective Abernathy asked looking at his partner with skepticism. "Because what I'm hearing, sounds like speculations from an unhappy, unfaithful wife."

"What do you mean speculations?" Detective Stokey said convinced Delores Clarkson's words amounted to a confession. "I heard her with my own ears say—"

"Say what Stokey!" Detective Abernathy said raising his voice. "She saw her husband murder that baby?"

"Of course not!"

"Well it damn well better be what you heard before you even think about arresting Charles Clarkston, and even then do you think it'll be that easy to arrest a man of Charles' status?" A look of self-assurance showed on Detective Stokey's face.

"Why wouldn't it be?" Detective Abernathy looked at his naïve partner and shook his head in disbelief.

"Man ain't no way in hell Charles Clarkston's lawyers are gon let you get within two feet of him despite what you think you heard his wife say!"

"Whose side are you on Abernathy?"

"I'm on the side of common sense and reality and right now man you ain't using either one!" Detective Stokey stared momentarily at his partner then picked up his menu obscuring his face.

"I'm about to make the most significant arrest in my life and prove that an innocent man's been wrongly convicted—at the risk of destroying my career and—"

"Naw man . . . what you're about to do is go down in history as the detective Charles Clarkston and his lawyer mopped the floor with!" Detective Stokey lowered his menu and looked into his partner's cynical eyes.

"Thanks for the vote of confidence Abernathy."

"Listen to what you're saying man—" Detective Abernathy's forehead wrinkled with frowns. "—do you really think there's a judge in this country that would dismiss the charges against Thomas Lee Simms, a poor Black man convicted by a jury of his peers of murdering an innocent baby?" Detective Abernathy looked anxiously around the restaurant and again to his partner. "And in exchange for Thomas Lee, you think a court is going to imprison Charles Clarkston the third a rich, well respected White man?"

"I think I'll order the T-bone steak." Detective Stokey said ignoring his partner's common sense question. "How's that sound?"

"It sounds like you out of your damn mind if you think this is an open and shut case."

"Well you know what Abernathy, I don't give a damn what you or anybody else thinks . . . I've got Clarkston by the cahoonas and I'm moving on it."

"Stokey man, talk to Mildred." Detective Abernathy said pleading, distressed by his eagerness to take down one of the most powerful men in the state. "Make sure you're on the right track."

"You think I should have the bake potato or steak fries?"

"Alright man—" Detective Abernathy said relenting. "—if you want to go up against Charles Clarkston and ruin a lifelong career you go right ahead." He looked at him with scolding eyes then picked up his menu. "Just don't come begging for breadcrumbs when you get down to your last penny."

"On second thought I think I'll have the bake potato, butter and sour cream, maybe some chives?" Detective Stokey said disregarding his partner's words of warning.

"You better hope you're right on this Stokey or it won't be Clarkston's cahoonas in your hands . . . it'll be yours in his."

"I wonder if I can get bacon bits added to that."

#

"Good Morning Andy." Mildred said when seeing him poke his head in her hospital door. "Not that I ain't glad to see you, but what brings you out here this early in the morning?" She asked sitting up in bed preparing to eat breakfast. He smiled.

"How are you feeling Mildred?"

"I was feeling fine until they put this stuff they calling food in front of me." She frowned at the tray containing a box of cornflakes, a boiled egg, a slice of wheat toast, a 4 oz. glass of orange juice and a 4 oz. carton of skim milk.

"I know it's not pig feet and rutabaga, but it'll keep you out of this place." Detective Stokey said. "That way you can keep helping me in proving Thomas Lee's innocence."

"I guess I should thank you and the good Lord for me living to see another day." She stated with gratitude. "They tell me it was you found me lying in there on the floor." Detective Stokey's eyes moistened as took hold of Mildred's hand and gently squeezed it.

"Don't you ever scare me like that again Mildred." He said lightly scolding her.

"Don't worry I don't plan on it." He hugged her. "How's the case coming along Andy?" Mildred asked struggling to open the small box of corn flakes. A victorious look formed on his face.

"I got him Mildred." She looked at him, unimpressed by his news. "Charles Clarkston . . . I got him!"

"Charles Clarkston ain't killed that baby Andy." Mildred said turning the box of cereal over trying to figure out how to open it.

"What do mean he didn't kill him Mildred, of course he did you heard Mrs. Clarkston . . . she practically admitted it."

"Delores ain't doing nothing but speaking from hurt and alcohol." Mildred said continuing to struggle with the box of cornflakes.

"Here, let me help you with that Mildred." Detective Stokey said removing the box from her hand and ripping it open then pouring the cornflakes in a bowl. "Okay, if it wasn't Clarkston then that leaves Mrs. Clarkston or the midwife." Mildred looked at him with displeasure as she tried unsuccessfully to open the carton of milk.

"Anna Louise would give her own life before she'd ever hurt a child." She said sitting the milk down and picking up the glass of orange juice attempting to remove the plastic cap on top. "I guess if I could ever get this stuff open I could eat it."

"I'll get that for you Mildred." Detective Stokey said removing the carton of milk from her hand and opening it, pouring it over the cornflakes. She looked with disappointment at the packs of artificial sweetener on her tray.

"I guess this must be the sugar." She said shaking her head with disapproval as he picked up the blue packets of artificial sweetener and sprinkled them over her cereal. "Thank you Andy." Mildred said continuing to watch as he removed the lid from the orange juice. "So when you plan on arresting Charles Clarkston?" She asked before putting a spoonful of the cereal in her mouth.

"I don't like it, but I see what you're saying Mildred." Detective Stokey said massaging his neck. "So tell me something—"

"I'm listening."

"What makes you so sure Clarkston didn't do it when Mrs. Clarkston clearly said he did?"

"Because Charles loves Delores—" Mildred said scowling as she put a spoon of cornflakes in her mouth.

"A wife who doesn't know the meaning of the word fidelity?" He shook his head in disbelief.

Love can sometimes be a funny thing." Mildred said looking at the boiled eggs as she continued scowling.

"Something uh, wrong with your eggs Mildred?"

"Yeah, they missing about six pieces of bacon that should be lying on this plate next to them."

"Mildred."

"A few slices of bacon ain't gon hurt none Andy."

"I know it's not pig feet but it all comes from a pig—" Detective Stokey silenced when seeing the insistent look on Mildred's face indicating that if he wanted more information he'd need to get her some bacon.

"I'll see what I can do." He said exiting the room in search of Mildred some bacon.

#

"Thank you for allowing me to be a husband to my wife Delores." Charles said kissing her intimately on the lips as she lay in his arms after a rare encounter of her sharing his bed with him, overnight. "It's been a long time since I've not had to share my wife with another man." Charles said applying a gentle kiss to her lips. "When I married you Delores it was like adding a sweet frosting to a very special cake." He gazed into her eyes. "And as fairytale go . . . . you were telling me I was the man of your dreams—" He paused. "—so then why Delores?"

"Why what Charles?" She said unmoved by his fond memories.

"Why would you betray me with Thomas Lee?"

"Why with any of the many men I've shared my bed with Charles?" She stated without remorse for her adulterous affairs. "The real question Charles—" Delores stared briefly at him. "—is why you?" He grabbed hold of her face and looked at her.

"Is this where I call you the whore that you are?" Charles said looking at her with contempt.

"Take your hands off me Charles!" She said raising her voice. "Where's Roosevelt?" Delores asked forcing his hand from her face. "After a boring night with you Charles I need a glass of wine." She sat up prepared to get out of bed. He forced her back down, pinning her to the bed. "You knew Thomas Lee and I were childhood friends, so why?"

"I have news for you Charles—" Delores looked him in the eyes. "—Thomas Lee's not the only friend you have that's enjoyed the grapes of your vineyard."

"You filthy whore!"
She laughed.

"I may very well be a whore Charles, but I'm your whore." He released her and turned away.

"As a little girl I always had this strange feeling something in my life was missing."

"Missing? What do mean missing?" Charles said unable to empathize with her heart-felt words. "For goodness sake Delores, you were raised with privilege and provided the best of everything!" He stated with a lack of understanding. "You had parents who adored you, the best schools money could buy, high standing in society and—" She cut him off.

"I didn't expect that you understand Charles."

"What's there to understand Delores? You had a life any young girl of standing would love to have and—"

"Tommy understood." She said with little regard to his feelings. Charles again turned to her and silently stared then burst into laughter followed by anger.

"Did he Delores? A poor Black man who'd never possessed anything in life of any worth unless I gave it to him!" Charles stated with arrogance. "How in the hell could he ever understand the life you and I were privileged to?"

"Privileged?" Delores sarcastically laughed. "Do you know what my society parents called me Charles?" Her eyes moistened with tears. "Their little showpiece."

"And you were . . . Delores you're beautiful!" She laughed out loud. "What?" Charles said puzzled by her humor.

"Is that why you married me Charles, because I was beautiful?"

"Partly, but I also because loved you Delores!"

"Love?" She continued laughing. "Do you even know what that word means Charles?" She asked seeing the muted look form on his face. "Of course you don't—your love's no different than my stoic parent's." He remained speechless. "And like my parents you have never been able to give me what I'm missing." Tears rolled down her cheeks. "But Tommy—" A loving smile displayed on Delores' face. "—he's different."

"Of course he's different Delores!" Charles yelled, hurt by her expressed feelings for her lover.

"Money and status isn't everything Charles, but you wouldn't know that because money and status is all you and the entire Clarkston family's ever known." He looked in her tear filled eyes.

"Then you tell me Delores, what else is there?"

"True love Charles!" She shouted.

"True love?" He sarcastically chuckled. "And you think that's what Thomas Lee gives you . . . true love?" Charles said amused. "Tell me how Delores when he has a wife?"

"Even with a wife Tommy gives me more love than you ever could or would be able to."

"Well guess what Delores?" He said looking at her with disgust. "There's a difference between love and lust—" She slapped him.

"Go to hell Charles!" She shouted, attempting to get out of bed. He grabbed hold of her.

"Are you really naïve enough to believe Thomas Lee loves you?" Delores looked into his humored eyes, but gave no reply. Charles continued grinning. "You fool, you really do!" He said grabbing hold of her face then staring her in the eyes. "If I hear about you going anywhere near that prison again—" He hesitated. "—I'll simply have your lover killed." Her eyes widened with fear. "Now get the hell out of my bed and go find Roosevelt so he can give you your morning bottle!" She slowly climbed out of bed then flashed Charles a look of disdain.

"I'll never love you the way I love Tommy!" Delores screamed.

"And I'll never give you a divorce Mrs. Charles Clarkston the third."

"I hate you Charles!" She bellowed. He laughed.

"You just stay the hell away Thomas Lee Simms!" She hurried from the room slamming the door behind her.

Chapter Fifteen

Carrie looked at Marietta with concern as she sat at the kitchen table chopping onions, celery and green peppers in preparation for her shrimp Creole. She worried that her coworker and friend had finally reached the breaking point.

"How's Mildred doing Marietta?" Carrie asked breaking the pin dropping silence in the room as she peeled shrimp over at the sink.

"Hospital supposed to be releasing her today." Marietta stated without looking up.

"That's good I know she was glad to hear that." Carrie shifted her eyes quickly in the vestibule making certain neither of the Clarkston's were within earshot then hurried over to Marietta. "So what happened when you took Ms. Delores to the hospital with you last week?" Carrie whispered.

"Ms. Delores ran her mouth so, by the time she stopped talking I thought for sure the police was gon be out here arresting Mr. Charles." Carrie's jaw dropped.

"Girl you lying!"

"I wish I was." Mildred said shaking her head. "You should've seen her—"

"I wish I had been!"

"Sometime Ms. Delores act just like a child, out there telling Aunt Mildred how her, and Thomas Lee was laying in each other's arm—" Carrie's mouth flung open.

"Girl, no she didn't!"

"Yeah, she did then she started calling my aunt—Aunt Mildred." Carrie burst into laughter. "Shhhhhh!"

"Did she say anything about what happened to her baby?" Carrie asked. Marietta shifted her eyes briefly in the vestibule then looked up the kitchen stairs.

"Wait until you hear this." Marietta again looked around. "Girl, Ms. Delores told Aunt Mildred she thought Mr. Charles had Anna Louise give her baby to a Black family." Carrie again burst into laughter.

"I knew that heifer was crazy!"

"Shhhhhhh!"

"Girl can't nobody hear me." Carrie said dumping the peeled shrimp into a large yellow bowl.

"You know Ms. Delores is light on her feet Carrie, you look up and she'll be standing there."

"Now where in the hell Ms. Delores, get some mess like that from?" Carrie said shaking her head. "She knows damn well when Anna Louise left this house she still had that baby in her own damn arms so what the hell is she talking about Marietta?"

"Shhhhhh!" Marietta again tried to quiet her mouthy coworker.

"Marietta I know you remember how Ms. Delores wouldn't let that baby go long enough for Anna Louise to even clean him up."

"I think we all remember that."

"Ms. Delores done lost her damn mind!"

"You know Anna Louise wouldn't have took that baby without Ms. Delores knowing it." Marietta said upset.

"Crazy heifer . . . what the hell's wrong with her Marietta?"

"That was that red wine talking." A stunned look displayed on Carrie's face.

"Red wine!"

"Keep your voice down Carrie!"

"Where in the hell she got red wine from in a damn hospital?"

"She had it inside her purse."

"What?" Carrie said again increasing her tone. "Damn drunk."

"Hush!" Marietta whispered as they continued preparing supper.

"They can't hear me."

"And get this Carrie—"

Carrie's excitement grew.

"Go on girl I'm listening."

"After she accused Anna Louise of taking her baby—" Marietta again looked around to ensure the Clarkston's weren't nearby. "—she accused Mr. Charles of killing him!" Carrie's jaw again dropped.

"Get the hell out here Marietta, no she didn't!"

"Shhhhhh!" Marietta rose from the table taking the bowl of chopped vegetables over to the sink. She again glanced up the kitchen stairs.

"Girl, if Mr. Charles heard her drunk ass, saying some mess like that I bet he'll divorce that heifer then!"

"I don't know what Ms. Delores was thinking telling Aunt Mildred that?"

"Marietta what's wrong with her?"

"Get me that bowl of fresh tomatoes out of the refrigerator so I can get started on my Creole sauce."

"That heifer got everything a woman could want." Carrie said on her way to the refrigerator. "Good looking husband—" Marietta quickly looked over at her.

"Carrie!"

"What?"

"I'm gon tell Buster on you in here looking at Mr. Charles like that!" She teased. Carrie removed the bowl of tomatoes.

"Girl you know Mr. Charles is good looking!"

"Well I practically raised him, so he gon always look like a little boy to me."

"Well I didn't raise him." Carrie said handing Marietta the tomatoes. "He was a full grown fine ass man when I met him." Carrie chuckled.

"Girl hush!" Marietta said grinning. "It's enough adultery going around to last a life time, don't you add to it."

"Adultery?" Carrie said reaching inside a base cabinet removing a pot for Marietta's shrimp Creole. "Damn Marietta all I said was Mr. Charles was good looking, I ain't said nothing about laying down with that man."

"Listening at Ms. Delores and all her crazy talk got me thinking—"

"Crazy, just like her." Carrie said running water in the large pot taking it over to the stove. "Ms. Delores' ass ought to be the happiest woman in the world . . . she rich, beautiful, living in this big ass house and got us doing every damn thing she don't want to do for herself, what more could she want?" Marietta looked her coworker in the eyes.

"I think Ms. Delores just want to be happy."

"Happy!" Carrie said slightly raising her voice.

"Hush now Carrie!"

"How in hell can Ms. Delores she have all this and not be happy?"

"Now that's something you gon have to ask her—" Carrie's eyes widened.

"Who? I ain't getting ready to ask that spoiled heifer nothing about her business." She said gathering the spices for Marietta's shrimp Creole. "If you asked me her ass is just use to having things her way!"

"Shhhhhhh!" Marietta said. "Mr. Charles or Ms. Delores hear you talking like that—"

"Good morning Marietta, Carrie." Roosevelt said startling them as he entered the kitchen.

"What the hell you doing sneaking up on us like that for Roosevelt?" Carrie said raising her voice.

"Good morning Roosevelt." Marietta said amused by Carrie's fright.

"I just wanted to let y'all know Ms. Delores on her way down, I didn't y'all wanted her to hear y'all in here talking about her." He quietly chuckled.

"Anything I got to say about Ms. Delores I'll say to her damn face."

"I know you will Carrie—but don't." Roosevelt said before smiling at Marietta. She blushed.

"You think you can keep from giving Ms. Delores anything to drink before—"

"Roosevelt!" Delores called out. "Would you get me a bottle of wine from the cellar?" She said suddenly appearing in the dining room being seated at the table. He shifted his eyes to Marietta.

"Ms. Delores don't you think you should put something in your stomach first?" Marietta stated. "Drinking wine on a empty stomach ain't no way to begin your day." Delores giggled.

"After spending a boring night with Charles—" Carrie looked quickly to Marietta and silently grinned. "—I need a glass of wine or an entire bottle." She laughed. Roosevelt intervened.

"Now Ms. Delores whatever you and Mr. Charles do in private—" She interjected.

"Will get me more jewelry, a diamond bracelet, a pearl necklace or perhaps even a new car!" Marietta and Carrie looked at one another trying to hold back their laughter. Roosevelt again intervened.

"Shame on you Ms. Delores speaking on your husband like that!" He said in Charles' defense. "Mr. Charles ain't been nothing but good to you—"

"He murdered by baby Roosevelt!" She shouted. "And you, Marietta and Carrie are hiding all it!" Carrie's jaw dropped. She looked quickly at Marietta.

"Delores!" Charles yelled coming down the stairs.

"I know you killed my baby you monster!" She cried out. "And that's just what I told Aunt Mildred." Charles looked in the kitchen at Marietta and Roosevelt. "And as soon as she gets out of the hospital she's going to tell the police—"

"Roosevelt."

"Yes Mr. Charles?"

"Please take my wife upstairs to her room." Charles said looking him sternly in the eyes. "Lock her in if you have to then get her psychiatrist over here so he can give her something to calm her down." Delores looked at Roosevelt then turned to Charles and again to Roosevelt as he approached her.

"You touch me Roosevelt and you're fired!" She shouted. He looked at Charles and awaited instruction. He nodded giving his permission. "Roosevelt reached for her arm.

"Don't touch me you nig—"

"Delores!" Charles shouted. He shifted his eyes to Roosevelt and again to his wife. "If you ever say that word in this house again, you'll be going on a special vacation, one that I guarantee you won't find the least bit delightful."

"Damn!" Carrie said whispering. "If that's what she's like after laying down with Mr. Charles—" She looked at Delores with troubled eyes. "—then he need to keep her ass out his bed."

"I apologize for my wife's rudeness Roosevelt." Charles stated uneasy by the awkward moment.

"No need in you apologizing for what Ms. Delores let come out of her mouth Mr. Charles."

"Delores dear I highly recommend you let Roosevelt take you back upstairs to your room or—" She interjected.

"Or what Charles?" She looked at him with defiant eyes. He cunningly smiled.

"Or I'll be the one calling the police confessing on behalf of my wife that out of disgrace, she murdered her love child fathered by Thomas Lee Simms." Marietta shifted her eyes to Roosevelt, horrified by Charles' consequential words to her son. "—and how the two of you simply tossed the unwanted child in the river." Carrie looked at Marietta seeing the fear in her tearful eyes.

"Dirty dog." She said whispering in Marietta's ear.

"Come on Ms. Delores—" Roosevelt said taking her gently by the arm. "—let me take you upstairs to your room." She looked at him with insolence but showed no resistance. "If you promise me you won't come back out I won't lock you in." He shifted his eyes to Charles. "You ain't no prisoner in here this is your home."

Charles watched as Roosevelt escorted his wife up the stairs before he entered the dining room being seated at the table. He picked up the morning newspaper.

"Marietta." She wiped the tears from her eyes, looking briefly at Carrie before entering the dining room.

"You need something Mr. Charles?"

"Since I've obviously missed breakfast and lunch—" He said from behind the newspaper. "—if you'll fix me a snack that should hold me until supper." She shifted her eyes to Carrie.

"Was it something in particular your wanted Mr. Charles?"

"I think I'll leave that up to your discretion, you know the kind of things I like to eat."

Chapter Sixteen

"Thank you for driving me home from the hospital Andy." Mildred said as he opened the passenger side door.

"It was my pleasure Mildred." He said helping her out of the car. "I figured it was the least I could do for all the help you've given me in trying to prove Thomas Lee's innocence." She held onto his arm as he escorted her up the stairs and on the porch. "If you give me your key Mildred I'll open the—"

"I'm gon stay right out here on this porch." She stated. "I been cooped up in that hospital for the last two weeks and I ain't getting ready to be cooped up inside that house." Detective Stokey quietly grinned. "I'm gon sit right here on this porch and soak up some sun."

"Are you sure Mildred?"

"If you ain't in a hurry, I could use your help in sitting down over here in my rocker."

"I always have time for you Mildred." He stated as he lowering her into the old rocking chair. "Did you need me to get you something Mildred, a glass of water, some buttermilk?" He teased. "You know I was kidding about the buttermilk right?" She giggled. "How about I grab you a nice cold glass of water?"

"That sounds good for now, but I'm gon need you to take me out a bag of them pigtails from the freezer." Detective Stokey looked at her with disciplining eyes.

"Mildred, your discharge instructions included a diabetic, low sodium diet and—" She interjected.

"I ain't ever heard of no sweet pig tails and if they salty it's 'cause whoever cooking done put too much salts in—" Mildred silenced when seeing the chastising look in his eyes. "—I guess I can live without eating pigtails, for today." Detective Stokey shook his head and silently chuckled.

"What am I going to do with you Mildred?"

"All I need you to do is keep working on that case until you get my nephew out of prison alive."

"I want you to know Mildred I'm doing everything in my power to make that a reality." Mildred reached over and took hold of his hand.

"I want you to make me a promise Andy—" She looked him in the eyes. "—no matter where this case leads you, I want you to promise me you won't go anywhere near my granddaughter." He looked at her with objection.

"Mildred you can't have it both ways." Detective Stokey stated respectfully. "You can't ask me to prove Thomas Lee's innocence then tell I can't follow every lead—" She snatched her hand away. He looked at her with apologetic eyes. "—I can't make you that promise Mildred, you know that in order for me to solve this I have to follow every lead." He looked at her with sympathetic eyes "Even, if it leads me to your granddaughter."

"Goodbye Andy."

"Come on now Mildred you know how this works—"

"Goodbye Andy!" She said raising her voice.

"Is it alright Mildred if I stop by tomorrow and bring you some of the foods your doctor recommended for you?" She gave no reply, refusing to look at him.

"Goodbye Mildred." He said walking off the porch headed for his car. "I'll see you tomorrow Mildred." She watched with bitter eyes as he climbed inside his car and back onto the road then drove away.

#

"You got any idea what you plan on ordering Stokey?" Detective Abernathy asked looking over the lunch menu as they sat in the rear of the Appetite Pleaser Café.

"It damn sure won't be the Ruben platter!" Detective Stokey said scrutinizing the sandwich section.

"I want to apologize Stokey for that little spat we had a few weeks ago."

"Is that what this *why don't we go have lunch* thing all about Abernathy?" Detective Stokey asked from behind the menu. "Well don't worry about it spats happens between partners."

"Naw Stokey man I should've taken you a little more serious about the Simms' case." Detective Abernathy said lowering his menu looking over at him. "I'm sorry man."

"Apology accepted . . . and you're right you should've." Detective Abernathy shook his head in response to his partner's sly remark then noted the green haired waitress.

"Miss!" He called out.

"Be with you in a minute." She said grabbing a pot of coffee off the warmer. He lightly kicked Detective Stokey under the table in response to the waitress' neon green hair.

"Hey." She said approaching them. "My name is Ella, what can I get you gentlemen to drink? Detective Stokey lowered his menu and looked up at her.

"I asked what you all were drinking." She said noting their sporadic gawks at her hair. "And stop looking at my hair!" She yelled. "It's not on the menu."

"That's refreshing to hear." Detective Stokey stated sarcastically, turning his attention back to his menu.

"Can you uh, give us a minute please Ella?" Detective Abernathy stated politely.

"And get us some coffee over here." Detective Stokey said annoyed by her aggressiveness.

"Old men can be such douche bags?" She said talking to herself as she walked away. Detective Stokey's mouth flung open. He looked across the table at Detective Abernathy.

"Did she just say what I think she said?"

"I don't know man I didn't hear nothing."

"Do I look old to you Abernathy?" Detective Abernathy obscured his face behind his menu, uncomfortable with his partner's question.

"Old?" He briefly hesitated. "Mature . . . how about that?"

"What the hell is that supposed mean Abernathy, mature?"

"The Philly Cheesesteak looks good." Detective Abernathy said diverting from the subject of his partner's aging process. "I wonder how much trouble it would be for them to add a couple slices of Swiss cheese and a some black olives."

"On a Philly Cheesesteak?" Detective Stokey said frowning.

"How's things coming along with the Simms' case man?" Detective Abernathy asked from behind his menu. "You any closer to finding out who murdered of that baby?" He asked sitting his menu down on the table. "So you think adding black olives would be too much?"

"It's your sandwich Abernathy you put whatever the hell you want to put on it, just don't ask me to taste it." Detective Stokey stated. "To tell the truth I think I'm stuck—"

"In deciding on what you want to order?"

"What?"

"On second thought, I think I will add black olives for a little more favor—what you think?" He again picked up his menu

"Are you even listening to me Abernathy?" Detective Stokey asked reaching over slightly lowering the oversized menu looking at his partner.

"You said you didn't know what you wanted to order for lunch."

"I'm trying to talk to you about the Simms' case, and all you can think about is adding black olives to a Philly Cheesesteak?" He said agitated.

"I heard you man . . . you said you were stuck right?" Detective Abernathy asked paraphrasing his partner's words. Detective Stokey ended his gaze at his partner and again turned his attention back to his menu.

"The pull pork sandwich looks good."

"Yeah man that does sound good." Detective Abernathy said sitting his menu down. "Maybe I'll order that instead of the Philly Cheesesteak." He thought for a moment. "On second thought I think I'll stick with my original order and include the black olives and Swiss cheese."

"Dammit Abernathy!" Detective Stokey said, frustrated. "Will you make up your damn mind?" Detective Abernathy's eyes widened in response to his partner's unprovoked outburst. "We've been sitting here for the last thirty minutes and there's still no food on the table!"

"You say that like it's my fault man."

"Waitress!" Detective Stokey called out beckoning Ella with his hand. She returned to their table, a cynical look on her face.

"Just so you know we don't puree any of our food in here." Detective Stokey's looked over at Detective Abernathy.

"Did she just say what I think she said?" He asked offended by her insulting words.

"I think I'll have the Philly Cheesesteak platter." Detective Abernathy said electing not to get involved in his partner's dispute with Ella. "And my friend here will have the pull pork platter." Detective Stokey quickly intervened.

"And can you get that coffee over here ASAP, no cream just sugar."

"Uh waitress." Detective Abernathy stated politely.

"Ella."

"Ella, if it wouldn't be too much trouble for the cook can he add a couple slices of Swiss cheese and some black olives to that Philly Cheesesteak?"

"That's up to the cook." She said snatching the menu from his hands. "Will that be all?" Detective Stokey briefly stared at her, his menu in still in his hand. Ella snatched it from him then walked away.

"Douche bag." She said underneath her breath.

"Where do they find these people?" Detective Stokey said talking to himself. Detective Abernathy quietly chuckled.

"So what did old lady Koffee say when you talked to her?"

"She said Clarkston didn't do it, but I'm not convinced I agree with her." Detective Abernathy looked at him and shook his head.

"Stokey man, do you like your job?"

"What?"

"I asked you if you like your job."

"Of course I like my job Abernathy, what the hell kind of question is that, and what does that have to do with the Simms case?"

"If Charles Clarkston had a hint you were even considering him as a suspect in the death of his wife's baby, I guarantee you your days as a detective would be over!"

"Were you even listening to me Abernathy?"

"Yeah I was listening man, and it sounded like you said you were thinking about retiring before Charles Clarkston got your ass fired!"

"You couldn't have been listening if that's what you thought you heard Abernathy or you would've heard me say Mrs. Clarkston made the statement that she was pretty certain Clarkston murdered her—"

"Two black coffees." Ella said interrupting their intense conversation. Detective Abernathy shifted his eyes over at her then back to his partner hoping Ella hadn't heard his damming accusation. "No cream or sugar."

"No!" Detective Stokey yelled. "Dammit I asked for sugar no cream!"

"That's not what I heard grandpa." She said sitting two cups on the table filling them with black coffee then reaching inside the pocket of her apron and removing several packs of sugar dropping them rudely on the table. Detective Abernathy watched as Ella walked away before he continued speaking.

"So tell me Stokey, what do you think would be Charles Clarkston's motive for killing that baby?" Detective Stokey looked at him in disbelief believing the answer to be obvious.

"Are you kidding me Abernathy? Clarkston's wife gave birth to her lover's child making Clarkston look like fool of the month, now you tell me what man would take that lying—" He abruptly silenced when Ella again returned to the table holding two large food filled white plates.

"I have two sandwich platters." She stated. "A Philly Cheesesteak platter—" She placed it on the table in front of Detective Abernathy. "—and a pull pork platter." Detective Stokey visually examined the sandwich after she sat the plate on the table.

"What the hell is this?" He said raising his voice.

"Is something wrong sir?"

"Yes Ella there's something very wrong!" He yelled continuing to examine the sandwich. "This pull pork looks a hell of lot like a Philly Cheesesteak!" She humped her shoulders.

"Then that's probably what it is." Detective Stokey opened the sandwich and looked inside.

"And it's drowning in Swiss cheese and black olives all over the damn place!" Detective Abernathy watched without interference as he stuffed fries in his mouth. "So what the hell happened to the pull pork I ordered?"

"That's a Chef question." She said in a matter of fact tone. "And I don't answer Chef—questions."

"Then get his ass out here and I'll ask him myself!"
Detective Abernathy intervened

"Uh, thank you Ella." He said deflating the impending confrontation. She looked at him and smiled.

"You're welcome sir." She turned to Detective Stokey and rolled her eyes. "Douche bag." His mouth flung open, staring angrily at her as she walked away.

"Can you believe that?" He yelled looking at Detective Abernathy's sandwich. "Open that bun!"

"What?"

"I said open the damn bun!"

"For what man? It's a Philly Cheesesteak you know that!"

He looked at Detective Abernathy with demanding eyes.

"Oh never mind." Detective Stokey said picking up the sandwich biting into it.

"Look at you Stokey man—" Detective Abernathy said disturbed by his explosive behavior. "Do you hear yourself?"

"What are you talking about, there nothing wrong with me?"

"You're letting this thing with Thomas Lee Simms make you crazy man!"

"Okay maybe I have been a little edgy lately."

"You think!"

"It's just when I heard Mrs. Clarkston in Mildred's hospital room—" Detective Stokey said picking black olives off his sandwich.

"You're treading in dangerous waters Stokey . . . you start messing with Charles Clarkston's wife and he's gon destroy you man!"

"She didn't even know I was there—"

"How in the hell could she not?"

"I hid in the hallway."

"You did what?" Detective Abernathy said troubled by his partner's questionable actions.

"I hid in the hallway she didn't even know I was there."

"Look man—" Detective Abernathy watched in awe as Detective Stokey opened multiple packs of the sugar and dumped them in his coffee. "—I know how bad you want to prove Thomas Lee's innocence, but you losing perspective Stokey!"

"And you're overreacting Abernathy."

"I know you think you might be onto something but—"

"Think?" Detective Stokey said stirring his overly sweetened coffee with his finger.

"Look—" Detective Abernathy said taking a quick swallow of coffee. "Huh?"

"Turn around . . . it looks like your number one suspect just walked through the door." Detective Stokey turned and looked into the irate eyes of Charles Clarkston.

"Now what the hell would he be doing in a dive like this?"

"I can guarantee you man it ain't for the exceptional cuisine." Detective Abernathy said watching as Charles headed their way.

"Detective Stokey." Charles said as he approached the two detectives.

"Mr. Clarkston—" Detective Stokey said masking his worry. "—funny meeting you—" Charles cut him off.

"My wife tells me you had Mildred Koffee interrogate her." Detective Abernathy bit into his Philly Cheesesteak trying to distance himself from the conversation.

"Interrogate?" Detective Stokey said appearing clueless. "I can assure you Mr. Clarkston I have no idea what you're talking about." He shifted his eyes briefly to his partner then back to Charles. "If your wife did speak to Ms. Koffee I think anything said between the two women would've been without my influence."

"Do you like your job detective?" Charles asked in a threatening manner. Detective Stokey looked across the table at Detective Abernathy.

"You know Mr. Clarkston I believe you're the second person today to ask me that question." He said biting into his sandwich, nervously chewing then swallowing. "And I'll give you the exact same answer I gave that person . . . of course I like my job or I wouldn't be doing it."

"Then I strongly suggest you stop all this nonsense about proving Thomas Lee Simms' innocence." Charles stated shifting his eyes briefly to Detective Abernathy then back to Detective Stokey looking him in the eyes. "Now!"

"Do you believe in our criminal justice system Mr. Clarkston?"

"I most certainly do that's why I believe Thomas Lee Simms is just where he belongs in accordance to a jury of his peers who decided he received just punishment for the crime he committed." Charles again glanced over at Detective Abernathy. "If it were up to me I would've given him death."

"Well that jury got it wrong Mr. Clarkston." Detective Stokey said looking him boldly in the eyes. "And you and I both know that prosecutor didn't have enough evidence against Thomas Lee to convict him of jaywalking."

"As I recall detective as witness for the prosecution you were very instrumental in Thomas Lee Simms being convicted?"

"Well I was wrong."

"Were you, detective?"

"Yes, I was."

"This is my final warning Detective Stokey." Charles said, shifting his eyes to Detective Abernathy a second time then turning his attention to Detective Stokey. "If you and Mildred Koffee don't stay the hell away from my wife I'll simply have to ruin you detective." He said glancing quickly over to Detective Abernathy then again to Detective Stokey. "Then I'll see to it that Ms. Koffee's house mysteriously burns to the ground." Detective Stokey shifted his eyes to his partner then stood, bravely looking Charles in the eyes.

"Let me tell you one thing Clarkston." He said unafraid. "If you go anywhere near Mildred Koffee my career will be the last thing I'll being worried about." Charles shifted his eyes yet again to Detective Abernathy before addressing Detective Stokey's threat.

"You've been warned Detective Stokey."

"And so have you Mr. Clarkston." The two men momentarily looked one to the other.

"I think you should know I'm prepared to do whatever it takes to preserve the Clarkston's good name, detective." Charles said shifting his eyes to Detective Abernathy then again to Detective Stokey. "You should also know my vengeance knows no boundaries."

"Does that include murdering an innocent baby Mr. Clarkston?" Charles gave no reaction to Detective Stokey's accusatory question. He shifted his eyes to Detective Abernathy a final time then turned and walked away. Detective Abernathy watched as he exited the café then looked across the table at his partner as he again sat down.

"Stokey man I'm impressed!" He said smiling. "You got more bite than a pit bull with an extra set of teeth!" Detective Abernathy said chuckling. "I just hope you realize you just declared war with Charles Clarkston the third." Detective Stokey maintained his silence as he again bit into his sandwich.

Chapter Seventeen

Detective Stokey slowed when seeing the large white sign with black letters saying "C.W. Brookside Sanitarium" in front of the huge, white brick building He drove up the steep driveway taking note of the building's many windows displayed in rows, designed to distinguish one floor from the other. Following the sign instructing visitor's to park in the rear, he thought of Mildred's cautioning words to stay away from her granddaughter as he parked and got out of his car walking towards the building in search of a door that would allow him entrance inside. His eyes slightly widened when seeing a large Black male quickly approaching.

"May I help you sir?" He said looking at Detective Stokey with suspicion.

"I'm uh, my name is Detective Stokey and I was told I could find Raynetta—" The man interrupted.

"Raynetta?" A confused look displayed on his face. "Why would a detective want to see Raynetta?"

"I'm uh, trying to solve a murder—" The man's eyes widened.

"A Murder?" He stated loudly, surprised by Detective Stokey's statement. "Raynetta's been here for the last twenty years, what would she know about a murder?"

"It uh, involves a family member of hers." The man frowned, still perplexed by Detective Stokey's reason for being there.

"Family member?"

"Yes uh—" Detective Stokey looked in the direction of the building. "—is there someone here I can speak with?" The large man stared at him, hesitant to assist.

"That depends on what you want to talk about?"

"I was uh, wondering if it would be possible for me to speak to Raynetta?" A peculiar look appeared on the man's face.

"Raynetta don't talk."

"Huh?"

"Come with me." He said walking towards the building then entering through the second door of three. Detective Stokey followed as the man inside the building, walking up two flights of stairs then down a long corridor containing several rooms with closed doors. They stopped at the nurses' station where two middle aged nurses—one Black, one White removed medication from their medication carts, dumping pills into various small soufflé cups.

"Hey Virginia—" The Black nurse looked up from her cart.

"You need something Vincent?"

"This gentleman says he's a detective here to speak with Raynetta." The White nurse stopped and turned gazing briefly at Detective Stokey, but said nothing as she again resumed her duties.

"Call Dr. Steinberg." Nurse Virginia said continuing to fill white soufflé cups with colorful pills. "I think he's in the therapy room."

"Alright." Detective Stokey watched as Vincent walked over to the desk and picked up the phone pressing three buttons. The sound of an intercom echoed.

"Dr. Steinberg, could you come to Nurse's Station Two please?" He said before placing the receiver back on its base. Detective Stokey massaged his neck as he looked around at the starch white halls with closed wooden doors. His attention suddenly drew to a small, white-haired gentleman wearing wire rim glasses in the distance, quickly approaching.

"Did you need something Vincent?"

"Yeah Dr. Steinberg, this gentleman said he's a detective here to talk to Raynetta." Dr. Steinberg shifted his eyes to Detective Stokey then again to Vincent puzzled by the unscheduled visit.

"Thank you Vincent." He said turning to Detective Stokey extending his hand. They shook.

"Welcome to C.W. Brookside Sanitarium . . . now how may I help you uh—"

"Detective Stokey."

"How may I help you Detective Stokey?"

The two nurses watched from the corner of their eyes as they continued opening and closing drawers on their medication carts.

"I was hoping I could uh, speak with Raynetta." An odd look formed on Dr. Steinberg's face.

"Speak to Raynetta?" He shifted his eyes to Nurse Virginia. "Are you sure it's the same Raynetta you're inquiring about?"

"Is there a problem doctor?" Detective Stokey asked growing impatient. Dr. Steinberg shifted his eyes again to Nurse Virginia.

"Detective Stokey . . . Raynetta hasn't spoken since—" He again looked briefly over at Nurse Virginia. "—what I'm trying to say is she hasn't spoken with any level competency since she was admitted here some twenty years ago." He looked at Detective Stokey with mystery. "May I ask what this is in regards too?"

"Well Doctor, uh—"

"Steinberg."

"I'm uh, trying to solve a murder and uh, Raynetta may have some valuable information—"

"Raynetta?" Dr. Steinberg said puzzled. "A murder involving Raynetta?" He again shifted his eyes to Nurse Virginia. "Detective Stokey may I ask of your acquaintance with Raynetta?"

"I'm a good friend of Raynetta' grandmother—" Dr. Steinberg's eyes widened with curiosity.

"Her grandmother?"

"Yes, Mildred Koffee she's uh—"

"Mrs. Koffee sent you here?"

"She uh, told me all about Raynetta and her childhood—" Dr. Steinberg looked again to Nurse Virginia then again turned to Detective Stokey.

"A wonderful mother and grandmother Mrs. Koffee is." Dr. Steinberg stated. "After Raynetta's mother Josephine passed away, Mrs. Koffee stepped right in becoming actively involved in Raynetta's treatment."

"Is that so?"

"Mrs. Koffee is the only person Raynetta's spoken with any kind of coherence since she's been here . . . so I'm told."

"So Raynetta is capable of speaking?"

"When she chooses . . . so I'm told." Dr. Steinberg looked around for Vincent. "Vincent!" He called out when not seeing him.

"I'm in here Dr. Steinberg." He said appearing in the corridor after exiting from one of the closed doors at the far end of the hall. "You need something?"

"Could you please take Detective Stokey to Raynetta's room?"

"Alright."

"Well Detective Stokey I hope Raynetta's able to give you whatever information it is you're looking for." Dr. Steinberg said extending his hand.

"I uh, hope she can too." Detective Stokey said hopeful. The two men shook.

"Come with me detective." Vincent said. "Raynetta's on the seventh floor, you want to take the stairs or the elevator?"

"The seventh floor?" Detective Stokey looked at him, overwhelmed by the thought of walking several flights of stairs. "Why don't we uh, take the elevator Vincent?"

"That's fine." Doctor Steinberg watched from the Nurse's Station as Vincent escorted Detective Stokey down the hall.

"Virginia?"

"Yes, Dr. Steinberg?"

"Get me the phone number for Mrs. Koffee I'd like to know if she's aware Detective Stokey is here to see Raynetta."

. . . .

"It's this way." Vincent said turning down the hall to his right which seemingly mirrored the one they'd just left. Detective Stokey followed. "Here it is." He said retrieving the master key from his left pants pocket, unlocking and opening the door. "She's in there." Vincent said then walked away.

Detective Stokey poked his head inside seeing a twin size bed situated in the middle of the room covered with a colorful handmade quilt.

"Raynetta?" He said moving further inside the room. His eyes drew to the slightly disheveled, attractive Black female sitting in a wooden rocking chair, her legs covered with a lap blanket identical to the quilt. She silently rocked seemingly unaware of his presence.

"Raynetta." Detective Stokey said softly as he advanced further into the room. She slowly turned and looked at him.

"I didn't see you come in Mr. Jonathan."

"Uh, no Raynetta my name is Andy—" She disregarded his words.

"You keep messing with me Mr. Jonathan sooner or later Momma gon catch us." She said removing the cover from her legs. Detective Stokey eyes widened, stunned by her unexpected gesture. He quickly approached and recovered her.

"Uh, no Raynetta—"

"You better hurry Mr. Jonathan before Momma come looking for me."

"Raynetta?" Detective Stokey said astounded by her obvious relationship with Congressman Cutter. "Can you understand what I'm saying?"

"Yeah I can understand what you saying Mr. Jonathan." She giggled. "You won't me to lay down in the bed so we can act like we married." She again uncovered her legs.

"No, no Raynetta—" Detective Stokey said, quickly recovering her legs. He nervously massaged his neck, uncertain how to address her trained response. "Raynetta my name is Detective Stokey and I'm a friend of your grandmother—"

"Did Grandma tell you what they done with my baby Mr. Jonathan?" She looked Detective Stokey in the eyes. "If Grandma told you about my baby then she must've told you about me and Mr. Jonathan?" Raynetta stated slightly incoherent.

"Yes that's right Raynetta your grandma told me everything, that's why I'm here." He sat on the bed and faced her. "Your grandma told me all about what Mr. Jonathan did to you, but can you tell me what actually happened Raynetta?" She looked away and stared at the wall.

"Mr. Jonathan been messing with me Grandma—" She stated then paused. "—now I got his baby growing inside of me." Raynetta looked at Detective Stokey as if he were Jonathan Cutter. "Daddy can't stand looking at me no more Mr. Jonathan, just like I ain't his little girl no more." Tears rolled down Raynetta's cheeks. "Look at me like something no better than the slop he feed the hogs." Detective Stokey removed a handkerchief from his shirt pocket and began wiping her tears. She caught hold of his hand and held it to her face. "After Ms. Vera had done brought my baby in this world—" Detective Stokey interjected.

"Who's baby Raynetta?"

"Your baby Mr. Jonathan—our baby." A huge smile formed on her face. "But Daddy and Momma won't let me see her." Detective Stokey's eyes widened.

"Her Raynetta? Are you saying you gave birth to a little girl?" His asked eager.

"Can I tell you a secret Mr. Jonathan?" She asked looking Detective Stokey in the eyes.

"Uh, of course you can Raynetta."

"Momma and Daddy don't know it, but between me and God I gave our baby girl a name."

"And you know what Raynetta—" Detective Stokey swallowed as his mouth dried. "—I would love to hear what you named your baby girl." She looked away then slowly turned back and again gazed in his eyes, smiling with excitement.

"Tell me Raynetta . . . I'm listening tell me about your little girl."

"Ms. Vera took our baby girl from me Mr. Jonathan like I ain't had no rights to have her." Tears again emerged from Raynetta's cheeks. "It was my body she came out of so that makes her mines, don't it Mr. Jonathan?"

"It certainly does Raynetta." She looked mysteriously at Detective Stokey. "Do you know what Ms. Vera done with my baby girl?" Raynetta said as her mind drifted.

"Stay with me Raynetta . . . you said you gave your baby girl a name?"

"Yeah I gave my sweet baby girl a name." She again smiled. "I named our baby girl Angel because that's just what she looked like, a little angel." A surprised look showed on Detective Stokey's face in response to hearing that Raynetta had actually seen her baby.

"You saw your little girl Raynetta?"

"Yeah I saw that beautiful baby girl." A large smile stretched across Raynetta's face. "Daddy told Ms. Vera to take her away and never let me lay eyes on my baby girl." Raynetta suddenly giggled. "But Ms. Vera believed in her heart a woman's got every right to see the child she brought in this world."

"You know what Raynetta I agree with Ms. Vera." Detective Stokey choked up with emotions.

"When I laid eyes on that little girl she was White as snow." She said giggling. "Nobody would ever believe a Black woman could birth a baby so white!" She continued giggling. "But Ms. Vera assured me she was my mines alright." Raynetta's joy turned into sadness. "That was the last time I saw our little Angel, Mr. Jonathan." Tears ran down her face and she began weeping.

"It's okay Raynetta, I'm sure one day you'll see you're little Angel again." Detective Stokey said trying to console her.

Raynetta's Story

Mildred looked at her pregnant seventeen year old granddaughter as she prepared to tell her of the relationship she shared with Jonathan Cutter in response to Mildred's insistence and promise not to tell Josephine and Ray Arthur.

I was in the library dusting the bookshelves Grandma like Mr. Jonathan told me . . . it sure was a lot of them books so I knew I wouldn't be helping Momma in the kitchen that day. Then Mr. Jonathan came in the library and closed the door, I didn't think much of it because he always been nice to me, but all his niceness changed.

"How's the dusting coming along Raynetta?" Jonathan asked, quietly closing and locking the double doors to the library.

"These books got enough dust on them to stuff a pillow." Raynetta said giggling as she continued dusting. Jonathan gazed at her from behind then walked over and embraced her around the waist.

"What you doing Mr. Jonathan?" Raynetta asked trying to wiggle her way out of his firm hold.

"Your Momma bringing you here to work was like waving a raw steak in front of a hungry lion!" He said tightening his grip.

"Mr. Jonathan I ain't but seventeen and daddy want me to wait until I marry before I—" Jonathan said cunningly grinning.

"How'd you like to play a game of make believe Raynetta?" He asked kissing her softly on the neck. She cringed. "How about I pretend I'm a seventeen year old boy and you can pretend that you're my girlfriend." He said as he lowered her down on the gold colored davenport.

"I think Momma need my help making supper Mr. Jonathan." Raynetta said nervous.

"Josephine's been preparing the Cutter family's supper since before you were born, she'll be alright."

"Then I need to be finishing up with my dusting."

"If you weren't so pretty maybe I could ignore you—" Jonathan said as he again planted his lips on Raynetta's neck. "—but you just about the prettiest girl of color I've seen . . . and the testosterone in me just won't allow me to resist you." He chuckled then kissed Raynetta passionately on the lips. She trembled with fear.

"I don't want to play Mr. Jonathan."

"Of course you do Raynetta because if you don't the Cutter family just might not find your momma's cooking satisfactory anymore and have to let her go." He looked in Raynetta's innocent eyes. "Now you wouldn't want to be the 'cause of that happening would you?" She shook her head no. He smiled. "Good, and if it'll make you feel any better Raynetta why don't we pretend we're newlyweds on our honeymoon . . . that sounds alright to you?" He kissed her lightly on the lips. "Now doesn't that sound like a fun game to play?" She gave no reply as he prepared to take away her innocence.

. . . .

Jonathan momentarily gazed at Raynetta still lying on the davenport, her eyes filled with guilt.

"Go on now girl get up off of that couch." He said pulling up his pants, buckling his belt. "We don't want anybody coming in here seeing you lying there like that now would we?" Raynetta remain frozen in place. "We don't want anybody to think we're in here doing anything naughty now would we?" Jonathan chuckled as he fastened the last button on his starch white shirt and adjusted his tie. "Get up now Raynetta and pull that dress down—honeymoons over!" He cunningly grinned as he watched her pulled the black maid's uniform down from around her waist and got up. "That wasn't so bad now was it?" He asked, smirking. Raynetta maintained her silence as she held back her tears. "Now remember what I told you Raynetta . . . don't tell anybody about our honeymoon they just might not understand and I could get in a whole lot of trouble!" She looked at him with confused eyes. "You see Raynetta you and I are husband and wife now." Jonathan cleverly grinned. "So you may as well get use to performing your wifely duties, you understand me girl?" She nodded backing away as he tried to embrace her. He grinned. "I think I'll have you do some dusting upstairs in the master bedroom tomorrow since the first Mrs. Cutter will be spending the entire day out of town at a fundraiser." He pulled Raynetta in his arms and kissed her intimately on the lips before releasing his hold then watched as she walked over to the bookshelves and picked up the duster to resume dusting. "Now you go ahead on and get back to your dusting and remember—this is our little secret, alright?" She nodded. Jonathan unlocked the double doors looking back at Raynetta before leaving the room. Josephine entered minutes later. "You still in here dusting Netta?" Raynetta gave no reply. "Well you can finish that up later, Mr. Jonathan's having a big dinner party's tonight and we got a whole lot of prepping, cooking and serving to do."

"Okay Momma." Raynetta said keeping her back turned to avoid looking at her momma, embarrassed by *the honeymoon* she'd just shared with Jonathan Cutter. "I just got a few more places to dust then I'll be right there Momma."

"You hurry up now Netta, that dust ain't going nowhere I need you in the kitchen." Josephine stated. Raynetta watched from the corner of her eyes as her momma hurried from the room.

#

"Ahhhhhhhhhhhh!" Raynetta screamed out. "Ahhhhhhhhhhhh!" Detective Stokey looked around, uncertain what to do.

"Can uh, I need help in here!"

"Ahhhhhhhhhhhh!" Raynetta continued crying out. "Ahhhhhhhhhh!"

"Help!" Detective Stokey shouted. "Is anybody out there, I need help in here!" Vincent hurried in the room and activated the call light then turned to Detective Stokey.

"I think you better leave detective." He said noting Raynetta's decompensated state. Detective Stokey quickly stood. "When Raynetta gets like this the only things gon calm her down is medication."

"I didn't do anything—"

"Don't worry about it detective this ain't nothing new for Raynetta." Detective Stokey massaged his neck as he watched Vincent struggle to remove Raynetta from the rocking chair.

"Did you need something Vincent?" A voice asked through the intercom.

"Yeah . . . Raynetta need some medication she down here acting up again." Detective Stokey observed Vincent holding her down on the bed after finally getting her out of the chair. An oversized orderly entered in the room to assist.

"What happened to her?" He asked shifting his eyes to Detective Stokey.

"You need to leave sir!" Nurse Virginia said as she hurried in the room carrying a syringe. Detective Stokey momentarily watched then exited the room, accessing the elongated hallway. He cringed at the ear piercing screams coming from Raynetta's room as he walked away.

"Dammit!" He said thinking out loud, shaking his head with remorse as he thought about Mildred's warning to stay away from her granddaughter.

#

"Marietta!" Charles yelled as he entered the house and stood in the vestibule. "Marietta!" He again shouted.

"Now why in the hell he bringing his ass up in here hollering like his ass is ain't got good sense?" Carrie said as she and Marietta changed the linen on a bed in one of the guest rooms upstairs. "I bet you it's got something to do with Ms. Delores' drunk ass."

"Ain't no telling." Marietta said agitated. "I know he better stop yelling at me like I'm his child, I raised him."

"Marietta!" Charles yelled out third time.

"Something wrong Mr. Charles?" Roosevelt asked entering the vestibule from the servant quarters in response to Charles' continuous shouting.

"Where's Marietta?"

"She upstairs cleaning as she does every day, did you need something?"

"I want to know where in the hell she gets off taking my wife to see Mildred Koffee!"

"Mildred is Marietta's aunt." Roosevelt said covering for her. "She was going to visit Mildred in the hospital and Ms. Delores insisted on going with her!"

"I don't want my wife around people like—" Charles abruptly silenced when seeing the offended look on Roosevelt's face.

"People like who Mr. Charles . . . me, Marietta and Carrie?" Charles' face flushed with guilt.

"Roosevelt you know that's not what I meant—"

"You call me Mr. Charles?" Marietta said as she entered the kitchen from the back stairs.

"Would you go upstairs and check on my wife Roosevelt?" He said wanting to speak with Marietta alone.

"If you wanting to know if she's sober she is for now." Roosevelt said shifting his eyes to Marietta seeing her headed for the vestibule. "Right now she's asleep." A concerned look formed on Charles' face.

"Is she feeling okay?"

"Yeah she's fine just been doing a lot of crying most of the day." A puzzled look formed on Charles' face.

"Crying? Why on earth would she be crying?" Roosevelt shifted his eyes to Marietta.

"That's something you gon have to ask Ms. Delores yourself Mr. Charles." He said electing not to inform him that the tears his wife shed were in response to her imprisoned lover.

"That'll be all Roosevelt."

"Yes Sir Mr. Charles." Roosevelt glanced briefly at Marietta before heading up the stairs to check on Delores and to eavesdrop from the upstairs hallway with Carrie on whatever Charles prepared to discuss with Marietta.

"Did you want to speak to me about something Mr. Charles?" She asked. He watched and waited as Roosevelt seemingly disappeared at the top of the stairs before speaking.

"I wanted to speak to you about taking my wife out to that hospital to see that—" Charles hesitated not wanting to upset Marietta. "—your aunt."

"Is that what Ms. Delores told you?"

"She also told me she was asked a multitude of questions by that—" He stopped. "—your aunt." Marietta gave no reply. "I don't want my wife anywhere near Mildred Koffee!" Charles said raising his voice. "She's poison and I don't want Delores around her!" He looked Marietta in the eyes. "Do you understand me?" He shouted.

"I'm leaving Mr. Charles—"

"What?" He said bewildered by her unexpected words.

"I said I'm leaving—" Charles' mouth opened and his eyes abruptly widened.

"Uh, leaving?"

"Yeah, I'm taking my grandbabies and moving up north to Ohio with a friend. He stared at her loss for words. "But I'll be sure to find somebody to replace me before I leave, bring her over here and let you meet her." A vacant look appeared in Charles' eyes.

"What uh—"

"Roosevelt or Carrie might also know somebody who might be interested—"

"Can we uh . . . can we discuss this later Marietta?" Charles said bewildered. "I uh, need to go upstairs and check on my wife, make sure she's uh, alright."

"Here he come Roosevelt." Carrie whispered when hearing Charles' voice near the stairs. They scattered from the hallway where they'd been listening then dispersed to various parts of the house. Carrie entering one of the guest rooms as Roosevelt moved swiftly down the backstairs into the kitchen.

"Marietta." Roosevelt said whispering. She turned seeing him in the kitchen then headed towards him. "You know you scared the hell out of Mr. Charles telling him you were leaving." He said quietly laughing. "I could hear it in his voice all the way upstairs."

"I really have been thinking about leaving here Roosevelt." Marietta said walking over and opening the refrigerator preparing to begin supper. Roosevelt's amusing moment ended.

"You have?"

"I'm thinking it's got to be something better in this world for me and—" He cut her off.

"Marry me Marietta!" Her mouth abruptly opened. "I'll take you wherever you want to go." Roosevelt said waiting for an answer. "Woman don't act like you didn't know I been in love with you all these years!"

"Roosevelt I got four grandbabies I'm raising and I ain't got time for no man in my life." He took hold of her hand.

"That's all the more reason you need to marry me, let me help you raise them children, now that Thomas Lee's in prison." An apathetic look displayed on Marietta's face.

"I don't know Roosevelt—" He raised her hand to his lips and kissed it.

"Promise me you'll think about it before you say no." He again kissed her hand. "You ain't leaving here without me woman!" Marietta blushed.

#

"I swear Abernathy it was like something straight out of a horror movie! Detective Stokey said as the two men stood in break room at headquarters. "I tell you that place made the very blood in my veins curdle . . .

and now I'm starting to have flashbacks." Detective Abernathy laughed. "I'm serious Abernathy when I got home that night I snatched the white sheets right off my bed and took them outback and threw in the garbage!" Detective Abernathy continued laughing as his partner re-lived the horrifying experience at the sanitarium. "Well aren't you going to say anything Abernathy?"

"Yeah, serve your ass right for snooping where Mildred Koffee told you not to."

"What are you talking about Abernathy?" Detective Stokey said trying to justify his betrayal. "You know how this works you have to go where your lead take you."

"I guess you're right man but—" Detective Abernathy walked over to the vending machine and looked through the glass window. "—all I know is Mildred Koffee practically begged you to stay away from her granddaughter."

"What do mean begged?" Detective Stokey said massaging his neck. "What Mildred asked me was to not let an innocent man die in prison." He stated manipulating the truth.

"You tell that to her when she finds out you went up there interrogating her mentally deranged granddaughter." Detective Abernathy said searching his pockets for change.

"What do mean interrogating . . . I did no such thing!" Detective Stokey stated in his defense. "How much do you need?" He asked noting his partner's fruitless search for change.

"A dime and a quarter." Detective Stokey reached in his pocket and removed a handful of coins.

"Here take it all." He said dumping the loose change in his partner's opened hands. Detective Abernathy inserted two quarters and two dimes in the machine then pushed the button, watching through the glass as a Milky Way bar dropped down.

"I hate to tell you Stokey but I got a feeling all that help you been getting from old lady Koffee is over man, look like you just threw a monkey wrench in your own plan."

"Thanks a lot Abernathy."

"Hey, I'm just telling you like it is."

"You know something—" Detective Stokey said reminiscing on his visit with Raynetta. "—there was something Raynetta said that added the biggest piece to the puzzle I've gotten yet."

"Oh yeah—" Detective Abernathy said chomping away on the candy bar. "—and what was that?"

"She kept referring to me as Jonathan Cutter."

"Ain't no mystery there Stokey, her momma work for the Cutter's for years." He turned around and looked Detective Stokey in the eyes. "I did a little checking and found out Raynetta hadn't been too long started working there herself before—" He silenced when seeing the cynical look in his partner's eyes. "What?"

"You're standing there telling me you did some checking on a granddaughter you clearly stated didn't exist?"

"Hey, what can I say, I was curious."

Detective Stokey stare momentarily at him.

"Anyway, she spoke as if—"

"Who spoke?" Detective Abernathy asked shoving the last of the candy bar in his mouth. Detective Stokey looked at him with disciplining eyes.

"Raynetta—now stick with me Abernathy!"

"I'm listening go ahead."

"She spoke as if she and the congressman actually had some sort of intimate relationship." Detective Abernathy began choking on the candy bar. "You alright Abernathy?" He nodded then swallowed.

"Whoa . . . hold up Stokey man before you take that ball and run with it—"

"Not ball Abernathy, facts."

"Well before you start repeating those facts you damn well better make sure your facts ain't a figment of Raynetta imagination—and don't forget man she's in that sanitarium for a reason."

"And don't you forget Abernathy that's the exact same thing she told Mildred before she went into that sanitarium, and we both know having a baby is no figment of the imaginations."

"Do you even know why Raynetta was committed in the first place Stokey?" A perplexed look appeared in Detective Stokey's eyes.

"I wish I did." He stated subconsciously watching as Detective Abernathy walked over to the vending machine and again looked inside. "But get this Abernathy—"

"Get what?" He said merely responding to his partner's voice as his eyes fixated on the assortment of sweets.

"She said something about her baby being born white as snow."

"Man ain't that the exact thing Mildred told you?" Detective Abernathy said as he again inserted two quarters and two dimes in the vending machine pressing the button for a second Milky Way. Detective Stokey watched in awe as his partner fed his sugar addiction, still troubled by Raynetta's puzzling words.

"I don't want you take this the wrong way Abernathy, but you're a Black man right?" Detective Abernathy sarcastically clapped.

"Damn you good man—mystery solved and just think it only took you twenty years of working with me to figure that out." He said looking at his partner with cynical eyes.

"Very funny Abernathy."

"Now that you've figure that out maybe you can solve the mystery of where I lost five dollars last week, you think you can—"

"Do you really think it's possible for a Black woman to give birth to an all White baby Abernathy?"

"As opposed to what Stokey . . . a striped one?" Detective Abernathy said half heartedly laughing. "Newsflash Stokey not only is it possible, but Black woman have been doing it since the days of slavery." A clueless look displayed on Detective Stokey's face.

"Doing what?"

"Having White babies who pass themselves off as White people because they could." A bewildered look entered Detective Stokey's widened eyes.

"You're telling me that it's possible for a Black woman to give birth to a completely White baby?"

"You'd be surprised by how many White people are actually Black, but because they don't have any Black features they passed themselves off as White." Detective Stokey's eyes lit up and a huge smile formed on his face as he realized he'd found another major piece to the puzzle.

"Well I'll be damn!"

"What?" Detective Abernathy said biting nonstop into the candy bar.

"Raynetta's baby daughter fathered by Jonathan Cutter was born White and that's why her parents wouldn't let her keep the infant." Detective Abernathy looked at him with a less than surprised look on his face.

"Stokey man ain't that what Mildred told you?"

"Yeah, yeah . . . what can I say Abernathy, I didn't believe her." Detective Abernathy began choking on the candy bar when sensing something brewing in his partner's head.

"Whoa . . . hold on Stokey man, are you crazy!" He said raising his voice.

"What are talking about Abernathy I haven't said anything."

"But I know you man and first of all you have no proof Jonathan Cutter was the one who even impregnated Raynetta, and secondly if that accusation ever reached the ears of anybody other than me, your next job's gon be shoveling dog poop at a pound somewhere up north."

"Calm down Abernathy." Detective Stokey stated making light of the situation. "To answer your first question no I'm not crazy, you should know you've only been working with me for forever."

"And I'm still not convinced man." Detective Abernathy said as his eyes again drew to the candy bars inside the vending machine. "I know you believe Thomas Lee Simms is innocent and I have to admit I'm beginning to think you just might be on to something but—"

"What do mean but?"

"Man you dealing with some pretty hard hitters, Charles Clarkston and now Congressman Cutter?"

"If you expect me to sit back and watch an innocent man spend the rest of his life in prison for a crime he didn't commit because it might upset the Clarkston's and Cutter's of the world, well they don't frighten me!" Detective Abernathy turned and looked at him, offended by his emasculating words.

"What? You think I'm a coward Stokey?" He asked.

"You tell me Abernathy."

"Man I got a wife and four kids that count on me to bring home the bacon and keep a roof over their heads!" Detective Abernathy said raising his voice in anger. "Unlike you Stokey who only have yourself to worry about feeding and keeping a roof over your head . . . if people like Charles Clarkston and Jonathan Cutter come after me—" He looked his partner firmly in the eyes. "—it ain't just me who gets hurt!"

"Look Abernathy I never said you were a coward—"

"You didn't have to man, that look on your face said it all!"

"Then I apologize if that's how I made you feel."

"Right now Stokey I'm the only one that's on your side man—"

"And I appreciate that Abernathy and—"

"But it's not just your neck that's on the chopping block anymore it's mines!"

"How so?"

"Man did you see how Charles Clarkston looked at me at the restaurant?"

"As a matter of fact Abernathy I did."

"Man he looked at me the same way he you and I don't have a damn thing to do with any of this mess!"

"If you want me to leave you out Abernathy I will."

"It's a little late for that don't you think Stokey?"

"I hate to tell you Abernathy but that's not the worst of it."

"What the hell you mean that ain't the worst of it?" Detective Abernathy said shaking his head in agitation.

"I think Mildred knows who murdered that baby." Frowns quickly formed on Detective Abernathy's forehead.

"Hold on one damn minute!" He yelled looking at Detective Stokey with angry eyes. "You're telling me Mildred Koffee's been putting you . . . and me through all this hell risking your career, and she knows who killed that baby?"

"Yes Abernathy that's exactly what I'm telling you."

"That's it!" Detective Abernathy shouted. "I'm going out there right now and arrest her old ass!" Detective Stokey looked at him with questioning eyes.

"On what charge?"

"What you mean what charge man, she's withholding evidence!"

"Can you prove that Abernathy?"

"What you mean can I—" Detective Abernathy stopped and shook his head in anguish. "Damn!" He shouted.

"My sentiments exactly."

"Okay, so where do you go from here Stokey!" Detective Abernathy asked infuriated. "Because from where I'm standing all you have is a bunch of invisible pieces to an invisible puzzle that may or may not fit together in any shape or form way that will help you solve a damn thing and . . . somehow you've managed to sank me into the same damn hot water you drowning in!" Detective Stokey looked at him and massaged his neck, loss for words.

Chapter Eighteen

Detective Stokey again met with Marietta behind closed doors at the Night Owl Nightclub.

"I want to thank you Marietta for agreeing to meet with me again I uh know it's always a risk when you do."

"You didn't find what you needed when you went to go see Raynetta?" She asked wondering if providing him information on Raynetta's whereabouts had been a mistake.

"Were you aware that the man she named as the father of her child was Congressman Cutter?"

"We all knew it was Jonathan Cutter who got that poor child pregnant." Marietta said shaking her head with upset. "And everybody in his house knew it as well including Mrs. Cutter!" Detective Stokey's mouth slightly opened, stunned by the accusation.

"Are you sure about that Marietta?"

"Raynetta told Aunt Mildred it was a time when Mrs. Cutter walked in the room and seen what her husband was doing to that child and walked back out." Detective Stokey's mouth again opened.

"You're telling me Mrs. Cutter allowed—"

"Look to me the Cutter's felt Raynetta working for them meant she belonged to them mind, body and soul."

"Were you uh, aware she'd been forbidden to see her baby after giving birth, Marietta?"

"You don't understand Detective Stokey, how Raynetta got with that child wasn't right—"

"Of course I understand but—"

"Then you tell me why anybody would want Raynetta to see that child knowing Ray Arthur wasn't gon let her keep it?" He massaged his neck, surprised by Marietta's position on the situation considering she herself had children.

"You don't think Raynetta had a right to keep a baby she brought into this world?" Detective Stokey asked empathetically. "That was her little girl." Marietta's mouth flung opened, shocked his knowledge of the sex of Raynetta's baby.

"Girl . . . only people knew what Raynetta gave birth was the folks in the room when Raynetta birth that child and Ray Arthur and neither of them would ever breathe a word to Raynetta."

"That's where you're wrong Marietta." A look of curiosity appeared in her eyes as she waited for Detective Stokey to reveal his source. "Somebody who actually gave a damn about Raynetta's feelings allowed her to see the child she brought into this world."

"Ray Arthur would turn over in his grave if he knew that." She stated in disappointment. "To him that baby was never born."

"Well to Raynetta she was, despite how her father may have felt and she had the right to see her little Angel." Marietta's anger heightened.

"What devil would destroy that child's mind by showing her that child?"

"I wouldn't exactly call the person who allowed a mother to see her newborn infant—" She cut him off.

"How's all that gon help Thomas Lee Detective Stokey?" Marietta asked raising her voice.

"Right now Marietta I'm not exactly sure how it'll help, but I just somehow know that it will." Detective Stokey stated with confidence. "I hate to be the one to tell you this Marietta, but I'm also certain Thomas Lee being convicted of murder had more to do with his affair with Clarkston's wife than the evidence the prosecutor actually had against him." Marietta's eyes widened, disturbed by the allegation.

"What you mean it had more to do with Thomas Lee messing around with Ms. Delores?" Detective Stokey took a deep breath and massaged his neck.

"What I'm saying Marietta is Clarkston may have used his influence to guarantee Thomas Lee's conviction."

"Uh, uh naw . . . you wrong about that detective." Marietta said refusing to believe Charles would frame her son, even though she knew in her heart he had. "Mr. Charles wouldn't do that to me." She said searching for justification for Charles' actions. Him and Thomas Lee just about grew up as brothers."

"But they weren't brothers Marietta." Detective Stokey stated, looking at her with realistic eyes. "And even a brother is capable of revenge if the other brother takes his wife to bed."

"Naw—"Marietta shook her head in denial. "—Mr. Charles wouldn't hurt me like that."

"Think about it Marietta!"

"I am and I don't believe that for one minute!" She said becoming upset. "All while Mr. Charles was growing up I treated him no different than I did my own son." Marietta's eyes filled with tears.

"Marietta it was Charles who insisted Thomas Lee be arrested for the murder of Baby boy Doe." She abruptly stood and walked over to the door preparing to leave.

"Is that why you call me here detective?" She said opening the door. "If it is then you wasted your time and mines."

"Marietta, wait!" She stopped and again turned to him.

"Wait for what detective? For you to tell me the one man who knew how much I love my son had him locked up knowing he could be murdered in that place." Detective Stokey looked at her with compassion.

"I know that's not what you want to hear Marietta, but I wouldn't lie to you." Tears roll down her cheeks.

"If I find out Mr. Charles had anything to do with Thomas Lee being locked up for murdering that baby—"

"Let me handle it Marietta, please." Detective Stokey said knowing she was no match for Charles Clarkston.

"It ain't your boy sitting in that prison wondering how long he gon to live detective." Marietta stated through her weeping. He walked over and embraced her.

"I know you're hurt and upset Marietta, but you have to let me handle this my way . . . which means you can't discuss what was said here today with anyone!" He looked at her with pleading eyes. "You have to promise me you won't say anything to anyone." He gazed into her eyes. "Thomas Lee's life depends on it." Marietta nodded.

"You get my boy out of that prison detective!"

"That's what I'm trying to do Marietta and I know in some way Raynetta's baby will lead the way."

"How?" Marietta asked, unconvinced. "Do you know how long ago that's been?"

"Did you ever hear anything about what happened to Raynetta's daughter after Ms. Vera delivered her?" Marietta looked at him with guilt.

"I didn't tell you this before detective but—" His mouth slightly opened troubled by her withholding information.

"You've been keeping things from me Marietta?" He asked, shocked by her admission. "Am I the only one who gives a rat's ass about Thomas Lee's freedom?" An empty look displayed in his eyes. "I don't understand."

"It's only four people who know what happened to Raynetta's baby after Ms. Vera left that house with it—Ms. Vera and the people she gave that baby to, but—"

"But what Marietta?"

"There's one other person knows who Raynetta's baby is." Detective Stokey's eyes widened, eager to hear Marietta's disclosure.

"Who Marietta?"

"I was never told and I never asked until recently."

"Okay, what were you told?" He asked anxiously massaging his neck.

"Besides Ms. Vera—" Marietta looked in his inquiring eyes. "—Aunt Mildred." Detective Stokey's jaw dropped.

"Dammit Mildred!" He shouted. "Why in the hell are you keeping things from me?" He said thinking out loud as he looked at Marietta. "Why didn't she just tell me? I could've saved myself a lot of time and patience and—" Marietta cut him off.

"Aunt Mildred would take it to her grave before she'd tell you or anybody else."

"Does she realize me having information like that could very well free Thomas Lee?"

"You do best to stay away from Raynetta too." Marietta said. Detective Stokey momentarily stared at her. "Aunt Mildred would give her life for that child."

"I don't understand." He stated upset. "What is it about this granddaughter that Mildred's so protective of her?" Marietta hesitated before answering.

"It's been rumored that Aunt Mildred ain't Raynetta's grandmamma, she's her momma." Detective Stokey's jaw dropped. A shocked look appeared in his eyes.

"What the hell!"

"The midwife brought Raynetta in this world said it wasn't Josephine's womb she pulled that child from, but Aunt Mildred's."

"Are you saying—" Marietta continued speaking.

"Had her late in life and out of wedlock, ten years after Daniel passed."

"Who's Daniel?"

"Aunt Mildred's husband."

"I don't understand, why hide it?"

"Aunt Mildred's a proud woman detective—folks knowing she birthed a baby by a man that wasn't her husband would bring shame on her and that child." Detective Stokey looked at Marietta unable to speak as he tried to understand Mildred's way of thinking. "She had Josephine and Ray Arthur raised Raynetta as theirs." Marietta looked inside Detective Stokey's disorientated eyes. "But you ain't heard that from me." He nodded.

"Of course not."

"Aunt Mildred ain't gon be too happy when she find out you went to go see Raynetta."

"I uh, hadn't planned on telling her." He looked at Marietta. "You uh, weren't going to were you?"

"By now detective if she don't know she will." He nervously massaged his neck.

"You think she's uh—"

"The minute you walked through that door asking for Raynetta, I'm sure them folks couldn't wait to tell Aunt Mildred."

"Dammit!"

"And depending on how mad Aunt Mildred is . . . your mission to get Thomas Lee out of prison might have to be done without her help." Marietta began walking away. "Bye detective."

"Huh?" He said startled by her voice as his mind remained occupied with Mildred's possible response to his visit with Raynetta. "Uh, thank you Marietta."

#

Detective Stokey looked apprehensively through his windshield as he turned down the road headed to Mildred's house. He swallowed the lump forming in his throat when seeing her through the screened door watching as he pulled in her driveway and parked, an infuriated look evident on her face.

"Well here goes nothing." He said to himself as he began getting out of his car. He gazed into Mildred's angry eyes as he walked towards her home.

"You lost?" She yelled from inside the house.

"Mildred I—"

"I asked if you was lost?"

"Mildred I tried to warn you—"

"And I told you to stay away from my granddaughter!"

"I'm sorry Mildred but it was necessary that I follow—"

"Dr. Steinberg called me wanting to know why a detective would be there wanting to speak with Raynetta about a murder." Detective Stokey looked at Mildred, loss for words. "I told him I couldn't think of a reason why!"

"Mildred I know you didn't want me to talk to Raynetta but—"

"Told me how you upset my granddaughter so, it took two hours for them to calm her down!"

"Please try to understand Mildred you know I have to follow every lead—"

"No matter who gets hurt?" She shouted.

"It wasn't my intent to hurt Raynetta, Mildred!"

"Intent or not that's just what you done!"

"Will it help if I say I'm sorry?"

"Are you?" Mildred stated, enraged.

"You know I am Mildred, but when solving a case like this people are going to get hurt—"

"Get off my property Detective Stokey, you ain't welcome here!"

"Mildred please just listen to me—" His eyes suddenly widened and his mouth flung open when seeing her stumble out of the door tumbling onto the porch, collapsing second after she pushed open the door. "Mildred!" He shouted. "Mildred!" He hurried onto the porch and knelt down at her side. "Help! Somebody help!"

Chapter Nineteen

Detective Stokey entered through the front door of the Appetite Pleaser Café rattled by his altercation with Mildred and her medical emergency.

"Over here Stokey!" Detective Abernathy called out when seeing him. Detective Stokey walked to the rear of the restaurant, joining his partner at the table.

"What? You couldn't wait for me to get here Abernathy?" He said when seeing him drinking a cup of coffee.

"Man you said noon and it's now—" Detective Abernathy looked at his watch. "— twelve thirty and besides it's only a cup of coffee."

"So where's mine's?"

"You took so long getting here man I drank it!" Detective Stokey's mouth flung open.

"What the hell you do that for Abernathy?" He shouted.

"Whoa . . . what the hell's wrong with you man?" Detective Abernathy said in response to his angry outburst. "All that over a damn cup of coffee?" He noted the distressed look on his partner's face. "Man what's going on with you?"

"Mildred found out I went to the sanitarium to see her granddaughter." Detective Abernathy shook his head in response to his partner's bad move.

"I tried to tell you man didn't I?"

"Yeah Abernathy you did."

"Well maybe it'll cheer you up to know I already ordered your lunch." Detective Stokey's agitation again magnified.

"What the hell you do that for?" He said screaming out, drawing attention to himself and his partner. "How the hell do you even know what I wanted?"

"Don't worry about it man—" Detective Abernathy said trying to remain calm. "I ordered us both today's special."

"I know I'll regret asking, but what is today's special?" Detective Abernathy smiled.

"The meatloaf platter!" Detective Stokey scowled.

"Meatloaf?"

"Yeah, what's wrong with that? You like meatloaf don't you?"

"Why not, I probably won't eat it anyway." He said in no mood to argue.

"Look Stokey if you don't want the meatloaf I'll order you something else."

"Don't worry about it."

"Look man if you don't want the meatloaf there's plenty of other things on the menu you can have."

"I said it was okay Abernathy I'll eat the meatloaf."

"You sure man because—"

"Dammit Abernathy!" Detective Stokey yelled. "I said I'll take the damn meatloaf okay!" Detective Abernathy momentarily stared at him, troubled by his excessive irritability.

"What the hell's wrong with you Stokey man?"

"Just when I thought my day couldn't get any worse—"

"Look man I told you I'd order you something else if you don't want the damn meatloaf!"

"This isn't about meatloaf Abernathy."

"Then what the hell's bothering you man?"

"One meatloaf platter—" The blonde haired waitress said sitting the large plate filled with fries next to a huge meatloaf sandwich in front of Detective Stokey. "—and a ham and cheese platter on wheat." Detective Stokey jaw dropped.

"I thought you said you ordered today's special for the both of us!"

"I did man, but I changed my mind at the last minute and ordered myself the ham and cheese instead." Detective Abernathy shifted his eyes to his partner's sandwich as he picked up the sandwich and bit it. "If I were you Stokey man I wouldn't let that meatloaf get cold, it loses favor." Detective Stokey stared momentarily at the sandwich then picked it up and bit it.

"Next time I'll be sure to be I'm on time." He stated sarcastically, thinking out loud.

"Uh waitress—" Detective Abernathy said. "—can my friend here get a cup of coffee with lots of sugar."

"Sure . . . will there be anything else?" She asked before turning to leave.

"You can bring me another cup too."

"Two cups of coffee with lots of sugar?"

"No sugar for me." Detective Abernathy stated. "The sugar is for my friend." She looked at Detective Stokey with reprimanding eyes then walked away.

"Now what the hell's her problem?" He said taking another bite from the meatloaf sandwich. "Did you see how she looked at me?"

"What?" Detective Abernathy said shoving fries into his mouth. "I didn't see anything." Detective Stokey silently stared at him.

"What man I didn't."

"Two black coffees." The waitress said returning with two cups filled with coffee, sitting them on the table then dropping several packs of sugars next to Detective Stokey's cups. "Will there be anything else?"

"Yeah, keep the coffee coming sweetheart." Detective Stokey said biting into his sandwich.

"Sure no problem."

"Man I thought you said you didn't have an appetite!" He glanced briefly over at Detective Abernathy, but continued eating. "So what's new with the Simms' case man?"

"I'm still trying to understand why Raynetta's father wouldn't let her keep her own baby, simply because the baby was White!" Detective Abernathy swallowed then looked at him.

"You ever been Black before Stokey?"

"What the hell kind of question is that Abernathy? Do I look like I've ever been Black?"

"That's why you don't understand man."

"You're Black Abernathy . . . you didn't turn out so bad." Detective Stokey said again biting his sandwich. "Black or White what difference does it make? You're a detective just like I am."

"Well answer me this Stokey, how long did your people have to fight before they could even be considered equal enough to be in law enforcement?"

"Don't start that equal rights rhetoric with me."

"Rhetoric?" Detective Abernathy said raising his voice. "Maybe it's best we end this conversation while we're still on the same team."

"Yeah, maybe we should."

"I know you've come up against a lot of pressure since you decided to prove Thomas Lee Simms' innocence, but remember Stokey it was your choice to do it."

"So would you prefer I leave an innocent man in prison Abernathy?"

"Have you forgotten a jury of Thomas Lee's peers thought differently and found him guilty?"

"I don't give a damn what that jury found!" Detective Stokey said raising his voice. He looked in Detective Abernathy's heated eyes. "I uh, I'm sorry Abernathy I uh, guess this case is taking its toll on me."

"You think!"

"Can we just go ahead and call it a truce?" Detective Stokey ask humbly.

"You can call whatever you want Stokey, but you need to hurry up and solve this damn case man because this thing is making you crazy!"

"Crazy?"

"Yeah Crazy!"

"Every time I think I have all the pieces to this damn puzzle, something else comes along and changes the whole damn thing which makes a cloudy picture even cloudier!"

"Can I make a suggestion?" Detective Abernathy watched as his partner added multiple packs of sugar to his coffee then stirred it with his finger.

"Why not, it couldn't hurt, and besides if I say no you'll just give it anyway."

"Take a day off man, go someplace where it's peaceful like the library."

"A library?"

"Yeah what's wrong with the library?"

"The last time I went to a library I met my third ex-wife."

"Okay then don't go to the library—stay home, but take a day off so you can gather all the pieces to your puzzle accumulated thus far and write everything down on those puzzle pieces." Detective Stokey quietly chuckled.

"Are you serious Abernathy?"

"Very."

"Okay, then what?"

"Start arranging the pieces in some kind of order until they paint a picture clear enough for you to determine what's important and what's not."

"You know Abernathy you may be onto something." Detective Stokey said taking another bite out of the meatloaf sandwich. "That almost makes up for this meatloaf platter I have to pay for even though I didn't order it.

"Hey man—" Detective Abernathy looked over at him. "—can you spot me on this ham and cheese?" Detective Stokey's jaw dropped. "I left my wallet at the home this morning after giving the kids lunch money for school." A cynical look formed on Detective Stokey's face.

"For once Abernathy you think you could surprise me and pay for your own damn lunch?"

"Why would I want to do that?"

#

"Let's see." Detective Stokey said to himself as he sat tucked away in a corner at the public library examining the multiple pieces of papers containing information gathered from Mildred, Thomas Lee, the Clarkston's staff, Ms. Vera and Raynetta. Also on the table laid a notebook and ink pen.

"Raynetta—" Detective Stokey said to himself. "—Mildred's granddaughter or possibly her daughter who gave birth to a baby girl, possibly fathered by Congressman Cutter over twenty years ago." Detective Stokey placed the pieces of paper mid-center of the rectangular table. "The baby was given away but only *closed mouths* know to whom." He said picking up the pen and writing. "Who could this child have been given to and how does it fit into the puzzle?" He moved a puzzle piece highlighted with a question mark to the right of the main piece. "Ms. Vera, according to Mrs. Clarkston took the infant from the house." Detective Stokey massaged his neck. His eyes suddenly widened when he remembered Detective Abernathy's words regarding Blacks passing as Whites. "Could that be what's going on here?" He asked himself. "Is Raynetta's daughter passing herself off as White? Of course she is—" He said throwing his hands up when realizing he'd added a significant piece to the puzzle. "All I have to do now is figure out who she is." He again threw his hands up. "Stokey you idiot—" He said slightly raising his voice. "Ms. Vera can tell me who she gave that baby to." Detective Stokey jotted it down in his notebook. "Talk to Ms. Vera and ask her about Raynetta's baby." He again added another puzzle piece to the equation. "I now know Baby boy Doe is the love child of Mrs. Clarkston and maybe Phony Tony?" He said glancing quickly around the library. "Could he have murdered that baby out of fear of Clarkston?" He said thinking out loud. He suddenly noticed a middle aged White female looking at him with peculiarity. Detective Stokey smiled. "Damn busybody." He said underneath his breath then turned back to the puzzle pieces. "So the questions of the day is who and why?" He placed a question mark on a puzzle piece and moved it to the center. "This is what I do know . . . Mrs. Clarkston gave birth to a baby—a Black baby boy who was later found floating in the river." He said in a low voice. "I just need to know now who in the hell had motive to want to see that baby dead?" Detective Stokey massaged his neck. "Clarkston, could his wife really be Black living as a White woman, if so is he not aware of it? He asked himself. "But if he is then he knew there was a possibility of her giving birth to a Black child no matter who fathered it, but would he really deny his wife the right to keep his own child?" Detective Stokey again glanced over at the woman in the library when noticing her annoying gawk. He ignored her. "Could Mrs. Clarkston be capable of tossing her own child in the river after being told she couldn't keep him finding it easier to live with than giving him away?" He jotted his theory onto a puzzle piece then placed it left of the center piece. Detective Stokey tapped his ink pen on the table as he contemplated on his clues.

"Shhhhh! The Librarian said as she returned books to the shelves. He looked over at her and nodded then suddenly threw his hands up.

"That's it!" Detective Stokey said raising his voice.

"Shhhhh!" The Librarian cautioned. He shifted his eyes over at her seeing the disciplining look in her eyes. A huge smile formed on Detective Stokey's face. "So Mrs. Clarkston is Raynetta's baby girl Angel, fathered by Jonathan Cutter, I wonder now if the congressman was aware of that?" He again tapped his pin on the table.

"Shhhhh!" The Librarian said reprimanding him with her eyes.

"Congressman Cutter—" Detective Stokey said to himself. "—you just moved to the top of my suspect list." He wrote the congressman's name on a puzzle piece and placed it at the top of the others. "You may not have thrown that baby in the river congressman, but you sure as hell know what happened to him after he left Mrs. Clarkston's arms."

Detective Stokey massaged his neck as he stood outside of Mildred's hospital room trying to build up the nerves to go in. He peeped inside then entered when seeing her eyes closed. He walked over to her bed and looked down at her.

"You freed my nephew yet?" She asked startling him as her eyes popped open.

"Dammit Mildred you scared the hell out me!" She humorously smiled. "How are you Mildred?" Detective Stokey asked relieved to see her awake.

"As long as I'm above ground I can't complain." She said slightly weakened. "They tell me it was you who saved my life."

"You know Mildred I've heard it said that you have nine lives, and after this I'm not so sure you don't." He stated masking his worry behind a chuckle.

"My doctor thinks I may have had a light stroke, but what do he know he's just the doctor." Mildred said amused. Detective Stokey grinned.

"Mildred I'm sorry I shouldn't have . . . I got you all upset and uh, now look."

"This ain't had nothing to do with you Andy, it was me going back to my old way of eating and not taking my medication like—"

"Mildred!" Detective Stokey said scolding her with his eyes.

"Maybe it's time for me to start listening at what them doctors saying."

"You think Mildred!"

"Kissing that floor twice been lesson enough for me."

"I'm warning you Mildred, no more pig feet, pig tails or buttermilk you understand me?"

"You figured out who murdered that baby yet?" She asked diverting from the subject of her eliminating pork from her diet.

"I wish I could say I had Mildred, but I seem to be stuck again."

"Tell me where you stuck, maybe I can help."

"Where should I begin?" He asked rhetorically. "Well I now know Mrs. Clarkston—" He looked at Mildred. "—is your great granddaughter, she's the baby taken away from your granddaughter Raynetta twenty something years ago."

"You sure about that Andy?"

"Something I'm sure you already knew." Mildred's eyes slightly watered as she neither confirmed nor denied his assumption. "I need you to help me Mildred please!" Detective Stokey stated.

"What else you got?"

"The one thing I can't seem to figure out is if Mrs. Clarkston son was actually her husband's." Mildred cunningly grinned.

"You better than I thought you were."

"I'm afraid that's where my brilliance ends Mildred." She giggled. "If I'm figuring this out correctly that brings me right back to Clarkston as the murderer." A perplexed look formed on his face. "But I can't see even Clarkston murdering his own son when he could've simply given the child away."

"Keep going Andy . . . you'll figure it out."

"Mildred?" He took a deep breath then massaged his neck as he prepared to confront her. "Do you know who murdered Baby boy Doe?" She looked at him and smiled but gave no reply.

"Dammit Mildred!"

Chapter Twenty

"I see you took my advice huh, Stokey?" Detective Abernathy said when entering the squad room seeing the puzzle pieces neatly arranged on his partner's desk.

"Yes, and you know what?"

"What?"

"It turned out to be just what was needed."

"So you figured out who murdered Baby boy Doe?" Detective Abernathy asked impressed. A look of defeat displayed on his face.

"I wish I could say I had Abernathy but I'd be lying." Detective Abernathy examined the puzzle pieces seeing some with words and others with question marks and a few containing nothing at all.

"You missed a few."

"Huh?" Detective Stokey said merely responding to his partner's voice as he remained engrossed in the puzzle, trying to mentally put the pieces together.

"You forgot to include the pieces saying you'll be buying Detective Fish a steak dinner or he'll be buying one for you." Detective Abernathy said laughing.

"Oh it's definitely Fish who'll be buying me the steak dinner Abernathy!" Detective Fish peeked from around his computer monitor.

"Did I hear somebody mention my name in reference to a steak dinner?"

"Yeah that's right Fish . . . I was just telling Abernathy here how—"

"You're ready to throw in the towel and admit there's no mystery suspect and that the jury convicted the right man." Detective Fish said, cynical.

"Very funny Detective Fish."

"How's that coming along anyway Stokey?"

"Wouldn't you like to know Fish?"

"Since I haven't seen any new arrest on the six o'clock news—"

"You just keep watching Fish and be prepared to buy me that T-bone steak."

"Don't hold your breath Stokey." Detective Abernathy intervened.

"Oh and uh, Fish—" He said laughing. "—I recommend Dom Perignon if you need recommendations on a good champagne."

"Spoken like a truly devoted partner." Detective Fish stated sarcastically.

"If you don't mind Detective Fish, my partner and I have a murder to solve." Detective Abernathy said although unconvinced his partner would actually be the victor.

"And after you're finished beating that dead horse maybe you can find the remains of Jimmy Hoffa." Detective Fish said bursting into laughter as his face again disappeared behind the computer monitor.

"Very funny, Fish." Detective Stokey said. "That guy really makes my tailbone ache."

"Don't let him get to you Stokey."

"Too late."

"Given the fact you have all these little pieces of paper, I take it things are finally coming together." Detective Abernathy asked.

"Why don't you just have a seat Abernathy, I'd hate for my findings to knock you off your feet."

"That good huh?" Detective Abernathy seated himself in the chair next to his partner's desk.

"And Abernathy?"

"Yeah man."

"Can you hold your comments until after I've explain the entire puzzle?"

"Yeah man I can do that."

"Thanks you, now let's see—" Detective Stokey turned his focus to the puzzle pieces. "—Raynetta . . . she's the major piece to the puzzle."

"How you figure that man?" Detective Abernathy asked interrupting.

"Because she gave birth to a daughter fathered by Jonathan Cutter twenty something years ago which leads straight to the murder of Baby boy Doe." Detective Abernathy's eyes widened.

"You gon have to do better than that Stokey if you expect me to believe anything you just said is gon free Thomas Lee.

"It's already been determined that Baby boy Doe is the son of Mrs. Clarkston right—" Detective Abernathy again interrupted.

"Determined by who Stokey man, you?" He said looking at him with doubt. "Or are you going by something Clarkston's staff told you?"

"What do mean . . . the information I received from the Clarkston's staff is credible."

"So tell me Stokey, which one of the Clarkston's staff is brave enough to repeat what they told you in a courtroom and in front of Clarkston?"

"Are you sure you're on my side Abernathy or should you be joining forces with Detective Fish?"

"Man you gon have one hell of a time proving what you saying Stokey?"

"Say your right—even if the Clarkston's staff won't testify I still have the midwife who delivered Mrs. Clarkston's baby." A skeptical look appeared on Detective Abernathy's face.

"Stokey man, are you serious?" He said slightly raising his voice.

"Will you keep your voice down Abernathy?" Detective Stokey said looking around the squad room. "If I wanted everybody to know I would've just made an announcement."

"Do you really think that midwife's going to admit she delivered the love child of Charles Clarkston's high society wife?" Detective Abernathy shook his head in response to his partner's naivety. "Man you've lost your damn mind!"

"Hey Stokey!" Detective Fish called out. "I just saw Charles Clarkston go in Lieutenant Porter's office." He chuckled as Detectives Stokey and Abernathy looked in the direction of the lieutenant's office seeing Charles Clarkston standing inside. "I'm sure we can all guess why he's here." Detective Fish said continuing to chuckle.

"Damn!" Detective Stokey said hoping the lieutenant wouldn't order him to stop his investigation. "I wonder what the hell he's demanding this time." Lieutenant Porter's door suddenly opened.

"Detective Stokey—" He said looking him directly in the eyes. "—in my office!" Detective Stokey massaged his neck.

"Calm down Stokey man." Detective Abernathy said seeing the anger in his partner's eyes as he rose from his desk. "You're almost there man, just a few more pieces to the puzzle and Charles Clarkston's gon regret he ever tangled with Andrew W. Stokey." Detective Abernathy said masking his fear over his partner's future with law enforcement.

"If I were you Detective Abernathy I'd talk some sense into my partner before he finds himself looking for work as a security guard at the mall."

"You know what Detective Fish?" Detective Abernathy said fed up with his mockery.

"What's that Abernathy?"

"Man you talk too damn much, and one of these days I'm gon replace your teeth with my toes!" Detective Fish abruptly stood.

"I guess now would be as a good of time as any to for you to try it Abernathy!"

"Sounds good to me!" Detective Abernathy began walking towards him.

"Hey!" Another detective in the room shouted grabbing Detective Abernathy by the arm. "We're all on the same team here, remember?" Detective Fish and Abernathy glared angrily at each other. "Do you detectives understand?" He yelled.

"Yeah, I understand." Detective Fish said again sitting down.

"Abernathy!" The detective said still holding him.

"Yeah man, I understand." He shifted his eyes over at Detective Fish before walking away, getting on the elevator and leaving.

. . . .

"Mr. Clarkston." Detective Stokey said looking Charles in the eyes as he entered the lieutenant's office. "You're a long way from your country club aren't you Mr. Clarkston?" Lieutenant Porter's eyes quickly widened, in response to Detective Stokey's rudeness.

"Detective?" Lieutenant Porter said slightly nervous. "Let's not get cute." Detective Stokey glanced over at him then again turned to Charles.

"Is it possible we could talk somewhere in private detective?" Charles asked humbly." A stunned look displayed on Detective Stokey's face, surprised by Charles' meek demeanor.

"Did I just hear you say you wanted to talk—to me?"

"I guess I can see how—"

"If you've come here to threaten me again Mr. Clarkston we can end this conversation right here and now."

"No Detective Stokey . . . I'm not here to threaten you." Charles shifted his eyes to Lieutenant Porter then back to Detective Stokey." I actually came here to help you." Detective Stokey's mouth slightly opened, he shifted his eyes briefly to Lieutenant Porter suspicious of Charles's sudden change of heart.

"You want to help me?" He said glancing over at Lieutenant Porter who quickly intervened.

"The interrogation room is available if you don't mind going—"

"The interrogation room is fine lieutenant." Charles said.

"Then I guess we'll uh, go to the interrogation room." Detective Stokey said stepping back from the doorway allowing Charles to exit the office ahead of him. Detective Fish watched in awe as Detective Stokey escorted Charles from the lieutenant's office and in the direction of the interrogation room.

"Here we are Mr. Clarkston . . . our interrogation room is right through that door." Detective Stokey opened it and allowed Charles to enter.

"Is it alright if I have a seat?" Charles asked looking around the room. "Please do."

"I'm sure you're curious as hell as to why I'm here Detective Stokey."

"I guess I'd uh, be lying if I said I wasn't." He said being seated on the other side of the table. Charles looked into Detective Stokey's inquisitive eyes.

"What I'm about to tell you detective could have negative consequences for my wife therefore I'm warning you, if you even think about arresting her—"

"Arrest?" Detective Stokey's heart pounded in his ears as he awaited a confession. Are you telling me—"

"I haven't told you anything yet detective."

"Are you sure you don't want your attorney here before you uh—" Charles interjected.

"Trust me detective if I thought for one moment I needed my attorney he would've accompanied me here today."

"So uh, what is it you're here to confess Mr. Clarkston?"

"You will never approach my wife Detective Stokey!" Charles stated adamantly. "And if one day for some reason you feel the need to be a hero and think for one moment think I would allow you arrest my wife, I guarantee you it will be your last day in law enforcement." Detective Stokey swallowed the lump forming in his throat.

"Okay, point taken." Charles looked at the one way mirror.

"If there's anyone out there listening detective would you be kind enough to ask them to leave?" Detective Stokey stood and walked over to the door then opened it. He looked out seeing no one then closed the door and again joined Charles at the table.

"Well Mr. Clarkston it looks like we have complete privacy."

"Good, now where were we?"

"What exactly is it you want to confess on your wife's behalf Mr. Clarkston?" Charles hesitated before continuing.

"I understand you went to the sanitarium to see Raynetta."

"As a matter of fact I did but how did you—"

"Who do you think covers the cost of keeping her housed at the C.W. Brookside Sanitarium?"

"You uh—"

"So naturally when a detective showed up requesting to see her I was immediately informed." Detective Stokey resisted the urge to shout as he awaited the impending confession. "I don't know if you've figured it out yet detective, but my wife Delores is the illegitimate child of Raynetta and Congressman Cutter."

"Angel." Detective Stokey said thinking out loud.

"So you know—"

"You've uh, talked to Raynetta?"

"Of course . . . as a Clarkston its' imperative we're familiar with the lineage of our prospective spouses." Charles stated with arrogance. "When I found no birth record verifying that my mother-in-law had ever given birth to a child, a very discrete . . . and expensive I might add, private investigator was hired." Charles again shifted his eyes to the one way mirror. "After some convincing, my wife's parents admitted they'd received Delores from the Black midwife who'd delivered her." Detective Stokey briefly massaged his neck. "It would appear detective there are some men who have little to no control when it comes to their libidos." An embarrassing look appeared on Charles' face. "Unfortunately our distinguished Congressman Jonathan Cutter is numbered amongst them." Detective Stokey remained silent. "It would also appear that dreaded woman Mildred Koffee is my wife's grandmother."

"Is that so?" Detective Stokey said as if hearing it for the first time.

"Because of Delores' extremely fair color she's been able to live her life as a White woman and being given to a prominent White family as an infant, her lineage was never questioned."

"Does uh, Mrs. Clarkston know that she's uh—"

"Black?" Charles said completing his question. "Of course not detective and you're not going to tell her!"

"That's a hell of a confession Mr. Clarkston to say the least, are you uh sure you don't want your attorney present?"

"Like I stated before detective, arresting my wife is not an option do you understand?" Detective Stokey massaged his neck.

"So tell me this Mr. Clarkston, what makes you so sure your wife is responsible for what happened to her son?" Charles readjusted his composure before speaking.

"Detective Stokey I love Delores very much—" Charles said, again readjusting himself. "—do you mind if I stand?"

"Go right ahead."
He rose from his chair and began pacing.

"Because I'm greatly in-love with my, I fear losing her and that's the reason I never told her of her ethnic heritage." Charles said turning to Detective Stokey. "My wife is quite fragile and she'd never be able to handle something of that magnitude and that is exactly why she will never see a day in court or an arrest." Detective Stokey momentarily remained silent, challenged by Charles' threat.

"Since you uh, obviously believe it was your wife who disposed of her son Mr. Clarkston . . . why don't you tell me what happened and we'll take it from there?" Charles continued pacing.

"Delores and I had quarreled that evening after I informed her she couldn't keep that infant."

"That infant?" Detective Stokey said bothered by his description of his wife's newborn child.

"You do understand why that wasn't an option don't you detective?"

"From your perspective Mr. Clarkston I do, but go on."

"Delores was angry out of her mind she just couldn't seem to understand why she couldn't keep that infant, and I couldn't exactly tell her the true reason why now could I?" He looked into Detective Stokey's eyes trying to read his thoughts.

"Ahem!" Detective Stokey cleared his throat. "I guess I uh, must be uh, catching a cold."

"A cold?" Charles stared momentarily at him then continued. "I was downstairs in the library when I saw Delores hurrying down the stairs carrying that infant wrapped in a blanket, and before I could stop her she rushed out the house." He again joined Detective Stokey at the table. "And when she returned home—" Charles hesitated. "—she no longer had that infant with her." Detective Stokey slowly stood.

"Mr. Clarkston do you realize you're telling me that your wife murdered an innocent—" Charles cut him off.

"And she will never spend a day in jail for it."

"Surely you don't expect me to just look the other way?" Detective Stokey said raising his voice.

"As a matter of fact detective that's exactly what I expect you to do."

"You'll have to excuse me Mr. Clarkston if I don't see things your way, but there's an innocent man in prison praying that he's not beaten to death by another inmate because he's been labeled a baby killer!"

"Thomas Lee deserves whatever he gets." Charles stated without remorse. "He dishonored my wife detective."

"You'll have to excuse me again Mr. Clarkston, but during my investigation I learned Thomas Lee wasn't the only man that—"

"There was a time detective when men like Thomas Lee would've been hung for committing such an act." Detective Stokey massaged his neck, enraged by Charles' words.

"You and I both know your wife's son could've been fathered by any number of men and—"

"The child was mines detective."

Detective Stokey's jaw dropped.

"The child was—"

"Yes detective . . . my wife's child was mines." Charles stated with coldness.

"And you told her she couldn't keep him?" Detective Stokey walked swiftly over to the one way mirror and looked at it. He took a deep breath and massaged his neck before again turning to Charles.

"Of course she couldn't keep him detective—my wife and I are of elite standing—"

"You and your wife Mr. Clarkston are murderers!" Detective Stokey said infuriated. "How in the hell could you allow your wife to just toss your son in the river simply because he didn't fit into your socially elite standing?" Detective Stokey yelled.

"I didn't allow my wife to do anything detective." Charles said offended by the accusation. "Had I known she was going to commit such an act—" A disturbed look formed on Charles' face. "—I would've simply tried to talk her into having the midwife give that infant to a suitable Black family."

"If you'll excuse me once again Mr. Clarkston . . . given your wife's reputation, how in the hell can you be so sure her child was yours?"

"Because detective—" Charles looked him arrogantly in the eyes. "—when you have a wife as active as Delores, you learn to keep very close tabs on her, especially during her times of ovulation." Detective Stokey's eyes widened, shocked by Charles' astonishing admission.

"Are you telling me you kept track of your wife's infidelity?"

"That's right detective, therefore I know without doubt that child my wife gave birth to I fathered." A brief moment of sadness appeared on Charles' face. He briefly lowered his head.

"Tell me something Mr. Clarkston—"

"What's that detective?"

"If your son had been born White—"

"Would I have allowed my wife to keep it?" He said completing Detective Stokey's unspoken words. A vacant look appeared in Charles' eyes. "I guess that's a question that will never be answered detective." Detective Stokey looked at him with loathing.

"You know what I think Mr. Clarkston?"

"I don't particularly give a rat's ass what you think detective." Charles stated smugly.

"I think you murdered that baby because your elite wife was about to make you the laughing stock at your blue blood society!"

"Do you really think I would murder my own son detective?"

"I don't know Mr. Clarkston you tell me?"

"I've said all that needs to be said." Charles stated then stood, walking over to the door as he prepared to leave. "If you're so certain I murdered my son detective—" He looked Detective Stokey directly in the eyes. "—then arrest me."

"Why did you even come here Mr. Clarkston?"

"I felt I owed you that much and I wanted to prevent you from ruining a perfectly good career as a detective from simply mentioning my wife's name in connection with Baby boy Doe." Detective Stokey massaged his neck as his agitation increased.

"You know damn well you haven't provided me with anything that would result in arrest of your wife and you could easily deny ever saying it."

"I believe I've explained to you detective that arresting my wife is not an option." A cunning smile formed on Charles' face. "Good day Detective Stokey." Charles looked at the Detective Stokey and smirked then opened the door. Detective Stokey watched, feeling helpless as Charles walked away.

"Dammit!"

#

"I see you back detective!" Big Mo' the daytime bartender at the Night Owl Nightclub said from behind the bar. "How you doing man?" Detective Stokey adjusted his eyes from the bright sunlight outside to the dimly lit night club.

"I'm still out here fighting crime if that's what you mean Big Mo."

"I don't care what nobody else say man, I think you gon get Thomas Lee out of prison!"

"Thanks for the vote of confidence Big Mo."

"Vote of confidence my ass—" Big Mo laughed. "—hell, I got a hundred bucks riding on it!"

"Well Bid Mo, consider yourself already a winner." Detective Stokey said as he proceeded through the establishment on his way to the back room. He knocked twice on the closed door then entered seeing Marietta and Roosevelt seated inside.

"Thank you for agreeing to meet with again." He shifted his eyes to Roosevelt greeting him with a nod.

"On the phone detective you said you had some new information." Marietta said hopeful.

"Yes, a confession." Her eyes quickly met with Roosevelt's.

"A confession?" A curious look appeared on her face. Who?" Detective Stokey joined her at the table.

"Do either of you think Mrs. Clarkston was capable of murdering her son?" Roosevelt vehemently shook his head no.

"Not Ms. Delores, she wouldn't crush a grape let alone murder her own child!"

"Did Ms. Delores tell you she killed her son detective?" Marietta asked, distressed by the thought.

"It wasn't Mrs. Clarkston who confessed to murdering her—" Marietta interrupted.

"Then why are you asking us if she could've done it?"

"It seems we have ourselves a problem." Detective Stokey said electing not to inform them of Charles's damning statement against his wife.

"What kind of problem you talking about detective?" Roosevelt asked.

"If neither of you believe Mrs. Clarkston could've murdered her son then that leaves me at a standstill."

"On the phone you said something about needing to speak with Congressman Cutter?" Marietta said shifting her frantic eyes to Roosevelt. He intervened.

"Mr. Charles is having a dinner party tonight for the congressman."

"Is that so?" Detective Stokey stated.

"Yeah, that Ol' devil running for re-election and like always Mr. Charles is endorsing him." Roosevelt laughed. "But he's got a real heavy contender running against him this time."

"Gary Grey . . . so I've heard." Detective Stokey said contemplating on his next move. "I remember him from his days as a snot nose assistant district attorney."

"Seems Congressman Cutter's got his eyes set on a seat in the senate, and knowing him he'd do just about anything to win." Roosevelt said grinning.

"What you needing to see him for?" Marietta asked confused by the request.

"I have information concerning the congressman I'm certain he would prefer not be brought to the attention of his constituents."

"What's that got to do with Thomas Lee?"

"A lot Marietta." Detective Stokey stated feeling encouraged. "I figure the congressman's eagerness to win has no boundaries."

"What you got in mind detective?" A cunning smile displayed on Roosevelt's face.

"Given the information I've obtained Roosevelt, it looks like I've got Congressman Cutter by the cahoonas." Roosevelt laughed.

"I hope this ain't got nothing to do with Raynetta." Marietta said ill at ease. "You ain't got no proof and Jonathan Cutter would never admit to it!"

"I have something even better Marietta." She looked over at Roosevelt then turned back to Detective Stokey, unconvinced.

"In reading the transcripts from Thomas Lee's trial I'm convinced his attorney neglected to call people to the stand who could've provided him with solid alibis clean up to the time he found Baby boy Doe."

"And I was one of them." Roosevelt said. "I tried to tell Thomas Lee's attorney that he came by here that morning to visit with his momma, but his attorney said he had all the witnesses he needed, and that prosecutor sure wasn't trying to hear nothing I had to say."

"Visit?" Marietta chuckled. "Came by here asking for money to buy beer to drink while he was out there on that fishing bank."

"I didn't tell Marietta, but Thomas Lee hit me up for a few dollars too!" Roosevelt said laughing.

"Apparently somebody didn't want that jury to hear anything that might cast doubt on Thomas Lee's guilt." Detective Stokey stated.

"You do whatever you have to do detective, just let us know what you need us to do." Roosevelt said.

"Thank you Roosevelt."

"I don't know who told you what detective, but it ain't no way Ms. Delores murdered that baby." Marietta stated with certainty. Detective Stokey looked at Marietta, not persuaded. "Aunt Mildred's been asking about you want to know why you ain't been out there to see her." Detective Stokey reddened.

"I was kind of hoping to be able to take Thomas Lee with me the next time I went out there."

"Go see Aunt Mildred, detective." Marietta said smiling. "I'm tired of hearing her asking about you." Detective Stokey's eyes slightly moistened as he chuckled.

#

Charles mingled amongst his many distinguished guest in the drawing room—looking around sporadically wondering why his wife hadn't yet joined them.

"Marietta." He called out when seeing her enter the room carrying a tray of hors d'oeuvres. She sat the tray on a table then made her way through the crowd of thirty over to Charles noting the slight look of embarrassment and worry on his face.

"Did you need something Mr. Charles?"

"Yes . . . my wife!" He said speaking in a low voice. "We're an hour into this thing and she has yet to join us." Marietta's stomach bundled with nerves.

"Truth is Mr. Charles—" Congressman Cutter intervened positioning himself between Charles and Marietta prior to her telling Charles of Delores' drunken state." Have you took a look at the polls lately Charles?" Congressman Cutter asked. "They're showing Gary Grey's numbers closing in on mines by a narrow margin." He said displeased. "Now more than ever Charles we need to find some skeletons." The congressman said whispering. "If you know what I mean." He turned slightly shifting his eyes to Marietta then took hold of Charles' arm and led him away. "Nobody in politics is that squeaky clean, we've just gotta dig deep—find some mud on that scoundrel that'll prove him unworthy to replace me as congressman of this district."

"I assure you Jonathan we have looked under every rock, stone and boulder—" Congressman Cutter cut him off.

"That's totally unacceptable Charles . . . everybody has a skeleton or two in their closet!" Charles half-heartedly listened as his mind remained occupied on his wife's absence.

"It just may be Jonathan that Grey may be the one exception to the rule."

"Nonsense!" Congressman Cutter stated. "Well if he doesn't have any skeletons I think its damn well time we gave him a few."

Charles looked over at Marietta and subtly nodded, instructing her to go find his wife. His attention suddenly drew to Roosevelt in the vestibule beckoning him.

"If you'll excuse me Jonathan, I see my butler is in need of my attention."

"You hurry back now Charles, this is of the utmost importance."

"Of course it is Jonathan." Charles stated sarcastically as he pulled away from the congressman's grasping hand on his arm and walked away.

"Roosevelt—" Charles said approaching him. "—would you happen to know why my wife's absent from an event that could damage our reputation as true American patriots?" A puzzled looked showed in Roosevelt's eyes.

"Marietta didn't tell you?"

"Tell me what Roosevelt?" He noted the disturbed look on Roosevelt's face. "Why don't we discuss this in the kitchen?" Charles said as he and Roosevelt walked in the direction of the kitchen.

"Did Marietta tell you Mr. Charles that Ms. Delores upstairs drunk out of her mind?" Carrie said as he entered the kitchen. Roosevelt looked at her with chastising eyes.

"What Roosevelt, she is!"

"Why wasn't I informed of this earlier?" Charles asked turning to Marietta. Roosevelt quickly intervened.

"We been going upstairs all day trying to check on her Mr. Charles, but she wouldn't open the door."

"So where in the hell did she get alcohol from?" Charles asked, upset.

"I'm thinking Ms. Delores must've come down sometime through the night and got a couple bottles and took them back upstairs with her, because she ain't asked me to bring her a bottle all day!" Roosevelt stated.

"Damn!" Charles said angered. "I want a lock on the wine cellar first thing tomorrow, it that understood." Carrie shifted her eyes to Marietta, but held her piece.

"Now Mr. Charles we don't want you worrying about Ms. Delores." Marietta said seeing the distraught look on his face. "You just go on back in there with your guest and—"

"That's right Mr. Charles you go on—" Roosevelt stated. "—we'll take care of Ms. Delores like we always do." Charles looked in the sympathetic faces of his staff.

"Thank you all." He placed his hand on Roosevelt's shoulder. "I sometimes wonder what I would do without my staff." He stated humbly.

"So you just go ahead and give your apologies for Ms. Delores being under the weather and we'll just keep on serving these hors d'oeuvres." Marietta said chuckling as she placed Cajun crab stuffed, mushroom caps on the sterling silver serving tray as Charles walked away to rejoin his guests.

"Charles?" Mrs. Cutter said hurrying over when seeing him enter the room.

"Good evening Mrs. Cutter."

"Where's your wife this evening?"

"I'm so very sorry Mrs. Cutter but I'm afraid Delores is—"

"Right is here." Delores said slurring her words. Charles abruptly turned, looking at her in astonishment as she slightly staggered down the staircase.

"Darling I thought you were lying down?" He said hurrying over to her, shifting his eyes in the kitchen seeing Marietta and Carrie watching. He subtly motioned for their assistance.

"Excuse me Mr. Charles?"

He promptly turned seeing Roosevelt standing in the vestibule.

"Will you please excuse me Mrs. Cutter I see my butler beckoning me."

"Will your wife being joining us this evening?" She asked.

"I'm afraid Mrs. Clarkston is a little under the weather and really shouldn't have gotten out of the bed." He said grasping hold of Delores' arm, escorting her into the vestibule with him. "Roosevelt, could you please take my wife back upstairs to her room?"

"Yes Sir Mr. Charles." Roosevelt took hold of her arm. "And there's a Detective Stokey's at the door waiting to see you." An astounded look appeared on Charles's face.

"Detective Stokey?" He said uneasy by the unexpected visit. "Did he say what he wanted Roosevelt?"

"Just said he wanted to see you." Charles glanced over at the partly opened front door.

"In that case would you have Carrie take my wife back upstairs so you can show the detective in?" He glanced quickly to his guests in the drawing room. "You can escort the detective into the library Roosevelt."

"Alright Mr. Charles." Roosevelt turned to leave guiding Delores in the direction of the kitchen.

"And uh, Roosevelt—" He again turned. "—after you've escorted the detective to the library would you please notify me?"

"Alright Mr. Charles." Charles looked into Delores' reddened eyes and shook his head with disgust before rejoining his guests in the drawing room.

Chapter Twenty One

"What's up baby killer?" A man's voice yelled out waking Thomas Lee up as he lay sleeping in the infirmary. Thomas Lee's eyes widened with fear when seeing a guard standing over him. "You think we gon let that detective get your ass off from throwing that baby in the river?" The guard shouted drawing back his fist viciously hitting Thomas Lee in the mouth busting his lip.

"Ahhhhhhhhhh!" Blood quickly covered Thomas Lee's mouth. "Man you wrong I didn't kill that baby and Detective Stokey gon prove it!"

"Shut the hell up!" The guard shouted. "That could've been my son asshole . . . my niece or nephew!" He again drew back his fist, connecting with Thomas Lee's eye.

"Ahhhhhhhhhhhh!" The guard looked at him with rage in his eyes.

"What the hell's wrong with you anyway you sick bastard?" The guard forcefully swung missing Thomas Lee face, blocked by a pillow he held up. "You think that pillow's gon protect your sorry ass, huh baby killer?" He snatched the pillow from Thomas Lee's hand. "I ought to smother your ass!" He said looking at Thomas Lee with fury. "What kind of man would throw an innocent baby in the river?" The guard shouted, again raising his fist, preparing to strike.

"Man I told you I didn't kill that baby!" Thomas Lee yelled as the painful blow of the guard fist landed on his arms as he threw them up, blocking the intended blow aimed for his face.

"Put you arms down baby killer so I can knock your ass out!" The guard said trying to knock Thomas Lee's arms out of the way. "You damn coward, get out of the bed so I can stomp your ass to death!" He grabbed Thomas Lee's legs and began pulling.

"Man that was my son, why would I kill him?" Thomas Lee said trying to reason with him. The guard's eyes widened, infuriated.

"What!" He screamed. "You killed your own damn son!" He screamed then viciously dragged Thomas Lee from the bed and onto the floor kicking him.

"Ahhhhhhhhhhhhh!"

"Eugene!" A man said in a low voice. "Man I just got word the nurse is on her way back."

"You lucky baby killer I was just getting ready to stomp your ass to death!" The guard said giving Thomas Lee a final kick in the side before hurrying from the room."

Charles huddled in a corner with Congressman Cutter away from his esteemed guests.

"Now there's a whorehouse out there in the country Charles—" Congressman Cutter said cunningly smiling. "—or so I've been told."

"Told Jonathan?" Charles said skeptical of the congressman's hearsay account.

"What I need you to do is find somebody who can entice Gary Grey out there then take as many pictures as they possible—without his knowledge of course—" Charles' ears deafened to the congressman's unscrupulous plotting as he watched Roosevelt open the front door and Detective Stokey enter defiantly waiting in the vestibule.

"If you'll excuse me Jonathan, I see I have an unexpected guest requiring my attention."

"It damn well better not be that Gary Grey!" Congressman Cutter stated.

"Of course it isn't."

"You hurry back now Charles, I'd like to have these *arrangements* taken care of before I leave here this evening." Congressman Cutter said whispering.

"Of course you do Jonathan." Charles said on his way to meet with Detective Stokey.

"Good evening Mr. Clarkston."

"Detective?" Charles said looking at him, curious of his drop in visit. "Roosevelt would you please escort the detective into the library, I'll join him in a moment?"

"Alright Mr. Charles."

"Thank you Roosevelt."

"If you'll just follow me Detective Stokey." Charles watched with apprehension as Roosevelt escorted Detective Stokey into the library then looked in the kitchen, momentarily watching as Marietta guided his wife up the kitchen stairs. He took a deep breath then glanced briefly in the drawing room taking note of Congressman Cutter impatiently waiting then headed for the library to join Detective Stokey.

"What exactly can I do for you detective?" Charles asked masking his worry, unsure if Detective Stokey had come to make an attempt at arresting his wife.

"Actually Mr. Clarkston it's not you I came here to see."

"Oh?" Charles said surprised.

"I understand Congressman Cutter's a guest here tonight?"

"That right . . . are you a supporter of his?" Their attention suddenly drew to the opening door and Congressman Cutter entering, suspicious of Charles' mystery guest.

"So this is where you disappeared to Charles!"

"Good evening Congressman." Detective Stokey said delighted by his intrusion. Congressman Cutter looked at him with unfamiliarity then extended his hand.

"Am I speaking to a loyal supporter that's planning on re-electing me as congressman?" Detective Stokey gave no reply as he shook the congressman's hand. "And I'm sure you've heard by now that I plan on running for a seat in the senate in the very near future?"

"If you gentlemen will excuse me I really need to check on my wife." Charles stated.

"Now don't you go too far Charles, we still have business to discuss." Congressman Cutter said as Charles hurried from the room. Roosevelt followed.

"Now where were we?" He said resuming his conversation with Detective Stokey.

"We were just about to discuss Raynetta." Congressman Cutter's fake smile faded.

"Who did you say you were again?" He asked rattled by the mention of Raynetta's name.

"Stokey . . . Detective Andrew Stokey."

"I don't think I'm aware of who you're speaking of Detective Stokey." Congressman Cutter half-heartedly chuckled. "I meet so many people as congressman names simply escape me." He said masking his knowledge of Raynetta.

"I find that quite odd since Raynetta and her mother Josephine were both in your employment—"

"Oh, that's right!" Congressman Cutter said as if he'd forgotten. "But that was over twenty years ago!" He looked at Detective Stokey with suspicion. "What would be you're your interest in past employees of mines detective?"

"Well congressman I heard your relationship with Raynetta went beyond employment—"

"I'm warning you Detective Stokey—" He said beginning to sweat. "—if you value your career I suggest we end this conversation right here and now!" Detective Stokey grinned.

"Another threat to end my career. . . . how original." He said unmoved by the threat. "Only it's not my career in jeopardy congressman it's yours." Congressman Cutter's eyes widened.

"How so?"

"One word of what I know about your overactive libido with a young Black girl over twenty years ago . . . and you won't find one voter in this state that would elect you as town-crier let alone congressman." He looked at Detective Stokey with disdain.

"What is this all about detective—blackmail?" Detective Stokey glanced around the enormous room filled with shelves of books then turned back to the congressman.

"I'm not in the business of blackmail congressman."

"Then why in the hell are you in here bringing up something I may or may not have knowledge of?"

"How would you like your supporters to hear the story of a woman I recently visited at the C.W. Brookside Sanitarium and how when seeing me she mistakenly thought I was you?" Congressman Cutter's forehead glistened with sweat. "Oh, and did I mention that all while she continued calling me Mr. Jonathan for some reason she seemed to think I was there to seduce her and—"

"You watch your step boy!" Congressman Cutter said infuriated. "I'm a very powerful man and I can destroy you with a single phone call."

"I'll keep that in mind congressman—" Detective Stokey said undaunted. "—while I'm making my own phone call."

"Now you look here you bastard!" He said raising his voice. "If you think—" Roosevelt opened the door and entered the room.

"Did you need something congressman?" He asked. "I heard your voice and I wasn't sure if you were beckoning me or—"

"Uh no, I was just uh, talking to the detective here and uh—" Detective Stokey intervened.

"A nice cold glass of cola would taste really good right about now Roosevelt, if you don't mind."

"I'll get that right away for you detective." Roosevelt said, again turning to Congressman Cutter. "You sure I can't get you something congressman?"

"Uh no . . . I'll be rejoining my loyal supporters as soon as I'm done speaking with the detective here." He said shifting his eyes to Detective Stokey then again to Roosevelt watching as he exited the room.

"I'm not quite sure what it is you want Detective Stokey, but why don't you come by my office tomorrow where we can discuss this matter in private?"

"How about we step outside on the front porch congressman?" Congressman Cutter momentarily stared at him. "Will that be private enough for you?" Roosevelt entered the room carrying the cola just as Congressman Cutter opened the door to exit.

"Here's your cola Detective Stokey." He said handing him the bottled drink.

"Thank you Roosevelt." Congressman Cutter watched as Roosevelt walked away. "After you Congressman." Detective Stokey said. He briefly hesitated then departed from the room followed by Detective Stokey.

"Now just what the hell is this all about detective?" He asked growing impatient as they stepped out onto the porch.

"It's about you congressman and seventeen year old girl name Raynetta and how you took advantage of that young girl, getting her pregnant then—"

"Now you hold on just one damn minute detective!" He said enraged. "That's a hell of an accusation without evidence to substantiate what you're saying!"

"Evidence or not congressman . . . an accusation like that is one that would definitely cost you your re-election and your bid for the senate."

"So tell me Detective Stokey just who in the hell's been feeding you that pack of lies?"

"Raynetta." Congressman Cutter's eyes abruptly widened. He momentarily looked at Detective Stokey then burst into laughter.

"You've got to do better than that detective, Raynetta's mind is so far gone she's lucky to remember her heads attached to her neck let alone an allegation of something that occurred twenty three years ago!"

"Twenty three years ago?" Detective Stokey said confirming his statement. "Is that an admission congressman?"

"Admission to what detective?" He said smirking. "And did I hear you say there was a child I'm supposedly had impregnated this Raynetta person with? Well, where is she?"

"She?" Detective Stokey cunningly smiled. "I don't recall identifying the gender of Raynetta's child congressman do you?"

"I uh, I guess uh—" He stuttered. "—I see what you're doing detective, you're trying to trick me."

"Trick you?" Detective Stokey massaged his neck. "The only thing I'm trying to do is figure out how your indiscretion with Raynetta is linked to the murder of Baby boy Doe." Congressman Cutter's mouth flung open.

"Now you hold on another damn minute!" He shouted. "I had nothing to do with what happened to that baby . . . now what happened between me and Raynetta—" He abruptly stopped seeing the satisfactory smile on Detective Stokey face.

"So you do remember Raynetta."

"Now look here detective, I don't know what the Sam-hell you're trying to pull here, but my moments of weakness don't have a damn thing to do with that murdered baby!" Detective Stokey listened to the congressman's continuous slip-ups and wondered if he even knew Delores was his illegitimate daughter.

"Do you even know who your daughter is congressman?"

"I don't know nor do I care to know."

"Would it surprise you if I informed you that Baby boy Doe was your grandson?" Congressman Cutter burst into laughter.

"In case you hadn't heard Detective Stokey—Baby boy Doe was Black or in addition to you being stupid you're colorblind as well!"

"And in case you've forgotten congressman so is Raynetta."

"If you have a theory of some kind detective I suggest you come right out with it and stop wasting my valuable time."

"Not a theory congressman . . . a proven fact."

"Proven by whom?" Congressman Cutter laughed. "Oh, that's right by poor demented Raynetta."

"You know congressman life can sometimes have a way of righting its own wrongs."

"And just what the hell is that suppose to mean?"

"It means a simple DNA test could easily link you to Baby boy Doe." Congressman Cutter's jaw dropped.

"You wouldn't dare try and force me into taking a DNA test." He said offended. "My attorneys would chew you up like bubble gum and spit you out like tobacco chew."

"Well you know congressman there is one person who can prove you're that baby's grandpa."

"And who the hell might that be detective?"

"None other than your biggest supporter." He looked at Detective Stokey puzzled by his unclear words. "Did you know there are Black people who look as White as me and you congressman?"

"You have five seconds to say what it is you came here to say detective before I have Charles throw your ass off of his property!"

"Why don't you do that Congressman, but not before I introduce your loyal supporters to your illegitimate daughter."

"What the hell are you talking about detective?" Congressman Cutter swallowed the lump forming in his throat "Okay, suppose I do take your word that I have this daughter . . . where the hell is she?"

"How much do you know about Delores Clarkston, congressman?" A impressive smile formed on the congressman's face.

"I know she came from a fine upstanding and very wealthy family who happened to be very dear friends of mines."

"She's also the illegitimate daughter you fathered with Raynetta." Congressman Cutter's jaw dropped.

"What the hell did you just say?"

"Delores Clarkston's your daughter congressman."

"That has to be the biggest lie I've heard all year, and that says a lot given I'm a politician!" He looked at Detective Stokey with mistrust. "Who sent you here you bastard, that jackass Gary Grey? Well you can just tell him—"

"This is not political congressman."

"Then you tell me just what the hell is it detective and what exactly you're after?"

"To prove Thomas Lee Simms is not the murderer of Baby boy Doe." Congressman Cutter lightly chuckled.

"I do believe a jury of Mr. Simms' peers already decided that detective." He looked Detective Stokey firmly in the eyes. "Now what the hell is this really about?"

"Exactly what I said it was."

"Hell, even Gary Grey's not fool enough to try and undue the guilty verdict of a baby killer."

"Thomas Lee Simms is no baby congressman." Congressman Cutter cleverly grinned.

"You know why I've been congressman for the last eighteen years detective?"

"Why don't you tell me congressman?"

"Because I know how to play the game."

"Game?"

"Yes . . . I understand what keeps the voters voting and what would make them fry your ass!" He looked Detective Stokey firmly in the eyes. "And freeing a convicted baby killer would definitely spark a flame." Detective Stokey massaged his neck as he prepared to make his request.

"Look congressman, I'm only asking you to provide me with some vital information the prosecutor apparently didn't think was important enough to present to Thomas Lee's defense attorney or a jury of his peers."

"And why would you give a rat's ass about that Detective Stokey?" He looked at Detective Stokey with skepticism. "And what the hell's in this for you?"

"I promised a man I would prove his innocence before he's beaten to death for a crime he didn't commit."

"That's a hell of a promise to make to a man convicted of murdering an innocent baby."

"I wouldn't have made it congressman if I didn't believe in his innocence."

"Say I do you this little favor detective—" Congressman Cutter shifted his eyes towards the front door. "—this damn well better be the last time I ever hear about your unproven accusations of an illegitimate daughter, do I make myself clear?"

"Crystal."

"Why don't you stop by my office in a couple days and—"

"Why don't I be there first thing tomorrow morning?" Congressman Cutter slightly chuckled as he relented.

"Make that very early tomorrow morning detective, say before office hours."

"And if for some reason you're not there congressman, I would advise you not to watch the evening news." Congressman Cutter cunningly grinned.

"You really should think about getting into the game of politics Detective Stokey . . . I would deem you to be a very worthy opponent."

"I'll keep that in mind." Detective Stokey said impressed by the congressman's flattering words.

"And detective . . . after Thomas Lee Simms walks out of that prison I hope you remember who made that possible when casting your vote."

#

"Stokey man I would not want to be walking in your shoes right now." Detective Abernathy said as the two men sat in the rear of the Appetite Pleaser Café.

"Well for once Abernathy you and I are on the same page."

"How so?"

"Right now I don't even want to be walking in my shoes."

"Welcome to the Appetite Pleaser Café." The waitress said as she approached. Detective Stokey looked up seeing a fortyish, blue eyed waitress with brunette hair holding a pad and pen in her hand. "Our special today is fish and chips would you like to try it?" She asked with a strong southern drawl. An enormous smiled stretched across Detective Stokey's face.

"What kind of fish are we talking about uh—" He looked at her name tag. "—Bridgette."

"What difference do it make what kind of fish it is Stokey?" Detective Abernathy said from behind his menu unaware of his partner's attraction to the waitress. "You either want it or you don't!"

"It might not make a difference to you Abernathy but—"

"Cod." Bridgette stated. "And it's fresh today."
Detective Stokey flash a flirtatious smile.

"Go ahead let me get the fish and chip platter, I wouldn't want it to seem like I'm hard to please." He said smiling. Detective Abernathy lowered his menu in response to his partner's obvious flirting, silently looking at him. "

"What?" Detective Stokey said.

"What if it was whitefish Stokey, would you still have ordered it?"

"That depends."

"On what man?"

"Sir, are you ready to order?" Bridgette asked shifting her eyes briefly to Detective Stokey. He winked. She blushed then again turned to Detective Abernathy.

"Yeah . . . I guess I'll have the fish and chip platter too." He said picking both menus up from the table, handing them her.

"Will that be all gentlemen?" She asked scribbling their orders onto her pad.

"Can we get two black coffees, one with sugar no cream?" Detective Stokey asked flirting with his smile. Bridgette blushed.

"I'll bring your coffee right over gentlemen." Detective Abernathy watched, amused as his partner fixated his eyes on Bridgette as she walked away.

"I ain't gon say a word man."

"Good! Then maybe for once we can eat lunch without arguing."

"You never did tell me what was said between you and Clarkston when he showed up at the precinct or is that classified?" Detective Abernathy said humored.

"You know Abernathy I don't know if I want to tell you."

"Okay, then don't."

"I'd hate to jeopardize your career." Detective Stokey teased.

"And I would hate for you jeopardize my career, so I guess we we're on the same page with that too."

"Two coffees . . . one black, one with sugar?" Bridgett said placing two cups filled with coffee on the table. She looked at Detective Stokey and smiled then dropped several packs of sugar in front of him.

"Thank you Bridgette." He said eager to say her name.

"You're welcome sir."

"Andy . . . just uh, call me Andy." He said flirting. She blushed.

"I'll bring your lunch out as soon as it's ready Andy."

"Thank you Bridgette." He again watched as she walked away then turned to Detective Abernathy seeing him shaking his head and quietly chuckling.

"Man, give me a break!"

"What?"

"You know she ain't doing nothing but trying to get a big tip out of you."

"You don't know that Abernathy?" He said opening several packs of sugar and dumping its contents in his coffee. "How do you know she's not just interested in me?"

"Because you have a lousy track record with woman, that's how." Detective Stokey's mouth abruptly opened. "Trust me man it's the tip."

"Feeling a little jealous Abernathy because you're married—"

"Happily married man and I don't want you making me look desperate just because you are."

"Desperate!"

"You gon tell me what happened with Clarkston or what?"

"So after he provided me with enough information to slap the cuffs on Mrs. Clarkston, he warned me that if I even came near his wife he'd deny everything he told me."

"Wow . . . on second thought forget I asked."

"Two fish and chips platters." Bridgett said flirting with Detective Stokey as she sat his plate on the table, first. He looked over at Detective Abernathy and gloated.

"Thank you Bridgett." He said flattered. Detective Abernathy watched in disbelief as his partner conceded to Bridgette's flirting.

"You know Stokey I believe the last time I had fish and chips was when you and your wife Marilyn invited me and Regina over for dinner." Detective Stokey's jaw dropped as he quickly shifted his eyes to Bridgette. She flashed him an angry look as she sat Detective Abernathy's plate on the table.

"Jerk." She said walking away.

"What the hell you do that for Abernathy?" Detective Stokey asked stunned by his partner's unexpected action. "You know I've been divorced from Marilyn for ten years!"

"Like I said man—" Detective Abernathy picked up his fish sandwich and bit it. "—she's playing you for tips man."

"Well just maybe I liked being played for tips did you ever consider that?" Detective Abernathy humped his shoulders.

"Your money, if you want to give it away to some waitress playing you for tips that you." Detective Stokey glanced over at Bridgette waiting on other customers then looked down at his fish sandwich.

"You didn't finish telling me what you did after Charles Clarkston told you he'd deny everything?"

"Forget it." Detective Stokey mumbled.

"Come on Stokey man you know she was playing you for tips!"

"I don't want to talk about it."

"Okay man if it means that much to you then I tell you what—" Detective Abernathy said trying to appease his sulking partner. "How about I leave here before you Stokey that way you can explain to Bridgette that Marilyn's your ex-wife."

"Do you really think she's going to believe that Abernathy?"

"Why not, it's the truth."

"Yeah, but Bridgette doesn't know that."

"Well that don't work just look at it this way."

"And what way is that Abernathy?"

"It wasn't meant to be." Detective Stokey looked at him with cynical eyes, watching as he stuffed his mouth with fries.

Chapter Twenty Two

"How are you feeling today Mildred?" Detective Stokey asked as he got out of his car and began walking towards her house. He humorously smiled when thinking about his first time coming there. A huge smile formed on Mildred's face as she delighted in seeing him.

"I've been better and I've been worse, but as long as I'm still above ground I'm doing just fine." She giggled. "The fact you here this early in the morning tells me you getting close to solving the case." Detective Stokey looked at her with mystery as he stepped up on the porch.

"My instincts tell me Mildred that you've known all along who murdered Mrs. Clarkston's baby." She gave no reply. "You know if you're withholding evidence I can—"

"Arrest me, Andy?" Mildred giggled. "You think that's gon help you with finding the person who murdered that baby?" He took a deep breath and massaged his neck, frustrated by her subtle challenge.

"Truth is Mildred I've done all I can do and—"

"Have you Andy?" She said looking at him with uncertainty. "If you've done all you can then I guess Thomas Lee was wrong in putting his trust in you." Detective Stokey's aggravation heightened.

"Dammit Mildred!" He said raising his voice "Why can't you just tell me who in the hell murdered that baby and stop with all the nonsense?" Mildred gave no reaction to his outburst.

You're a good detective Andy and I know if you dig just a little deeper you'll figure it out." He looked at her with irate eyes.

"What is it Mildred . . . you want the credit for solving the murder of Baby boy Doe?" He said losing his temper. "Okay you can have it!" She giggled.

"Sometimes folks appreciate things a little more when they work a little harder to get it."

"Why are you doing this Mildred?"

"Instead of getting mad at me it would do you more good to look at the puzzle pieces you got and—" He cut her off.

"To hell with those damn puzzle pieces!" He shouted.

"That man bothering you Mildred?" A man from across the streets asked as he stepped out on his front porch. "You need me to come over there?" Detective Stokey swiftly turned to him.

"Take your ass back in that house and mind your own damn business before I come over there and arrest your ass for obstruction of justice!"

"I'm alright Bennie!" Mildred said amused. "He just blowing off a little steam, but he gon be alright." Detective Stokey momentarily stared at her then walked away.

"Goodbye Mildred."

"Let the evidence lead you Andy and not your beliefs or feelings." He abruptly stopped.

"I've done that and it led me to Clarkston and his wife!"

"Did it Andy?"

"If not the Clarkston's then who Mildred?" He asked, agitated. "But you keep telling me that I'm wrong even though I have confessions from both Clarkston's each accusing the other!"

"And ain't either one of them got guts enough to cut the head off a chicken." Mildred said laughing. "Follow the steps of the last person who seen that baby alive and I guarantee you gon find your killer." His agitation grew.

"But doesn't that again lead me back to Mrs. Clarkston?"

"Was Delores the last person to see that baby alive, Andy?" Mildred asked mysteriously.

"You're telling me she wasn't?" He looked at her with inquiry. "Clarkston said out of his own mouth she was." Detective Stokey said massaging his neck.

"I think Delores the only one can to tell you that." His eyes displayed further confusion. "I guess you wondering now how you gon talk to her without Charles' permission?" Mildred cunningly smiled.

"That uh, did kind of cross my mind, you have any ideas?"

"I'll let you know when and where you just be there." He looked at her and smiled.

"Are you sure you've never been a detective Mildred?" He said chuckling.

"I learned a long time ago Andy folks love to talk, especially when they got ears willing to listen." She giggled. "I've always been a listener."

#

"How are you holding up Thomas Lee?" Detective Stokey asked as he entered the infirmary seeing him sitting on the side of the bed eating breakfast.

"Besides having my ass kicked around like a football—" A look of alarm formed on Detective Stokey's face.

"Are you alright Thomas Lee?"

"I'm breathing ain't I?" He grimaced as he rubbed his sore ribs. "Man they talking about putting me back on the block." Thomas Lee's eyes filled with fear as he shook his head with hopelessness. "If they do that I'm a dead man walking."

"If it's any consolation Thomas Lee, I want you to know I'm doing everything I can to prove your innocence."

"It ain't that I don't appreciate it man, but that don't mean jack in here . . . these dudes think I killed that baby and that's all that matters." Thomas Lee picked at the food on his tray. "Once I'm back out there, I give it a day before I'm dead." Detective Stokey massaged his neck.

"Thomas Lee if you'll just—"

"Just what man!" He yelled. "Start numbering my days, because we both know it won't be long!"

"Thomas Lee just give me—"

"I ain't ready to die man!" He cried out. Detective Stokey looked at him with timid eyes, empathizing with his fear.

"I won't let that happen, Thomas Lee—"

"How you gon stop it man!" Thomas Lee shouted. "You ain't in here, so how in the hell you gon stop anything huh?"

"Give me two weeks and—"

Thomas Lee leaped up off the bed.

"Two weeks . . . hell naw!" He said frantic. "I got to get out of here now!" He said anxiously looking around. "That's what I'm gon do, I'm breaking out of here!"

"Thomas Lee—"

"Naw man, I ain't trying to hear a damn thing you got say I'm getting my ass out of here!"

"Try to calm down Thomas Lee I promise you you're not going to die in here."

"Man you can't promise me a damn thing, but I tell you what you can do—" Thomas Lee looked him firmly in the eyes. "—you can help me escape." Detective Stokey's eyes widened.

"Thomas Lee that's not the answer."

"It's gone be my answer!" He looked nervously around as he tried to figure out a way to escape. "So I guess I'm supposed to sit around and wait until one of them big ass guards come and shank my ass?"

"Thomas Lee just let me—"

"Man, get your ass out of here and leave me alone."

Detective Stokey looked at him loss for words and prepared to leave.

"Hey man—" Thomas Lee said looking at him with humble eyes. "Tell my momma I want to see her." Detective Stokey nodded then walked away.

#

Thomas Lee watched with moistened eyes as Marietta entered the visitor's room looking around at the numerous inmates and their guests—their lips seemingly moving continuously. He quickly wiped the tears forming in his eyes, believing this would be the last time he'd see his mother before being murdered by a fellow inmate or guard. Marietta held back her tears as she approached him being seated across the table from her only son, both displaying illegitimate smiles.

"Thanks for coming Momma."

"I never thought I'd see the day I'd be coming to see my son in a place like this." She said looking nervously around. "It would hurt your daddy's heart if he saw—" He cut her off.

"I ain't trying to hear nothing about Daddy, Momma!" Thomas Lee said raising his voice. "Where the hell he is at anyway Momma? Do you even know?" Marietta abruptly stood.

"This ain't about your daddy, Thomas Lee . . . it's about you!" He looked at her with apologetic eyes.

"I'm sorry Momma, sit down." Marietta hesitated then again sat. "How you been doing Momma? I know this ain't been easy, you waiting on them folks to call and tell you I been killed in this place." He reached over to touch her hand.

"No touching!" A guard shouted. Marietta quickly turned around, startled by the commanding voice.

"Can't even touch your own momma's hand." She said upset. "You still a human being!" Thomas Lee shook his head as he looked over at the guard.

"Not in here Momma, you just another one of society's throwaways and I ain't even that." He said discouraged. "To these folks I'm one of the worst monsters to ever walk through that gate and at anytime, anyone of these men would cut my throat just as soon as to look at me."

"Don't be talking like that Thomas Lee!" Marietta said frightened.

"That's why I sent word for you to come see me Momma."

"I didn't come here to hear that kind of talk, you hear me Thomas Lee?" Her eyes watered with tears.

"Hear what Momma that your only son gon die in here?" He looked her in the eyes. Marietta turned away as tears rolled down her cheeks. "Look at me Momma." He said as his own eyes watered. "This might be the last time you see me breathing Momma." She slowly turned and looked in her only son's tear filled eyes. "I want you to know one thing Momma—" He looked at her with sincerity. "—I didn't kill that baby."

"I know you didn't Thomas Lee, I didn't raise you to be no murderer."

"How did you raise me, Momma?" He asked looking at her with disrespect. Marietta quickly stood.

"I ain't getting ready to go through this with you again Thomas Lee." She stated in anger.

"Come on now Momma sit down let me get this off my chest while I'm still breathing." She looked around the room then eased back into her chair. "Why Momma?"

"Why what Thomas Lee?" She snapped.

"Why you let Daddy treat you like that?" He asked trying to hold back his anger. "That lowdown rascal would be gone for weeks at a time Momma then he would just walk back through that door smelling like another woman's perfume and you always took his trifling ass back!"

"Stop it Thomas Lee!" Marietta said weeping.

"What was it Momma, you was scared of living your life without him? Is that what it was Momma?" Thomas Lee asked without compassion. "Daddy wasn't no real man Momma, he was an imitation of one!" Tears flowed down Marietta's face, hurt by Thomas Lee's truthful words. "Yeah he looked like a man, smelled like a man and had all the things that make a man a man—" He looked at his mother as a fool. "—but he wasn't no real man . . . so why Momma?"

"Don't you talk about your daddy like that Thomas Lee!" Marietta said enraged. "Your daddy was a good man and he always put food on the table—" Thomas Lee cut her off.

"When Momma?" He said challenging her untruth. "When did Leroy ever put food on the damn table?" He said raising his voice. 'cause I never seen him so much as bring home a loaf of bread that you didn't pay for!" Marietta's weeping intensified.

"Is that why you wanted to see me Thomas Lee?"

"Naw Momma, that ain't why." He said feeling remorseful. "I wanted to see my momma before I left this world."

"You ain't going nowhere Thomas Lee 'cause I ain't ready for you to!" Marietta stated through her tears.

"It ain't your call Momma!" She stared briefly at him and again stood then hurried away. "I love you too Momma!" Thomas Lee said mad at himself for unleashing the bitterness he felt for his father out on her.

Chapter Twenty Three

Charles buried his face behind the morning newspaper as Marietta placed a breakfast of French toast, bacon and a vegetable omelet in front of him.

"Marietta?"

"Yes Mr. Charles?"

"If there's any way you can convince my wife to join me on a vacation to the south of France to visit with her parents I'd be eternally grateful."

"I don't know what you think I can do." She said masking her hurt from knowing of his involvement in Thomas Lee's conviction. "I'm sure Ms. Delores parents would love to see her." She said sitting a glass of orange juice on the table before returning to the kitchen to retrieve the coffee pot. She wondered if Charles taking Delores out of the country meant that perhaps she had murdered her baby. "What made you want to take Ms. Delores to go see her parents?" Marietta asked as she returned to the dining room with the coffee.

"My wife's been through a lot lately as you very well know." He lowered the newspaper, watching as she filled his cup. "I'm worried that if she continues on that path she'll—" He abruptly silenced; a blank stare entered his eyes.

"You alright Mr. Charles?"

"Just see what you can do." He said again obscuring his face behind the newspaper.

"Alright, but you know once Ms. Delores makes up her mind ain't no changing it." Marietta said forcing a slight chuckle.

"Yes, but she'll listen to you." Charles peeped from behind the newspaper when receiving no response. "Am I right?"

"I guess we'll find out."

"Please do what you can Marietta."

"Alright Mr. Charles I'll do my best."

"Thank you Marietta." Her eyes met with Carrie's as she returned to the kitchen.

"What the hell's he running from?" Carrie said whispering as she loaded dishes in the dishwasher. Marietta glanced in the dining room to ensure Charles' focus remained on the newspaper then turned to Carrie with moistened eyes.

"What's wrong Marietta?" Carrie asked surprised by her friend's tearfulness.

"If Mr. Charles leaves here with Ms. Delores, Thomas Lee ain't coming out of that prison alive." She said silently weeping.

"Girl you know Ms. Delores ain't going nowhere with Mr. Charles." Carrie said amused. "She don't like his ass enough to be traveling that far with him." Marietta quietly grinned through her tears.

"You alright Marietta?" Roosevelt asked as he entered the kitchen from the servant's quarters. "What's got you in tears this early in the morning?"

"Marietta!" Charles called out.

"Now what the hell he want?" Carrie said. "You want me to go see what he want Marietta?" She shook her head no then quickly wiped away her tears.

"Did you need something Mr. Charles?" Marietta asked returning to the dining room.

"Why don't you go ahead and pack my wife a bag." He said laying the newspapers on the table, picking up his fork beginning to eat. "I'd like to leave here no later than a week from today."

"Pack just one bag Mr. Charles?" Marietta asked shifting her eyes in the kitchen when sensing the gazing eyes of Carrie and Roosevelt. "You sure that's gon be enough?" Charles noted the uneasy look on her face.

"Is everything alright Marietta?"

"No Mr. Charles it ain't."

"Oh?" He said surprised. Marietta's tried to think of what to say, not wanting him to know of her discovery.

"Ms. Delores ain't been looking too well lately."

"She looked perfectly fine at supper last night." Charles said dismissing Marietta's concern.

"You know if I didn't know better I'd swear I heard her throwing up this morning."

"If you're thinking my wife might be pregnant—" Marietta discretely shifted her eyes in the kitchen seeing Carrie and Roosevelt's opened mouths. "—she's not."

"You sure Mr. Charles? You can't be too sure with a young woman like Ms.—"

"I had a vasectomy." Marietta's mouth slightly opened as she again glanced in the kitchen seeing the widened eyes of Carrie and Roosevelt.

"What you choose to do with your body Mr. Charles is your business, but since you was the one brought it up—"

"Good morning dear." Charles said as Delores entered the vestibule from the stairs wearing a purple silk nightgown and matching robe. Marietta shifted her eyes in the kitchen a third time seeing Carrie and Roosevelt quickly resuming their daily duties.

"Morning Ms. Delores . . . give me a few minutes and I'll get started on your breakfast."

"I'll just take a glass of orange juice this morning Marietta."

"You feeling alright Ms. Delores?" She asked looking at her with peculiarity. Charles intervened.

"Will wonders ever cease?" He stated sarcastically. "How refreshing to see my wife drinking anything that even resembles a normal breakfast." She flashed him a contemptuous look then turned her attention back to Marietta.

"Marietta . . . could you and Carrie please turn the bedroom nearest to my room into a nursery?" Marietta's mouth abruptly opened, shocked by Delores' unexpected request. Charles showed no reaction to his wife's hopeful words.

"You pregnant Ms. Delores?"

"Not yet Marietta, but the only way I'll join my husband in France is if he promises me that upon our return—" Delores cleverly smiled. "—we'll be returning as three. Charles slightly choked on the food in his mouth.

"You alright Mr. Charles?" Marietta asked.

"Delores dear I hardly think this is right time for us to be discussing our personal affairs." He shifted his eyes to Marietta then back to his wife. "Uh, Marietta would you please excuse us, I'm sure you have other duties to attend to before you begin preparing our evening's supper."

"You still want me to pack Ms. Delores a bag for y'all trip after I finish doing the laundry, cleaning rooms, prepping supper and—"

"Yes Marietta if it wouldn't be too much of a bother."

"How long you and Ms. Delores plan on being gone?"

"Marietta would you please bring me the glass of orange juice I requested?" Delores asked diverting from the subject of the trip. Marietta turned to leave. Charles gazed silently at his wife as he digested her impossible ultimatum.

"Roosevelt!" Charles called out. Roosevelt hurried from the butler's pantry where he'd been eavesdropping and entered the dining room through the kitchen to eliminate suspicion.

"Yes Mr. Charles?"

"Make sure my wife remains sober until I return home this evening." Charles said picking up the newspaper again obscuring his face.

"I'll try Mr. Charles . . . but you know how Ms. Delores can be when she—"

"Just do it!" Charles yelled. Marietta shifted her eyes to Roosevelt in response to Charles' unnecessary hostility.

"Did you remember I asked you to serve garlic stuffed roast beef for supper Marietta?" Charles asked from behind the newspaper. "Congressman Cutter and his wife Winifred will be joining us this evening."

"Got it already chilling in the refrigerator."

"Thank you Marietta." She walked away, returning to the kitchen to retrieved Delores' orange juice. Roosevelt followed. Carrie watched with widened eyes as they both entered.

"Whenever y'all ready to quit on his ass just let me know." She said whispering, angered by Charles' intolerable temperament.

#

"I got your message Marietta." Detective Stokey said entering the back room of the Night Owl Nightclub where she awaited. "You said it was urgent?"

"I thought you needed to know Mr. Charles planning on taking Ms. Delores out of the country." An alarmed look appeared on his face. He massaged his neck.

"Did he say why?"

"Claim he want to take Ms. Delores to go see her folks, but told me to pack only one bag . . . look to me he don't plan on coming back."

"Dammit!" Detective Stokey said raising his voice. "Is there any way you can stall him? I need a few more weeks before I can prove Thomas Lee's innocence!"

"You might have a lifetime with what Ms. Delores holding over his head." Marietta said lightly chuckling. An inquisitive look displayed in Detective Stokey's eyes.

"What's uh, she holding over him?"

"Said she want Mr. Charles to have her pregnant before they get back." Detective Stokey's anxiety heighted as he remembered Charles' statement, on he and his wife's societal standing.

"Is that so?"

"Only thing is Mr. Charles snuck and had his self fixed." Detective Stokey's eyes widened, stunned but somewhat delighted by Marietta's news.

"Fixed? As in vasectomy fixed? "

"That's what he said this morning before Ms. Delores walked in the room." Detective Stokey grinned.

"Then I guess he won't be able to make good on that promise now will he?" He stated with ambiguity. "Hopefully that'll delay his plans for little while, but I still need to find a way to meet with Mrs. Clarkston." He said thinking out loud.

"Aunt Mildred's gon be giving you a call with the place and time." A huge smile formed on Detective Stokey's face.

"I guess one day I'll figure out how a woman her age that barely leaves home and sits on her porch all day, with her phone inside the house can get so much accomplished." He quietly grinned. "You sure your Aunt Mildred's never been a detective?" They laughed.

#

Marietta's attention drew to the back door as Roosevelt entered the house followed by Delores after they'd spent the last few hours in the vegetable garden outback, picking tomatoes, peas and pulling carrots from underground.

"Mmmm! That smells delicious Marietta." Delores said sniffing. "What is it?"

"Garlic potato soup."

Delores' eyes light up.

"That's my favorite!"

"I know . . . and to go with that soup I made you a roast beef sandwich with Swiss cheese on a onion roll, and Carrie made you a watercress salad." Delores looked at the two women with childlike eyes.

"What are you two up too?" She said, curious. "It's not my birthday so—" She looked at Marietta. "—what's going on?"

"Why don't you go ahead and get washed up Ms. Delores so we can serve you your lunch?" Carrie said spooning soup into a bowl. Roosevelt looked at Marietta with inquisitive eyes, wondering what her and Carrie were up to as Delores washed her hands at the kitchen sink then entered in the dining room being seated at the table.

"Here you go Ms. Delores." Carrie said placing a cloth napkin across her lap as Marietta placed the bowl of the soup on the table.

"Roosevelt would you get me a bottle of wine to go with this delicious lunch?" Delores asked sipping soup from her spoon. He shifted his eyes to Marietta.

"Now you heard what Mr. Charles said this morning Ms. Delores!"

"Charles is my husband Roosevelt, not my father."

"Father or not Ms. Delores I been instructed not to give you any wine."

"Go ahead Roosevelt—" Marietta said. "—a little red wine with Ms. Delores' lunch ain't gon hurt none." His eyes widened with concern.

"Marietta you heard Mr. Charles, he said—" She cut him off.

"I'll get it." Marietta said on her way to the butler's pantry to retrieve the wine. Roosevelt hurried in behind her.

"You feeling alright Marietta?" He asked puzzled by her actions.

"I'm feeling just fine Roosevelt, why?" She asked taking a bottle of wine from the cupboard.

"Mr. Charles said he wanted Ms. Delores sober when he got back home from work." Roosevelt said, anxious. "You know once Ms. Delores starts drinking she ain't gon stop until she drunk!" Marietta handed him the bottle of wine.

"Here . . . go give it to her." His jaw dropped.

"You know I can't do that Marietta, if Mr. Charles said he don't want her—"

"Give it here." Marietta said removing the bottle from his hand. "I'll take it to her." He quickly caught hold of Marietta's arm, troubled by her behavior.

"What's going on Marietta?"

"Ain't nothing going on, why?"

"Ms. Delores been doing just fine, ain't had a drink all day, I don't understand why you want to mess that up!" Roosevelt said frustrated. Marietta popped the cork on the bottle then filled a long stem glass and handed it to him.

"Taste this."

"You know I don't drink Marietta."

"Taste it!"

"Now Marietta—" She put the glass up to Roosevelt's lips and watched as he took a sip.

"What you taste?"

"Red wine . . . maybe a little watered down." He took another sip.

"I thought you said you didn't drink?"

"Anymore, that's probably what I should've said." Marietta's mouth slightly opened, surprised by his subtle admission.

"After a few glasses of regular wine Ms. Delores ain't gon know the difference." Marietta handed him a bottle of regular red wine. "Take this in there and pour her a couple glasses then switch bottles." She looked into Roosevelt's worried eyes. "It ain't your job to keep Ms. Delores sober." Marietta stated with defiance. He looked at her with mystery.

"I guess I never knew you were so sneaky Marietta."

"Being married to an alcoholic can make you do things you never thought you'd do." She said as he removed the bottle from her hand cunningly smiling at her. "What?"

"You thought anymore about what I asked you?"

"What?" Marietta said trying to evade his question.

"You know what woman." Roosevelt leaned in and placed a light kiss on her lips. "I asked you to marry me . . . that's what!"

"Roosevelt!" Delores called out."

"Be there in a minute Ms. Delores." He said gazing in Marietta's eyes before applying another kiss to her lips. She blushed. "You may as well say yes because I ain't gon stop asking until you do." He placed a final kiss on her lips. She watched as he walked away carrying the bottle of wine then girlishly smiled.

#

"Man where you taking me?" Thomas Lee asked terrified as he followed a guard through the dimly lit tunnel located underneath the prison. The guard turned and faced him.

"Shut the hell up!" He glared briefly at Thomas Lee before continuing down the hall.

"If you gon kill me just go ahead and do it now!" Thomas Lee said raising his voice.

"Keep walking!" The guard shouted. Thomas Lee trailed the guard around a corner, stopping just outside a closed door. Thomas Lee swallowed the lump in his throat, watching as the guard unlocked and opened the door.

"Get your ass in there!" He yelled, pushing Thomas Lee inside the room containing a round table, two chairs and a small mattress on the floor. Thomas Lee fell on the floor and prepared himself for a brutal beating or death. "Get your ass up off that floor and sit down!" The guard yelled standing over him. Thomas Lee quickly got up and sat at the table. He watched with apprehension as the guard walked out and shut door.

"Yeah, they getting ready to kill my ass!" Thomas Lee said looking around the room. "I knew I should've escaped last night the minute the nurse turned her back." He said talking to himself. "It's gon kill my poor momma burying me . . . I hope they don't beat to where can't nobody recognize me." He said trembling. "I hope whatever they do it's quick, I don't want to be in pain for too long—" His eyes drew to the door when hearing it unlock. Thomas Lee's mouth dried as he awaited his tormentor or executor to enter.

"Tommy!" Delores said excited. His eyes widened as she rushed in and wrapped her arms around his neck. Thomas Lee quickly threw up his hands to avoid touching Delores as his eyes remain on the guard. "I've missed you so much Tommy!" She said passionately kissing him as he continued holding up his hand.

"I ain't touching her, she touching me!" He said—his eyes still focused on the guard as Delores placed his arms around her waist and romantically kissed him. "She kissing me man . . . make sure you tell that to the warden that, you see what she doing!" The guard momentarily watched, amused then closed and locked the door as Thomas Lee's again raised his hands.

"What you doing here Delores?" He asked terrified.

"Marietta told me you wanted to see me . . . you do want to see me don't you Tommy?" She again kissed him.

"Why would my momma say something like that knowing it could get me killed?" He said quivering with fear.

"So I called Papa in France—" Delores stated sounding like a spoiled brat. "—you know he'll do anything to please his little showpiece." She giggled. "So here I am Tommy!"

"Do Charles know you here?" He asked looking over at the door.

"Of course not silly." Delores said unsnapping his orange jumpsuit. Thomas Lee quickly caught hold of her hands removing them.

"What you doing Delores?" He said looking over at the closed door. "You trying to get me killed?"

"It's okay Tommy." She said continuing to unsnap his jumpsuit." He again took hold of her hands.

"Stop Delores!' Thomas Lee yelled. "What's this some kind of set up?" He asked as she tugged at the jumpsuit trying to take it off. "What is this, a dying man's rite of passage or something?"

"No silly." Delores said guiding his hands to the buttons on her button-down red dress. "Aren't you going to undress me Tommy? I'm wearing your favorite color!" She kissed him. "I know how much you love the color red."

"Why would they let me and you—"

"You don't want me Tommy?"

"You know damn well I do!" He said confused. "But I ain't getting ready to die for it." Delores giggled.

"You're not getting ready to die silly!" She said lying down on the mattress. "I've missed you so much Tommy." He watched as she completely undressed. "Well come on silly we don't have all day." Thomas Lee momentarily hesitated looking over at the door then joined her on the mattress where they engaged in intimacy.

#

"Hey Stokey you got a visitor man." Detective Abernathy said as he stepped off the elevator and headed towards the squad room.

"A visitor?" He said raffling through the multitude of papers scattered across his desk. "If it's not Mrs. Clarkston I don't want to see any—" He silenced when looking up and seeing Mildred.

"Good morning Mildred?" He said surprised to see her.

"I guess if Mohammad won't come to the mountain, the mountain gon have to come to him." She giggled. Detective Stokey shifted his eyes over to Detective Abernathy who humped his shoulders. "Is there somewhere we can talk?"

"The interrogations room's free Stokey." Detective Abernathy said opening a box of donuts over to his desk.

"Uh, is that going to be okay with you Mildred?"

"I guess it's a good a place as any as long as you don't try to arrest me." She said chuckling.

"Of course not Mildred." Detective Stokey said shifting his eyes to his partner, shaking his head when seeing him stuffing a powder donuts in his mouth. "If you'll follow me Mildred I'll take you to our interrogation room." Detective Fish watched in awe, curious of Mildred mysterious visit.

"It's good to see you here Mildred . . . out of your comfort zone." He teased as they entered the room.

"I come out when I have to."

"You've found a way for me to meet with Mrs. Clarkston yet?" He asked closing the door, eager to hear her answer.

"When is the last time you went to go see Thomas Lee?" She asked, smiling.

"My uh, last visit didn't' go so well, but I've been meaning to—" He stopped, seeing the tell-tale look on Mildred's face. "Are you serious?" She smiled. "Are you telling me she's at the prison with Thomas Lee right now?" Mildred's smile widened. "Just let me grab my jacket then we can go."

"You don't need me."

"You're not coming Mildred?"

"That ain't no place for an old woman to be." She giggled. "I led the horse to the water now it's up to you to drink." She stood.

"Thank you Mildred." Detective Stokey stated with gratitude. "You uh, need a ride home?"

"Don't worry about me you just get out to that prison before Delores leaves."

"I owe you big Mildred."

"I'm gon hold you to that Andy." She said watching as he rushed from the room on his way to the prison to question Delores Clarkston.

#

Thomas Lee fastened the last snap on his jumpsuit, watching as Delores buttoned her red dress. He wrapped his arms around her, they passionately kissed.

"They gon let you come back or is this it?' He asked placing multiple light kisses to her lips.

"Do you want me to come back Tommy?" A huge smile stretched across his face.

"Hell yeah I do!" He again kissed her. "Ain't no women in this place Delores, except the nurses."

"What about Dorothy Jean?"

"There you go again." Thomas Lee released her. "Why you always got to bring up Dorothy Jean?"

"Because she's your wife."

"I know that Delores!" He said raising his voice. "I didn't hear you say nothing about Dorothy Jean before you, laid down with me."

"I'm sorry Tommy I didn't mean to—" The door suddenly opened.

"Times up Simms!" The guard said. Thomas Lee ignored his forceful command as he again embraced Delores in his arms and applied a final kiss to her lips.

"You just make sure you come back, soon." He said smiling.

"Bye, Tommy." She watched as he walked over to the guard and exited the room.

"I'll be back to let you out as soon as I put him back in his cage."
The guard said flashing Delores a seductive smile before closing the door. She
sat down at the table and awaited the guard's return. She looked up when
seeing the door again open, a startled look displaying in her eyes as Detective
Stokey walked in.

"How are you Mrs. Clarkston?"

"Who are you?"

"My name is Detective Stokey."

"What do you want?" Delores asked uncertain of his intent.

"I guess the real question would be what are you doing here?"

"Well it's not what you think." She said getting up from the table.
Detective Stokey cunningly grinned.

"Of course it is Mrs. Clarkston."

"Wasn't that Thomas Lee I saw leaving here, with a smile on his face
the size of a hyena's?"

"Please don't tell Charles."

"Now that depends."

"On what detective?"

"Why don't you go ahead and take a seat Mrs. Clarkston." He said
masking his excitement, confident he'd have the case solved by the time he left
there. Delores looked at him with frightened eyes as she again sat down.

"What do you want Detective Stokey?"

"I just needed to ask you a few questions."

"Questions?" She said with apprehension. "What kind of questions?"

"About your son." Delores' anxiety increased.

"Why are you asking me about that? I didn't kill my baby if that's why
you're here." She looked at the closed door. "Where's that guard?" She
nervously stood. "I'm ready to leave now."

"I promise you Mrs. Clarkston this won't take long at all, please be
seated." Detective Stokey said joining her as she again sat. "You see Mrs.
Clarkston I believe you know who murdered your son."

"Well you're wrong detective!" She said agitated. "Do you think if I
knew who murdered my baby I would allow Tommy to be locked up in this
awful place?" Detective Stokey contemplated her question.

"You know Mrs. Clarkston, I don't believe you would." He observed
her nervous demeanor. "But you know what I do think—"

"And what's that Detective Stokey?"

"I think—" She cut him off.

"If you're thinking Charles murdered my son you're wrong." She
again stood. "Now if you don't mind I'd like to go."

"Please Mrs. Clarkston . . . I have a few more questions I'd like to
ask." She again sat. "Your husband said the last time he saw your son you were
fleeing from your home with him." Delores looked at him, surprised by

Charles' admission. She gave no reply. "When you left there that night Mrs. Clarkston where did you go?"

"I went to go and see Tommy." She said nervously looking over at the door. Detective Stokey's heart seemingly dropped into his stomach when hearing her damning words. "Are you saying you gave your son to Thomas Lee?"

"Yes—no, that's not what I'm saying detective." She said anxiously twirling her hair. "I went to go see Tommy to give him his son when Charles said I couldn't keep him—" Her eyes slowly watered. "—but when I arrived he wasn't there."

"So Mrs. Clarkston—" Detective Stokey said sympathetic to her tears. "—what did you do then?"

"I tried to give our son to Tommy's wife, Dorothy Jean—" A stunned look formed on his face.

"Dorothy Jean?"

"Yes, but she wanted nothing to do with me and Tommy's son." Detective Stokey massaged his neck as he listened to Delores account of what happened. "She called me and my son filthy names and told me to get him away from her home then she went back inside and slammed the door in my face."

"Was Thomas Lee aware you had left your son there at his home?" He asked realizing her story again moved Thomas Lee to the top of the suspect list.

"I don't know, but I just knew when Tommy came home and saw our beautiful son he'd make Dorothy Jean accept and love him just as he did." A knot formed in Detective Stokey throat as the finger continued pointing in the direction of Thomas Lee. "Now can I go Detective Stokey?" She asked looking at the clock hanging on the wall. "I really must get home before Charles returns home from work." Delores again stood. "He'll wonder where I—"

"Just one more question Mrs. Clarkston."

"One more and that's it!" She said becoming upset.

"Was there anybody else who may have seen you and your son at the Simms' home beside Dorothy Jean?" Delores thought for a moment.

"No—yes, there was a neighbor lady who saw the entire thing." She said hurrying over to the door. "May I go now detective?"

"Uh yes, just knock on the door."

"Guard!" Delores called out pounding on the door. Detective Stokey watched as she rushed from the room the minute the door opened. He processed the information she'd given him, his thoughts now turned to Dorothy Jean's neighbor Rita and what, if anything she might know.

"Okay ladies." He said to himself. "Which one of you, are going to tell me what happened to the baby after his momma left him there?" He massaged his neck. "If she left him there like she said she did."

Chapter Twenty Four

Dorothy Jean watched from her front porch as Detective Stokey pulled in her driveway and parked then got out and began walking towards her house.

"I thought I told you to stay away from here Detective Stokley?" She yelled.

"I just wanted you to know I'm narrowing in on suspects!"

"You done arrested Delores Clarkston and her rich husband yet?" She said shifting her eyes over at Rita seated on her front porch next door, watching. "I heard she was the last one to see that baby alive." Dorothy Jean stated again shifting her eyes to over to Rita. Detective Stokey's heart pounded in his chest when hearing her verify part of Delores' story.

"Is that so?"

"Yeah, that's so." She said as he continued walking towards her house. His eyes drew to Rita as she stood and began walking towards Dorothy Jean's house.

"You know Mrs. Simms there's not a whole lot of people who knew that."

"Everything alright Dorothy Jean?" Rita asked glaring at him.

"I don't know Rita—" She said with her eyes fixated on Detective Stokey. "—this detective here sounds like he might be trying to interrogate me without reading me my Miranda Rights. Detective Stokey again looked over at Rita.

"Is that what you think I'm doing Mrs. Simms because if you do you have the right to remain silent—" He said trying to read the blank gaze in her eyes. "—and if you think you need an attorney you have the right to one of those too."

"Say your peace detective then get off my property!"

"As I was saying—" Rita cut him off.

"You might want to wait for your attorney Dorothy Jean." She said looking at Detective Stokey with mistrust. "You know how police around here got a way of putting words in your mouth you never spoke."

"Well now Ms.—"

"Johnson . . . my name is Rita Johnson and you can quote me on that."

"Well Ms. Johnson if I decide to consider Mrs. Simms as a viable suspect I'll be certain to read her Miranda Rights, and at that time if she request an attorney I won't ask her another question until she has one."

"Well in case you didn't know it Detective Stokey . . . Dorothy Jean works for an attorney and I'm sure he won't have no problem representing her."

"I have no problem with that Ms. Johnson."

"Coming out here intimidating good Black folks." Rita said gawking at him as she joined Dorothy Jean on the porch.

"As I was saying—" Detective Stokey proceeded. "—there were only a few people who knew Mrs. Clarkston was the last person to be seen with her son alive, so you want to tell me how you knew?" He asked shifting his eyes to Rita then back to Dorothy Jean. "Did you see Mrs. Clarkston the night before her son was found floating in the river Mrs. Simms?"

"Get off my property Detective Stokley!" She shouted taunting him my mispronouncing his name. "Unless you arresting me—"

"Arrest you Mrs. Simms?" He stated. "I never made any such claim."

"In case you hard of hearing detective I'll tell you again." Dorothy Jean looked at him with maliciousness. "Get your ass off my property before I—"

"Good day Mrs. Simms." Detective Stokey said shifting his eyes over at the growling, barking dogs as he walked away. "If you have information that can help prove your husband's innocence Mrs. Simms I don't understand why you wouldn't want to provide it!"

"Goodbye Detective Stokley!" Dorothy Jean yelled.

"Oh, and Mrs. Simms . . . I thought you might like to know that for some reason your husband's being allow to have conjugal visits." Detective Stokey said opening his car door. "I saw him right after he'd had his first visit yesterday." He said hesitating before getting in his car. "That was a hell of a smile he had on his face . . . must be nice, a man being allowed to have those kinds of visits with his wife." He said starting his engine. "But if it wasn't you that left a smile like that on your husband's face—" He looked at her. "—then I guess we both know who did." Dorothy Jean shifted her eyes to Rita then back to Detective Stokey, watching with fury as he backed out of her driveway onto the dirt road and drove away.

\#

A large lump formed in Thomas Lee's throat as he saw the infuriated look on Dorothy Jean's face as she walked pass the guard, headed towards him in the visitor's room. His stomach filled with butterflies as he wondered if she'd somehow heard about Delores' recent visit.

"How you doing Dorothy Jean?" He said attempting to mask his fear as she sat across the table from him. He looked in her eyes trying to read her thoughts as she maintained her silence. "You uh—" He nervously swallowed the lump in his throat.

"That Detective was at the house yesterday." Thomas Lee's fright magnified, beams of sweat covered his forehead, certain Dorothy Jean had learned of Delores' visit. "He must be out of his damn mind coming to my house asking me questions!"

"What uh, kind of questions he was asking you Dorothy Jean?"

"Sounded almost like he was accusing me of murdering Delores' baby!"

"What?" Thomas Lee said using the collar of his jumpsuit to wipe the sweat from his forehead, seeing the enraged look in Dorothy Jean's eyes. He swallowed the second lump he felt forming in his throat. "What the hell he bothering you for?"

"These folks allowing you to have special visits Thomas Lee?" Dorothy Jean asked out of the blue. His stomach bundled with nerves as he searched for an answer other than the truth.

"What you talking about Dorothy Jean?" Thomas Lee said trying to mask his guilt. "Why you asking me something like that?"

"Detective Stokey went out of his way to let me know Delores been coming out here to see you." Thomas Lee's eyes widened.

"He lying Dorothy Jean!" He said raising his voice.

"Keep it down!" A guard yelled. Thomas Lee looked swiftly over at him then turned back to Dorothy Jean.

"I ain't seen Delores since they locked me up!" He said upset by her apparent knowledge of his conjugal visits, concerned they might end. "I'm in here fighting for my life and you come out here with some mess—talking about Delores coming up here to see me!" Dorothy Jean looked at him, uncertain what to believe. "You must be messing around yourself you coming up here accusing me!" He said again raising his voice.

"I told you to keep it down!" The guard shouted. "I have to say it again your ass going back in your cage." Thomas Lee ignored him.

"Then why would that detective say that Thomas Lee if it wasn't true?"

"Baby you know I love you." He said reaching over taking hold of Dorothy Jean's hand.

"No touching!" The guard again yelled.

"Baby, why would I be trying to mess with Delores when I'm trying to make things work for us?" Thomas Lee said looking her in the eyes, sounding sincere.

"I should find out who his lieutenant is and go tell him how Detective Stokey's been coming out to my house harassing me." Thomas Lee's anxiety accelerated.

"Don't do that Dorothy Jean!" He said panicked. "You upset that man he might stop helping me, then who gon get me out of here?" Thomas Lee again wiped beads of sweat from his forehead with his jumpsuit collar. "Baby all I want to do is get out of here and come home to you—my wife!" He stated sounding sincere. "I wish they would give me visits like that Dorothy Jean . . . you know damn well you'd be the first one to know about it." He winked. She blushed.

#

Mildred watched from her front porch as Detective Stokey got out of his car and began walking towards her house.

"From that look on your face seems you done figured out who murdered that baby." She said as he stepped on her porch and sat down in the chair to her right.

"Somehow Mildred the satisfaction I thought I'd feel from finding the truth is suddenly not so sweet."

"Victory ain't always gon be sweet Andy, especially when innocent people get hurt in the midst of the battle." He momentarily looked up in the sky.

"She did it Mildred." He stated with a dazed look in his eyes. She just tossed that baby in the river like he was fish bait." Mildred noted the sorrowed look in Detective Stokey's eyes. "What the hell would make a woman murder an innocent baby?"

"Folks can do a lot of things don't make since to nobody but them." Detective Stokey's eyes moistened as he looked up at the sky. "He didn't asked to be born Mildred." He said standing up. "But how do I prove it and will it be enough to set Thomas Lee free?" Mildred continued her silence. "She would never confess and I doubt her love for Thomas Lee would be enough to compel her to do so." Detective Stokey looked at Mildred and shook his head in anguish. "How in the hell do I tell Thomas Lee that in proving his innocence, I'll be destroying the woman he loves?" He gazed at Mildred with empty eyes, loss for words.

"You ain't gon have to prove it Andy, she gon come to you." A look of doubt showed in his eyes.

"I'm sorry Mildred but I have to disagree with you on that, I just don't see it happening."

"You been agreeing with me all this time Andy what's making you doubt me now?"

"It's not that I don't believe you Mildred, it's just that—"

"Murdering a baby ain't a easy thing to do, I'm sure by now it's got to be getting the best of her."

"I sure hope you're right Mildred."

#

"Which dress do you think makes me look the prettiest Marietta, the pink one or the yellow one?" Delores asked elated as she looked in the mirror holding the pink dress against her body.

"Well I guess—"

"Maybe I'll wear this yellow one!" She said tossing the dress on the bed before Marietta could answer then grabbing the yellow one draped across a Queen Anne chair. "I'm so excited I feel like I'm about to burst!"

"So I guess you finally changed your mind about going on vacation with Mr. Charles." Marietta said in response to Delores' notable enthusiasm.

"That's not why I'm so happy Marietta!" She said hurling the yellow dress onto the bed then hurrying inside her enormous closet removing a red dress pressing it against her body as she again admired herself in the mirror. "Don't you think this red would simply drive any man absolutely wild?" She asked, exhilarated.

"Looks like Mr. Charles gon be in for a real treat."

"Charles?" Delores giggled. "Don't be silly Marietta this dress isn't for Charles it's for Tommy!" Marietta's jaw dropped.

"Thomas Lee?" She said confused by Delores' statement.

"Well since you're Tommy's momma I'm going to tell you first." Delores said somewhat giddy. Marietta's heart pounded in her chest as she waited to hear Delores' news.

"Just between me and you—" A glowing smile formed on Delores' face. "—I've been spending time with Tommy at the prison." Marietta temporarily lost her balance, gently landing in the Queen Anne chair.

"Are you alright Marietta?"

"Naw I ain't alright!" She yelled. "What you mean spending time with Thomas Lee?" Marietta said continuing to yell.

"You know." Delores smiled as a naughty teenager. "We've started our relationship again Marietta!" A horrified look entered Marietta's eyes.

"Ms. Delores you telling me you been lying up with Thomas Lee out at the prison?" Delores blushed.

"Just like we did at the motel."

"You trying to get my boy killed?" Marietta shouted. "Mr. Charles find out you going out there he gon—" She abruptly stopped then hurried from the room in tears.

Roosevelt and Carrie's attention drew to the kitchen stairs when hearing Marietta weeping as she rushed down the kitchen stairs in tears.

"What's wrong Marietta?" Carrie asked assisting her into a chair at the table. Roosevelt watched, concerned by Marietta's obvious upset.

"Is Thomas Lee alright?" He asked thinking perhaps he'd been murdered.

"Ms. Delores, Ms. Delores—" Marietta said unable to convey the origin of her distress. Roosevelt's eyes widened with alarm.

"Did something happen to Ms. Delores?" He asked, panicked.

"She been going up to that prison—"

"She what?" Carrie yelled. "No she ain't taking her trifling ass up there messing with that man!" She said infuriated. "What the hell's wrong with her?" Marietta tried to speak as she continued sobbing.

"If Mr. Charles find out—"

"Damn!" Carrie said shaking her head. "I ought to go up there right now and whup that heifer's ass—damn tramp!"

"So that's where she's been going for the past three weeks like clockwork." Roosevelt said as he recalled her mysterious absences. "I saw her getting ready to leave here one day last week and when asked her where she was going—" Carrie interjected.

"I bet her ass didn't tell you she was on her way up to that prison to fu—"

"Carrie!" Roosevelt said cutting her off.

"Ms. Delores is getting on my last damn nerve!" Carrie said raising her voice. "Why in the hell would that prison let her take her ass up there messing with Thomas Lee, she ain't his wife!"

"I tell you one thing—" Roosevelt said gently rubbing Marietta's back as she continued weeping. "—it had to be somebody with a great deal of influence and discretion to pull that off without Mr. Charles finding out."

"And Ms. Delores's ass knows plenty of folks with that kind of influence and money." Carrie stated.

"Well I'm off!" Delores said entering the vestibule from the stairs."

"Wait a minute Ms. Delores!" Roosevelt said trying to stop her.

"Bye!" She rushed out the front door ignoring Roosevelt's beckoning.

"If it wasn't for the fact I know Mr. Charles would take it out on Thomas Lee—" Roosevelt intervened.

"And us!"

"I'd tell him my damn self what his wife been doing while he at work." Carrie said as Marietta continued weeping.

#

Detective Stokey sat at his desk with his head rested in his hands as he thought of how although the victory of knowing Thomas Lee hadn't murdered Baby boy Doe, he couldn't stop agonizing over the impending fate of who he believed to be the real murderer. He also thought of how the death of an innocent baby could've been prevented by Marietta's truth.

"Hey Stokey!" Detective Fish called out from his desk.

"What do want Fish?" He said in no mood to tolerate his coworker's taunting.

"Looks like you have a visitor." Detective Stokey looked up seeing Detective Abernathy escorting Dorothy Jean in the direction of the interrogation room." He looked at him, curious if Dorothy Jean had come to offer information that would lead to the arrest of Delores Clarkston. Detective Abernathy humped his shoulders in response to the inquiring look in his partner's eyes indicating he had no idea why she was there. Detective Stokey rose from his desk and followed, arriving at the interrogation room just as Detective Abernathy escorted Dorothy Jean inside. He momentarily stood outside of the two-way window watching as Dorothy Jean sat down at the table then turned his attention to Detective Abernathy as he exited the room, closing the door behind him.

"What's going on Abernathy?"

"She came in this morning Stokey man . . . said she wanted to talk to you." He looked at Detective Stokey and humped his shoulders. "Your guess is as good as mines."

"Thank you Abernathy." Detective Stokey said massaging his neck.

"You got any idea why she's here?"

"If my hunch is right, I think perhaps she's about to tell me she witnessed Mrs. Clarkston murder her son." Detective Abernathy's jaw dropped.

"Are you serious man? Delores Clarkston killed her own son, damn!"

"There were only four people who saw Mrs. Clarkston with that baby before Thomas Lee found him in the river, and all fingers are pointing to that baby's mother."

"You really think Delores Clarkston murdered that baby?" Detective Abernathy asked looking at his partner in disbelief. "What would be her reason for murdering her own son?"

"I don't know Abernathy . . . I hope that's what Dorothy Jean's about to tell me."

"And if she did witness, Mrs. Clarkston murder her son then what?" Detective Abernathy asked. "Charles Clarkston already warned you that he'd destroy you if you came anywhere near his wife so—"

"I guess I'll cross that bridge when I get to it Abernathy." Detective Stokey took a deep breath as he prepared to enter the room.

"I'm glad I'm not you man that's all I got to say." Detective Abernathy said as he walked away.

"I'm glad you aren't me either Abernathy." Detective Stokey said before opening the door and entering. "Mrs. Simms?" Dorothy Jean looked up at him. "Thank you for coming in." He sat down across the table from her. "Can I get you anything, a coke or uh—"

"I ain't slept one night since that baby died." She said looking down at the table. Detective Stokey attentively listened as he awaited her eye witness testimony.

"Are you sure you want to speak to me without an attorney?" He asked covering all his bases, due to her having withheld evidence. She looked briefly up at him and again hung her head.

"What happened to that baby was wrong . . . he ain't asked to be born." Detective Stokey swallowed the spit in his mouth as it dried.

"Why don't you tell me what happened Mrs. Simms?" He said sympathizing with the tears rolling down her cheeks.

"He also ain't asked to die." She stated.

The Confession

Delores stepped on the Simms' front porch, her newborn son cradled in her arms.

"Tommy!" She called out pounding on the door. It suddenly swung open. Dorothy Jean stood on the other side. "Where's Tommy?"

"What you doing bringing your ass over here to my house Delores?" She said enraged. Delores looked down at her son swaddled in the blue baby blanket.

"Charles won't let me keep him."

"Well you damn sure can't leave him here!" Dorothy Jean shouted.

"I'm giving him to Tommy so he can—"

"The hell you are!" Dorothy Jean yelled looking at Delores with disdain. "Get your cheap trifling ass off my porch before I beat you bloody, and take your bastard son with you!"

"I want Tommy to have his son."

"Well Thomas Lee ain't here, so you take that thing back home to your husband and y'all figure it out."

"When will Tommy be back?"

"Heifer did you hear what I said?"

"Dorothy Jean, please!" Delores said desperate, her attention drawn to her infant son as he began to cry.

"You got five minutes to get your ass off my porch slut, and take that crying thing with you."

"I don't care what you think of me Dorothy Jean, but Thomas Lee Jr.—" Dorothy Jean's eyes widened with fury.

"What you say heifer?" She shouted. "I know damn well you didn't name that thing after my husband!" She drew back her hand and forcefully slapped her.

"Ahhhhhhhhhh!" Delores cried out.

"You must be out your damn mind bringing that thing around here expecting me and my husband to raise it!"

"Can you just call Tommy and tell him I'm here with his son?"

"You think I'm gon call my husband Delores and tell him his hoe is out here at our door with her bastard child?" Dorothy Jean again slapped her.

"Ahhhhhhhhhhhh!" Delores again hollered out. "Dorothy Jean please, I'm giving him to you and—"

"If you don't get your ass off my property—"

"Charles won't let me keep him and I don't have anywhere else to take him." Delores suddenly shoved the infant in Dorothy Jean's arms and hurried away.

"Come back here Delores!" Dorothy Jean shouted watching as she climbed in her car and sped away. "This thing ain't getting ready to come between me and my husband—come back her heifer!" Dorothy Jean suddenly noticed Rita sitting on her front porch having witnessed the altercation.

"Everything alright Dorothy Jean?" She asked walking across the yard headed over to Dorothy Jean's house.

"Naw everything ain't alright, you saw what that wench just did!" Rita stopped at the bottom of Dorothy Jean's stairs curious of the crying infant concealed inside the blanket.

"That heifer brought this thing over here talking about he belongs to my husband!"

"Well do he?"

"This thing ain't none of Thomas Lee's!" Dorothy Jean shouted.

"How you know Dorothy Jean, ain't Thomas Lee been messing around with that woman?"

"That don't mean this thing belong to him!" Dorothy Jean shouted looking down at the blanket covered infant. "From what I heard this thing could belong to any Black man in the county."

"But that would also include Thomas Lee too, Dorothy Jean." Rita said trying to reason with her irate neighbor.

"Ain't you got something else you need to be doing Rita besides standing over here giving your opinion that ain't no damn body asked you for?"

"If that's your way of telling me to mind my own business I can—"

"It is." Dorothy Jean yelled. Rita looked at the crying infant hidden beneath the blanket.

"Just let me take a look at him see if he got any resemblance to Thomas Lee."

"Hell naw . . . he don't look like my husband!"

"How you know Dorothy Jean you ain't even looked at him." Rita said stepping up on the porch, removing the infant from Dorothy Jean's arms. The newborn quieted. She pulled back the blanket seeing the Bi-racial baby. He again began to cry. "Awww Dorothy Jean this baby is beautiful!" Rita said smiling. "And he do have Black folk features."

"Then you take him Rita!" Dorothy Jean shouted in hysterics. Rita placed a kiss on the infant's cheek.

"I would love to but this is between you, Thomas Lee and Delores Clarkston."

"You can have that thing Rita because he ain't staying here with me and my husband!"

"I don't know what y'all plan on doing Dorothy Jean, but the first thing you need to do is take this precious little boy in the house and feed him."

"I told you now Rita . . . that thing ain't coming in my house!" Rita looked at her neighbor with compassionate eyes.

"Dorothy Jean girl take this baby in the house and feed him." Rita picked up the diaper bag Delores left on the porch and handed it to Dorothy Jean. "Here, take this baby and I'll carry the diaper bag."

"Get that thing away from me Rita before I flush it down the toilet!" Dorothy Jean yelled. "It ain't got nothing to do with me."

"Well at least take this diaper bag."

"Give it here!" Dorothy Jean snatched the bag from Rita's hand then entered the house, dropping it on the floor then hurrying to her bedroom, slamming the door.

"You just as handsome as you can be." Rita said talking to the infant as she removed a bottle of milk from the diaper bag. "And your daddy gon just love you to death." She said beginning to feed him.

· · · ·

Detective Stokey massaged his neck stopping Dorothy Jean when concluding that she and not Delores Clarkston had murdered Baby boy Doe.

"Uh, Mrs. Simms—" She slowly looked up at him. "—I think it's time for me to read you your Miranda Rights and if you'd like an attorney I need to inform you that you have the right for one to be here—do you understand." Dorothy Jean nodded.

"*You have the right to remain silent. Anything you say can and will be used against you in a court of law. You have the right to an attorney. If you cannot afford an attorney, one will be provided for you.* Do you understand what I just said Mrs. Simms?" She again nodded.

"I want to finish detective."

"Are you sure?" She subtly nodded.

The Confession Continues

Rita knocked softly on the bedroom door.

"Dorothy Jean I'm getting ready to leave now, I'm finished feeding this precious baby and he's laying in here on the sofa sleep." Rita looked over at the sleeping baby boy and smiled before exiting the house. Dorothy Jean slowly opened the bedroom door when hearing the front door shut. She entered the living room then walked over to the sofa, briefly watching as the infant lay asleep on his back.

"I hate you Thomas Lee!" Dorothy Jean yelled out in anger as she thought of Delores giving birth to her husband's child, something she'd never been unable to do. "If you think I'm gon raised that heifer's child Thomas Lee you got another thing coming!" She said thinking out loud as she wrapped the infant in his blanket and picked him up, grabbing the diaper bag from the floor and storming out of the house hurrying to her car. Dorothy Jean opened the front door and laid the infant on the seat then rushed to the other side and got in, driving frantically down the dark roads until arriving at the river and parking. She remained momentarily in her car, looking over at the infant before picking him up and grabbing the diaper bag, quickly getting out of the car. She rushed over to the river bank laying the infant on the ground. "Must think I'm a damn fool—" Dorothy Jean said tossing the diaper bag in the river. "—we gon see who the fool is Thomas Lee!" She stared at the blanket swaddled infant then picked him up and hurled him in the river. "How you like that Delores?" Dorothy Jean shouted. "You think you gon use your bastard child to come between me and my husband, well you think again you trifling ass wench!"

. . . .

Detective Stokey remained speechless as he listened to Dorothy Jean recall her unthinkable act. His mouth dried as he swallowed the enormous lump in his throat, blown away by her heart wrenching confession. Dorothy Jean continued.

. . . .

"I stood there holding that thing in my arms that was gon come between me and my husband and all I could think about was how Thomas Lee had betrayed me with Delores Clarkston, and in my mind all I could see was them making love and laughing at me." Detective Stokey's stomach bundled with nerves as he heard the sound of pure evil in Dorothy Jean's voice. "After I had thrown that thing in the river, I went home and I told myself what I done was justified . . . if I couldn't bear children for my husband, wasn't no other woman was gon do it either." Dorothy Jean said looking briefly at Detective Stokey then again lowered her head. He held back his fury as he listened to the unthinkable act of a scorned wife. "When Thomas Lee got home that night I made no mention of Delores or that little crying thing she brought to my house thinking I was fool enough to raise it." She abruptly silence then looked up at Detective Stokey without remorse.

"Ahem!" He cleared his throat. "Would you uh, please excuse me Mrs. Simms?" Detective Stokey said overwhelmed by her repulsive words. "I uh, I need to grab a glass of water—you sure I can't bring you back a soda?" He asked struggling to keep from regurgitating the contents in his stomach in her presence. He gazed momentarily into Dorothy Jean's eyes hoping to see a sign of repentance, but saw nothing.

"Detective?"

"Yes Mrs. Simms?" He said hoping this would be the moment she declared remorse for her wickedness.

"I'll take a soda if it's no bother."

"A soda?" Detective Stokey said barely able to speak. "I uh, can uh, do that." He slowly rose from the table and walked over to the door then stopped. He looked back at Dorothy Jean and shook his head in disbelief before opening the door then exiting the room.

"Stokey man you alright?" Detective Abernathy asked when seeing him re-enter the squad room, hurrying in the direction of the restroom. He followed his partner inside, noting the distraught look on his face and the look of horror in his eyes.

"She did it Abernathy." Detective Stokey said standing at the sink. He vomited.

"What the hell?" Detective Abernathy said alarmed by his partner's behavior. "Stokey man you sick?"

"She murdered that baby." Detective Stokey said slightly dazed. "She just tossed him in the river without conscience."

"Who? Delores Clarkston?" Detective Abernathy asked watching as his partner again lower his head in the sink and vomit. "Stokey man you need me to bring you something?"

"She's pure evil Abernathy." Detective Stokey said, his stomach in knots as he again vomited in the sink. "He was an innocent baby Abernathy . . . and she just tossed him in the river like he had no right to live." Detective Abernathy noted the tears in his partner's eyes.

"You still ain't said who Stokey?"

"Thomas Lee's wife . . . Dorothy Jean." Detective Abernathy's jaw dropped.

"Are you serious man . . . Thomas Lee Simms' wife murdered that baby and let him go to prison for it?" Detective Stokey nodded. "Damn! What you gon do now man?"

"What do think I'm going to do Abernathy?" He said raising his voice. "I'm going back in here and arrest her sorry ass!" Detective Stokey turned to his partner before again lowering his head and vomiting in the sink. "Just as soon as my stomach settles."

"Did she say why she did it?"

"Lunch—"

"What?" A baffled look formed on Detective Abernathy's face. "Man, pull yourself together Stokey!"

"I was saying why don't we discuss this over lunch?"

"Lunch?" Detective Abernathy scowled. "You think you ought to be eating anything man?" He continued scowling. "Better yet . . . are you gon be able to keep anything down?"

"I don't know Abernathy—" Detective Stokey said splashing water on his face. "—but if not I guess I can always watch you eat."

"You're joking right?"

"Do me a favor Abernathy—"

"What's that man?"

"Can you take Mrs. Simms a coke, I uh, told her I'd bring her one?" Detective Abernathy's eyes widened.

"Seriously?"

Chapter Twenty Five

Thomas Lee thought about the early years of his relationship with Dorothy Jean when they were teenagers as lay in bed in a death row cell, put there to isolate him from the general population, an order by newly re-elected Congressman Jonathan Cutter. He wondered what went wrong.

"Simms!" A guard called out.

"Yeah."

"Mr. Gordano's here to see you." The guard said unlocking and opening Thomas Lee's cell then leading him in the direction of an isolated visitor's room.

"Who?"

"Your lawyer?"

"My lawyer . . . man I ain't seen his ass since that jury found me guilty!" The guard unlocked and opened a steel door leading to a small room. "But I don't remember his name being Gordon."

"Gordano!" The guard said correcting him.

"What?"

"Your lawyer's name is Gordano." Thomas Lee looked at the impressively dressed gentleman inside the room awaiting his arrival.

"Thomas Lee Simms?"

"Yeah I'm Thomas Lee, who the hell are you?"

"I'm Robert Gordano your attorney." He extended his hand to shake. Thomas Lee ignored it.

"I ain't got no money to pay you if that's why you here."

"Your attorney's fees have already been paid Mr. Simms." Thomas Lee's eyes widened.

"What? By who?"

"I'm not at liberty to say."

"Then tell me this man—"

"What that?"

"Why you showing up here now?" Thomas Lee asked, annoyed. "The trial is over, I been convicted, and they sent my ass to prison . . . so ain't nothing left for you do."

"Please have a seat Mr. Simms."

"And what the hell happened to my appeal?"

"Mr. Simms . . . would you please be seated?"

"Man what's this all about?" Thomas Lee asked sitting down. "I ain't seen you since they slam that steel gate behind my ass." He looked Mr.

Gordano directly in the eyes and waited on an explanation. "What? You came to apologize for these guards beating the hell out of me whenever they had a bad day or—" Mr. Gordano interrupted.

"Guards?" He said rummaging through his black leather briefcase. "I'm sorry Mr. Simms I wasn't aware of that."

"If you ever brought your ass up here you would've known just by looking at my bruised face, black eyes, broken arm and cracked ribs!" Mr. Gordano's mouth slightly opened.

"Were you aware that someone has confessed to the murder of Baby boy Doe?" Thomas Lee's jaw dropped.

"Who? Charles Clarkston?" He said shaking his head, confirming what he slightly suspected. "I knew his ass had something to do with killing my son."

"It wasn't Mr. Clarkston—"

"Oh I see—" Thomas Lee said looking at him with distrust. "—y'all getting ready to cover up for his rich ass!"

"I hate to be the one to tell you this Mr. Simms but—"

"Tell me what?"

"The person who confessed to the murder was your wife Dorothy Jean." Thomas Lee quickly stood.

"Hell naw!" He yelled shaking his head with disbelief. "My wife ain't killed my son . . . what y'all trying to do exchange one Simms for another?" Thomas Lee's eyes moistened with tears.

"She's already given the District Attorney a signed confession and—"

"Hell naw!" Thomas Lee again shouted. "What y'all do talked Dorothy Jean into saying she done it to save me?" He said pacing through the room. "Man where my wife at I need to see her."

"I'm sorry Mr. Simms, but your wife's already been arrested." Thomas Lee's eyes widened with fear.

"You telling me y'all done already locked my wife up?" He shouted.

"That's usually what being arrested means—"

"Hell naw!" Thomas Lee flashed him an angry stare. "Dorothy Jean ain't done that, I know my wife and she ain't got that kind of hate in her." He looked at his lawyer. "So you tell her to plead not guilty!"

"I'm not your wife's attorney Mr. Simms." Mr. Gordano stated solemnly.

"You can still help her though can't you?"

"I'm not her attorney."

"Then what the hell you doing here man?" Thomas Lee yelled out, enraged.

"As your attorney Mr. Simms I wanted to inform you that the prosecutor's willing to discuss your release."

"Man I need to see my wife!" Thomas Lee shouted. "And why Detective Stokey didn't come and tell me? Is he responsible for this?"

"An attorney for some reason has filed a motion to have your wife's confession thrown out."

"Man I need to see Detective Stokey!" Thomas Lee said frantic. "My wife can't go to prison, she ain't gon make it in there!" Mr. Gordano rose from the table and prepared to leave.

"I'm truly sorry Mr. Simms."

"I don't need you to be sorry man—" Thomas Lee hollered out pounding his fist on the table. "—I need you to get my wife out of jail!" The guard immediately entered.

"Everything okay in here?" He looked at Thomas Lee. Mr. Gordano subtly nodded then stood.

"Hey man, tell Detective Stokey I said let me do my time and leave my wife alone!" Mr. Gordano looked at Thomas Lee with sympathetic eyes.

"I can speak to him Mr. Simms, but because your wife confessed I don't see how anyone can—"

"Just do what I asked you too!" Thomas Lee shouted.

"Let's go Simms!" The guard shouted. Mr. Gordano walked over to the door.

"Goodbye Mr. Simms."

"Hey Gordano!" Thomas Lee said. Mr. Gordano turned around. "Tell my wife I would die in here for her man." Thomas Lee stated with sincerity. "Promise me man you gon tell her that I said that okay?" Mr. Gordano nodded then opened the door and left. Thomas Lee laid his head on the table and wept.

#

Charles silently watched as Marietta placed a plate of ham, waffles and a vegetable omelet on the table in front of him next to his orange juice.

"I'll be back with your coffee."

"Thank you Marietta." He said picking up the glass of orange juice and taking a sip. "I guess kudos should go out to Detective Stokey." Charles stated as Marietta poured his cup of coffee. "He seems to have found someone to confess to the murder of my wife's son." Marietta's mouth flung open.

"Somebody to confess? A perplexed look formed on Marietta's face. "Who?"

"Apparently an individual came forward, confessing to being the actual killer of Baby boy Doe."

"Did they say who?"

"As a matter of fact Marietta they did." Charles made no attempt to hide his dissatisfaction. "The alleged guilty party is none other than Thomas Lee's wife." Marietta gasped, horrified by the unexpected news. "Rather convenient wouldn't you say."

"You sure they said it was Dorothy Jean?" Marietta asked, unknowingly overfilling Charles' cup.

"Marietta!" He stated calmly.

"Huh?"

"The coffee." She looked down seeing spilled coffee on the white silk tablecloth.

"I'm sorry Mr. Charles." Marietta said as her mind remained occupied on thoughts of Dorothy Jean confessing to the murder. "Let me go get a towel so I can clean that up."

"And after you've finished, you can bring my breakfast into the drawing room." Charles said standing up.

"I can't see Dorothy Jean doing something like that?" Marietta said thinking out loud.

"I guess good things really do come to those who wait." Charles stated cynically underneath his breath.

"You say something Mr. Charles?" Marietta asked still deep in thought.

"Yes . . . don't forget to bring me another cup of coffee."

#

"Hey Stokey!" Detective Fish called out from his desk when seeing him enter the squad room. "It looks like you win—technically."

"What the hell's that suppose to mean Fish?"

"Well you didn't actually solve the case it sorta dropped into your lap." He stated pessimistically. "But I guess you're still entitled to that steak dinner."

"Aren't you forgetting something Detective Fish?"

"I don't know am I?"

"Yes, my bottle of champagne!"

Detective Fish laughed.

"It was a confession Stokey!"

"Confession or not . . . the agreement was if I freed Thomas Lee you'd buy me a steak dinner and a bottle of champagne." Detective Abernathy intervened.

"Looks like you've been dealing with a welcher all along Stokey." He said looking at Detective Fish as a fraud.

"Just be grateful you're getting the steak dinner!" Detective Fish sarcastically chuckled. "It was a confession."

"You know what Fish?"

"What's that Stokey?"

"I think I'll pass on the steak."

Detective Fish's jaw dropped.

"Oh no Stokey . . . a deals a deal!"

"If you're not going to follow-thru on the original bet Fish then just forget it."

"The bet was a steak dinner and a bottle of champagne and that's just what you're getting Detective Stokey!" Detective Abernathy again intervened.

"Look Stokey man, why don't you let me and Regina take you out for that steak dinner and bottle of champagne?" Detective Stokey quickly turned to Detective Fish and smirked.

"It's a date Abernathy."

"Detective Stokey?" A woman's voice stated interrupting his victorious moment. He turned his attention away from his welching coworker seeing Marietta. "I need to talk to you if you ain't too busy."

"Never to busy for you Marietta." Detective Stokey said getting up from his desk.

"This conversation's not over Stokey!" Detective Fish said watching as the detective escorted Marietta in the direction of the interrogation room.

"Why don't you go ahead and have a seat Marietta." He said as they entered the room. "Now what can I do for you?"

"Did you forget to tell me something?" She asked as he joined her at the table.

"You're here about Dorothy Jean?" He said, briefly looking down as he prepared answer her question.

"Is it a reason why you didn't tell me about her confessing to the murder of that baby?"

"Marietta I uh—" She cut him off.

"I had to hear it from Mr. Charles."

"I'm sorry Marietta it's just that I've been so busy trying to get Thomas Lee released I guess it slipped my mind."

"Did Dorothy Jean say why?" He massaged his neck when recalling the morbid confession.

"Marietta you uh, don't want to uh, hear the details of—"

"I been knowing Dorothy Jean since she was a child and I ain't ever seen her do nothing to hurt another human being."

"Sometimes Marietta people do things no one would ever imagine they were capable of doing, when they've been hurt." Detective Stokey's heart pounded in his chest as he reluctantly remembered Dorothy Jean's confession.

"I told Thomas Lee nothing good was gon come from his adulterous ways—" Marietta said upset. "—messing around with other women right there in Dorothy Jean's face." She looked into Detective Stokey's sympathetic eyes. "But murdering an innocent baby, I just can't see Dorothy Jean doing that no matter how bad Thomas Lee hurt her!"

"I'm sorry Marietta—"

"Don't be sorry for me detective, be sorry for Dorothy Jean." He swallowed the newly formed lump in his throat as he masked his true feeling about sympathy for Dorothy Jean. "Can I see her?"

"As a matter of fact Marietta she's still here at the station, I can arrange for you to meet with her if you'd like." She nodded.

#

Marietta entered the visitor's room at the jail seeing Dorothy Jean sitting on the other side of a glass window. The two women looked one to the other as Marietta sat down both hesitating before picking up their phones to speak.

"I guess they gon be letting Thomas Lee go soon?" Dorothy Jean said trying to read the look on Marietta's face.

"Is that why you said you murdered that baby Dorothy Jean?"

"I said it Ms. Marietta because I done it." She stated coldly. "That baby ain't had no business being here." Dorothy Jean said slightly dazed. "Should've never been born." A horrified look appeared on Marietta's face in response to her daughter-in-laws callous words. "I know you were there the day Delores brought that thing in this world Ms. Marietta—"

"Dorothy Jean—" Marietta interrupted. "—Ms. Delores' baby didn't belong to Thomas Lee." Dorothy Jean looked at her mother-in-law with skeptical eyes.

"That heifer stood right there on my front porch Ms. Marietta and told me that little crying thing was my husband's—even tried to give it to Thomas Lee."

"Dorothy Jean!" Marietta looked at her with remorse in her eyes. "Thomas Lee couldn't father Delores child or nobody else's."

"What you trying to tell me Ms. Marietta?" Dorothy Jean asked, unconvinced by her troubling words. Marietta's eyes watered with tears.

"Doctor told me a long time ago Thomas Lee would never have children." Dorothy Jean's mouth slightly opened. "I never could get up the nerves to tell him, so I let him believe you were the reason y'all never has kids."

"I don't believe you Ms. Marietta . . . wasn't nothing wrong with my husband."

"Think about it Dorothy Jean, as many women as Thomas Lee's been with—"

"I ain't trying to hear about my husband's adulterous ways Ms. Marietta!" Dorothy Jean yelled.

"Have you ever known a woman to ever claim Thomas Lee as father to her child?"

"Delores Clarkston did!"

"Ms. Delores brought somebody's child in this world, but it wasn't Thomas Lee's."

"Then you tell me Ms. Marietta why was that child look Black?"

"When Ms. Delores gets drunk she'll lay down with any man—Black, White, it don't much matter."

"I know Thomas Lee didn't know she was that kind of woman or he would've never touched that filthy—"

"Yeah he knew Dorothy Jean." Marietta said looking into Dorothy Jean's tear filled eyes.

"You telling me I'm getting ready to spend the rest of my life in prison and my husband couldn't even have Children?" Dorothy Jean momentarily gazed at her deceitful mother-in-law then hung up the phone and walked away.

#

Thomas Lee's eyes lit up when seeing Detective Stokey waiting on the other side of the gate, there to pick him up after his released. The prison gate slowly opened then closed after Thomas Lee passed through. He looked at Detective Stokey and smiled then leaped for joy elated to have his freedom.

"Keep walking Thomas Lee you're a free man!" Detective Stokey said grinning.

"Man you my hero!" Thomas Lee said as he hurried towards him with tears in his eyes. The two men shared a brief hug.

"You ready to go home?" Detective Stokey asked feeling victorious. The luster in Thomas Lee's eyes abruptly diminished.

"Ain't nothing at home for me to go home to detective." He said looking Detective Stokey in the eyes. "My wife ain't there . . . I ain't got my son—" Detective Stokey gently patted Thomas Lee on the back, masking his disdain for Dorothy Jean.

"You'll be alright Thomas Lee." Detective Stokey stated then paused. "Your uh, wife wants to see you Thomas Lee."

"Man I ain't ready to see her!" Thomas Lee said becoming upset. "She murdered my son man!" Detective Stokey massaged his neck as he resisted the urge to tell Thomas Lee the child wasn't his.

"Why don't we just plan on going to the jail and if you change your mind before we get there we'll turn around and I'll take you to lunch, how's that sound?" He said trying to cheer Thomas Lee up.

"Thanks man."

"You're welcome Thomas Lee."

"Where you talking about taking me to lunch anyway man?"

"It's a place called the Night Owl Night." Thomas Lee's mouth flung opened.

"Man, get the hell out of here!" He said amused. "What the hell you know about the Night Owl?" Thomas Lee laughed.

"I know they have great jerk chicken there."

"Man after eating that prison slop I could use some good food!"

"I have a better idea Thomas Lee."

"And what's that?"

"Why don't we go by and see Mildred—"

"Koffee?" Thomas Lee yelled as his eyes widened. "Hell naw, man I just got out of prison . . . I don't want the first woman I see to be Mildred Koffee!"

"I guess I uh, can understand what you're saying Thomas Lee, but remember if it wasn't for Mildred you'd still be behind bars." Thomas Lee shook his head with slight protest.

"Yeah, you're right man."

"You like pig tails?"

"For lunch?" Thomas Lee frowned. "Hell naw!"

Chapter Twenty Six

"Hey Stokey!" Detective Fish called out from his desk when seeing him enter the squad room that morning being seated at his desk.

"If it's about that steak dinner you reneged on Fish you're too late, Abernathy and his wife Regina and her very attractive friend Pauline—" A huge smile stretched across Detective Stokey's face. "—have already honored your bet and I can assure you it was far more interesting than spending an evening listening to your constant yelping Detective Fish.

"Thanks for the, *I don't give a damn* report—" Detective Fish stated sarcastically. "—but I was only trying to let you know that Lieutenant Porter said he wanted to see you the minute you walked through the door."

"Fish you jackass!" Detective Stokey said abruptly standing. "Why didn't you just say that?"

"Because you were so busy yelping about your evening with Abernathy and his wife—" Detective Fish mocked. "—oh yeah, and your blind date Pauline, you didn't give me a chance."

"Well that blind date Detective Fish may one day become the next Mrs. Andrew Stokey."

"I won't hold my breath." Detective Fish said chuckling. "If she's dense enough to marry you how good of a catch could she be?" "Well don't expect to find your name on the guest list Fish."

"I wouldn't come if you promised me a steak dinner and a bottle of champagne."

"Welcher—"

"Detective Stokey!" Lieutenant Porter said interrupting the detective's daily squabble.

"You wanted to see me lieutenant?" Detective Stokey said shifting his eyes briefly to Detective Fish then again to the lieutenant.

"In my office now!"

"We'll finish this later Detective Fish." Detective Stokey said on his way to the lieutenant's office.

"Whenever you're ready Detective Stokey."

"Close the door detective." Lieutenant Porter said sitting at his desk. Detective Stokey's anxiety heightened as he closed the door. "Sit down detective."

"What's up lieutenant?" He asked being seated in front of the lieutenant's desk.

"The Simms' case—" Detective Stokey interjected.

"I know it took a lot longer than the time you allotted but—"

"Great job!" Lieutenant Porter said smiling. Detective Stokey's mouth flung open.

"What?"

"I have to admit, there were times when I thought you were chasing a hurricane in a row boat trying to prove a convicted man's innocence, especially one found guilty of murdering a baby but—"

"It was Mildred Koffee, lieutenant." Detective Stokey said ensuring Mildred received the credit. "She was the one who gave that row boat the horsepower it needed to catch up with that hurricane."

"Well it looks like Thomas Lee Simms owes you, and you owe Mildred Koffee . . . Congratulations!" Lieutenant Porter extended his hand. The two men shook. "Be sure and close the door on your way out." A puzzled looked appeared on Detective Stokey's face.

"That's it?"

"Yes, what did you expect a T-bone steak and a bottle of champagne—now get back to work you have real cases to solve."

"Uh, okay . . . thank you lieutenant." Detective Stokey rose from his chair and took a deep breath, proud of his career altering victory. "I guess I'll uh, get back to work then." He said walking over to the door and opening it.

"*For he's a jolly good fellow, for he's a jolly good fellow*—" Detective Stokey's jaw dropped when seeing his coworker giving him a standing ovation. "*—for he's a jolly good fellow—which nobody can deny.*" An enormous smile displayed on his face as his coworkers applauded, each taking turns shaking his hand.

"I bet you think you're some kind of hero now don't you Stokey?" Detective Fish said seated at his desk. "Well I've got news for you—"

"And what's that Officer Fish?"

"That's Detective Fish, and the news is . . . I have the best bottle of champagne you've ever drank!" He said removing a bucket of ice from underneath his desk containing a bottle of Dom Perignon. Detective Stokey's eyes lit up. "Congratulations Andy." Detective Fish said popping the cork.

"I guess this means I need to remove your name from the suggestion box as who not to include in the Secret Santa exchange this year?" Detective Stokey stated teasing. He looked over at his partner who saluted him with a subtle nod as he stuffed powder donuts in his mouth, the chest of his navy blue shirt covered with powder sugar.

"Man being in this prison makes me nervous." Thomas Lee said as he and Detective Stokey entered a small room containing a round table and four chairs, there to see Dorothy Jean. "This place is a lot nicer than that zoo they caged me up in." Thomas Lee said looking around reminded of his own incarceration. He sat down, resting his head on the table.

"Relax Thomas Lee you're a free man now." Detective Stokey said pacing through the small room, ill at ease about seeing Dorothy Jean.

"I guess it's gon take a minute for that to sink in." Thomas Lee said slowly dozing off—snoring. Detective Stokey's attention drew to the opening door. He watched as a female guard escorted Dorothy Jean in the room.

"Thomas Lee." He said tapping him on the shoulder. Thomas Lee's eyes gradually opened.

"Yeah, what is it?"

"Wake up your wife's here." Thomas Lee looked up at Dorothy Jean then stood.

"How you doing Dorothy Jean?" He said taking her in his arms, kissing her gently on the lips. "They treating you right in here?"

"As well as they can treat a person that's locked up for murder." She said forcing a smile. He gave no reply. "It's been two weeks since they freed you Thomas Lee—" Dorothy Jean shifted her eyes to Detective Stokey then again to Thomas Lee. "—where you been?"

"Ahem!" Detective Stokey cleared his throat. Thomas Lee looked over at him. "I'm uh, going to let you to spend some time with your wife alone."

"Thanks man—" He subtly nodded. "—for everything."
Detective Stokey likewise nodded then exited the room. Dorothy Jean pulled out of Thomas Lee's embrace then sat down at the table. He also sat.

"So what you got to say Thomas Lee?"

"What you want me to say Dorothy Jean?" She looked into his eyes questioning eyes.

"It's funny how one day your main thought is what you gon cook for supper and the next day—" She half heartedly grinned. "—you wondering if you gon spend the rest of your life behind bars."

"Why Dorothy Jean?" Thomas Lee asked looking at her, wondering what would make her commit such an act. "Why you killed my son?"

"Look like Delores gon finally have you all to herself." Dorothy Jean said dismissing his question.

"Only thing Delores gon be doing is staying right there with Charles!" Thomas Lee stated knowing that's what Dorothy Jean wanted to hear. "Messing with her is what 'caused all this mess in the first place." She looked at him, doubtful.

"And the minute Delores come wagging her tail—" Dorothy Jean sarcastically chuckled. "—you gon be on her like fleas on a dog."

"Come on now Dorothy Jean this ain't about Delores." Thomas Lee said feeling guilty.

"Detective Stokey told me what you said." An uneasy look formed on his face, uncertain of just what the detective had told her.

"A man says a lot of things when he locked up behind bars Dorothy Jean."

"Said you sent word you would die in that prison for me." Thomas Lee gazed into her eyes then leaned in and kissed her on the lips. "Did you mean that Thomas Lee or was that just one of them things a man say when he behind bars?" He grinned then again kissed her.

"I meant every word of that baby." Thomas Lee said placing another kissed on her lips. "I love you Dorothy Jean and if I could, I'd trade places with you."

"I bet you would." She said humored. "Then you'd finally have more women than you can handle." She chuckled. A large smile formed on Thomas Lee's face.

"I hadn't looked at it that way." His smile widened. "I know a lot of men would love to have a opportunity like that!" He said cunningly grinning as he thought about it. "I want you to know Dorothy Jean I'm gon wait for you." Her eyes moistened with tears.

"Don't." She said. "We both know I ain't ever gon get out of here Thomas Lee."

"Don't say that Dorothy Jean!" He said hopeful. "Detective Stokey gon get you out of here just like he did me!"

"You were innocent Thomas Lee . . . I ain't." Tears ran down Dorothy Jean's cheeks. "I want you to forget all about me, find yourself a good woman."

"Come on now Dorothy Jean don't be talking like that!" She suddenly chuckled.

"What you laughing for?"

"Try to make sure your next woman ain't attached to a husband."

"Now you sound like Momma." Thomas Lee said chuckling. "I love you Dorothy Jean." They passionately kissed.

"Ahem!" Thomas Lee looked over at the door seeing Detective Stokey.

"I guess that means times up huh?"

"Don't come back no more Thomas Lee." Dorothy Jeans said as tears erupted from her eyes.

"Let's go Simms." The female guard stated. She rose from the table and exchanged a final hug and kiss with Thomas Lee.

"I love you girl."

"I love you too Thomas Lee." She said walking away. Thomas Lee watched as Dorothy Jean exited the room.

"You uh, you alright Thomas Lee?" Detective Stokey asked seeing tears in his eyes.

"Naw man, I ain't gon be alright until I see my wife walk out of this place."

#

"Damn!" Thomas Lee said as he looked through his wedding album seeing photos of him and Dorothy Jean's wedding day. He thought of the possibility of her spending the rest of her life in prison and silently wept. His attention drew to knocking at the front door. Thomas Lee wiped the tears from his eyes as he closed the photo album. "Now who the hell is that?" He said thinking out loud as he walked over to the living room window, peeping through the curtain. "Damn!" He said shaking his head, agitated when seeing Delores on the porch wearing a bright red dress. "What the hell Delores doing over here?" Thomas Lee said to himself, hesitating before opening the door.

"Hi Tommy!" She said wrapping her arms around his neck the minute she entered. She romantically kissed him. "Welcome home!" She again kissed him.

"What you doing here Delores?" She kissed him a third time. "Did you hear me girl?" She placed a fourth kiss to his lips. Thomas Lee shook his head as he closed the door.

"Of course I heard you Tommy, aren't you happy to see me?" He took a deep breath and looked into her excited eyes.

"Naw, yeah . . . I don't know Delores." He said confused. "What you think gon happen if Charles finds out you over here?"

"Let's run away together Tommy." Delores said placing a seductive kiss on his lips.

"What you talking about us running away Delores?"

"Let's run away, go someplace where nobody would think to find us!" She said overjoyed. "I'll divorce Charles and we can get married . . . I love you so much Tommy." He removed her grasping arms from around his neck and walked away sitting down on the sofa. Delores hurried over and sat on his lap then kissing him repeatedly on the lips.

"Hold on now Delores!" She wrapped her arms around his neck and placed another kiss on his lips.

"We belong together Tommy and now that Dorothy Jean's gone it seems just like it was fate?"

"Fate!" Thomas Lee shouted. Delores looked in his eyes, ignoring the anger showing inside as she again attempted to kiss him. He quickly turned his head avoiding her kiss. "Get up!"

"Why Tommy what did I do wrong?"

"Get your ass up now Delores!" He said raising his voice. She slowly rose being seated on the sofa next to him. "My wife being in prison ain't no damn fate!" He said disturbed by her thoughtless words. She pouted.

"I'm sorry Tommy."

"You think I'm happy about my wife being locked up maybe for the rest of her life Delores, huh?" Thomas Lee yelled.

"Don't be mad at me Tommy it's just that I love you so much and I thought—"

"Thought what Delores?"

"I thought you loved me too Tommy."

"I do." He said beginning to mellow. "But—"

"But what Tommy?"

"Ain't you got a husband Delores?" She kissed him lightly on the lips.

"It's not my husband I'm in love with silly." Delores giggled. Thomas Lee gazed in her inviting eyes then embraced her in his arms, passionately kissing her.

"Anybody know you here?"

"Charles had a business meeting tonight and Marietta's not going to say anything." His eyes widened, agitated by her carelessness.

"You told my momma you was coming over here Delores?"

"I didn't tell anyone Tommy, but I'm sure Marietta had some idea that I would be." She again kissed him.

"What make you say that?"

"Only because she knows how much I love her son." She said kissing him seductively on the lips.

"You can't be doing this Delores, you gon get my momma fired."

"Oh silly . . . Charles would never fire Marietta if I told him it would be over my dead body." She giggled.

"Is that right?" Thomas Lee smiled. Delores kissed him on both sides of his neck then moved her mouth to his lips.

"Stop now Delores." He said passively pushing her away. "I promised my momma I wouldn't be messing with you like this no more."

"You didn't mean that did you Tommy?"

"Yeah, no . . . I don't know Delores!" She continued applying intimate kisses to his neck and lips.

"It sure was nice Tommy—" She placed a seductive kiss to his willing lips. "—us being together at the prison."

"Huh?" Thomas Lee said succumbing to her seduction. He again embraced Delores in his arms and passionately kissed her on the neck and lips then lowered her onto the sofa to engage in intimacy.

#

"Marietta have you seen Ms. Delores?" Roosevelt asked concerned about her unscheduled absence from the home.

"The last time I saw her she was upstairs in her room trying on dresses again, I guess her and Mr. Charles got another dinner engagement somewhere tonight." Marietta stated. "But he never told me not to cook dinner."

"You know he been trying to keep Ms. Delores' ass busy every since they released Thomas Lee." Carrie said amused. A peculiar look displayed on Roosevelt face.

"Come to think of it, Ms. Delores ain't said nothing to me about her and Mr. Charles going out this evening either."

"Maybe she didn't think it was none of your damn business Roosevelt." Carrie stated sarcastically as she peeled shelled shrimp over at the sink. "Ol' trifling heifer."

"Carrie!" Marietta looked briefly at her as she gathered items from the refrigerator in preparation for her jambalaya. "If I didn't' know better I'd think you was jealous." Marietta teased.

"Jealous my ass!" Carrie said laughing. "That heifer can't cook, clean, stay sober and can't even make up her damn mind about if she want to be with Mr. Charles or that no good Thomas Lee!" Roosevelt quickly shifted his eyes to Marietta. "I saw that heifer about forty five minutes ago sneaking out the back door." Carrie said amused. Marietta's heart pounded in her chest.

"Ms. Delores is a grown woman she ain't got no reason to be sneaking nowhere."

"Well did she tell you she was leaving before she left?" Carrie asked cynically. "That's what Mr. Charles gon want to know if he get home before her ass do."

"Aww hush Carrie!" Roosevelt said sympathetic to the worried look in Marietta's eyes.

"Do you remember what Ms. Delores was wearing Carrie?"

"Yeah girl she had on a loud ass red dress . . . left her looking like a damn cherry Popsicle!" Carrie said bursting into laughter. "Why you ask?" Marietta shifted her eyes to Roosevelt.

"I sure hope she ain't over there messing with Thomas Lee." Roosevelt said with a panicked look on his face.

"Now y'all know damn well that's where that heifer's is!" Carrie said disregarding Marietta's feelings. "Especially, now that Dorothy Jean's locked up tighter than a fat woman in a petite size girdle." She again burst into laughter.

"Carrie!" Roosevelt said chastising her.

"You know I'm right Roosevelt!" She looked at him then briefly shifted her eyes over at Marietta. "That man's wife barely behind bars and Ms. Delores got her whorish ass over there doing who knows what?" Roosevelt reluctantly grinned. "I guess we know all what she doing." Carrie said disregarding Marietta's nervous demeanor.

"I'm sure Thomas Lee was glad to see her coming after spending all that time behind bars!" Roosevelt said joining in Carrie's naughty conversation.

"Roosevelt!"

"What Marietta? That man was locked up for six months, and you know as well as I do what he was like before he got locked up." He cunningly grinned. "You want me to go over there and bring Ms. Delores back Marietta?"

"She found her way over there let her find her way back." Marietta stated, defiantly.

"What if Mr. Charles gets home before she do?" Roosevelt asked worried.

"Let me get started on my jambalaya." Marietta said diverting from Delores' taboo behavior. Roosevelt shifted his eyes to Carrie, surprised by Marietta's uncharacteristic reply.

#

"You better get on back home Delores." Thomas Lee said as they lay cuddled on the sofa.

"I wish we could lay here like this forever Tommy." Delores said basking in the moment. Thomas Lee placed a smooch on her lips then sat up.

"Get up." She pulled him back into her arms and romantically kissed him.

"Stop now Delores, get up girl." She placed a quick kiss on his lips.

"Help me up." She said giggling. Thomas Lee took hold of her arms and assisted her into a sitting position. She again wrapped her arms around Thomas Lee's neck and romantically kissed him then sat on his lap.

"Get on now Delores!"

"Do I have to Tommy?" She said as he lifted her up from his lap.

"Yeah you do." Delores kissed Thomas Lee, fumbling as she tried to button her dress, half buttoning it. "Charles ain't getting ready to come over here and kill me over you girl."

"Bye Tommy." She said placing sporadic smooches on the lips. "I love you Tommy."

"I know you do Delores." He said as she opened the door to leave, flashing him a big smile.

"Bye Tommy."

"Bye Delores."

#

Roosevelt, Marietta and Carrie abruptly looked in the direction of the back door seeing Delores as she rushed in.

"Is Charles home yet?" She asked speaking just above a whisper.

"Where you been Ms. Delores?" Marietta asked raising her voice.

"I had some last minute shopping I needed to do and—" She fluffed her hair with her fingers. "—you wouldn't believe how crowded those stores were." She observed the doubtful looks on their faces. "Why are you all looking at me like that?"

"It's a good thing Mr. Charles ain't here." Carrie stated unconvinced. "Ain't no way in hell he would believe no mess like that!" Delores' mouth slightly opened.

"Carrie!" Roosevelt stated.

"What Roosevelt . . . if she been shopping all day like she said where in the hell are her bags?" Carrie said challenging Delores' untruth. "And look at her dress, damn thing ain't even buttoned right." Delores quickly looked down realizing in her haste she'd incorrectly buttoned it.

"Okay!" She said looking at Marietta. "I didn't go shopping, I went over to speak with Tommy—" Carrie burst into laughter.

"Speak? Since when do speaking with a man involve you taking off your damn clothes?"

"Carrie!" Roosevelt said.

"I didn't want Tommy sitting over there all alone in that house." Delores said trying to explain. "I thought maybe he'd like to have some company." Carrie again burst into laughter.

"I bet he did!"

"Carrie!"

"What Roosevelt?"

"Looks like I'm gon have a talk to my son." Marietta said as her stomach ached from tension.

"I know you don't want me and Tommy to be together Marietta." Delores stated. Carrie intervened.

"Be together!" She looked at Delores, stunned by her statement. "Ms. Delores how in the hell you gon be with Thomas Lee when you got a husband?" Delores looked briefly at her then turned her attention back to Marietta.

"Tommy and I talked about getting married and leaving here." Marietta shifted her eyes to Roosevelt too angry to speak.

"Now Ms. Delores I'm pretty sure Mr. Charles ain't gon let you divorce him." Roosevelt said trying to reason with her irrational thinking.

"Did Thomas Lee say he was planning on marrying you Ms. Delores or did you tell him that's what you wanted him to do?" Marietta asked convinced Delores initiated the conversation.

"I may have suggested it Marietta but Tommy didn't say no."

"We can see that by the way your clothes practically hanging off you." Carrie stated humored.

"Roosevelt, take Ms. Delores upstairs so she can clean up and changed before Mr. Charles get home." Marietta said trying to hold her temper.

"No!" Delores stated with defiance. "I'm not a child . . . and I'm perfectly capable of finding my own way upstairs." She said looking at

Marietta. "I won't be made to feel ashamed of my love for Tommy and his love for me." She shifted her eyes to her half buttoned dress then walked away.

"Aww hell!" Carrie stated. "Y'all we gon have to start looking for new jobs, if Mr. Charles find out she been over there laying up with Thomas Lee he gon fire all our asses." Carrie shook her head as she resumed peeling shrimp. "Ol' trifling heifer."

Chapter Twenty Seven

"Is my wife all packed and ready to go Marietta?" Charles asked from behind the evening newspaper as she filled his glass with ice tea.

"You know Ms. Delores . . . she change her mind like a new mother change diaper." Marietta chuckled as she walked to the other end of the table and filled the empty glass where Delores would be sitting.

"Would you please go upstairs Marietta and let my wife know supper's ready?"

"I'll go right now." She said sitting the pitcher of ice tea in the center of the table, returning to the kitchen and walking up the back stairs. "Ms. Delores—" Marietta said knocking on her bedroom door. "—Mr. Charles wanted me to let you know supper's ready."

"I'm not hungry Marietta." Delores said through the closed door.

"Well you gon be the one to tell Mr. Charles that."

"Can't you tell him for me Marietta?"

"I think it would be best if it came from you since he's planning on y'all leaving here this weekend for France." The door quickly opened.

"This weekend!" Delores said stunned by Marietta's news. "I don't recall agreeing to travel to France with Charles this weekend or any other weekend."

"That's all the more reason you need to be joining your husband for supper."

"Marietta would you please tell Charles I'll be right down?"

"I sure will."

"Thank you." Delores again closed the door.

Carrie watched as Marietta returned downstairs.

"Is she coming down?"

"Yeah she's coming?"

"I guess it's getting ready to be showdown at the OK Corral then." Carrie said quietly chuckling. "All I need now is a box of popcorn and a glass of that red wine Ms. Delores can't seem to get enough of." She burst into quiet laughter.

"Carrie!" Marietta whispered.

"What Marietta!" Carrie said aggravated. "I'm sick of Ms. Delores' spoiled ass always wanting to have her way."

"Marietta is my wife coming down?" Charles asked becoming impatient.

"She should be down any minutes now Mr. Charles."

"If not could you please go back upstairs and see what's keeping her?"

"I know what's keeping her—" Carrie said whispering. "—that damn guilt from her lying up with Thomas Lee!" She said, amused. "And while you up there you might want make sure she ain't hiding Thomas Lee's ass up there somewhere." Carrie teased.

"Thomas Lee ain't no fool."

"He a man ain't he?"

"Maybe I'll take a little peek in her room this time." Marietta said in response to the skeptical look on Carrie's face.

"If my wife's not down in the next five minute you can begin serving dinner, but before you do I'd like it if you would check on her again."

"I'll go right now." Marietta said hurrying up the kitchen stairs hoping not to find Thomas Lee in her room.

"Thank you Marietta." She arrived at Delores' bedroom and raised her hand to knock on the door then hesitated before knocking.

"Ms. Delores?" She again opened the door.

"Yes Marietta?"

Marietta discretely peeped inside the room.

"Mr. Charles is getting worried."

"Let him worry I don't care."

"Now Ms. Delores you don't want to start making your husband suspicious—"

"I don't know what to do Marietta!" Delores said bursting into tears. Marietta's mouth slightly opened in response to Delores' sudden outburst. "Come here baby." She said embracing her in her arms. "Now what you talking about you don't know what to do?"

"About my life with Charles." Marietta gently rubbed her hair.

"Mr. Charles wouldn't know what to do without you Ms. Delores." Marietta lightly chuckled. "So the best thing for you to do is stay right here with your husband and be one of them high sadity woman that spend all day shopping and going to fancy luncheons representing Mr. Charles and the Clarkston family." Delores giggled through her weeping. "I know you love my son Ms. Delores, but I ain't ever known Thomas Lee to be faithful to no one woman."

"Things are different with me and Tommy."

"I know that's what you want to believe Ms. Delores but—"

"Tommy loves me Marietta!"

"In his own way Ms. Delores I'm sure he do, but in the four years you been messing around with Thomas Lee he ain't once left Dorothy Jean to be with you." Marietta looked into Delores' vulnerable eyes. "You ever ask yourself why?"

"I know Tommy Marietta and I know he—"

"Ain't no different than that no good daddy of his." Marietta stated. "He love the women and the women love him." Marietta chuckled then used her apron to wiped away Delores' tears. "Now you go ahead on Ms. Delores and put on a dress in your husband's favorite color so you can join Mr. Charles downstairs for supper and y'all can discuss your trip to France." Delores looked at Marietta with childlike eyes.

"Thank you Marietta."

"Now I'm gon give you ten minutes to come downstairs and join Mr. Charles before I come back up here and dragged you to that dinner table." Marietta teased. Delores giggled. "I'll let Mr. Charles know you on your way down." Marietta turned to leave.

"Marietta—" She again turned. "—would it be so bad to have me as your daughter-in-law?"

"Don't keep Mr. Charles waiting."

#

"Damn!" Thomas Lee said when seeing Marietta through the window headed for his house as he stood in the kitchen preparing a late breakfast. He shook his head in response to her forcefully knocking at his door.

"It's open Momma." He said calling out from the kitchen. Marietta opened the door and entered. "You want some of this breakfast I'm cooking Momma?" Thomas Lee asked as she entered being seated at the table. She silently stared at him. "You looking at me the same as you done when you caught me and Dorothy jean in my bed when I was sixteen." He said grinning. "Now before you say anything Momma—Delores came over here to me."

"What's wrong with you Thomas Lee?" She said raising her voice. "Dorothy Jean locked up in prison, maybe for the rest of her life and you in here, laid up with Ms. Delores!" Thomas Lee shifted his eyes briefly over at her as he removed a slice of ham from the skillet sitting it on his plate next to the buttered grits and scrambled eggs.

"You sure I can't fix you plate Momma?" He said trying to avoid their conversation on Delores.

"And why you just now eating breakfast anyway?"

"Food don't care when you eat it Momma." He laughed. Marietta looked at him with chastising eyes, unamused.

"Got Ms. Delores coming home with her clothes half buttoned, barely hanging on her." Thomas Lee humorously smiled as he sat down to eat.

"You told me to stay away from Delores Momma and I did!" He looked briefly down at his plate then into Marietta's disappointed eyes. "I knew I should've cooked me some biscuits to go with this." He turned to Marietta. "What you think Momma? You think I should cook some biscuits?"

"I ain't come here to talk to you about no biscuits Thomas Lee!" She said raising her voice as he walked over to the counter and removed two slices of bread from a loaf then returned to the table. "I guess a couple slices of bread ought to do." He said shifting his eyes over at her. "It ain't my fault if Delores acts like she can't get enough of me Momma." He cunningly grinned.

"And you talked about your daddy and the kind of man he was." Marietta said looking at him as a hypocrite. "Look to me you walking right in his footsteps."

"So what you want me to do Momma?" Thomas Lee asked folding the slice of bread then filling it with scrambled eggs. She gave no reply. "I'm a man Momma." He said biting the makeshift sandwich. "And if Delores or any other woman come at me like that—" A deviant smile formed on Thomas Lee's face. "—I'm gon do what a man do."

"No matter who gets hurt Thomas Lee?" He stabbed his fork in the ham and raised it to his mouth then bit it.

"I ain't trying to hurt nobody Momma." A cunning smile formed on his face. "I'm just giving the ladies what they want . . . I squeezed, teased, and aim to please. He said laughing. Marietta abruptly stood.

"You keep playing with fire Thomas Lee and sooner or later you gon get burned!" He humorously smiled as she opened the front door and walked out slamming it shut behind her.

#

Marietta rushed through the back door of the Clarkston mansion after her fruitless visit with Thomas Lee.

"Carrie!" She called out hurrying over to the sink, washing her hands and putting on her starch white apron then walking swiftly over to the refrigerator. "Carrie!" She repeated.

"You called me Marietta."Carrie said coming out of the family room where she'd been watching television, noticing the distressed look on Marietta's face. "What's going on Marietta?"

"How come you ain't start dinner for me?" Marietta asked as she removed a package of spare ribs from the refrigerator taking them over to the sink. "How am I supposed to have these ribs ready in time for dinner?"

"Slow down Marietta!" Carrie said looking at her with concern. "Mr. Charles called and said he was taking his Ol' trifling wife out to dinner tonight."

"Carrie!"

"What Marietta . . . ain't Ms. Delores still taking her ass over there messing around with Thomas Lee?"

"You gon get enough of talking like that about Ms. Delores." Marietta said giving warning. "She gon mess around and one day hear what you saying about her."

"Like I give a damn!"

"Well you better." Marietta said looking at her with reprimanding eyes. "Me and Roosevelt need you here . . . Mr. Charles ain't gon find nobody else to put up with Ms. Delores' trifling ass." Carrie's mouth flung open.

"Marietta!"

"I earned that one." They laughed.

"I guess I better go on up here and help *the lady of the house* pick out something to wear for dinner tonight." Carrie said mockingly.

"Did Mr. Charles say where he was taking her?"

"Naw, but wherever it is . . . it's gon be damn expensive."

"Why you say that?"

"Cause he's trying like hell to keep his wife away from Thomas Lee!" Carrie said bursting into laughter as she headed up the stairs. Marietta walked over to the refrigerator and put the spare ribs in the freezer.

"Marietta!" Carrie yelled hurrying back downstairs. "That heifer done slipped out of here!" Marietta's anxiety heightened.

"You checked all the rooms upstairs Carrie?" She asked, panicked. "Where's Roosevelt?"

"He's in his room sleep."

"Go wake him up and ask him if Ms. Delores said anything to him about going anywhere today."

"Marietta let that man sleep!" Carrie said aggravated. "Ms. Delores ain't no child if she want to get her ass in hot water let her."

"You know how Mr. Charles—" Carrie cut her off.

"Marietta that's his trifling ass wife let him deal with her." She said looking into Marietta's worried eyes. "Maybe it's time he did." Marietta's heart pounded as her apprehension soared.

#

"Marietta!" Charles called out as he entered through the front door excited about the evening he'd plan for him and his wife. He hurried upstairs to retrieve the diamond bracelet he bought with the intent of giving it to Delores to wear for the evening. He reached inside a dresser drawer and removed the case containing the bracelet then hurried from his bedroom, returning back downstairs. "Marietta!"

"Did you need something Mr. Charles?" She asked coming from the servant's quarters where her, Carrie and Roosevelt watched television.

"Yes . . . is my wife is she ready?" He asked eager. Marietta's mouth quickly dried.

"I ain't seen her Mr. Charles."

"Ain't none of us seen her ass." Carrie said from inside the servant's quarters hoping Charles heard her.

"Hush Carrie!" Roosevelt stated.

"She might be upstairs in her room sleep it's been about a hour since we last checked on her." Marietta said trying not to arouse Charles' suspicion.

"Would you be a dear Marietta and go check for me please?"

"I sure will Mr. Charles." She said knowing in her gut Delores' absence involved Thomas Lee. "Did you want me to leave her alone if she's sleep?"

"Of course not . . . get her up we have dinner reservations!" Charles said holding the black velvet jewelry box in his hand. "I want to give Delores the diamond bracelet I had made especially for her." Marietta's stomach filled with butterflies. "Would you like to see it Marietta?" He asked elated.

"I already know it's nice." Marietta said as she approached him. Charles quickly opened the box displaying the sparkling piece of exquisite, extremely expensive jewelry.

"That's beautiful Mr. Charles and I know Ms. Delores gon just love it!" She said masking her nervousness behind a forced smile.

"Yes, my wife does love fine jewelry." Charles said admiring the bracelet. "And Marietta would you please make sure she's appropriately dressed."

Marietta slightly trembled as she headed up the stairs knowing Delores wouldn't be there. She stopped when hearing the back door open then close. Delores rushed in halting when seeing Charles standing in the vestibule.

"Charles, you're home early." She said shifting her eyes to Marietta frozen in place on the stairs.

"Where the hell have you been?" Charles yelled taking note of her slightly disheveled appearance and the tell-tale look in her eyes. She looked at him loss for words, unwilling to answer his question.

"I asked you where the hell have you been Delores." He shouted, grasping hold of her arm.

"I was uh—"

"Don't even bother trying to lie!" Charles said staring her in the eyes. "Do you think I don't know you've been sneaking around with Thomas Lee?" He shifted his eyes to Marietta then back to his wife. Marietta's eyes widened with fear. "Is that why you've had such a difficult time making your mind up about our travel to France?"

"Oh, oh." Carrie said looking at Roosevelt as they listened from the servant's quarter.

"You're hurting me Charles!" Delores cried out. Roosevelt stood and prepared to go to her rescue. Carrie caught hold of his arm.

"Where you going Roosevelt?" She whispered.

"I can't just stand here and let Mr. Charles hurt that girl!"

"That ain't got nothing to do with you." She said trying to stop him. "You go out there trying to help Ms. Delores you gon find yourself in jail."

"Then I guess I'll just be going to jail." He said exiting the room. "Did you call me Ms. Delores?" Roosevelt stated. Charles quickly released her arm when seeing him headed towards the vestibule.

"And how long have you known about my wife being with Thomas Lee since his release from prison Roosevelt?" Charles asked gazing into Roosevelt's courageous eyes.

"Mr. Charles you know I ain't ever had nothing to do with Ms. Delores' personal affairs, and I ain't about to stand here and let you put me in the middle of all this mess!" Roosevelt said raising his voice." Charles shifted his eyes to Marietta.

"I'm quite sure you knew my wife was seeing your son Marietta and I'm holding you personally responsible!"

"Mr. Charles I've talk to Thomas Lee over and over, I even went over there this morning and tried to tell him to leave Ms. Delores alone, but—"

"But what?" Charles shouted.

"It's Ms. Delores who won't leave him alone." Marietta said becoming upset. A frightened look displayed on Delores' face.

"I should fire every last one of you!" Charles stated, infuriated.

"Fire us for what?" Carrie yelled from the kitchen, unleashing her anger. "It ain't our job to keep your wife's ass out of Thomas Lee's bed!"

"Carrie!" Roosevelt said trying to quiet her.

"Maybe you ought to talk to your wife, let her tell you why she can't stay away from Thomas Lee!" Charles quickly took hold of Delores by the arm.

"Roosevelt!" Marietta called out, frightened by Charles' aggressiveness. "Bring Ms. Delores up here before Mr. Charles do something he gon regret."

"I'll get her Marietta." Carrie said entering the vestibule, easing Delores' arm from Charles' firm grip. "Come on Ms. Delores let me take you to your room before all our asses end up in jail." Charles watched in anger as Carrie led his wife upstairs.

"You want me to go ahead and start cooking supper Mr. Charles or were you and Ms. Delores still going out to dinner?" He momentarily stared at her then stormed out the house."

#

Thomas Lee lay on the sofa watching television and drinking beer. He scrambled to his feet when hearing the sound of screeching tires in his driveway, followed by footsteps on his porch then pounding at his front door. He peeped through the curtain seeing Charles frantically beating on the door. Thomas Lee dropped to his knees when seeing the pistol Charles held in his right hand. He crawled over to the phone sitting on a table by the window and quickly called his momma.

"Clarkston's residence."

"Let me speak to my momma Roosevelt?" He said panicked as Charles continued hammering at the door.

"Hold on a second Thomas Lee."

"Hello."

"Momma this crazy man's out here trying to break down my door!" Thomas Lee said whispering as he again peeped through the curtain. "And he got a pistol in his hand!" Marietta's heart raced. "This man getting ready to kill me Momma!"

"Who Thomas Lee?"

"That crazy ass Charles!"

"What you mean he getting ready to kill you?" She yelled looking quickly to Roosevelt, horrified by Thomas Lee's words.

"He out here with a crazy ass look in his eyes and I know Momma—" Thomas Lee again peeped out, still down on his knees. "—if he get in here he gon kill me Momma!"

"Kill you?" Marietta said horrified.

"Yeah Momma I told you he got a gun!"

"Didn't I tell you to stay away from Ms. Delores?" Marietta screamed in the phone.

"Open this door Thomas Lee I know you're in there!" Charles shouted as he rammed his body against the door. Thomas Lee quickly crawled to the back door in preparation to run out then stopped when rationalizing he would never make it to his truck parked out front before Charles could shoot him.

"Come out here Thomas Lee so I can shoot you like the animal that you are!"

"You hear that Momma?"

"Thomas Lee!"

"What Momma?" He said crawling in a back bedroom then trying to open a window to escape.

"Open this door Thomas Lee!" Charles said continuing to shout as he butted his shoulder against the door.

"What I'm gon do Momma?" Thomas Lee said crawling to a second bedroom when unable to open the window in the first. "This man is gone mad!" He stated snatching the curtains down, trying desperately to open the window being unsuccessful. "What the hell's wrong with all these windows that they stuck?" He said talking to himself.

"Let him in Thomas Lee." Marietta said. His jaw dropped.

"Did you hear what I said Momma?" Thomas Lee said continuing his efforts to open the window. "That man plan on killing me Momma!" He looked around the room, anxious to find something to pry the window open.

"Mr. Charles ain't gon kill you Thomas Lee."

"Well that gun in his hand, say different Momma."

"Let him in Thomas Lee!"

"Momma!" He shouted snatching a wire hanger from the closet trying to shove it underneath the window. "If I let that man in here and he kill me Momma my blood gon be on your hands."

"Just crack open the door and hand Mr. Charles the phone let me speak to him."

"You sure Momma?"

"Yeah I'm sure now go ahead and do it!" Thomas Lee crawled in the kitchen and grabbed the black skillet off the stove then returned to the front door.

"I got my momma on the phone Charles!" He yelled crouching at the door. "She want to speak to you man." He said trembling. "I end up dead she gon know it was you who done it!" Charles gave no reply Thomas Lee slowly opened the door to a crack, his hand shaking as he handed Charles the phone.

"Stay out of this Marietta!" Charles yelled. "This is between me and Thomas Lee!"

"Mr. Charles I know you angry about what's been going on with Ms. Delores and my boy, but killing Thomas Lee ain't gon stop Ms. Delores from doing what she do!" Marietta said trying to reason with him. "Instead of being over there trying to hurt my boy you need to be speaking to Ms. Delores seeing why she so unhappy—" Charles cut her off.

"Unhappy!" He shouted. "What reason would my wife have to be unhappy?"

"That's something you need to be asking her."

"My wife was fine until Thomas Lee confused her—"

"You know that ain't true Mr. Charles . . . Ms. Delores took up drinking not too long after you married her."

"If you don't keep your son away from my wife Marietta, I swear to you I'll kill him!" Charles bellowed. Marietta dropped the phone and began weeping. Roosevelt picked it up.

"Mr. Charles?"

"Roosevelt?"

"That right." He said upset by Marietta's distraught state. "I know you upset with Thomas Lee, but Marietta ain't had nothing to do with it and you know it!" Roosevelt said raising his voice.

"I would never do anything to hurt Marietta."

"You hurting her now!" Roosevelt yelled. "—over there trying to kill her son."

"I won't continue to allow Thomas Lee to dishonor my wife!" Charles shouted.

"Mr. Charles I don't mean you or Ms. Delores no disrespect—" Roosevelt swallowed the lump forming in his throat. "—but Ms. Delores been with many men besides Thomas Lee—" Charles dropped the phone and stormed away. Thomas Lee peeped through the curtain when hearing the phone drop then the sound of Charles' car speeding away.

"Crazy ass man!" Thomas Lee said standing to his feet slightly unbalance with fear. He opened the door and stepped out on the porch picking up the phone, holding it to his ear.

"Mr. Charles you there?" Roosevelt asked.

"He left Mr. Roosevelt." Thomas Lee said feeling his heart pounding in his chest. "Tell my momma I'll talk to her later."

"Alright son." Roosevelt said angered by what Thomas Lee had just put his momma through. "I'll let her know."

Chapter Twenty Eight

Roosevelt and Carrie watched from the kitchen as Charles entered the dining room the following morning still wearing his bed robe and appearing to be slightly dazed as he joined his wife at the dining room table.

"Is it Saturday already?" Delores said when seeing him in his robe. "Marietta I think I have a craving for waffles this morning." She said already intoxicated.

"Now what the hell's wrong with Mr. Charles?" Carrie whispered, alarmed by his peculiar behavior.

"I don't know." Roosevelt said observing him. "Look like I might need to call his doctor he ain't looking right."

"If you was married to Ms. Delores' ass you wouldn't be looking right either." Carrie said amused. Roosevelt looked at her with reprimanding eyes as he prepared to check on Charles. "What you getting ready to do Roosevelt?" He dismissed Carrie's question and walked away.

"You alright Mr. Charles?" Roosevelt asked taking note of the blank stare in his eyes.

"Charles?" Delores said slurring her words as she looked at him with peculiarity. "What's wrong with him Roosevelt?"

"I don't know Ms. Delores." He said alarmed by Charles' refusal to speak. "You want me to call his doctor?"

"Where's Marietta?" Roosevelt shifted his eyes briefly in the kitchen to Carrie before responding. "I haven't seen her this morning Ms. Delores."

"Marietta!" She called out.

"She ain't here Ms. Delores." Carrie said entering the dining room.

"What do mean she's not here?" Delores asked looking at Carrie with perplexity. "Is she ill?" Carrie ignored her.

"You want me to help you get Mr. Charles to the den Roosevelt so he can lie down?"

"I'll get him." Roosevelt said placing Charles' left arm around his neck, standing him to his feet. "You go ahead call the doctor, the number's taped on the inside of the cabinet door."

"Alright."

"Come on Mr. Charles let me take you in the den so you can lay down." Charles eyes remained stationary as he continued his unresponsive stupor.

"If anything changes Roosevelt I'll be in here in the kitchen cooking that spoiled heif—" Carrie stopped. "—Ms. Delores her waffles after I call Mr. Charles' doctor." Carrie returned to the kitchen searching for the doctor's number amongst the many numbers listed on the inside cabinet door. "Which doctor is it, I see about twenty numbers wrote on this damn door?"

"It's Dr. Rogers."

"Okay I see it." Carrie quickly called the doctor alerting him to Charles' alarming behavior.

"I sure hope Marietta's feeling better tomorrow." Delores said certain she would soon become her mother-in-law.

"She ain't sick." Carrie said removing a large yellow bowl from the cupboard before going in search of the canister of flour. "She having family problems right now."

"Did something happen to Aunt Mildred?" Carrie abruptly stopped in response to Delores' reference to Mildred as *Aunt Mildred*.

"This ain't got nothing to do with Mildred."

"Is it her grandchildren?"

"Her grandchildren are doing fine too." Carrie said adding baking powder and salt to the bowl or flour.

"Then what is it?"

"That's Marietta's business."

"Then I'll just ask her tomorrow when she returns." Delores said giving no thought to Charles' current condition.

"She ain't gon be here tomorrow either." Carrie said trying not to unleash her anger on her employer. A puzzled look showed on Delores' face.

"I don't understand what you're saying—" Carrie cut her off.

"Truth is Ms. Delores, Marietta ain't coming back she quit!" Delores' eyes widened as she rose from the table slightly unbalanced.

"Why?" She asked concerned. "We've always treated Marietta like one of the family, why on earth would she quit?"

"Mr. Charles." Carrie said mixing eggs and milk into the batter.

"Charles?" Delores staggered towards the kitchen." Marietta and Charles have been squabbling for years." She giggled. "I'm sure whatever little spat they may have had can be reconciled with a simple apology." She said in a matter-of-fact tone.

"Then I guess Mr. Charles didn't tell you."

"Tell me what?"

"He took his crazy ass over to Thomas Lee's house yesterday carrying a gun and trying to kill that man!" Delores placed her hands over her mouth, shocked by Carrie's news. "Like to been scared poor Marietta to death."

"Is Tommy alright?" She asked upset. "I've got to go see him, make sure he's okay."

"Sit down Ms. Delores!" Carrie said looking her firmly in the eyes.

"What?"

"I said sit your ass down." Delores' mouth abruptly opened.

"Why are you talking to me this way?"

"It's been enough devilment as it is!" Carrie said raising her voice. "Thomas Lee's wife killed your baby . . . Mr. Charles trying to kill Thomas Lee—" Delores watched in awe as Carrie walked over to the trash can and dumped the batter inside.

"What are you doing?"

"And your spoiled ass in the middle of all this mess!" Delores' jaw dropped.

"You can't talk to me that way I'll have Charles fire you when he—"

"When he's what Ms. Delores?" Carrie said looking at her with contempt. "Come out of whatever the hell it is got him looking like a damn zombie? Or did you even notice?"

"Of course I noticed Charles is my husband!"

"Your husband?" Carrie sarcastically laughed. "When in the hell has Mr. Charles being your husband ever meant a damn thing? Did it mean anything when you was over there laying your ass up with Thomas Lee?" Delores looked away.

"I'm going in here right now and have Charles—"

"I don't give a damn what you have Mr. Charles do I quit!"

"Good!" Delores shouted.

"Selfish ass heifer?" Carrie said walking towards her. "You got a husband most women would kill to have he's rich, handsome and for some reason he seem to love your trifling ass!" Delores placed her hand over her open mouth shocked by Carrie's biting words.

"Charles!" She yelled.

"He can't hear you Mr. Delores, you done ran that poor man crazy 'round here running up behind Thomas Lee's no good ass." Delores' eyes widened. "Why don't you leave that man the hell alone?" Carrie shouted. "He got a wife and her name ain't Delores!"

"Get out of my house!" Delores screamed.

"I hope you do take your ass over with Thomas Lee, let you see what it's like being with a poor Black man that can't keep his ding-a-ling in his pants."

"Get out!"

"You gon find out it's a lot easier being Thomas Lee's hoe than his wife."

"Get out!" Delores bellowed.

#

"Hey old man." Marietta said as she entered the Clarkston Mansion through the back door seeing Roosevelt at the stove cooking. He turned sharply in response to her voice. A huge smile formed on his face.

"Hey Marietta!" They hugged. "It sure is good to see you."

"What you doing in here cooking?" Marietta asked looking around. "Where's Carrie?" Roosevelt shook his head.

"She quit after Ms. Delores fired her." A complex look formed on Marietta's face in response to Roosevelt's confusing statement.

"What?"

"Carrie couldn't keep that big mouth of her shut!" He said speaking just above a whisper. "Told Ms. Delores just what she thought of her." Marietta's mouth abruptly opened.

"I told Carrie about always talking so much!" She stated upset.

"And Ms. Delores didn't like what she said one bit." Roosevelt said amused.

"What did Mr. Charles have to say about it?" Marietta asked. Roosevelt shook his head, distressed by Charles' unchanged condition.

"Mr. Charles ain't been doing too good Marietta." She gasped.

"What you mean he ain't doing good what's wrong with him?" Roosevelt lowered his eyes and he continued shaking his head then again looked at Marietta. She noted the worried look on his face.

"Ain't said two words in the last two days."

"You call his doctor?" Marietta asked, panicked.

"Yeah, he been out here every day . . . still ain't figured out what's wrong with him."

"Is he that bad?"

"Can't tell—" Roosevelt stated. "—doctor ain't been doing nothing but asking Mr. Charles a bunch of questions he ain't answering."

"Is he gon be alright?"

"Yeah, Mr. Charles gon be just fine Marietta." Roosevelt said with confidence. "He just exhausted from years of having to walk in his father and grandfather's shoes." He shook his head with empathy. "And dealing with Ms. Delores ain't made it no easier."

"I've known Mr. Charles since he was a little boy—"

"Then you saw how the whole family ain't done nothing but pampered and molded that boy." Roosevelt said. "Wouldn't let him be who he was, wanted him to be just like them."

"And that's something Mr. Charles ain't ever wanted to be." Roosevelt nodded in agreement. "He always been a kind man—"

"Until he married Ms. Delores." Roosevelt said grinning.

"I knew from the first time I met that girl, Mr. Charles was getting in over his head." Marietta stated. "She was spoiled and selfish just like Carrie said she was."

"And don't seem like she ever really loved Mr. Charles." Roosevelt said shaking his head. "But Ms. Delores ain't the reason Mr. Charles in the shape he in." He said looking at Marietta with humble eyes. "It was you Marietta." Her mouth quickly opened in response to the accusation.

"Me?"

"Like you said . . . you been caring for Mr. Charles since he was a boy, having you around gave him something to hold on to, something he needed being that his daddy's deceased and Mrs. Clarkston off somewhere in a nursing home."

"Mr. Charles ain't always treated me right Roosevelt you know that."

"I know Marietta, but he just trying to prove he can run things like his daddy and granddaddy done." Roosevelt said in Charles' defense. "But you can't let him get to you Marietta." Her eyes moistened with tears.

"Mr. Charles was the 'cause of my boy being locked up for the murder of that baby." Marietta said heartbroken by his betrayal. "Then pulling a gun, talking about killing Thomas Lee—" Roosevelt interrupted.

"Mr. Charles wasn't gon hurt Thomas Lee Marietta, he was just hurt and angry that's all!" He looked into Marietta's tearful eyes and embraced her. "But I can't say I blame him for going over there scaring the hell out of Thomas Lee for messing around with his wife all these years." He looked at Marietta. "But I'm thinking right now Mr. Charles feeling pretty bad about how he hurt you in doing so."

"If you think I'm gon apologize to Mr. Charles for quitting—"

"Marietta I wouldn't dream of asking you to do that." Roosevelt said. "But I know it would mean an awful lot to Mr. Charles if you came back to work." He hesitated. "You are back ain't you?" He looked at her with pleading eyes then kissed lightly on the cheek. She blushed.

"Yeah Roosevelt I'm back."

"And everything's alright with you Mr. Charles?"

"Yeah Roosevelt everything's alright with me and Mr. Charles."

"Good." He placed another kiss on her cheek. "Now why don't you go on upstairs and let Mr. Charles know you here, something tells me he gon suddenly feel like talking."

"Thank you Roosevelt." She smiled.

"Now if you really want to thank me marry me." He said. Marietta's mouth slightly opened. "You know I ain't giving up right?" She kissed him lightly on the lips.

"Who said I wanted you too." His eyes lit up as he watched her walked away, headed upstairs to reconcile with Charles.

#

"Hey Thomas Lee!" A female bartender at the Night Owl Nightclub said as he entered through the front door.

"Hey sweetheart." Thomas Lee said looking around the partially filled establishment before sitting down at the bar.

"How you doing baby?" She said placing an unexpected kiss on his lips. He smiled delighted by the kiss. "I heard they had freed you."

"And it's good to be a free!"

"What you drinking tonight baby?" She asked flirtatiously. Thomas Lee noted her discretely remove the wedding ring from her finger, sliding it in her pant pocket. He blushed.

"What you recommend sweetheart?"

"Let me give you my phone number in case you want to call me whenever you feeling lonely." Thomas Lee's blushing smile grew as she jotted her number on a napkin and slid it over to him. "You remember me don't you baby?"

"Yeah I remember you—Brenda right?" She blushed.

"Beverly . . . but that's close enough." He suddenly thought of Dorothy Jean's warning about staying away from married women as he eased the napkin from Beverly's hand and put it in his shirt pocket.

"So when can I expect to hear from you?" She asked, seductively. He took hold of her hand.

"As soon as your husband give me permission to lay down with his wife." She grinned.

"So what make you think I'm married, you don't see a ring on these fingers do you?"

"It was when I sat down here at this bar." He said looking her in the eyes smiling. She giggled. "Why don't you bring me a beer sweetheart while I'm thinking over your proposition?" She looked inside his inviting eyes and removed the ring from her pocket, sliding it back on her finger. "What time do they free you from this place?" Thomas Lee asked looking her at with lust in his eyes and a big smile on his face. She girlishly blushed then walked away to get his beer.

"That depends on how long you willing to wait."

"Hey sweetheart let me get that in the bottle?" He Lee said when seeing her reach for a glass.

"However you want it baby." She stated. Thomas Lee grinned. "That'll be three-fifty." She said returning with the bottled beer. Thomas Lee's eyes widened.

"For one beer?"

"That's the price you pay when you want it in the bottle."

"Then pour it in a glass and throw that bottle away." Thomas Lee teased as he handed her a five dollar bill. She placed the bottle in front of him and began walking away.

"Keep the change right?"

"Hell naw . . . you better bring me my damn change!"

"Chump."

"Oh, so now I'm a chump?" Thomas Lee said watching as Beverly walked over to the register. "Go ahead sweetheart and keep the change." He winked.

"I was gon do that anyway baby." Thomas Lee grinned as he stood and walked away being seated at a table. He glanced around the bar remembering the many woman he'd picked up in there over the years. His eyes drew to a fiftyish, attractive female coming from the kitchen with a platter of jerk chicken wings, placing them on the table of the gentleman seated next to him.

"Waitress!" Thomas Lee called out to her. She looked at him and walked away ignoring his beckoning call then returned to the kitchen. The gentleman at the next table quietly laughed.

"That's Ms. Lorraine and she don't like being called waitress." He said continuing to laugh.

"So what I need to call her to get me a plate of them wings?"

"Just call her cook."

"Cook?"

"Yeah, she like for people to think she's the best cook in all of Louisiana and I'm inclined to agree with her . . . Ms. Lorraine!" The man hollered out. "You got a customer wanting a plate of some of your good Ol' chicken wings!" He said licking his fingers as he dissected the wings on his plate.

"Man I thought you said she wanted to be called cook?"

"She do but her name is Lorraine." Thomas Lee took a swig of his beer then noted Beverly watching him. He grinned.

"One order of jerk chicken wings." Ms. Lorraine said speaking over the loud music as she sat the plate on Thomas Lee's table. "That'll be seven dollars." His eyes widened.

"Damn!" He yelled. "Do it cost any less if I go back there and cook them myself?" She looked at him unamused as he reached in his pocket and pulled out a ten dollar bill then sat it on the table. He looked at her as she reached over to retrieve the money then grasped hold of her hand and gazed in her eyes. "What do I have to do to see you after you done cooking chicken?" Thomas Lee asked flirting.

"Dry that milk from behind your ears first because baby you're young enough to be my—" She stopped and looked at him with familiarity. "Don't I know you?" Ms. Lorraine asked. "Ain't you that man they convicted of killing Baby boy Doe . . . Ms. Marietta's boy?" Thomas Lee looked around hoping patrons not yet hearing of his overturned conviction hadn't heard her. "What you want from me?" She asked looked in Thomas Lee's alluring eyes. "I guess you have been locked up for a while, but baby Ms. Lorraine don't give away nothing for free!" Thomas Lee looked at her, offended by her challenging words.

"And Thomas Lee don't pay for nothing he can get for free!" She momentarily stared at him, insulted by his words.

"Well that's your loss."

"Go sit your old ass down somewhere Lorraine!" The man sitting at the table next to Thomas Lee said. "That young man ain't hardly gon waste his money paying for nothing you offering other than these chicken wings!"

"How you know Curtis?"

"I'm an old man myself and I wouldn't give you change for a dollar!" He burst into laughter.

"You go to hell Curtis." She said turning back to Thomas Lee. "Wait a minute—" She cunningly smiled. "—I bet I do have something you'd be willing to pay for?"

"And what's that sweetheart?"

"Your family . . . like to keep a lot of secrets." She said cleverly smiling. "A lot of folks ain't heard yet that it was your wife Dorothy Jean—" Ms. Lorraine silenced when seeing the infuriated look on Thomas Lee's face. "—killing that baby was done in vain."

Thomas Lee looked at her with angry eyes.

"What the hell you talking about?" She cunningly grinned.

"Information like that cost money." He stared briefly at her, curious of her mysterious words. "Why don't we go someplace where we can talk in private?"

"What's wrong with right here?" Thomas Lee asked slightly nervous. She shifted her eyes seeing Curtis peering over at her then again turned to Thomas Lee.

"What I'm about to say is for your ears only." She again shifted her eyes to Curtis. "Now let go of my hand so I can get my money for that chicken!" Thomas Lee released it. Ms. Lorraine shifted her eyes to Curtis a third time then back to Thomas Lee. "Follow me." He rose from the table.

"Hey Curtis man watched them chicken wings for me, grabbed a few if you want."

"Yeah I can do that." He said looking at Thomas Lee with probing eyes in response to him preparing to accompany Ms. Lorraine. "Man you gon—"

"Hell naw!" Thomas Lee said shaking his head with strong objection. "This is strictly business man." Curtis shifted his eyes to Ms. Lorraine then resumed dissecting his chicken wings. Thomas Lee trailed her to a back room becoming nervous as he watched her closed the door. "Money first." She said holding out her hand.

"How much?"

"Twenty dollars." Thomas Lee's mouth flung open.

"Twenty dollars!" He said removing a twenty dollar bill from his wallet. "I don't know what you got to say that's worth twenty dollars, but it damn well better be something I don't already know!" Thomas Lee stated as she snatched the money from his hand.

"Can we at least sit down?"

"We ain't gon be back here that long." Ms. Lorraine said sliding the twenty dollar bill inside her bra. "Besides, twenty dollars won't gon get you but five minutes."

"Five minutes?" Thomas Lee yelled.

"Take it or leave it." He looked down at his watch.

"You got my money so start talking."

"Dorothy Jean didn't know it—"

"Know what?"

"You and next door Rita, been more than just neighbors." She said grinning. "And all the while she's pretending to be Dorothy Jean's friend."

"Don't play with me woman!" Thomas Lee said raising his voice. "Now tell me something I don't know."

"You got a lot of eyes in your neighborhood Thomas Lee."

"Then maybe I need new neighbors . . . what else you got?"

"Dorothy Jean didn't have to murder that baby." Ms. Lorraine stated with vagueness. Thomas Lee's anxiety increased as his patience grew thin.

"Say what you got to say old woman or give me back my damn money!"

"You're not the one who fathered Delores Clarkston's son." She cunningly grinned. Thomas Lee stared at her with fury in his eyes then shook his head with disbelief.

"You don't know what the hell you talking about that boy was mines!

"Times up."

"The hell it is!" He shouted. "You gon give me something more than that!"

"You should've took me up on my first offer." Ms. Lorraine said seductively smiling. "You might've gotten that information for free."

"You crazy if you thought I was gon pay you for—" He thought for a minute. "—hell naw!"

"That's your loss." She said quietly grinning. "But it's gone cost you another twenty dollars if you want to know what I know. Thomas Lee looked at her with mistrust, but remained curious of what she knew. He reached inside his pocket and removed his wallet. Ms. Lorraine watched as he took out another twenty dollar bill, quickly snatching it from his hand.

"I know damn well you gon give me more than what you just did." He said upset.

"Ms. Marietta didn't tell you—"

"Tell me what?" He yelled.

"I guess it ain't easy for a momma to tell a man-child he can't make babies." Frowns stretched across Thomas Lee's forehead.

"What the hell you talking about old woman?"

"It wasn't Dorothy Jean that couldn't make babies—" She grinned. "—it was you didn't have enough fish swimming upstream to fertilize a egg like they suppose to." Thomas Lee looked momentarily at her then walked away, unable to speak as he stood facing the door. "Since you still got a few minutes left I guess I can tell you something else you didn't know. He again faced her.

"Something like what?"

"When Ms. Mildred's granddaughter Raynetta gave birth to that White baby—" An odd look showed on Thomas Lee's face.

"What the hell you talking about?" He said, clueless. "What White baby? And who the hell is Raynetta?"

"Ray Arthur wouldn't let her keep that White baby that's what drove her crazy—"

"Now you really trying to play me." Thomas Lee said looking at her with contempt. "Because what you saying ain't got a damn thing to do with me!" Ms. Lorraine cleverly smiled.

"Folks love to talk—" She grinned. "—and from what I've heard you know Raynetta's baby real well." She said teasing Thomas Lee with the information.

"I don't know nothing about no Raynetta or her White baby, so now you just wasting my time and my money."

"You won't feel that way once I tell you who that baby is."

"I don't care who Raynetta's baby is, like I said that ain't got nothing to do with—"

"Delores Clarkston."

"What about her?"

"She's Raynetta's baby!" Thomas Lee's confusion deepened as his anger mounted.

"Now I know you lying!" He said infuriated. "Delores is White and so are her parents!" Ms Lorraine burst into laughter.

"Delores is Black as you and me, she just happened to take on her daddy's color." Thomas Lee shook his head unconvinced.

"Hell naw, I don't believe that."

"You don't have to believe me just go ask your Aunt Mildred."

"Aunt Mildred? What you talking about?"

"You mean she didn't tell you?"

"Tell me what?" He shouted.

"Delores Clarkston's your cousin baby!" Ms. Lorraine said deviously chuckling. "Talk about your kissing cousins."

"Shut up old woman before I—" Thomas Lee walked angrily towards her. He quickly stopped when seeing her reach inside her apron pouch, removing a small caliber pistol. She chuckled.

"If you ever change your mind about spending a little time with Ms. Lorraine you know where to find me." She seductively grinned. "And I ain't your cousin." She burst into laughter.

"Don't count on it." Thomas Lee said opening the door and walking away.

Chapter Twenty Nine

"Let me in Tommy!" Delores said pounding on his door.

"Get on away from here Delores!" He yelled from inside the house. "I ain't got time for you now . . . go away and leave me alone!"

"Why are you doing this Tommy?"

"Charles ain't getting ready to kill me over you girl!" Thomas Lee said hearing Ms. Lorraine's words remained in his head as Delores continued banging on the door. "You hear me Delores?"

"I'm not going anywhere Tommy, open this door!" Thomas Lee paced throughout the living room, sporadically peeking out the drapes as he tried to remove Ms. Lorraine's words, revealing Delores' true identity from his head.

"Leave me alone now Delores."

"Get your ass away from that man's house and leave him alone like he said Ol' lowdown heifer!" Delores swiftly turned in the direction of the voice seeing Rita standing on her front porch.

"Who are you?" Delores asked.

"I'm the woman that's getting ready to become your worst damn nightmare and Thomas Lee's next wife." Rita said stepping down off her porch.

"Go away this between me and Tommy." Delores said knocking on the door. "Tommy!"

"Think you better than us poor folks don't you?" Rita said looking at Delores with disdain.

"I never said that and I don't even know you—"

"What you say wench?" Rita yelled crossing over into Thomas Lee's front lawn. "Up there living in that big ass mansion, got Black folks waiting on you and your uppity husband, hand and foot—" Delores interjected.

"It's not like that." She said nervous. "Marietta, Carrie and Roosevelt are just like family—"

"Hah!" Rita shouted. "Family my ass—"

Thomas Lee suddenly opened the door.

"Tommy!" Delores quickly embraced him.

"What the hell you doing over here Rita?"

"You better be careful with that one Thomas Lee." She said shifting her eyes to Delores then back to Thomas Lee. "I heard she's a witch . . . going around here casting spells on poor Black men."

"What you talking about Rita?"

"Look at her—think she's better than us Black folk." She said jealousy of Delores. "Because of that wench, Dorothy Jean's in prison."

"Naw, Dorothy Jean put herself in prison when she decided to do what she done."

"You just better hope her rich husband don't come back over gunning for your ass Thomas Lee, got you hiding out in your own house like a turkey on the day before Thanksgiving." An emasculated look displayed on Thomas Lee's face.

"That man had a gun Rita!"

"And?" She said looking at him as a coward.

"Get on away from here Rita this ain't got nothing to do with you."

"I need to talk to Delores and you gon respect that." He looked at her with inviting eyes. "I'll get with later."

"Yeah, you do that." Rita said walking away, looking at Thomas Lee with intimate eyes. She smiled. "But don't say I didn't warn you." She looked at Delores and rolled her eyes.

"Who was the woman Tommy?"

"Nobody you need to be worrying about." He said shifting his eyes over at Rita then back to Delores. "You just get in house Delores."

#

Detective Stokey pulled into Mildred's driveway and parked. He looked around as he got out of his car and began walking towards her house.

"Mildred!" He called out when not seeing her sitting in her old rocker on the front porch. He massaged his neck, concerned about her absence. "I brought you some pig feet, buttermilk, and fried cabbage!" He said teasing. "Mildred?" Detective Stokey again called out as he walked up on the porch peeping through the back door. "Mildred, are you in there?" His heart pounded in his chest as he nervously reached over and turned the doorknob. The door opened. "Mildred?"

"You looking for me." She said stepping from behind the door startling him.

"Dammit Mildred!" He yelled. "You scared the hell out me."

"You had that coming Andy." She said scolding him. "I ain't seen you but once since they set Thomas Lee free." She suddenly silenced. "Did I hear you say something about pig feet, buttermilk and fried cabbage?" Mildred asked coming out on the porch.

"Now Mildred I was just uh—"

"Teasing with me?" She giggled. "I know you was Andy." He hugged her.

"How have you been Mildred?"

"Well, I'm still above ground." She said grinning being seated in her old rocking chair. "Come on sit down with me Andy." He sat in the chair to her right. "I got a visit yesterday from my niece."

"Marietta?" Detective Stokey smiled. "How's she doing?" Mildred giggled.

"You got a black suit?"

"Huh?"

"I asked if you had a black suit."

"As a matter of fact I do but—" She cut him off.

"She tell me Charles Clarkston went out to Thomas Lee's house one day carrying a pistol talking 'bout killing him." Detective Stokey's eyes widened.

"Let me guess . . . he's taken up with Mrs. Clarkston again?"

"Charles just about scared poor Thomas Lee nearly to death!" Mildred burst into laughter.

"I can't say Thomas Lee didn't deserve it." Detective Stokey said humored. "What is it about Mrs. Clarkston that he just can't seem to stay away from her?"

"You got that backwards Andy." He looked at Mildred with oddity.

"Huh?"

"It's Delores can't seem to stay away from Thomas Lee." Mildred giggled.

"Oh!" Detective Stokey flushed with redness.

"I think if Charles Clarkston wanted to kill Thomas Lee, he'd already be dead."

"Really Mildred, so you uh, think Clarkston's capable of murder?" He asked still convinced Charles has something to do with the murder of his wife's baby, despite Dorothy Jean's confession.

"What was it you was saying about pig feet?" Mildred asked diverting from the subject of Charles and murder.

"Please tell me you're not eating pigtails and pig feet again Mildred."

"I'm an old woman Andy and I been eating that way all my life and it ain't gon be easy to just turn it off like a water faucet."

"Now Mildred you know—"

"Why don't you run on in the house and fix us both a plate of pigtails, grits, and some of them fried tomatoes?" Detective Stokey massaged his neck. "And while you in there, why don't you grab both of us a can of beer." Detective Stokey's eyes widened.

"Beer Mildred?"

"Not too many people know, but I drink me a cold beer every now and then."

"What else is it about you Mildred I don't know?" She cleverly smiled.

"I'll share that with you after supper." She giggled. Detective Stokey's face reddened.

"Now Mildred I uh, thought we had uh, discussed—"

"You still think I'm trying to get you in my bed Andy?" Mildred said, humored.

"I uh—"

"I'm starting to think maybe that's where you want to be." She burst into laughter when seeing the frightened look on his face.

"Did I hear you say there were pig feet on the stove Mildred?" Detective Stokey said embarrassed by the conversation.

"And after we eat, I'll tell you what I heard from a little birdie."

"A little birdie?" He looked at Mildred with curious eyes. "Do you know something about other crimes that have taken place Mildred?"

"Let's just say I got a whole lot of puzzle pieces just waiting to be put together." He chuckled.

"You know what Mildred?"

"What's that Andy?"

"Give me one reason why I shouldn't arrest you for withholding evidence?"

"Because not even you want to see a eighty three year old woman behind bars." Detective Stokey laughed then entered the house to retrieve the pig feet, grits, fried tomatoes—and beer.

#

Marietta's slightly balked, startled when seeing Thomas Lee enter through the back door of the Clarkston mansion.

"I need to talk to you Momma!" He yelled.

"What you doing here Thomas Lee?" She whispered. "Are you crazy, coming here to Mr. Charles' house to see his wife?"

"Momma the hell with Delores I'm here to see you!" Marietta's anxiety heightened when noting the fury in Thomas Lee's eyes as he walked towards her. "Why you been lying to me Momma?"

"Lying . . . about what Thomas Lee?"

"You know what I'm talking about Momma!" He grabbed Marietta by the arm. "What I'm talking about is how my wife murdered a baby wasn't even mines Momma!" Thomas Lee said looking in Marietta's guilt ridden eyes.

"Thomas Lee I—" He cut her off.

"I don't want to hear it Momma!" He said raising his voice. "What kind of woman are you Momma?" He asked as his eyes watered with tears. "You let me make a fool out of myself Momma, believing Delores' baby was mine." Marietta stood speechless. "I talked to a woman named Ms. Lorraine and she told me everything—"

"That Ol' witch!" Marietta stated with bitterness.

"Well that Ol' witch told me something you didn't Momma." He looked deep in Marietta's eyes. "I couldn't make babies with Delores or no other woman Momma and you knew it!" Marietta's heart raced seeing the hurt in her beloved son's eyes.

"I wanted to tell you Thomas Lee but—"

"But what Momma?" He shouted. She opened her mouth to speak, but nothing came out. "You know what Momma—"

"Turn your momma loose boy!" Roosevelt said entering the kitchen seeing his firm grip on Marietta's arm. Thomas Lee quickly turned.

"This ain't got nothing to do with you Mr. Roosevelt!"

"Hush Thomas Lee before Ms. Delores hear you."

"I don't give a damn about that Momma!" Thomas Lee turned momentarily to Roosevelt.

"This between me and my momma Mr. Roosevelt so turn your old ass around and go back to wherever you came from—you hear me?"

"I can't do that son."

"I ain't your son old man!" Thomas Lee yelled, tightening his grasp on Marietta's arm. "Or is he Momma?"

"Being a old man Thomas Lee, I wouldn't even try to—"

"Shut the hell up!" Thomas Lee shouted.

"Thomas Lee!" Marietta cried out upset by his aggressive behavior towards Roosevelt.

"I don't know what's got you all fired up this morning Thomas Lee—" Roosevelt said sympathizing with his tears. "—but hurting your momma ain't gon help."

"She lied to me Roosevelt." Thomas Lee said crying. "My own momma made a fool out of me and got my wife put in prison." Did you know about Delores too Momma and who she really is?" A perplexed look formed on Marietta's face.

"What you mean who she really is? What you talking about Thomas Lee?" Roosevelt quickly intervened.

"I been working with your momma for a long time now Thomas Lee and she's one of the finest woman I've ever known." He said diverting from the subject of Delores. "I stay here working despite the aches and pains running through my body—"

"Your old ass is here because Charles is paying you to be!"

"Naw Thomas Lee I'm here because—" He looked at Marietta. "—it gives me another day to see Marietta's sweet face." She smiled, touched by Roosevelt's words. "I've been in love with your momma for many years Thomas Lee and I'd marry her today if she'd say yes."

"You stay the hell away from my momma old man!" Thomas Lee yelled, again tightening his grasp on his momma's arm.

"Ahhhhhh . . . you hurting me Thomas Lee!"

Roosevelt took a step forward.

"Don't bring you old ass over here Mr. Roosevelt I'm telling you now man, with the way I'm feeling I won't think twice about hurting your old ass!"

"I'm pretty sure you would Thomas Lee but I'd rather you hurt me than your momma."

"Stay out of this Mr. Roosevelt!" Thomas Lee shouted. "I ain't here to hurt my momma I just want some answers." He turned to Marietta as tears streamed down his cheeks. "I just want to know why Momma, why you didn't tell me?" Marietta's eyes filled with tears.

"I didn't want to hurt you Thomas Lee, make you feel like—"

"Like what Momma . . . less than a man?" He said completing her unspoken words. "Well I do." Thomas Lee said shaking his head with self-pity. "I do Momma."

"I'm sorry Thomas Lee."

"It's too late for you to be sorry Momma." He looked into her sympathetic eyes. "Dorothy Jean getting ready to waste away her life locked up behind bars and for what Momma!" He yelled.

"Thomas Lee I'm sorry—"

"Bye Momma." He released her arm then turned to Roosevelt. "I would never hurt my momma old man, like you I love her too." He momentarily stared at Marietta then turned and walked away exiting the house.

"Tommy!" Delores said hurrying down the kitchen stairs wearing a blue silk nightgown and robe. She looked at Marietta. "Was that my Tommy?" Roosevelt looked over at Marietta and shook his head.

#

"Hey y'all!" Carrie said entering through the back door of the Clarkston's home seeing Roosevelt and Marietta in the kitchen prepping for the evening supper. They quickly turned in response to her voice.

"Carrie!" Marietta said hurrying over and hugging her.

"Hey Carrie what you been up to?" Roosevelt asked giving her a hug. "It's good to see you."

"You back?" Marietta asked returning to the sink to resumed shucking cobs of corn.

"Where's Mr. Charles?"

"He's at work but—" She cut Marietta off.

"Where's Ol' trifling ass Ms. Delores?" Roosevelt quickly intervened.

"Ms. Delores is upstairs and I'm telling you now she ain't in much of a forgiving mood since Thomas Lee won't have nothing to do with these days if that's why you here." Carrie's mouth flung open. She looked over at Marietta.

"I guess Mr. Charles must've really scared the hell out of Thomas Lee when he went over there gunning for him." Carrie said laughing.

"Now how you find out about that Carrie?" Marietta asked, surprised.

"Girl you know how talk gets around, especially when it's something juicy!" Carrie giggled. Roosevelt reluctantly grinned.

"I stopped by there one day last week to check on my son and to see what he meant by Ms. Delores' real identity—" Roosevelt quickly interjected.

"I wouldn't put too much thought into Thomas Lee's words Marietta, you saw how upset he was—" Carrie intervened.

"I bet he was even more upset when they slammed that prison gate behind Dorothy Jean's crazy ass!" She stated without considering Marietta's feelings. "Who would've ever thought she was that damn crazy?" Carrie suddenly silenced. "I guess you never know what people capable of doing."

"And when I stopped by there yesterday Thomas Lee was drunk out his mind!"

"Drunk?" Carrie said shocked. "Marietta, Thomas Lee don't drink like that do he?"

"Noooooooo!" Delores screamed out from upstairs. Carrie flinched.

"What the hell was that?" She asked looking at Marietta and Roosevelt startled by the ear bursting shrill.

"Ms. Delores." Roosevelt said shaking his head with pity. "She's been doing that every day since Thomas Lee broke it off with her." Carrie's eyes widened, astonished by the break-up.

"Damn!" She looked at Roosevelt. "Do Mr. Charles know that?"

"Yeah he knows." Marietta said rinsing the shucked corn off before putting it in a bowl. "He's been talking about sending Ms. Delores to a sanitarium."

"Let me grab a garbage bag for you Marietta—" Roosevelt said hurrying over to the pantry. "—help you clean up that corn shuck." Carrie shifted her eyes to Marietta with inquisitiveness.

"Marietta I don't see how y'all can stand all that damn screaming!"

"Girl it ain't been easy."

"Marietta's right." Roosevelt said stuffing corn shuck in the garbage bag. "Got on my nerves so bad one day I tried to give her a bottle of red wine!" Marietta's mouth abruptly opened.

"Roosevelt!"

"What Marietta? That screaming was wearing my nerves out!" He said shaking his head. "Do you know she wouldn't even touch the stuff . . . I end up drinking it myself." Roosevelt said humored.

"Marietta you telling me all that damn yelling ain't getting on your nerves?" Carrie asked then turned to Roosevelt. "You better than me, Roosevelt 'cause, I would've funneled that damn wine down her throat!" He chuckled.

"I never said it wasn't getting on my nerves." Marietta said sitting down at the table preparing to shave the kernels from the cobs of corn. "But her lying up with Thomas Lee was getting on my nerves a hundred times worse."

"I don't know about y'all, but I'm damn curious what would ever make Thomas Lee leave Ms. Delores alone?" Carrie said looking briefly at Roosevelt with probing eyes. "I know that's your son Marietta, but pistol or no pistol it ain't like Thomas Lee to turn down no—"

"Carrie!" Roosevelt cut her off.

"I'm still trying to figure out what he meant when he ask me if I knew who Delores really was?" Marietta said ignoring Carrie's truthful words.

"You coming back to work Carrie?" Roosevelt asked, again diverting from the topic of Delores' identity.

"Hell naw!" Carrie said chuckling. "And give up my piece a mind!" Roosevelt grinned. "I ain't sure I'm ready to be bothered with Ms. Delores's spoiled ass again, plus Buster been talking about us leaving Louisiana and moving to Florida to be near his momma."

"Must be nice having a husband wanting to take you away from all this mess?" Marietta said glancing over at Roosevelt when sensing his stare.

"Noooooooo!" Delores bellowed. "Answer the phone Tommy!"

"Damn!" Carrie shook her head. "I don't know how in the hell y'all put up with that all damn day!"

"Let me go and see if I can calm her down." Roosevelt said. "And just in case I can't let me take her one of them pills her doctor prescribed." He stated opening the cabinet and removing a bottle of sedatives, taking out a pill before heading up the kitchen stairs.

"Girl what's going on between you and Roosevelt?" Carrie asked with intrigue. "I saw how he was looking at you . . . got his old ass around here trying to do his work and yours!" She burst into laughter. Marietta blushed.

"He did ask me to marry—"

"Marietta!" Roosevelt shouted as he rushed back down the stairs in hysterics. Marietta's heart pounded in her chest.

"What's wrong Roosevelt?" She asked believing something to be wrong with Delores.

"Ms. Delores called Thomas Lee and—" Carrie cut him off.

"Why in the hell won't she leave that damn man alone?" She said agitated. Marietta's knees weakened when seeing the horrified look on Roosevelt's face.

"What's wrong Roosevelt?" She asked.

"It's Thomas Lee, Marietta!"

"What about him?" She shouted as butterflies filled her stomach. "Mr. Charles killed my boy, Roosevelt?" Marietta asked, quickly rising from the table.

"Person answering Tommy Lee's phone said ambulance took him to the hospital—"

"Noooooooo!" Marietta screamed dropping to her knees. "Mr. Charles killed my boy!"

"Get up Marietta." Roosevelt said assisting her to her feet. "Come on sit back down." A worried look showed on Carrie's face.

"What's going on Roosevelt?"

"Seems Thomas Lee got drunk—" Roosevelt shifted his eyes to Carrie then back to Marietta. "—wrapped his car around a tree."

"Noooooooo!" Marietta bellowed.

"Is he dead Roosevelt?" Carrie asked expecting the worst. A hopeless look appeared on Roosevelt's face.

"Not yet, but it's plenty bad . . . don't look like he's gon make it."

"Noooooooo!" Marietta again cried out.

"Come on Marietta let me take you out here to the hospital before Thomas Lee leaves here." Roosevelt said assisting her from the chair, comforting her with his embrace as she wept.

Chapter Thirty

"Thank you Roosevelt." Charles said from behind the morning newspaper after Roosevelt placed a breakfast of pork sausage patties, Cajun grits, a vegetable omelet and beignets next to his glass of orange juice. "Have you spoken with Marietta, how's she doing?"

"Been spending most of her days out at the hospital with Thomas Lee—"

"Tommy!" Delores said slurring her words as she staggered down the stairs, entering the dining room intoxicated. "I want to see Tommy!" Charles lowered his newspaper and looked at over at her with disdain. Roosevelt quickly intervened.

"Ms. Delores, can I get you some breakfast?"

"No!" She yelled. "I want Tommy!"

"Roosevelt, would you please take my wife back upstairs to her room?"

"Come on Ms. Delores . . . let me take you back upstairs so you can lay down."

"No!" She stated with defiance. "I'm going to the hospital to see my Tommy." Charles stared at her, annoyed by her insistence on seeing her former lover. Roosevelt interjected.

"Well you can't go out there wearing your nightclothes Ms. Delores." He said shifting his eyes to Charles. "Why don't you come on back upstairs so you can bathe and put on your prettiest dress?" He said, again shifting his eyes to Charles. "Then we'll see if the doctor's are allowing Thomas Lee to have visitors today."

"You're right Roosevelt." Delores said running her fingers through her hair. "I wouldn't want Tommy to see me looking like this." She giggled. Charles watched in anger as his wife rose from the table and staggered into the vestibule then headed up the stairs.

"Roosevelt?"

"Yes Mr. Charles?"

"Would you see to it that my wife's anticipated visit to the hospital never happens?" Roosevelt nodded then turned to leave. "And Roosevelt—"

"Yes Mr. Charles?"

"I never learned exactly why Carrie left our employment."

"I think the best person to speak to about that is Carrie."

"Would you please let her know I'd like to speak to her when I return home from work?"

"I sure will."

Charles laid down the newspaper and began eating.

"I . . . we still need her."

"She'll be glad to hear that."

"And I'll take my coffee now."

#

Marietta rested her eyes as she sat in the chair next to Thomas Lee's bed listening to the beeps of his heart monitor and praying they wouldn't stop.

"You want me to run downstairs to the cafeteria and get you something to eat Marietta?" Roosevelt asked concerned that she'd not eaten since breakfast—yesterday.

"Naw . . . I couldn't eat nothing if I wanted to, but if you want to go grab something go ahead."

"Woman you ain't ate since yesterday!" Roosevelt said subtly chastising her. "Now I'm going down here and bring you back something if it ain't nothing but a sandwich." Marietta rose from her chair and walked over to Thomas Lee's bed, looking down at him.

"Is egg salad alright?" Roosevelt asked observing as she rubbed Thomas Lee's bruised and swollen face wrapped in white bandages. She nodded. "I don't know what I'd do if I lost you Thomas Lee." Marietta said taking hold of his hand. "He just about the only child I got left." A puzzled look showed on Roosevelt's face.

"What you mean Marietta I thought you had a daughter in Ohio?"

"I had three children Roosevelt." She said looking him in the eyes. "I had a daughter named Tonya she died when she was just five years old." Marietta paused. "Got hit by a car." Roosevelt looked at her with sympathetic eyes.

"As long as I've known you Marietta, you ain't ever speak about having a deceased child."

"Speaking on the death of your child ain't easy." She said looking briefly at him then again to Thomas Lee. "When Denise got herself hooked on them drugs after getting with the wrong man, leaving her four children here for me to raise, seem like Thomas Lee was all I had left." Her eyes filled with tears. Roosevelt walked over and embraced her in his arms.

"You got me Marietta if you willing to have me."

"Spoiled him—" She said dismissing Roosevelt's pleading words. "—look the other way when Thomas Lee done wrong even when he started messing around with Ms. Delores."

"Thomas Lee's a grown man Marietta!" Roosevelt said troubled by her blaming herself for his wrong doing. "Been troubled every since he was a young boy." Marietta looked at him. "A boy needs his father Marietta." Roosevelt said with compassion. "And you know as well as I do Leroy ain't ever been a father to Thomas Lee—" He gazed into Marietta's eyes. "—or a husband to you."

"How he doing?" Marietta's quickly turned seeing Mildred enter the room accompanied by Detective Stokey.

"Ain't been no change since he came in here five days ago." Roosevelt answered on Marietta's behalf.

"What the doctors saying?" Mildred asked.

"Just keep saying wait and see." Marietta said silently weeping.

"I'm uh, truly sorry Marietta." Detective Stokey stated. "If there's anything you need I'm here." She looked at him and nodded. He turned to Roosevelt.

"You doing alright Roosevelt?"

"Until all this happened—" Roosevelt silenced. "How's things going with you detective?"

"I was on top of the world after freeing Thomas Lee's and now this."

"You done something nobody ever believed could be done." Roosevelt said. "You gave Thomas Lee his freedom." Detective Stokey nodded then turned to Mildred.

"Uh, Mildred I think I'll let you spend time with your family and uh, I need to get back to the precinct."

"Thank you for bringing me out here Andy."

"No problem Mildred." He shifted his eyes to Thomas Lee recalling the day he picked him up from the prison. Detective Stokey's eyes moistened.

"Keep me posted will you." He stated before exiting the room.

"I want to see my Tommy!" Delores's voice yelled out in the hallway. Marietta looked at Roosevelt.

"I didn't bring her out here." He said in his defense. "When I left home she was upstairs in her room sleep and Carrie was—" Marietta interrupted.

"Carrie?"

"Yeah . . . Mr. Charles hired her back, realized he needed her."

"I hope that ain't the reason Ms. Delores is drunk." Marietta said, worried.

"Since when do Ms. Delores need a reason?"

"Roosevelt!" Marietta subtly scolded him.

"Marietta?"

"Yeah you right."

"Excuse me." A nurse said entering the room. "There's a lady out here stating that she's Mr. Simms' fiancée?" Marietta shifted her eyes to Mildred.

"I'll take care of it." Roosevelt said. "Last thing you need to be worrying about is Ms. Delores, you just see about Thomas Lee." An inquisitive look appeared in Mildred's eyes. "I'll bring you something back after I take Ms. Delores home."

"Don't worry about trying to come back tonight Roosevelt you just make sure Ms. Delores is alright."

"Mr. Charles told her plain as day this morning, not to come out here to this hospital!" He said agitated.

"You know Ms. Delores don't pay Mr. Charles no mind." Marietta said slightly amused. Roosevelt kissed on her cheek and prepared to leave.

"Call me and let me know how things are going no matter how late it is alright?" Marietta smiled and nodded.

"It was good seeing you again Mildred." He said placing a kiss her on the cheek then walking away joining Delores in the hallway.

"Roosevelt!" She called out when seeing him. "They won't let me see Tommy!"

"Doctors got him sedated Ms. Delores he wouldn't know you was here anyway." He said taking hold of her arms. "I think it's best he don't be disturbed."

"I just wanted to tell him that I love him Roosevelt!"

"I'm sure he already knows that Ms. Delores."

"You think so Roosevelt?"

"I'm pretty sure he do, now come on let me take you back home."

Mildred looked at Thomas Lee with a heavy heart then turned to Marietta.

"How you holding up?"

"I don't know what I'll do Aunt Mildred if Thomas Lee don't make it."

"He gon be alright." Mildred said looking into Marietta's tear filled eyes. "Its gon take a little while, but he gon pull through." She looked at Marietta with an inquiring stare in her eyes." Now tell me what's going on with you and my brother-in-law?" Marietta lightly chuckled believing Mildred to be teasing.

"Right now Aunt Mildred I ain't got time for your brother-in-law or no other man."

"Well he sure seems to have time for you?"

"You gon have to tell me who this mysterious brother-in-law of yours is 'cause I don't know who in the heck you talking about Aunt Mildred."

"Roosevelt."

Marietta's eyes widened, stunned by Mildred's unexpected words.

"Roosevelt?"

"He was married to my sister-in-law Marlene before she passed—" Mildred stopped to think. "—must be fifteen years now."

"How come I didn't know that, Aunt Mildred?"

"Did you know my sister-in-law Marlene?"

"I ain't never even heard of her before."

"That's why you didn't know." Mildred lightly chuckled. "Roosevelt's a good man Marietta and it looks like he's ready to make you wife number—" She abruptly silenced when seeing Marietta's mouth open. "So I take it things ain't got no better between Delores and Charles." Mildred said changing the subject from Roosevelt.

#

Charles' face remained buried behind the morning newspaper as he sporadically took swallows from his coffee.

"Are you and Carrie preparing breakfast again this morning Roosevelt?" He asked as Roosevelt filled Delores' glass with orange juice.

"Look like its gon be that way for a while since Marietta ain't got no intentions on leaving Thomas Lee's side until the doctor say he's out of danger." Charles lowered his newspaper and looked over at his wife in response to Roosevelt's reply. She ignored him.

"How is Thomas Lee?" Charles asked, again shifting his eyes to his wife. She quickly looked to Roosevelt longing to hear his answer. "I understand he's awake now."

"That's right Mr. Charles, and his doctors expect him to have a full recovery over time." Charles watched as Delores' eyes widened, excited by the news.

"I'm sure Marietta's quite relieved to hear that." He said sounding slightly disappointed by Thomas Lee's prognosis.

"Did the doctor say when Tommy could come home Roosevelt?" Delores asked, unable to hold back her concern. He shifted his eyes to Charles before answering.

"No Ms. Delores he didn't."

"That will be all Roosevelt." Charles said obscuring his face behind the newspaper blocking his wife's face from his view. She looked at Roosevelt and mouthed the words *thank you*.

#

"Did you see the look on Mr. Charles face when Ms. Delores asked when the doctor was gon release Thomas Lee from the hospital?" Carrie said whispering as she and Roosevelt prepped the evening supper.

"It wasn't the look on Mr. Charles' face I noticed." Roosevelt said amused. "It was the look in Ms. Delores' eyes when Mr. Charles said Thomas Lee was woke!" Roosevelt silently chuckled.

"I just hope she don't take her ass back out there claiming to be Thomas Lee's fiancée again . . . Ol' crazy heifer."

"I better call out to the hospital and let Marietta know Ms. Delores is aware Thomas Lee's woke." Roosevelt stated.

"You going back out there tonight Roosevelt?"

"Yeah, did you want to go with me?"

"I would but Buster starting to complain—won't me home right after work to get his supper on the table." Roosevelt laughed.

"That's because you got that man spoiled." He teased.

"One of these days I'm gon tell Buster to cook his own damn supper!"

"I don't know about that Carrie." Roosevelt said teasing.

"Why?"

"Once you get a man spoiled like that he ain't gon be, too pleased if you stop . . . might go looking elsewhere for a woman who'll do what you won't."

"Anyway—" Carrie said dismissing Roosevelt's opinion. "—when you go out to the hospital let Marietta know we praying for Thomas Lee."

"I sure will." Their attention drew to Delores emerging from the kitchen stairs wearing bright red dress, red shoes and carrying a red purse.

"You going somewhere Ms. Delores?" Roosevelt asked shifting his eyes briefly to Carrie.

"I don't think where I'm going is any of your business Roosevelt."

"Now Ms. Delores you ain't planning on going back out to the hospital, are you?" He asked. Carrie looked at her and awaited her reply. "Now Ms. Delores you know Mr. Charles don't want you going out to that hospital—" She interjected.

"Well Roosevelt I don't give a damn what Charles, you or Carrie want." Delores said walking pass him and Carrie heading for back door. Roosevelt stepped in front of the door, blocking it.

"Move out of my way Roosevelt!" Delores yelled.

"I can't do that Ms. Delores."
She shifted her eyes to Carrie.

"I'm going to ask you one more time Roosevelt to get out of my way!" He looked into her demanding eyes and stepped aside.

"Roosevelt!" Carrie said urging him to stop her.

"I'm gon let Mr. Charles deal with it Carrie . . . I'm tired."

"Good!" Delores stated with defiance. "And don't worry about preparing my lunch, I won't be back by then." They watched as she pushed opened the back door and walked out.

"Ol' spoiled heifer!" Carrie stated.

#

Marietta stood at Thomas Lee's bedside feeding him from his breakfast tray.

"Look like we gon have to make room for you somewhere at my house after the doctor discharge you." She stated.

"You ain't got—ta do that—Mom—ma." Thomas Lee said his speech temporarily impaired. "Dor—thy—Jean ca—take—care of me—jus—fine."

"You don't start eating more the doctor ain't gon let you come home." Marietta said diverting from the subject of Dorothy Jean electing not to remind him of his wife's incarceration.

"Tommy!" Delores said hurrying in the room. Marietta's mouth flung open, shocked by Delores unexpected visit.

"What you doing here Ms. Delores?"

"I've missed you Marietta!" She said hugging her. A huge smile spread across Delores' face when turning to Thomas Lee. "Hi Tommy." He looked at her with unfamiliarity as she wrapped her arms around his neck, kissing him on the cheek. "I been worried sick about you Tommy." He shifted his eyes to Marietta for clarity.

"You don't remember Ms. Delores, Thomas Lee?" Marietta asked, alarmed.

"Don't be silly Marietta of course my Tommy remembers me." She kissed him lightly on the lips.

"Tom—my?" He said confused. "Who—is—" Marietta intervened.

"That's Ms. Delores, Mr. Charles' wife . . . you remember Charles don't you Thomas Lee?" He nodded and smiled.

"Yeah—my frien—Charles—I gro—up with—im."

"Did Tommy's doctor say when he'll be going home Marietta?"

"Now Ms. Delores you know—" She interjected.

"With Dorothy Jean being in prison somebody's going to need to take care of Tommy and since we have so many rooms he can stay right there with us where you'll be able to take care of him!" Marietta looked at Delores, troubled by her belief that Charles would allow Thomas Lee to live in his home.

"Wha—she tal—bout—Mom—ma?" Thomas Lee asked agitated from hearing Delores speak on Dorothy Jean's incarceration. "Wher—my wife!" He said raising his voice. Marietta looked at Delores with disciplining eyes.

"I think you need to leave Ms. Delores."

"I didn't mean to upset Tommy, Marietta . . . I just wanted to—" Marietta cut her off.

"Thomas Lee's blessed to be here, but his mind still ain't healed." She stated upset. Delores' eyes moistened as she looked at her former lover, clueless to her identity.

"I'm sorry Marietta—" She said crying.

"I know you are Ms. Delores."

"I'll go ahead and leave." She leaned down and kissed Thomas Lee intimately on the lips. "I love you Tommy, bye." She hurried from the room in tears. Thomas Lee looked at Marietta, confused by Delores' kiss.

"Mom—ma—why tha—White la—dy—kiss me?"

#

"I'm back here Stokey!" Detective Abernathy said when seeing him enter the Appetite Pleaser Café.

"Did you order already Abernathy?"

"No . . . I thought I'd let you order your own food this time."

"I wouldn't have mind if you had ordered for me, now I have to wait for the waitress to come over, take my order then take it to the kitchen and—" He silenced when seeing Bridgette approach.

"A pull pork platter." She said sitting the food filled plate in front of Detective Abernathy. "Would you like a refill on your coffee sir?"

"Yes thank you." He said shifting his eyes to Detective Stokey.

"Are you ordering anything . . . Andy right?" Bridgette stated. A large smile stretched across Detective Stokey's face.

"Give him the same thing I'm eating." Detective Abernathy said in response to his partner's frozen stare at Bridgette. "He'll also have coffee with lots of sugar and cream." Detective Stokey intervened.

"Just sugar, no cream." His stationary smile remained as he continued his gawk at her.

"Another pull pork platter and a coffee?" Bridgette said flattered by Detective Stokey's unrelenting stare. "I'll bring that right out." She turned to leave.

"Not so fast." Detective Stokey said opening up his menu. "I think I'll have a cappuccino." Detective Abernathy's eyes widened in response to his last minute change.

"Cappuccino Stokey?"

"Isn't that what I said?" He stated looking across the table at him.

"So that's a pull pork platter and a cappuccino? I'll bring that right out." Bridgette flashed Detective Stokey a flirtatious smile then walked away. He watched with widened eyes as she returned to the kitchen to place his order then turned back to Detective Abernathy seeing the disapproving look in his eyes.

"What?"

"You know that cappuccino don't come with free refills right?"

"Of course I know that Abernathy—didn't I just solve the Thomas Lee Simms case?" He stated proudly.

"Man I sure hope you don't let that go to head." Detective Abernathy said biting his sandwich. "How's Thomas Lee doing anyway?" He asked with his mouth full.

"He uh, he's good—" Detective Stokey stated with vagueness. "—he has a little memory loss but he's good even if he doesn't remember me." Detective Abernathy choked on his chewed food.

"You alright Abernathy?"

"Whoa!" He said quickly swallowing. "Hold on Stokey, did you just say Thomas Lee Simms has no idea of who you are man?"

"Yes Abernathy that's what I'm telling you."

"Wow!" Detective Abernathy shook his head. "I'd heard his accident was serious but—" A sympathetic look displayed on his face. "—I didn't know it was serious enough to where Thomas Lee wouldn't remember the man who set him free . . . do he even remember being locked up?"

"Marietta hasn't said anything to me, but get this Abernathy—"

"Get what?" He said again biting into his sandwich.

"Apparently he doesn't remember Mrs. Clarkston either." Detective Abernathy's again choked, reaching quickly for his coffee taking a swallow.

"Are you serious man?"

"And Mr. Clarkston couldn't be happier."

"Yeah I bet!" Detective Abernathy said washing down his food with another swallow of coffee before taking another bite from his sandwich.

"That pull pork must be pretty good you're going at it like a hungry bear after hibernation."

"It tastes alright."

"What do you mean it taste alright?" Detective Stokey said reaching over and picking up a fallen piece of pork off his partner's plate putting it in his mouth.

"Man why you eating off my plate?" Detective Abernathy said continuing to chew. "You can't wait for them to bring you yours?"

"What are you talking about Abernathy . . . I wasn't eating off your plate—"

"The hell you wasn't!"

"I just picked up a few scraps lying on the plate to see how it tastes, and it taste pretty good!"

"One pull pork platter and a cappuccino." Bridgette said sitting the plate on the table. "I'll be right back with that cappuccino."

"No problem I'm not going anywhere." Detective Stokey said flirting, watching as she walked away. Detective Abernathy looked at him and shook his head.

"I see you back at it."

"What's wrong with that?"

"You didn't see that rock on her finger man?"

"Rock? I didn't see any rock?"

"She's married man!"

"What are you talking about Abernathy I didn't see a wedding ring on Bridgette's finger?"

"Seen it or not man it's there."

"No it's not!"

"I guess we'll see when Bridgette gets back here with your no refill cappuccino."

"Did I tell you that Lieutenant Porter wants me to start working the cold cases?"

"Seriously?" Detective Abernathy said, ambiguous. "Congratulations man and good luck!"

"He wants me to start with the Williamson case."

"Yeah I remember that case."

"Wanted to know if I was interested in having you continue as my partner."

"No!" Detective Abernathy said stuffing fries in his mouth. "Working cold cases—" He shook his head. "—not interested."

"Then I'll just tell the lieutenant I pass."

"Naw man if you want to work on cold cases Stokey, don't let me stop you."

"Here's your cappuccino Andy." Bridgette said sitting the cup on the table. He discretely shifted his eyes to her hand noting the ring on her finger.

"Nice ring."

"Thank you . . . my ex-husband gave it to me on the day we got married." He looked briefly over at Detective Abernathy.

"Ex-husband?"

"But when my boyfriend proposed I figured since I already had a ring why not use it!" Detective Abernathy quietly chuckled.

"Can I get you anything else Andy?"

"I think I have all I need."

"Well you gentlemen enjoy your lunch." She said walking away. Detective Stokey momentarily watched then turned and looked into his partner's glaring eyes.

"I'm not sure I got what it takes to solve cold cases anyway." He said massaging his neck.

"Maybe you don't if you missed that big rock on Bridgette's finger." Detective Abernathy said laughing.

"So what do think?"

"I think you're too good for her man."

"Not the waitress, about us working cold cases." Detective Stokey said biting into his sandwich.

"Then I guess you didn't hear me when I said no."

"Good, then it's settled." Detective Stokey stated. Detective Abernathy looked at him, not surprised by his disregarding his objection.

"Do you remember why the Williamson case went cold in the first place Stokey?"

"Yeah, it was never solved."

Detective Abernathy looked at him sarcastically in response to his simple reply.

"There were no witnesses, very little evidence and—"

"See that's where you're wrong Abernathy, according to Mildred—"

"Whoa!" Detective Abernathy stated with objection. "Man I know you ain't counting on Old lady Koffee to solve every cold case that comes across your desk?"

"Why not? She help me solve the Thomas Lee Simms case didn't she?" Detective Stokey said confident in Mildred's abilities. "And besides, she's already said she could lead me straight to the killer."

"Wait . . . you're telling me Mildred Koffee's been sitting back on information that could've solved that case fifteen years ago?"

"It would seem so."

"That's it!" Detective Abernathy said agitated.

"What?"

"As soon as we get done eating, I'm going right out there and arrest her old ass for obstruction of justice and don't you try to stop me Stokey!"

"That's fine." He said in a matter-of-fact tone.

"What you mean that's fine?"

"If you want to arrest Mildred go right ahead." Detective Abernathy looked at him, suspicious of his approval.

"And you're okay with that?"

"Why not?"

"So why are you okay with that man?"

"Because the minute you arrest her, the case goes right back into the cold case files."

"How you figure that?"

"Do you actually think Mildred would give you information that you could use against her? She too smart of a lady for that—"

"Are you gentlemen doing alright over here?" Bridgette asked returning to their table.

"Let me have another one of those cappuccinos." Detective Abernathy shook his head in response to his partner's indulgence.

"Another cappuccino coming up." Bridgette turned to leave.

"And Bridgette—" She again turned.

"Did you need something Andy?"

"Yeah . . . keep um' coming." Detective Abernathy looked at him, stunned by his out of character spending.

"You spending kind of big ain't you Stokey?"

"Why not, it's not going to cost me a dime."

"Oh, Lieutenant Porter's picking up the tab or something?" Detective Abernathy asked stuffing fries in his mouth.

"No Abernathy you are."

He began choking, again reaching for his coffee taking a drink.

"Whoa—" He swallowed. "—I never said I was paying for your food man!"

"I know, but I accidentally forgot my wallet at the precinct."

"Here's your cappuccino Andy." Bridgette said sitting it on the table. Detective Abernathy intervened.

"Uh, Bridgett—"

"Did you need something sir?"

"Unless there's free refills on those cappuccinos make that one his last."

"Are you sure?"

"Yeah he's broke." She looked at Detective Stokey and rolled her eyes.

"Dead beat."

Detective Abernathy laughed as she walked away.

Chapter Thirty One

"Roosevelt?" Charles said from behind the morning newspaper as Roosevelt sat a plate containing a breakfast of chicken fried steak, Cajun grits, a vegetable omelet and two beignets, next to his glass of orange juice.

"Yes Mr. Charles?" Roosevelt said pouring coffee in Charles' cup.

"Do you have any idea when Marietta will be returning?"

"She should be back tomorrow."

"Oh?" Charles said masking his enthusiasm.

"Thomas Lee's doing a lot better and Marietta's oldest granddaughter gon be taking care of him.

"I'm sure Marietta's quite please about that." Charles said withholding his true feeling about Thomas Lee's recovery.

"Ahhhhhhhhhhhh!" Delores screamed out. Charles looked down at his watch.

"I see my wife's right on cue." He said from behind the newspaper. "I'm starting to wonder if she has her clock set for her annoying daily shrills."

"Sounds like Ms. Delores just now waking up." Roosevelt stated.

"A few months in a sanitarium should give her time to adjust to Thomas Lee's unfortunate memory loss which appears to have erased all memory of my wife as his lover." Charles stated laying the newspaper down on the table as he prepared to eat.

"Well that ought to give our ears a few month of rest." Roosevelt said with an unapologetic look on his face.

"I didn't hear that Roosevelt." Charles said fully aware of how taxing his wife had been on the staff.

"What you want us to do about her this morning Mr. Charles?"

"Same as always." He said unmoved by her sporadic outburst. Roosevelt looked in the kitchen at Carrie and nodded. She removed a small bottle of Lorazepam and a dropper from the cupboard then placed a few drops in a glass of orange juice then headed upstairs with the juice.

"Did you need anything else Mr. Charles?"

"Yes Roosevelt could you make certain my wife's presentable when the limousine arrives this afternoon to take her to the sanitarium?"

"Was it anything in particular you wanted Ms. Delores to wear?"

"Yes, she has this bright red dress she seems to be quite fond of."

"I know just the dress you talking about."

"Good." Charles said continuing to delight in his breakfast. "That'll be all Roosevelt."

#

"It's good to have you back Marietta." Charles stated with graciousness. Marietta smiled as she sat a plate of grits covered in grillades and gravy, a vegetable omelet and two beignets in front of him as he continued reading the morning newspaper.

"I'll be back in a minute with your coffee."

"Marietta?" Charles lowered the newspaper and looked at her with humble eyes. "I just wanted to say congratulations." She smiled.

"Thank you Mr. Charles."

"All this time you and Roosevelt here working together—I never imagined the two of you would be married." Marietta giggled.

"I guess that makes two of us Mr. Charles."

"I hope you two enjoy the honeymoon I gave you as a wedding present." Charles said holding back his tears. "It's the least I can do, and don't worry about what's going on here while you're away, I'm sure Carrie and the additional staff I've hired will do just fine." Marietta's eyes moistened.

"I think you can do without me and Roosevelt for one week." She teased.

"And thank you for cutting your honeymoon short so you could be here for my wife's return home."

"You don't have to thank me Mr. Charles I'm looking forward to being here when Ms. Delores gets back home." An endearing smile displayed on Marietta's face. "I've missed her." A modest look appeared on Charles face.

"So have I." He smiled. "I think she's finally accepted that Thomas Lee doesn't—" Charles abruptly stopped. "—does he?"

"Naw Mr. Charles he don't remember Ms. Delores?"

"Then I guess we're halfway there." He said forcing a slight chuckled. "Now if only my wife could do the same it would make my life as her husband much easier."

"Ms. Delores truly do love you Mr. Charles, she just need time to realize it."

"Maybe my wife does love me Marietta—" Charles stated with uneasiness. "—but it's your son she's in-love with."

"Its gon be alright Mr. Charles."

"Thank you for saying that, Marietta."

They exchanged a mutual smile then Charles again obscured his face behind the morning paper.

THE END